UNRULY WOMEN

The Politics of Confinement and Resistance

KARLENE FAITH

Seven Stories Press
New York

Originally published by Press Gang Publishers, November 1993

First Seven Stories Press Edition July 2011

The quotation by Hyemeyohsts Storm on p. 9 is from *Seven Arrows* (New York: Ballantine Books, 1972), p. 213

Seven Stories Press
140 Watts Street
New York, NY 10013
www.sevenstories.com

College professors may order examination copies of Seven Stories Press titles for a free six-month trial period. To order, visit http://www.sevenstories.com/textbook or send a fax on school letterhead to (212) 226-1411.

Book design by Jon Gilbert

Library of Congress Cataloging-in-Publication Data

Faith, Karlene.
 Unruly women : the politics of confinement and resistance / Karlene Faith. --
1st Seven Stories Press ed.
    p. cm.
Includes index.
ISBN 978-1-60980-137-3 (pbk.)
1. Female offenders. 2. Women prisoners. I. Title.
HV6046.F25 2011
365'.6082--dc23
                                        2011018084
Printed in the United States

9 8 7 6 5 4 3 2 1

*For the constancy and inspiration of
their leadership in the struggle for justice, this book is dedicated to Kim Pate
and Filis Iverson, and to the memory of
Claire Culhane.*

*This book is also dedicated to all the
unruly women, men, and children
whose resistances to social injustices are
the hope of the world.*

CONTENTS

CHAPTER TWO
CONTEMPORARY PERSPECTIVES:
THE CRIMES AND THE THEORIES / 57

CHAPTER THREE
THE PUNISHMENT: INVOLUNTARY
CONFINEMENT / 121

CHAPTER FOUR
WOMEN CONFINED / 183

CHAPTER FIVE
INSTITUTIONALIZED VIOLENCE / 229

CHAPTER SIX
GOING TO THE MOVIES / 255

CHAPTER SEVEN
EDUCATION FOR EMPOWERMENT:
CALIFORNIA, 1972–1976 / 275

ACKNOWLEDGEMENTS

M Y PRIMARY DEBT is to women who, over the years, have entrusted me with the material of their lives.

This book was written in Vancouver, British Columbia between January and August 1993; the commitment behind it was formed in California, beginning in the late 1960s, where my work as a prisoners' rights advocate was joined with the work of scores of prisoners, community activists and scholars with a social conscience. With enduring respect, I give thanks to friends who were also my comrades and mentors in the work of learning about and resisting the injustices of criminal "justice." These included: Bill Barlow, Ellen Barry, Mary K. Blackmon, Herman Blake, Norman O. Brown, Jaki Christeve, Catherine Cusic, Jean Gallick, Tracy Gary, Laraine Goodman, Georgia Griffin, Rafael Guzman, John Isbister, Popeye Jackson, Stephanie Klein, Debra Miller, Rose Mohrstein, Bill Moore, Madeline Moore, Anne Near, Holly Near, Tanya Neiman, Huey Newton, Leslie Patrick-Stamp, Tony Platt, Diane Ramsey, Frances Reid, Karen Rian, Michael Rotkin, Nick Royal, Ted Sarbin, Pat Singer, Mattie Smith, Page Smith, Sin Soracco, Norma Stafford, Lia Stahrlite, Nancy Stoller, Michael Strange and Cris Williamson.

I have benefited from the work of many US, British, and Canadian academic feminists who, as referenced in this text, have conducted invaluable research in the area of women, crime and punishment.

The process of selecting material to be included here has been guided in part by the work of undergraduate students at SFU and on California university campuses. Students' probing questions and thoughtful commentaries have enriched my own understandings, and I have been continually inspired by the ways that students translate the fruits of their classroom labours into work in the community.

Special thanks to Kathleen Kendall for her timely research rescue missions, her long-distance camaraderie, and the generosity of her spirit.

Vancouver, B.C. / August 31, 1993

On the eve of the reissue of this book, my gratitude extends to the staff at Seven Stories Press, notably Crystal Yakacki, who has been a great friend and supportive ally in this project. I also thank Dan Simon, Ria Julien, Liz DeLong, Veronica Liu, Anne Rumberger, Ruth Weiner, and Jon Gilbert for their significant contributions.

In the course of doing this work, I have been steadily inspired by two remarkable friends, Liz Elliott and Jennifer Wysong, who have demonstrated extraordinary courage in the line of fire.

Finally, a big thank you to my adult children, Craig, Kimberly, Todd, and Brent for their steady support for the work of social justice.

Vancouver, B.C. / May 27, 2011

PREFACE

I WROTE THIS BOOK over a period of nine months in 1993, while working at Simon Fraser University in British Columbia. Press Gang, a Vancouver women's publishing collective, issued the first and second printings (1994–96), but soon afterward the collective dissolved. All of their publications went to another small, local enterprise, Raincoast Publishers, for distribution. Shortly after that agreement, Raincoast gained Canadian distribution rights for the Harry Potter series, and the little company that could was suddenly a major national success story. Press Gang books sat unattended on the storage shelves while Raincoast faced the challenge of meeting the demand for J. K. Rowling's books. And now Seven Stories Press has rescued my orphaned book. When Crystal Yakacki called to ask if I'd be interested in reissuing *Unruly Women*, I was delighted. For years I've respected Seven Stories publications, and I appreciate being associated with them.

I am especially pleased that this book is available again, with a new cover that illustrates a key contradiction of prisons: on the one hand, the drab, gray, sterile, fenced-in space designed for social outcasts, and, on the other hand, the vibrant personalities and colourful assortments of women who are cast out.

My earliest contact with criminal justice, in the late 1940s, did not breed confidence in the system. As a kid in a small prairie railroad town, I frequented the public library on the top floor of the town hall across the street from where we lived. The local jail was in the basement, and, as I would pass by the barred ground-level windows, I'd see dejected men sprawled on the cement floor with a naked light bulb swaying, casting eerie shadows. It frightened me to realize that there were people on earth, right in our town, who were willing to lock up other people. One awful day I watched the school wrestling coach and an armed cop beat up someone I loved and then shove him into a police car. He was a young adolescent who played the saxophone and was an excellent dancer. He was poor and didn't have a dad to defend him, so they sent him to a jail for juveniles for the crime of defying the coach. The idea of people with guns forcing people who hadn't even hurt anyone into cages felt really terrible to me.

In 1961, while married with three small children and doing office work, I found a book in the library listing hundreds of agencies that hired North Americans to work in countries all over the world, both government jobs and in the private sector. They arranged and paid for the move and transportation, so it was equal opportunity for people like ourselves who lived from one pay cheque to the next. A year later we boarded a plane bound for Europe, our first time flying, and it felt like winning the sweepstakes.

Moving to France with my family was the start of a life of adventure, living, studying, and working in different cultures on varied continents, and it was mostly very wonderful. However, in every country where I spent time I was disturbed to learn that it was invariably a despised and feared minority group that was most likely to be incarcerated, even though their crimes were no more serious or frequent than those of the dominant culture. For example, in France it was the Romany people (aka gypsies) who were locked up; in Eritrea, East Africa, where I worked with the Peace Corps and my fourth child was born, it was Muslims; in Jamaica it was the Ras Tafarians, with whom I was doing research, who were persecuted.

In 1967, I returned with my children, after almost five years away from North America, to live in California, where I was active in the civil rights, antiwar, and women's liberation movements. Many radical thinkers recognized the uses of law enforcement in practices of discrimination, and the class and race prejudices that fueled the prison industry. It was not coincidental that in Canada it was people from First Nations who were most apt to be arrested, convicted, incarcerated, and denied parole, and that in the United States it was African Americans and, increasingly, Latinos. To understand class divisions and racism at its core required an understanding of the ways criminal justice helped sustain those injustices, and I wanted that understanding. Further, as a feminist activist, I wanted to understand why it was that women in the criminal justice system were so invisible. In 1970–1971 I was teaching at the infamous Soledad state prison and was shocked that even though a lot of the men in the class had a sister, aunt, mother, or girlfriend in prison, they had no idea where the women's state prison was located. It was as if imprisoned women disappeared. Hence began what became part of my life work, helping to bring their stories to light.

Over the years, both prisoners and outsiders have asked me why I would voluntarily spend so much time in prisons. One answer is that I'm a student of history, culture, and politics, and prisons offer a transparent, microcosmic view of how power abuse is inherent to capitalist culture. As activists, we need the facts, and fighting social injustice requires going to the source and gathering the data. Another reason I continued with prison work most of my adult life was that I liked to visit my friends inside. While prisons are sickening, the people in them are often uplifting. It's inspiring to know people with gumption who are able to transcend dehumanizing circumstances. Their resilience inspired this book.

This book was also motivated by the hope that it could serve as a useful resource for prisoner rights activists. In Canada, the book directly catalyzed the organization of Strength in Sisterhood (SIS), a cross-country network of former prisoners who did advocacy for incarcerated or newly released women. Similar to the influence of the Critical Resistance movement in the US, the public testimony of these women—in media interviews, conferences, university lectures, published articles, political rallies, court hearings, and official governmental investigations—has had an influence on how people think about prisons, even if the archaic practices of punishment persist. In 2011, the global prison industrial complex is vaster than ever, including private prisons, while abolitionists continue to promote saner and more civilized responses to people that breach the law.

A couple of years after original publication, it was gratifying to attend an international academic conference and be told by at least a dozen professors that they were using *Unruly Women* in their classes in Canada, the US, Great Britain, and Australia. Likewise, the international responses from human rights activists were positive, and in 1994 a panel of judges gave the book the VanCity B.C. Book Prize for the best work focused on women. The publicity brought the work to the attention of policy makers and various authorities that often agreed that prisons, as we know them, should be abolished.

In the mid-1990s, together with other advocates including former prisoners, I consulted at length with Justice Louise Arbour, who led an official inquiry into harm done to women in the federal Canadian prison. Her report contained strong recommendations for limits on punishment, such as restricting solitary confinement to one month's duration. People in the business of punishment, however, have generally ignored her judgements. Their defiance of the esteemed Justice Arbour's authority underscores the lawlessness of prisons, which operate with remarkable autonomy and lack of judicial oversight. (Arbour subsequently saw more results as the head of the war crimes tribunal in the Hague; from there she was appointed to a seat on the Supreme Court of Canada, and eventually she was appointed High Commissioner of Human Rights with the United Nations.)

In my writing I wanted to reflect the varied points of view of those who are incarcerated, and Press Gang Publishers distributed free copies of the book to prisoners who requested it. Women who have been or are in prison who read the book reassured me that they felt accurately represented by it. I also learned that some female wardens had recommended the book to their male and female guards. But the fundamental picture hasn't changed—for over a century. Women's prison populations have significantly expanded since the 1980s, though their crime rates have not generally increased, and there are still many fewer women than men who are incarcerated. Drug and theft offences still dominate women's criminal convictions. Some of the women's prisons I describe have been closed or used for a different prison population, such as minimum-security men or youth, with the women shifted to other prisons. The bars, cells, and walls are interchangeable, even when forward-thinking administrators attempt to provide constructive options. A woman who spends her day working in a prison garden, studying accounting, learning to read, experiencing a sweat lodge, or training dogs, may appreciate the diversion, but will still be locked in her cell four times a day to face the door for a "body count." She will still be told when to stand, sit, walk, sleep, arise, work, and eat, and she will be vulnerable to being sent to solitary confinement if she offends a guard or other staff member. She will not forget that she is in prison.

Having previously visited and taught in men's prisons, and not normally prone to stereotyping, when I first went to women's prisons, in 1972, I nevertheless expected to meet the bull dykes of Hollywood prison movies. Instead, they covered the gamut of sheer normalcy, most aged twenty to forty. Some were beautiful, some wholesome-looking, others sophisticated, and others tough; most were young mothers, some were articulate, others mumbled, some looked beaten down, others had chutzpah to spare, some were funny, others were contemplative. Some had been in and out of prison all of their adult life, for possessing an illegal drug or stealing. For others, prison was a new experience. Relatively few had hurt anyone. With about 600 prisoners in the California state prison for women in 1972, sixteen had been convicted of first-degree murder and half of these had killed an abusive spouse, years before the emergence of the battered woman defence. Contrary to the grotesque stereotypes, there were no monsters.

Less than 5 percent of all lawbreakers are ever caught, charged, convicted, and incarcerated. Prisoners are selected by the criminal justice system according to gender, age, class, and colour, predominantly young men from urban black and Hispanic ghettoes and barrios in the US and First Nations communities in Canada. Like her male counterpart, a black or brown girl living in urban poverty is much more likely to be locked up than a white girl from the suburbs, even if they're both using illegal drugs or shoplifting to acquire makeup and clothes.

Those selected for prison generally lack a skilled defence lawyer. Inside they are subjected to physical, emotional, and mental abuse, despite progressive rhetoric from those prison administrations that wish to be seen as humanitarian. In virtually every prison, body cavity searches (tantamount to rape), solitary confinement, being constantly under suspicion and surveillance, the absence of adequate medical care or healthful diets, among other abuses, combine to erode prisoners' well-being even when they're high-spirited. Prisons are the most blatant evidence of the inequities that constitute capitalist culture, a junction where all social injustices converge. As for gender, this book considers why there are still so many fewer women than men who are imprisoned, whether the system is more lenient toward women, and why women's minority status within the criminal justice system has resulted historically in systemic discrimination against them.

There have always been prison reformers who sought either more humane treatment of prisoners or more effective means of punishing them. I never wanted to be known as a reformer because it was clear to me that prisons cannot be structurally reformed. They can be prettified, and staff members and outsiders can develop interesting programs. But whenever a group of people with weapons is given the authority to lock up and control a stigmatized group, abuses are inevitable. Despite surface niceties in some prisons, everyone is suspicious of everyone else, with good reason. After forty-five years of advocating for prisoners' human rights, it still shocks me to hear about incidents such as: a woman stripped naked and chained to a plank on the floor of a cold concrete cell; guards witnessing a prisoner's suicide and not intervening; women punished with solitary confinement for attempting suicide; mothers denied visits with their children; prisoners forced into sex with guards; a woman shot in the leg while trying to escape, and put in solitary without attention to her wound. Given the intentionally grim environment, it's not shocking that such events occur. What shocks me is the persistence of such punishments over the course of more than a century and the normalizing of brutality by those who are licensed to inflict it.

I naïvely believed, when I started this work decades ago, that if more people were aware of the injustices of the so-called justice system, there would be a public outcry. Parallel to the surge in new prison construction starting in the 1980s, and as resistance to it, the prison abolition movement has indeed grown in the past few decades, as has the restorative justice movement, or what some of us call transformative justice. Many more former prisoners are speaking publicly, as are high-ranking officials, on the idea of using prison only as a last resort, and certain enlightened communities are restoring justice by attending to the needs of both those who have caused harm and their victims. At the same time, now that corporations are running privatized prisons with forced labour, and selling lucrative stock, more people than ever are directly profiting from prisoners, few of whom are among the most dangerous people in society.

If the state were to confine only those who present a danger to others, very few women would be locked up and many fewer children would lose their mothers to the punishment industry. Every nation on the planet is most apt to convict and imprison people from underclass minority groups. In Western nations, many fewer people would be imprisoned if racism was eradicated from arrest, prosecution, and sentencing traditions. With a saner system, tax revenues could be redirected into education, job training, affordable housing, parks, community gardens, music, arts, child care, conflict resolution, and health care, including mental health and substance abuse programs—all as a means of strengthening communities and thereby reducing crime. There are many ways to hold people responsible for their actions, with constructive intent and outcome. It makes no sense at all to spend billions of dollars locking up impoverished women who are not dangerous, but this is what happens, across the globe, for all the reasons I go to great lengths to explain in the pages ahead.

Karlene Faith
Vancouver, B.C.
February 2011

INTRODUCTION

THE UNRULY WOMAN is the undisciplined woman. She is a renegade from the disciplinary practices which would mold her as a gendered being. She is the defiant woman who rejects authority which would subjugate her and render her docile. She is the offensive woman who acts in her own interests. She is the unmanageable woman who claims her own body, the whore, the wanton woman, the wild woman out of control. She is the woman who cannot be silenced. She is a rebel. She is trouble.

The unruly woman of Western societies is a product of the bourgeois imagination and the politics of patriarchal relations. Her crimes are the impolite crimes of the woman who lacks the resources to wrap herself in the cloaks of middle-class femininity. The "bad girl" of cultural stereotyping is the product of class-biased, racist and heterosexist myths. Historically and to the present, her appearance, actions and attitudes have been offensive to the dominant discourses which define, classify, regulate and set penalties for deviance. She is socially constructed as undeserving of the "protections" of the woman who is confined within the parameters of gender conformity.

As the flip side of the hysterical woman of the 19th century, who was perceived as the victim of her womb-inducing fantasies and in need of medical and psychiatric intervention, the unruly woman of this book asserts her untamed power in acts of resistance. When apprehended for crossing the boundaries of legality she is criminalized and punished as much for her betrayal of Womanhood as for her witting or unwitting failure to submit to The Law. In the chapters to follow I examine female transgressions against social order and the ways by which women's crimes and punishments refract the ideological constructions of gender.

Beginning with an historical overview, in Chapter One I establish the context for the witch hunts. Between the 15th and 18th centuries, untold numbers of women were executed on the charge of copulating with the Devil. This fear of undisciplined female sexuality resulted in increasing social controls over women's lives. The punishments for prostitution, scolding, adultery, killing one's husband and infanticide likewise signified the social imperatives for women of all classes to be properly confined within the walls of the patriarchal familial structure.

In addition to their apprehension for sex-specific offences, women of "the dangerous classes" were a significant presence in social crimes against nascent capitalism. With men they resisted the gentry's appropriation of common lands, protested worker-displacement by technology and industrialization, and organized popular demonstrations against high food prices in a new market economy. The gendered ideology of the nuclear family, as entrenched within the 19th century Victorian era, reiterated female subservience as a means of controlling women's unruly impulses. This misogynist continuum reappears in the 20th century in the form of Pre-Menstrual Syndrome, as appropriated by and exploited through the discourses of law and medicine in attempts to mediate the natural, even if generally latent, monstrosity of femaleness.

In Chapter Two I review contemporary literature which demystifies the "female offender," and I present an array of theoretical issues that new feminist scholarship has introduced through and against the discipline of criminology. The discussion focuses on modern crimes by women, namely the categories of prostitution, property crimes, illegal drug offences and crimes of violence, with an emphasis on the continuum between victimization and criminalization. Prostitution is understood as an issue of self-determination, whereby young women often lay claim to their bodies as a means of escaping sexual abuse in the home and as a livelihood choice in a gender-stratified economy. At the same time, prostitution is understood as the continued exploitation of females as commodified sex objects who are then blamed for societal ills, such as the spread of AIDS.

The most common female crimes are theft and fraud, which on the surface are straightforwardly economic in nature. However, as discussed, significant recent increases in female property crimes are also a gender issue, stemming from an intensification of the feminization of poverty between the 1970s and 1990s. In Canada, the proportion of women incarcerated for illegal drug offences has decreased in recent decades; however, the question of ownership of the female body has resurfaced with increasing prosecutions and regulations of female drug users relative to fetal risk. In this as in other female crimes, it is primarily women living in poverty who are most vulnerable to state expropriation of their bodies. Finally, in this second chapter, I discuss the low rate of violence committed by women and the contradictory explanations for women's lesser danger to society. The increasingly successful plea of Battered Woman Syndrome as a mitigating defence in the courts is a clear indicator of both a growing recognition and a social reification of women as victims.

Everyone in the world is potentially confined and constrained by the exigencies of their social position and the particular boundaries imposed by class, colour, sex/gender, culture, ethnicity, age, familial status, physical or mental ability, and so on, within the contexts of political, legal and other historically situated limitations. To be confined within a penal (or mental) institution is linked to these other constraints, sometimes directly, but as an experiential variation it is quite another matter. For over a century, in Western nations, involuntary confinement has been the standard punishment for those whose crimes are deemed serious by the courts. In Chapter Three I review the historical construction and ideologies of prisons for women, and contemporary debates concerning the viability of segregated institutions. With particular focus on prisons in Canada and California, I critically question the usefulness of custody, security and surveillance represented by modern institutions, given that most women who are incarcerated do not represent a danger to society.

Discussion of the "pains of imprisonment" is juxtaposed against a review of institutional programs and services designed to respond to the social and psychological needs of prisoners, which are not unique to women in prison and which are exacerbated by the fact of imprisonment itself. I also discuss the challenges faced by women who are employed as the guards of women locked up; the challenges faced by women upon release from prison; and reasons why prisons do not succeed either in reducing crime or in addressing the social, political and economic inequities that result in selective criminalization and incarceration.

The most common response to involuntary confinement is not acquiescence but rather resistance, which takes many forms. Chapter Four offers discussion of specific categories of women who populate institutions, and ways by which they seek to ameliorate their circumstances. This chapter opens with a discussion of the ways by which First Nations peoples in Canada have been oppressed and subordinated through racist assimilation practices of the dominant culture. Native women in prison exemplify a post-1960s trend among prisoners to form organized alliances with those who share cultural identity. In the spirit of self-determination, they are reclaiming their heritage and demanding that prison officials accommodate their cultural traditions and healing rituals. Given that Native women are significantly overrepresented in Canadian prison populations, this development has important political implications for "correctional" philosophies.

The majority of incarcerated women are young single parents, and this is the second group discussed in Chapter Four. Very often their crimes are the consequence not of bad parenting but rather of the effort to sustain themselves and their children with inadequate resources. A primary negative effect of incarceration of women is the harm caused by their separation from their dependent children, and I consider the question of whether or not a woman should be entitled to keep her children with her while serving her prison sentence.

The question of sustaining intimate relations with loved ones while serving prison time segues to the bonds formed between women who are incarcerated with one another. Self-identified lesbians are a small minority of female prison populations. However, women who are locked in prison for any significant length of time commonly develop special friendships which break down lesbophobic prejudices so commonplace in societies at large. The phenomenon of women loving women in prison has been the subject of some of the most reactionary studies on incarcerated women, and the purpose of this discussion is to dispel common myths and to affirm the positive aspects of these relationships.

The discussion in Chapter Five is concerned with empirical questions about the levels of violence committed by female prisoners against one another. In particular, the academic literature is examined for the purpose of setting to rest the notion that women in prison engage in more interpersonal violence than do male prisoners. Other sections in this chapter consider institutionalized violences against prisoners as perpetrated in the guise of medical treatment and in the name of custody and security. I also examine self-injury, or "slashing," as the most common form of violence within women's prisons.

Women in prison commonly remark that they feel safer in prison with other women than they ever felt in the "free" world. However, as discussed, this view would not hold in those institutions where female prisoners are raped by male staff, an issue that prior to the 1990s was shrouded in secrecy.

The myth that women in prison routinely assault one another has been perpetrated most effectively and dramatically by the media. In Chapter Six I identify a wide assortment of primarily Hollywood films which have capitalized on the historical fears of women as the embodiment of evil. These include campy films which demonize women as latter-day witches who do Satan's dirty work, and dark films which warn against "emancipated" women who become masculinized bull-dagger terrorists and who, when locked in prison, rape other women and engage in violent mayhem. Teenagers are not exempt from this exercise in stereotyping, and some of the more predatory celluloid characters are those featured in bad-girl reform school movies. Capping this cyclical Hollywood trend is a new, more insidious genre which moves out of the cheap B-grade movie formula into highly touted feature films, in which beautiful and seductive "independent" women metamorphose into monsters who threaten decent men and their decent families. These films, which have had major success at the box office, emphatically make the point that "women's liberation" is a dangerous social development.

Returning from the realm of cultural myth to concrete, carceral reality, the last chapter of this book recounts a revolutionary prison education program conducted in the California state prison for women between 1972 and 1976. A collaborative effort between prisoners and feminist allies from the "free" world, this program was sponsored by the University of California at Santa Cruz. The academic curriculum introduced prisoners to critical theory in the humanities, the social sciences and the arts. The program also featured a wide range of political and cultural workshops facilitated by community activists, and celebrations with music and artistic performances. The consciousness-raising and unifying effects of this program raised the antagonism of prison guards and security officials, and ultimately the program was cancelled. The lasting results, however, were politically significant in their effects on the prisoners who participated, and as a means of demystifying female prisoners and educating outsiders as to the functions of the state in maintaining control over criminalized populations.

• • •

At the outset, I need to explain what I mean by "political minority," a term I use frequently in this book. During the 1960s and 1970s it was common to refer to people of colour as belonging to the "Third World." The phrase was coined in 1962 by Dr. Julius K. Nyerere, the first president of decolonized Tanzania (formerly Tanganyika) in East Africa, as a way of identifying nations throughout the world that were overthrowing colonization status and claiming independence from both capitalist and communist regimes. Minority groups in Western nations, including Aboriginals, descendants of people forced into slavery and recent immigrants, similarly identified as Third World peoples. However, due in part to the exigencies of assimilation policies and the politics of new independence movements, the term "Third World" is no longer so widely accepted, and the concept of "race" has been discredited as a flawed anthropological device. Thus, throughout this text I make reference to women from "political minority" groups to indicate not only women of colour or of Aboriginal heritage, but also those women of European origin whose poverty renders them similarly vulnerable to biased criminal justice practices.

• • •

The majority of women who enter the criminal justice system have been victims of violence, and women are more often in court seeking redress for crimes against them than as offenders. The mass media likewise give more attention to harms done to women than by them. As a random example, on April 29, 1993, while I was working on the draft of this introduction, my hometown newspaper (the *Vancouver Sun*) reported not a single incident in which females were perpetrators of crime. It did, however, report many male crime stories, including crimes against women and children as in the following paraphrased items:

> In the small city of Kamloops, in the interior of British Columbia, "spousal abuse" cases tripled in 1992 due to "increased societal pressures and the poor economy." A female family lawyer and the Legal Services Society complain that the police are not doing their job, and still treat wife-battering as a "family problem" rather than as a serious crime, "even when weapons have been involved and injuries [are] apparent." (A6)

A young man in Ontario is angry about having to spend a month in jail for causing serious injury to his girlfriend's face; from his perspective, he shouldn't have been charged because, in his words, "I didn't hit her that hard." (A10)

A judge in Saskatchewan modified an earlier decision to restrict press coverage of the trials of nine adults, including a police constable and two former police chiefs, who are charged on eighty-three counts of sexual [ritual] abuse of children in an unlicensed "childcare" facility. He ruled that although the media should have access to the proceedings, testimony from the children will not be made public. (A10) [It later came to light that women were involved in this case.]

A former Crown prosecutor in New Brunswick was sentenced to five years in prison for sexually assaulting six women, in a six-month period, whose sexual assault cases he was handling as the prosecutor. He confessed to assaulting them by forcing them to "re-enact their sexual assaults" because, as he explained it, he wanted to be sure of the details of the offences against them. His defence was that he was depressed at the time. In his ruling, the judge accepted this mitigating defence and the guilty lawyer will be eligible for parole in two years. (A10)

In Vancouver, a "sexual predator" who was defended by a female lawyer was convicted of sexual assault against eleven different women, ages nineteen to fifty-one, who were attacked on the street or in their own homes over a period of four years. The significance of the case was that it was solved by matching traces of the perpetrator's semen with his DNA profile. (A1, B1)

As I discuss in various sections of the text where I critique "essentialist" tendencies in feminist theory, it is a mistake to generalize women as innocent victims of inevitable male violence. We are all innocent and we are all guilty; there are no purely "bad" or "good" people. Violence is a learned response based on socially constructed power relations, and in many cultures women have been routinely violent against children, in the name of "discipline," just as men have "disciplined" women and children—as well as exercising violence against one another in the names of order, honour, defence, vengeance, sport, God, and country. Historically, sexual violence has been almost entirely a male practice, and both male and female children, as well as adult women, have been pervasively victimized.

It is not a central purpose of this book to focus on women as victims or survivors of violence; however, the global commonality of this experience among women informs the construction of women as "offenders." The continuum from victimization to offending is at the heart of this work. The feminist insistence that we should refer to female targets of male violence not as victims but as survivors has clear merit when it suggests that the prior victim is in a process of recovery. When the harm done leads to self-defeating actions the indicators are that the victimization has not yet been overcome. At the same time, however, many "criminal" and other antisocial behaviours constitute rebellions which demonstrate that the "offender" is in fact a survivor in resistance against the status quo.

There are important connections between women who are selectively labeled criminal for random or impulsive illegal rebellions, and unruly women whose legal defiances signify deliberate rejection of the values that sustain existing hierarchical power relations. Whether an action is considered a crime or deviancy, or a behaviour is socially tolerated, depends entirely on the historical and cultural contexts and the particular configurations of power which issue formal and informal judgements.

Whether or not they are labeled "criminal," unruly women do what ordinary women do. They feel love and fear; they try to make a living or to find someone to support them; if they are mothers they care for their children the best they can; they get lost in dreams of how life might be, if only . . . . And along the way, if they are truly unruly women, they get into trouble. Most female rebels have been victimized in some way, and most victims have the capacity to resist and to become active players in social transformation.

* * *

Clearly feminists need to be critical of androcentric and misogynist work as a means of resisting constructions of knowledge which erase, denigrate or distort the realities of women, and as a way to sharpen our own analyses and to begin to repair the damages to women caused by the lies of history. For example, prior to the 1970s, an expansive "scholarly" literature on the witch hunts utterly failed to acknowledge that during the most fervent periods of persecution and slaughter it was almost entirely women who were the victims. It wasn't until the advent of Second Wave feminism that women interjected the important observation that the witch hunts were inextricably linked with fears of and social controls over women. Subsequent criminalization of female sexuality, as manifest most conspicuously in the attempted regulation of prostitution, likewise can now be explained in terms of social and political power imbalances which subordinate females on the grounds of sex and gender.

As feminists, we must also look critically at our own assumptions, formed in part through flawed or clouded prisms of reality, as a necessary step in the process of naming our lives as we experience them. We can resist the prejudices upon which social divisions are sustained, and we can resist the institutions and social structures of oppressive ideologies. We cannot, however, presume now or into the future to have arrived at a definitive set of knowledge or understandings. In the social sciences, new knowledges have never entirely displaced old ideas. The very authority to identify "empirical truths," and to interpret observable, testable "facts," is dependent on existing power relations within given social contexts. But as new materials are produced, ideas can be reconstructed in new configurations of "truth" which allow for previously silenced groups to name themselves and to describe their own experiences.

I am privileged to be able to enter into the discourses of social change and, at the same time, I am humbled by the challenge of breaking silences. By giving name to lies about women who have been historically denied a forum for speaking in their own voices, we open the doors to the cacophony of dissent and reaction. We also expand our range of vision so as to more clearly see that, through their actions of resistance, unruly women have persistently articulated a refusal to acquiesce.

> *You, Red Star Woman, if within your being you have a love for people, then write this upon your Belt, the Shield of Women. It is one of your Gifts. Write the Signs of Truth in all things upon your Belt, and you will grow. Your sisters and brothers will see plainly your Name, and from their Shields you will also learn theirs. Your dreams and your fears should also be plainly written, because then you can receive Gifts from your brothers and sisters to help you become a Whole Woman. You will learn and they will learn.*
>
> (Hyemeyohsts Storm, *Seven Arrows*)

CHAPTER ONE

Historical Perspectives: From Witch Hunts to PMS

EVERYWHERE in the Western world, girls and women from both dominant (white European) and minority cultures offend the criminal law much less than do men, historically and to the present. One can also discern historical continuity in the kinds of offences for which women are punished. This first chapter sketches examples of early social practices, primarily in the context of English Common Law, whereby condemned women were punished for their transgressions.

The subordination of Anglo-Saxon women in the contexts of North American majority populations is rooted in the shaping of power relations in early England, a process vividly reflected in and reinforced by the world of crime and punishment. The sins/crimes described below, ascribed primarily to unruly white women in England and Canada between the 15th and 19th centuries, betray some of the ways by which both men and women were schooled in gendered and class ideologies. These ideologies invested female bodies with dangerous sexual powers, and signified the power of male-governed common law to maintain "community standards" for female behaviours.

Social historians, since the 1970s, have been giving new attention to patterns of crime and punishment in early England. Rarely are these studies focused on women, beyond brief sections or fleeting references, but perusal of the work reveals cumulative insights into serious female crime. The first set of offences I will discuss can be categorized as Sex and Gender Crimes, starting with witchcraft. The witch hunts epitomized the notion that undisciplined women, by virtue of their sex, have the power to lure, terrorize and endanger mortal beings. Further, the radical significance of the witch hunts problematizes and intensifies the gendered meanings of other early female offences to be discussed, including prostitution, scolding, adultery, killing one's husband and infanticide.

The second section focuses on Property Crimes, including: offences set forth under the Black Act of 1723, which protected the gentry's property interests; activities of the Luddites in the 19th century, who protested industrialization because it robbed people of work; and popular "mob" protests against high food prices, over several centuries. Unlike those who committed individualistic acts of theft or vandalism, or most sex/gender crimes, the tens of thousands of women who participated in popular illegal protests were explicitly expressing the will of the common people, male and female.

Sex and property crimes consisted of actions or ascribed characteristics which offended the church, the patriarchs, the gentry, new medical professionals and the emerging capitalists—all of whom constituted The Law. Gender role standards were entrenched through contradictory reiterations of biological determinism. On the one hand, based on maternity, females had an innate moral superiority, which explained why so few women committed crime; on the other hand, female crime (despite its infrequency relative to male) was evidence of women's natural, physiological inferiority and sexualized propensities for evil and chaos. This latter point of view resurfaces, late in the 20th century, in the form of the Pre-Menstrual Syndrome defence, as discussed in the third section in relation to early female crime theories.

Throughout this chapter I make chronological and geographical leaps, back and forth, which I hope will not be disconcerting to the reader. My intention is to illustrate that neither the continuities nor discontinuities in attitudes toward women follow a tidy linear pattern. The contradictions are heightened in some historical periods and contexts, and in others they recede. It is important to not confuse the present with the past; it is likewise important to not underestimate the effect of the past on the present or the ways by which historic breaks are the result of human decision and agency.

SEX AND GENDER CRIMES

Witchcraft. Mythical stories abound, globally and transhistorically, of witches, sorcerers, diviners, fortune-tellers, shamans, enchanters, and so on, of both sexes. Often these myths position women as villains in a sexual war.

> *Of Adam's first wife, Lilith, it is told*
> *(The witch he loved before the gift of Eve,)*
> *That ere the snake's, her sweet tongue could deceive,*
> *And her enchanted hair was the first gold.*
> (D. G. Rosetti, "The Lady Lilith," circa 1855)

As another example, from Bohemia at the end of the 7th century, comes this story:

> After a long period in which women had governed the affairs of Prague, when the men tried to take over all decision-making the women refused to submit to their rule. A young woman named Wlasca, who was a "born leader," had designs on getting "complete control over the men." To her friends, who trusted her special powers, she gave a potion which immediately caused them to "loathe their husbands, brothers, lovers and the whole male sex." These witches then killed almost all of the men, laid siege to the castle, and ruled for seven years. (Baroja, 1975: 92)

Ancient superstitions and fears of supernatural powers served (then as now) as informal social control, and produced conformity and obedience to "higher" authority. From a functionalist point of view, community solidarity is strengthened when authorities (of the state, church, universities, medicine, law) can covertly or overtly identify a single consensual enemy, against which "the people" can rally. This diversionary tactic is employed most earnestly during times of economic instability and political or spiritual upheaval. Scapegoating, in particular, has been useful historically both as a way of re-entrenching the status quo and as a direct or indirect impetus for hegemonic shifts. Recent Western examples include the 1940s Hitlerian holocaust against Jews, homosexuals, the mentally ill, the physically disabled and Gypsies, and the North American anti-Communist movement in the 1950s. Witch hunts are useful to garnering patriotic commitment and to the "cleansing of the race." In the 1990s, the image of the evil witch is conjured up by Robert Bly, the big daddy of the back-to-real-men movement. As observed by Susan Faludi in a mixed workshop, Bly exhorts the men in the group to avoid blaming anyone for their circumstance by declaring "There's a witch in the room who is doing this to us," thereby, as Faludi interprets it, representing "the feminist monster in a form men can revile without apology" (Faludi, 1991: 311).

Witch hunts have recurred frequently throughout recorded history, not as a linear, teleological pattern but rather as shaped by specific social and political contexts. Between the 13th and 15th centuries, late-medieval witch hunts targeted men as well as women, throughout Europe and in England and Scotland. Over time, fewer men were charged, and increasing numbers of women were convicted of the crime in both ecclesiastical and secular courts. However, until recently scholars have virtually ignored the glaring fact that women were the vast majority of victims of witch hunts. By the end of the 15th century, at the dawn of the Renaissance, witch hunts erupted with a new fervour that signaled major social changes, "an explosive force, constantly and fearfully expanding . . ." (Trevor-Roper, 1975: 121). What scholars have ignored is that this "explosive force" was undisguised fear and hatred of women.

A view of women as an irresistible but evil temptation to innocent men is a Biblical theme which has resurfaced in both popular culture and the law with historical irregularity, but never more profoundly than in the case of the witch hunts. In the early Western world it was the Roman Church that most clearly defined and set punishments for crimes of witchcraft, but following from the Reformation in the 16th century the new Protestants were quick to pick up the chants. Martin Luther believed that witches should be burned even when they weren't hurting anyone, because God clearly commands through the Bible that "they must be slain—witches and enchantresses shall be put to death" (Trevor-Roper, 1975: 130). The Protestants and Catholics were warring with each other but they collaborated in the witch hunts.

It is not against Canadian law to *be* a witch, but it is against the law to *pretend* to be one (*Canadian Criminal Code,* 1993):

365. Every one who fraudulently
  (a)   pretends to exercise or to use any kind of witchcraft, sorcery, enchantment or conjuration,
  (b)   undertakes, for a consideration, to tell fortunes, or
  (c)   pretends from his [or her] skill in or knowledge of an occult or crafty

science to discover where or in what manner anything that is supposed to
have been stolen or lost may be found, is guilty of an offence punishable
on summary conviction.

This would suggest that the law is not willing to acknowledge witchcraft as
something real that can be practiced by otherwise mortal human beings, but
it nevertheless forbids generating public or private fears of or beliefs in witchcraft. The law's apparent intent is to protect society from the harm caused by
induced fear, even if the fears are groundless. We may believe in supernatural
phenomena, religiously oriented or otherwise, but, as a going-on 21st century
society, the vast majority of the Canadian population would probably not seriously and openly profess to believing that certain women copulate directly
with Lucifer, Satan, the Prince of Darkness, the Devil, as a literal being (in the
supernatural guise of a man, or an animal) and thereafter exercise evil powers
on earth in collusion with Him.

There are contradictory views of the Devil in Christian mythology. On
the one hand, the Devil was God's adversary, whose immeasurable powers to
cause terror and harm were independent of and in conflict with God's will.
Henry Lea, turn of the century historian of the Inquisition and witchcraft, is
quoted in reference to a single parish in Germany where six hundred witches
were burned. He says:

> Christendom seemed to have grown delirious, and Satan might well smile at the
> tribute to his power in the endless smoke of the holocausts which bore witness to his
> triumph over the Almighty . . . . Could any Manichean offer more practical evi-
> dence that Satan was lord of the universe? (Parrinder, 1963: 25–26)

On the other hand, the Devil could be useful. His evil energies could be har-
nessed by the Holy Trinity (God the Father, His Son Jesus Christ and the Holy
Ghost) to perform punishment on someone guilty of mortal sin, as suggested
by St. Paul in a moral tirade against fornication:

> . . . with the power of our Lord Jesus Christ,

> To deliver such [a fornicator] unto Satan for the destruction of the flesh that the
> spirit may be saved . . . . (1 Corinthians 5:4–5)

By the 15th century, a Western witch was most commonly thought to be someone who sexually surrendered herself to the Devil, and became slave to his evil, supernatural powers. As encoded in church documents discussed below, given natural female lust and a deceptive nature, and given that the Devil was male, women were better suited to this perverse activity than were men. It was woman's unruly sexual character which engaged her in witchcraft. Female behaviours which, in the 20th century, would be diagnosed as psychosis were, in the pre-Enlightenment era, viewed as evidence of willful coitus with embodied evil.

Aboriginal communities in early Canada attributed to women special powers which Europeans interpreted as the negative power of witches, and which might well have led to persecution or death for some indigenous women at the hands of white men. However, no woman was ever officially executed for witchcraft in Canada, which was in the early processes of formation as a newly colonized nation during the latter stages of the witch hunts. In the early 18th century one woman was charged with "complicity in a case of witchcraft," and then acquitted (LaChance, 1981: 160–61).

Considerable attention has been given to the witch trials in Salem, Massachusetts, where, between March and September 1692, hundreds of women were charged with witchcraft. Of these, fourteen wild women, who used bad language or were otherwise perceived as uncontrollable, were executed by hanging or pressing (Hansen, 1969; Williams, 1981; Wilson, 1993). "Evidence" of their powers included being able to "fly through the air," attributed to six of the women accused. Others were accused of myriad offences such as causing a cow to stop giving milk, raising storms at sea, making hogs chase men, being able to walk in rain without getting wet, and possessing "familiars," small animals (such as dogs, cats and birds) sent by the Devil to assist them in their evil deeds (Wilson, 1993: 61–63). Many of the accused confessed that they were witches, themselves convinced (under tormenting inquisition) that Satan had so empowered them. A number of men in Salem were also accused, but there were relatively few of them and almost all were thought to be contaminated by female relatives who had the Devil's powers.

By the late 17th century, Spain, which had been home to the Inquisition, was among the European countries that executed the fewest women for witchcraft. One of the Spanish Inquisitors, Salarzar Frias, had carefully examined 1,800 early cases of confessions, and he concluded that the "witches" were subjects of delusions and that confessions had been forced under torture. Given his prominence and influence, he was persuasive to the authorities in discouraging future witch trials (Parrinder, 1963: 26).

Between the 15th and 18th centuries, uncounted women in England, Scotland and central Europe were imprisoned, hanged, guillotined, drowned in hot oil, and in other ways tortured and executed for witchcraft. When women were burned at the stake, as they were in France and Germany among other nations (though not generally in England), it was to ensure that their bodies would not be resurrected (Hansen, 1969: 34). The church made the judgements, then handed the guilty bodies over to the state for execution (Parrinder, 1963: 25). We lack exact knowledge of the numbers of women executed overall but estimates range from several hundred thousand to nine million killed between the 15th and 18th centuries (Ehrenreich and English, 1973; Klaits, 1985: 86–103; MacFarlane, 1970). In some cases mothers and daughters were executed together (Lea, 1957, vol. 2: 849).

Because witches were thought to exercise supernatural power, it was believed they could cause harm without having physical contact with their victims. Sharpe cites the case of the luckless Margery Stanton who, in 1578, was convicted of the following offences: bewitching a horse; killing chickens; tormenting a man; causing a woman to swell up as if pregnant; making a cow give blood instead of milk; and causing a child to become ill (Sharpe, 1984: 78–79). Most seriously, witches were thought to kill children (including "the unborn") as sacrifices to Satan. It was commonly believed that witches did their evil deeds under cover of darkness, and that they had the ability to fly. As in Salem, it was believed that they could project themselves into the form of an animal and that they also bonded with animal "familiars," or imps, who facilitated their witchcraft. At a time when domesticated animals in the home were uncommon, an unmarried woman who kept cats or other small animals for company would be a likely suspect (Parrinder, 1963: 42–51). In effect, to be executed "witches" needed only to be accused, and during periods of frequent executions all women must have lived with the fear of being suspected. This would account for the vociferous accusations by women against women, publicly demonstrating their opposition to Satan's work so as to circumvent accusations against themselves.

Any woman associated with an odd or disastrous occurrence would be vulnerable not only at the time but for the rest of her life, since such events could be recalled at trials many years later. Accused witches were blamed for every social and private malady: diseased animals; impotence; unwanted pregnancy; illness; death; bad weather; quarrels; disappearance of objects; bad crops; injuries; fires; and so on. A witch also had the power to send demons and bad spirits into other people's bodies, including children (Boguet, 1929: 8–14). If these infected individuals were themselves charged with witchcraft they might escape punishment by accusing whomever they believed had cursed them.

Fluctuations over the centuries in the enthusiasm with which women were dispatched to their deaths accompanied fluctuations in the gendered political economy and in church-state relations. The numbers of women executed accelerated in the late 15th century at least in part as a result of a significant documented presented to the courts by the Roman Church. In 1486, Pope Innocent VIII commissioned two Dominican monks, Heinrich Kramer and Jacob Sprenger, to write a handbook on the detection, apprehension and punishment of witches. Between them they had served as Inquisitors at the trials of over fifty women. Their *Malleus Maleficarum* (*The Witches' Hammer*) is a disturbing, misogynist document on women as evil by nature. It is a guide to all the different ways a woman could reveal her propensity for witchcraft, and advocates execution of all witches. Virtually any woman, by their observations, could be a witch:

> All wickedness is but little to the wickedness of a woman . . . . What else is woman but an unescapable punishment, a necessary evil, an evil of nature, painted with fair colours . . . . Woman [is] more bitter than death . . . because of the first temptress, Eve. (Kramer and Sprenger, 1486/1948: 42–44)

> [Women] are feebler both in mind and body . . . more carnal than a man. When a woman weeps, she labors to deceive . . . . The world now suffers through the malice of women . . . . Woman is beautiful to look upon, contaminating to the touch, and deadly to keep . . . . [Woman is a] liar by nature . . . . They cast wicked spells on men and animals. All witchcraft comes from carnal lust, which is in women insatiable. They consort even with devils. It is no matter for wonder that there are more women than men found infected with the heresy of witchcraft. (Ibid.: 44–47)

The monks' graphic portrayals of women as suffering from natural/unnatural insatiable lust and overwhelming sexual passion, and the violences that should be done unto them, served the function of pornography. With five printings this book was an early bestseller among the literate population. It sat on magistrates' podiums throughout Europe, and provided a strong religious basis for the legal conviction of witches (Summers, 1948: xiv). Men were only occasionally executed for witchcraft following from the publication of the *Malleus Maleficarum*, through the 17th century. Those found guilty were commonly husbands who refused to testify against their wives, and were thus believed to be themselves conspirators with the Devil (Klaits, 1985: 68–69; MacFarlane, 1970: 160).

The Bible itself exhorted against witches, and the increasing sexualization of witchcraft corresponded to a rise in Christian fundamentalism (Klaits, 1985: 68–69). In Exodus 20:13, Moses is told "Thou shalt not kill." In Exodus 22:18, however, he is told "Thou shalt not suffer a witch to live." Although it was a sin to take a human life, it was not a sin to execute a witch; it was a way of fighting the Devil. Given all the hardships attributed to the Devil's powers, it was reasonable that people would want to help rid the earth of Him and his representatives—except when one was herself the target of accusation.

Kramer's and Sprenger's influence spread throughout Europe with lasting effects, as evidenced (and referenced) in the testimony of a late 16th century French lawyer, Henri Boguet, who aggressively hunted down witches in France and wrote about the necessity of killing them. In explaining why women were suited to witchcraft he both echoes the monks and anticipates Freud:

> The Devil uses them so because he knows that women love carnal pleasures, and he means to bind them to his allegiance by such agreeable provocations. Moreover, there is nothing which makes a woman more subject and loyal to a man than that he should abuse her body. (Boguet, 1929: 29).

Who were these witches so feared by the church, state, emerging medical profession, bourgeoisie and, finally, the population at large? Modern history has generalized the victims of witch hunts to be women without men to give them legitimacy and respectability, women easily scapegoated because they lacked the protections enjoyed by married women. So-called spinsters (literally, one who spins) and widows were thought to be specially vulnerable, as were vagabond, homeless women. Any unemployed woman without male support would be at risk.

Contemporary archival work on witch hunts demonstrates that it was not just poor, single, older women who were targeted, or rebel-saints like Joan of Arc, or the healer-midwife wise women, but rather that very ordinary women were likewise victims of accusation and execution (Klaits, 1985: 86–103). Married women were by no means exempt, and although the rich were usually spared, this was not always the case. In some provincial villages virtually all women were executed, and in such scenarios the war against the Devil was clearly a war of the fathers against their wives, mothers, sisters and daughters.

The most famous and politically significant of the witches, Joan of Arc (Jeanne d'Arc), was executed by fire in 1431 at age nineteen on the grounds that she was a trafficker in witchcraft (Lightbody, 1961: 23). She was charged as "a sorceress, a divineress, a false prophet, one who invoked evil spirits, a witch, a heretic, an apostate, a seditious blasphemer rejoicing in blood . . ." (Lang, 1909: 274). Moreover, she cropped her hair and wore masculine garments (Sackville-West, 1936: 325–28). Her head, and probably other body parts, was shaven before execution, because it was believed that witches would otherwise hide special painkilling drugs in their hair to reduce the likelihood of involuntarily "confessing" during tortures (Boguet, 1929: 125).

The medical profession became increasingly professionalized, formalized and legitimized during the Ages of (so-called) Reason and Enlightenment (17th and 18th centuries), and the church and state colluded with physicians in the suppression of traditional healers and midwives. Kramer and Sprenger believed that "no one does more harm to the Catholic Faith than midwives," and because infant mortality rates were high it was easy on this basis to accuse midwives of witchcraft (Porringer, 1963: 114). These women became key targets of witch hunts, and physicians were employed to verify guilt (Ehrenreich and English, 1973; MacFarlane, 1970). Indeed, Kramer and Springer specified that physicians above all others were eminently qualified to confirm the presence of the Devil's powers in women suspected of witchcraft (Summers, 1948: xliii). This was a shift from such traditional tests as throwing the woman into the water: if she sank she was innocent, though she might drown; if she floated she clearly had supernatural powers and was then executed.

The use of physicians as an "alternative" to metaphysical, pre-science judgements was a singularly unifying historical moment in the triumvirate of church, law and medicine (Ehrenreich and English, 1979). The "scientific" means by which physicians identified witches was through locating "Devil's marks" on their bodies, as explained by a lawyer in the 17th century who describes these signs as follows:

> some big or little Teat upon their body, and in some secret place, where he [the Devil] sucketh them. And Besides their sucking, the Devil leaveth other marks upon their body, sometimes like a blew or red spot, like a flea biting; sometimes the flesh

is sunk in and hollow (all which for a time may be covered, yea taken away, but will come again to their old form). And these the Devil's marks be insensible, and being pricked will not bleed, and be often in their secretist parts, and therefore require diligent and careful search. (Dalton, 1630, quoted by Gareau, 1992: 20)

The witch hunts accelerated anew in the 17th century and then tapered off; by the middle of the 18th century executions for witchcraft had virtually ceased. The newly literate gentry took credit for being civilized enough to combat the superstitions of the common people, and they gave up the witch hunts long before the common people gave up their fears of witches (Parrinder, 1963: 32). But the witch hunts did not, in fact, cease due to the good will of the gentry, despite their desire to be seen as gentlemen of a new order. (As one historian stated, with tongue in cheek: "It was lucky for the witches that England was aristocratically governed" [Ibid.].) Rather, the witch hunts came to an end due to a convergence of historical tensions and political events.

Radical feminists most commonly decry the witch hunts as genocidal exercises in misogyny, or "femicide" (Radford and Russell, 1992). In this vein, Marianne Hester theorizes convincingly that the witch-craze was an effort "at maintaining and restoring male supremacy" (1992: 27). During the 15th to 17th centuries women had wide-ranging responsibilities, and exercised considerable autonomy at home, in the marketplace, as single or married women earning their keep, and as possessors of important knowledges. Marriage was not exalted for all classes until the 18th century, during the same era in which the notion of private property was entrenched among the ruling classes. The witch hunts were the historic prelude to legislating women as private property, to be tamed of their wild natures and kept under surveillance.

The advent of popular science and taxonomical methods of classification which scientized every detail of everyday life; an increasingly sophisticated medical profession which pathologized women as the source and manifestation of physical and social disease; the weakening of religious authority; the introduction of parliamentary governance; the Industrial Revolution; the emergence of capitalism; and, the introduction of the pre-Victorian father-right nuclear family as basic to an orderly economy—all these served to challenge beliefs in witches (as well as, more benignly, in goblins and other folkloric beasts). The social and political emphases shifted from executing women to controlling them in the home. This was not an innovation. It had long been idealized, through religious authority, that when a man marries he can expect his wife to obey him, as expressed in the 16th century by Thomas More in his vision of Utopia, the perfect society:

> Husbands are responsible for punishing their wives, and parents for punishing their children, unless the offence is so serious that it has to be dealt with by the authorities, in the interests of public morality. (1516/1965: 104–5)

The notion that men had to work at controlling women was not innovative; however, it was an invention of the pre-Victorian Enlightenment era to suggest that women were incapable of heinous crime unless driven or influenced by their husbands. Historically, this was a short-lived illusion.

It is somewhat remarkable, given a substantial literature on the witch hunts, that so little attention was given to their significance in the construction of sex/gender power relations. Male academic theorists, no less than purveyors of conventional wisdom, have studiously avoided acknowledging that these killings of women cumulatively constituted a holocaust against women. Functionalist anthropologists, for example, sound gender neutral when theorizing that beliefs in witchcraft have been able to meet "a necessity of social existence . . . it enables people to put a name to their anxieties" (Mair, 1969: 199). Kluckhohn theorizes that "the image of the witch as capable of every forbidden act allows people to contemplate such acts with a clear conscience . . . it 'affirms solidarity by dramatically defining what is bad'" (Ibid.: 201). Such theories, reductionist though they may be, might have partial validity in the feminist framework if it can be recognized that it came to be women who were defined as bad.

In another example of this failure to recognize the double standard and the sex-gender power relations behind the witch hunts, an historian speculated that women, due to their peculiar microbiological makeup, were uniquely affected by a poisonous ergot fungus, from which derives the hallucinogen lysergic acid diethylamide-25 (that is, LSD) (Matossian, 1989). By this theory, the highly toxic mold, which grows on rye grain, caused stricken women to behave unpredictably and strangely, and caused others to fear them. One could as easily theorize that a poisonous fungus caused the hysteria exhibited by church and state authorities who invented and constructed the crimes of and punishments for witchcraft. Approximately thirty thousand women at one time in just one region of France were suspected of being witches, and alarmists declared that every country on the continent was "infested with this miserable and damnable vermin" (Boguet, 1929: xxiv).

These hysterical men and their institutions, periodically and in different forms over time, are and always have been actively resisted—by other men as well as by women. Of the countless women who adamantly resist late 20th century vestiges of witch hunts, many do call themselves witches. Ranging in age from teenagers to the elderly, these women's beliefs are the antitheses of the doctrines of contemporary satanic and similar cult forms; the rituals and practices of contemporary "good" witches are likewise antithetical to those of hate cults at large. Hate groups in 1993, from churches which condemn and reject homosexuals, to the Ku Klux Klan, to those practicing femicide by rape and torture of women in Bosnia, practice straightforward and ritualistic physical and/or psychic violence, and constitute the modern harbingers of the same paradigms and ideologies which governed the witch hunts.

Contemporary witches, according to their orientation, practice combinations of many ancient as well as new age approaches to expressing one's faith and respect for the planet, its inhabitants, and our universal environment. What they do, depending on who they are, is inclusive of the following and much more: spiritual self-help and consciousness-raising; formation of "covens" (a word with the same origin as "convent"); divination and meditation; singing praises; searches for past lives; developing physical health and sacred sexuality; imagination and dream work; pagan chants and healing rituals, with emphasis on solstice celebrations; visualization; ecological preservation; transformational exercises; revival of goddesses whose representations have cyclically appeared, then disappeared, for over 30,000 years; study of Aboriginal shamans, Celtic supernatural traditions, and witches in Africa, the Middle East, the Caribbean, Latin America and Europe; cultivation of The Feminine, and channeling of loving, open, focused personal energies; adoption of political ideas and impulses of radical feminism; and, physical and psychic convergences of woman-power.[1]

The new witches, like crones of yore, form communities and look to the natural elements to inform them of their roots and connectedness. They write new liturgies. Most explicitly reject the hierarchical, patriarchal features of Christian, Jewish and other faiths and doctrines, and the state formations, professions and institutions that have evolved from patriarchal traditions. They rename themselves. Z Budapest, a Hungarian refugee, was arrested in 1975 for reading Tarot cards in Los Angeles. (Only licensed ministers, priests, rabbis and so on were legally entitled to foresee the future.) Z became a significant teacher and healer of women. In the 1990s a California theology professor named Starhawk is similarly a respected elder in the world of witchcraft and goddess worship as resistance. There are others. They are everywhere.

Prostitution. In the time-worn adage, prostitution is the world's oldest profession. Others retort that pimping came first. The pimp is the manager, the slave-owner, the profiteer, the brutalizer, the self-serving leech and parasite. The pimp is also the state, the economy and society at large, which construct the market for prostitutes.

There are at least five analytic approaches, or discourses, that provide frameworks for analyzing prostitution. A *gender* analysis considers means by which the female body is mystified, commodified and exploited to serve male interests. An *economic* analysis examines class stratification and the exclusion of women from well-paying jobs. A *religious* analysis identifies prostitution as a moral issue, usually presented with the burden of sin on the woman who prostitutes, not on the man who buys her services. A *legal* analysis examines the continuities and discontinuities in legislative and juridical processes, and patterns of punishment. Finally, a *medical* approach is concerned with devising social controls over health and safety.

None of the above-named discourses are mutually exclusive; rather, numerous conditions converge in the creation, perpetration and condemnation of street prostitution. In the 19th century, bourgeois men had unambiguous authority over women; economic conditions compelled women to prostitute themselves; moralists condemned the commercial sex activity that gender relations and economic conditions produced as inevitable; and law and medicine converged in methods of social control over prostitutes.

In the 1860s, England's Parliament passed the Contagious Diseases Acts, a medical approach to prostitution which gave the police broad powers to confine women on untried charges of prostitution so they could be tested for infections. The purported intent was to stamp out sexually transmitted diseases, but health measures were foregone in favour of punitive treatment of the women. Prostitutes who were servicing soldiers were especially targeted, but the sweeping police powers to confine any woman who was a suspect resulted in countless arrests and "medical" violations of women who were not working as prostitutes. Women in England united to oppose these Acts, under the leadership of Josephine Butler. Given the feminist thrust of the campaign, it was surprisingly successful in altering public opinion, although the Acts were not repealed until 1883, almost two decades later (Valverde, 1991: 81).

In his discussion of female crime in England between 1660 and 1800, J. M. Beattie accounts for the higher rate of female arrests in urban rather than rural settings with "the likelihood that informal sanctions would have been more effective and would have been used more readily . . . [in] the country-side" (Beattie, 1986: 240). Sharpe concurs that women engaged in full-time prostitution were rare outside London and other urban areas, noting that apart from notable village bawdy houses, the typical rural prostitute was a part-timer, usually "a vagrant, wandering from parish to parish augmenting her income by soliciting en route." Even in the cities, women worked primarily "on an amateurish and opportunistic basis" (Sharpe, 1984: 110, 116). By the mid-19th century, so many women in England were homeless and, many of them, working as occasional prostitutes that when "prostitutes, vagrants and tramps" were excluded from tallies of "criminal" populations, in the late 1860s, the number of females in this demographic was reduced from 54,703 (1860) to 11,445 (1870) (Zedner, 1991: 21).

As opportunities for single women to find a job or a husband decreased in the countryside, they flocked to the cities. With increased urbanization, unem-ployment was rampant and single women were vulnerable to pimps, madams and other entrepreneurs in the sex industry who emerged amidst other capi-talist enterprises. The urban environment was blamed for exacerbating tastes for fancy clothes and entertainments which, in combination with various vices, led to "social disorder, rebelliousness, idleness, and crime," including a demand for prostitution (Beattie, 1986: 241). Full-fledged brothels prolifer-ated, and arrests were routine. Women could even be arrested for "talking [obscenely] at unseasonable time of night" (Sharpe, 1984: 116).

In 18th century London, women, not men, were arrested for keeping bawdy houses, seducing poor women with money and entrapping them in the business. Sharpe describes one such madam who, on occasion, "would make her girls start a fight in the street, and then have pickpockets work the crowd that gathered to watch" (Ibid.: 115). The punishment for running a bawdy house was commonly confinement to the pillory, a public degradation ritual. The head and wrists were held by tight openings in a wooden frame, rendering the prisoner immobilized and exposed to the elements and public humilia-tions. Crowds of contemptuous citizens gathered to heap rotten vegetables and vile epithets against morals offenders in particular.

Houses of correction functioned in 18th century England as places of con-finement for petty offenders awaiting trial. These places were filled with the poor and homeless, unmarried mothers, errant servants, and prostitutes, who constituted up to a third of those incarcerated (Ibid.: 117). Many male offenders were sent to the army, a jail of another kind (Beattie, 1986: 498). Such people, male and female, children and adults, were perceived as lazy, corrupt and inherently dangerous to the status quo and to the emerging religious, political and economic ruling classes.

At the same time that prostitutes in England were judged as sinners and social danger, so were they exploited by authorities for their sexual currency. Female convicts who were transported from England to the colonies, during the 18th and 19th centuries when this form of banishment became an alternative to the death penalty, were being punished primarily for petty theft. But even those who hadn't been prostitutes in the home country were forcibly used as prostitutes by the male convicts and guards on the ships, and they were virtually condemned to prostitution once they arrived in Australia. Upon arrival (if they didn't die of disease or abuse en route) their situation didn't improve.

. . . whether she was concubine to one man or available to all she was still considered a whore. Since there was virtually no escape from the colony which required women to be whores, there was no escaping whoredom. . . .

So strong was the idea that all women in penal colony Australia were whores that women who were not convicts became its victims too. Aboriginal women carried a double burden. As women, they were seen as sexual objects and fair game for white men; as members of a subject people they were also victims of the whole range of indignities bestowed by a brutal invading colonialism which considered itself to be the master race. . . .

It was deemed necessary by both the local and the British authorities to have a supply of whores to keep the men, both convict and free, quiescent. The Whore stereotype was devised as a calculated sexist means of social control and then, to absolve those who benefited from it from having to admit to their actions, characterized as being the fault of the women who were damned by it. (Summers, 1975: 270, 276, 286)

Some 18th century prostitutes who had somewhat more voice in the matter refused to be intimidated, as demonstrated by a group of Canadian women who, when confronted by law enforcement officers seeking to arrest them for lewd behaviours, chased after the police with wooden clubs and managed to take the warrant from them (LaChance, 1981: 160). By the end of the 19th century, prostitution was singled out as the most despicable social evil in Canada, but, as Val Verde notes, proposed reformers differed in their approaches: some wanted harsh, legal punishments whereas doctors thought prostitution to be a sign of mental illness (Valverde, 1991: 77). Moralists distinguished between fallen women, pathetic lost souls who needed saving, and real sinners, real prostitutes, who contaminated and corrupted men, and defiled the family.

On the west coast of Canada, prostitution flourished in mining towns during the Gold Rush, and in other isolated areas where men gathered in work crews. The practice likewise extended to urban areas. Prominent among Canadian social reformers who generated moral panics about prostitutes was Emily Murphy (1922), the first female magistrate in the British Empire and one of the women who challenged Canada's high court decision that women could not sit in the Senate because they did not qualify as "persons." After a ten-year struggle, in 1929 the British Privy Council overturned the court's judgement and women were persons at last. Prostitutes, however, were another matter. Even women who engaged in what would now be thought to be normal courtship behaviour were denigrated as "occasional prostitutes" (Ibid.: 83). More rescue homes were established, continuing a tradition begun mid-19th century for "fallen" women, wherein Chinese prostitutes, among others, were converted to Christianity (Ibid.: 88). The bulk of female (as well as male) prisoners in Ontario jails in the 19th century were Irish immigrants, most of them fine-defaulters charged with drunkenness, idleness, disorderly conduct, vagrancy and prostitution-related offences. The Women's Christian Temperance Union, among other groups, argued that customers should be no less liable than prostitutes (Backhouse, 1991: 237), a point of view which was not enacted into policy until late in the 20th century.

Women who were not of British origin were particularly suspect, and racism was a major factor in prosecution. Although women of African heritage constituted just three percent of the population in Nova Scotia in the late 19th century, they constituted 40 percent of women incarcerated for prostitution (Fingard, 1988: 71). For some women without resources "jail provided one of the few opportunities to live in safety and comfort" (Ibid.: 77). Backhouse (1991), in the most complete study to date of women and the law in 19th century Canada, observes that women of African origin were overrepresented in jails in Halifax and in Calgary, and Japanese and Chinese women were overrepresented on the West Coast. Explicit racism was especially expressed toward First Nations women, whose punishments were harsher and who were charged without convincing evidence, although they did not yet constitute a significant portion of Canadian female prisoners. Discriminatory prosecution also negatively affected Quebec prostitutes, and Roman Catholic prostitutes in Nova Scotia. In addition to street prostitution, young, unmarried and impoverished women found work in brothels throughout Toronto and other emerging cities. At least one woman, in London, Ontario, made a lucrative living running a brothel and successfully invested in real estate (Backhouse, 1991: 233, 241–42, 244–59).

Federal legislation in Canada between 1869 and 1892 sought to prevent the entry of young women into prostitution, by providing criminal penalties to homeowners who permitted girls under age sixteen to participate in sexual activity under their roof, and by making it a crime for anyone, including parents, to defile or encourage defilement of females under age twenty-one. Arguing against both sinfulness and sexual exploitation of women, social reformers wanted prostitution eradicated. However, in the process, they were harassing women for whom selling sex was work, their livelihood.

It is axiomatic that many men would not want to make or enforce laws against prostitution. Rationalizations abounded for society's inability to control prostitution, and in 1937 a theory was presented that justified leniency. Kingsley Davis, a functionalist US sociologist, hypothesized that prostitution saved marriages and stabilized society. In his view, prostitution provided restless men with necessary outlets and variety for their naturally healthy sexual appetites, and prostitutes served men in war and men too repugnant to attract women to marry them.

From this functionalist view, buttressed by the essentialist perspective of men as having uncontrollable appetites for sex, prostitution is a social service which society could scarcely do without. This view had prevailed for some time among judges, who exhibited relative leniency to prostitutes. Backhouse remarks of 19th century Canadian judges, "It appears that much as the judges believed in the legal regulation of sexuality, they also viewed prostitution as something of a 'necessary social evil,' required to accommodate male sexual needs" (Backhouse, 1991: 330).

Davis's theory is problematic because it essentializes male/female behaviours as biological phenomena. It fails to recognize that prostitution is itself socially constructed and laden with issues of power. If men really do have uncontrollable sexual aggressiveness, how does one explain such highly valued male-Enlightenment concepts as free choice, reason, rationality, individual choice and self-control? And how could any woman ever trust any man, if male sexuality is hormonally uncontrollable? Contemporary sociological theorists refute the sex-functionalist explanation and instead examine the socio-economic conditions, legislative shifts, enforcement practices and gender factors that produce prostitution (see, for example, Lowman, 1988). More than any other offence, prostitution signifies the historical continuum of sexualization of female criminality and criminalization of female sex. Much more will be said about prostitution in Chapter Two, where we will examine its significance in the contemporary context.

Scolding. Common laws against defamation, rumour, gossip, slander and so on were derived from a presumption of community consensus of gender role behaviour:

> It would seem that scolding, so often written off by historians merely as a joke, contains some important clues not only to [early English] views on harmony and order, but also on attitudes to differences in behaviour between the sexes. (Sharpe, 1984: 89)

When a wife in early England scolded (nagged or berated) her husband, she was committing a common-law offence. A woman's husband was her Master. His authority extended from God through the King to all Men. It was a man's duty to govern his wife and children (and, if he had any, his servants). It was a woman's duty to obey, submissively. Scolds were tried in court by a jury, as if criminal, until the mid-18th century, when their trials, like those of witches, shifted to "the justice's parlour" (Sharpe, 1984: 93).

The woman who criticized her husband, who bossed him, who insulted him, or who in any way showed her rejection of his authority, was a shrew, or a scold, subject to public humiliation. She could be locked into the pillory, or run through town while being lashed. She also could be chained and whipped in a public square, demonstrating to other women the penalty for betrayal of the female gendered role. She could be made to wear the "brank" (or "scold's bridle"), a metal apparatus which fit over the head and into the mouth, with sharp points that cut into the woman's tongue if she attempted to speak (Dobash, Dobash and Gutteridge, 1986: 19–20; Underdown, 1985: 123). The purpose of each of these punishment rituals was to silence dissident women, and to publicly buttress the ideal of the compliant, obeisant wife.

Given that a scolded husband was likewise not fulfilling his gender duty, he too could be publicly humiliated, through straightforward ostracism or the satire of a charivari. For example, in one public ritual, as depicted in a popular 17th century chapbook and play, "The Pinder of Wakefield" (Capp, 1984: 216), a village boy was selected to dress up as the nagging wife and a man took the role of the berated husband. They were seated backward on a donkey, with the "wife" beating on her "husband's" back with a ladle while raging and shrieking at him. Paraded through town, the guilty couple's neighbours, and people from neighbouring towns, followed behind mocking and taunting their impersonators (Underdown, 1985: 123). It was not only women, then, whose behaviours were circumscribed. Just as women were being trained to be passive, so were men being trained to be authoritarian. Shakespeare made fun of the process in his comedy "The Taming of the Shrew," where he says "Such duty as the subject owes the prince, Even such a woman oweth to her husband."

Adultery. In the 17th century crime and sin were hardly distinguishable, and in 1650 English Parliament declared female adultery to be a criminal offence, meriting the death penalty though it was seldom enforced (Sharpe, 1984: 92). Ridicule and shaming were the more common responses, as fictionalized by Nathaniel Hawthorne in *The Scarlet Letter* (1850), the colour "scarlet" designated by the Bible to signify sin and harlotry (Isaiah 1:18, and Revelations 17:1–6). Given a double standard rationalized as physiological differences in sexual needs, men were not generally condemned by one another for acting on extramarital sexual interests. Women, on the other hand, were expected to uphold the Biblical admonition of faithfulness to the husband who owned her as property. The cuckolded husband was publicly shamed by the placement of a ram's horns over his door, symbolizing his failure to hold on to his wife. The guilty wife could be thrown into a deep pond, strapped to a "ducking stool," or "cucking stool" as the method was called when used for charges of adultery (Capp, 1984: 215–16).

Hill observes that women made significant status gains during the mid-17th century, due in part to the "economic activities forced on them by the absence of husbands on military service or in exile" (1961: 167). The return of husbands once again restricted women's activities in the public sphere, a common post-war syndrome. One can observe on the basis of modern evidence that it is precisely at those historical moments when women have effectively demonstrated competencies that sex/gender constraints and disciplines are tightened.

In Canada in the 19th century, continuing the English and European tradition, adultery by women was considered much more serious than adultery by men. Men were admonished from the pulpit to be monogamous, but they could have discreet extramarital relations with relative impunity, whereas a woman's adultery would not have been tolerated. Marriage was a social institution to which women owed an unquestioning obedience. As discussed by Vogel in the French, English and Prussian contexts, "it is not only the property right of a private person that is at stake here, but the collective interest of society represented by the state," at a time when the possibility of divorce raised fear of how women would behave if they enjoyed sexual freedoms (Vogel, 1992: 148–50, 164).

It was rationalized that strict monogamy on the part of women was essential to knowing correct descent of blood lines and male inheritance, a theory originally proposed by Friedrich Engels in the 19th century (Engels, 1884/1976). This notion, which buttresses any male impulse to control women, is confirmed by a 19th century legal authority, who observed as follows:

> . . . it is true that the wife's infidelity is followed by results of a graver character than those which follow the infidelity of the husband, and it is therefore in the interest of society that one should be punished more promptly and more severely than the other. (quoted in Backhouse, 1991: 191)

In both England and Canada until the latter half of the 20th century, adultery was virtually the only ground upon which divorce could be granted. However, women whose husbands were adulterous stood little chance of divorcing them unless their husband's overall behaviours toward them were exceptionally violent and outrageous by any standard (LaChance, 1981: 168), and even then only if the women themselves were perceived as entirely virtuous and, upon separation, living under protection of male relations. Women had the status of minor dependents, and the law practiced judicial paternalism. In Canada, as elsewhere, women were subject to private penalties, such as the French woman who, in the 18th century, punched a priest and was later beaten up by her husband, as his way of demonstrating to her, as he told the judge, that "he was opposed to all acts of violence." Similarly, in the only recorded case of female shoplifting in this period, the woman's husband "gave her a flogging when he learned what she had done" (LaChance, 1988: 11, 14).

Given the sparse population in Canada prior to the 19th century, and the strict gender controls over women's lives, few women had the opportunity to commit adultery and during the 18th century only one woman was convicted of this crime. She was publicly flogged and then confined to prison where, for three years, she was kept in the company of incarcerated prostitutes (Ibid.: 17). Both men and women were exhorted to practice marital faithfulness, to ensure the reproductive order of society and the moral behaviours of its population. However, the notion of property rights as it applied to women "sustained the double standard of adultery in . . . law and legal arguments" (Vogel, 1992: 163). Women were expected to be both more virtuous than men and in greater need of social controls; thus they were more universally condemned when they failed. Official 19th century punishments imposed on the increasing numbers of women convicted of adultery included primarily floggings and imprisonment. Even more punishing was a woman's state-imposed loss of status as a wife and a mother.

Petit Treason. The British Treason Act of 1351 differentiated between high treason, signifying "breach of loyalty" to the King, and petit treason, signifying "breach of loyalty to an immediate lord" (Hill, 1961: 288). The act stipulated that if a wife killed her husband, generally by poison, knives or blows to the head, it would constitute a treasonous act second only to attacking the monarch; to kill her master was an affront to God, the King and the entire patriarchal lineage. To premeditate the murder of one's husband was an aggravated form of homicide, an affront to hierarchical male authority as the foundation of the state and social order. The guilty woman was a traitor to gendered power relations and thus a threat to the male-dominant status quo.

The woman convicted of petit treason was burned at the stake instead of being hanged, the punishment for murder and many lesser crimes. As a form of leniency, a woman "could be strangled prior to being burned," but apparently this happened only rarely in practice. Women who were not penitent were shown no mercy by the crowds of hostile spectators who viewed these public executions (Gavigan, 1989–90: 360).

In a rigorous examination of petit treason law, Shelley Gavigan argues that according to historic context and form, the law has been uneven as an expression of patriarchy. She concludes: "With the elimination of the aggravated penalty of burning at the stake (1790), and the ultimate repeal of petit treason altogether (1828), married women who killed their husbands achieved a measure of formal equality previously denied them" (Gavigan, 1989–90: 336).

These changes toward formal "equality" occurred with the shifts toward Enlightenment notions of a man's responsibility for his wife's behaviours, and the Victorian penchant for stricter demarcation lines between the public and private spheres. Far from being equal, women were men's natural inferiors and it was at least in part the husband's failure if a wife was insubordinate. The shift away from burning, from the capital crime of petit treason, and from public executions, also coincided, significantly, with the pre-19th century shift away from the gallows for less serious crimes and toward imprisonment (Beattie, 1986; Foucault, 1979; Ignatieff, 1978).

Canadian historian J. M. Beattie speculates, from his research on crime in early England, that women convicted of petit treason were victims of wife battering, and that their murders of their husbands were probably forms of self-defence (Beattie, 1986: 100). Certainly this has been the Western pattern in the 20th century—that is, women who kill their husbands are commonly battered women (Browne, 1987). But now women don't burn. As discussed in the next chapter, in the 1990s such women are increasingly granted leniency, acquittals, clemency and pardons, if they qualify for the Battered Woman Syndrome defence. Such a defence would have been unthinkable two centuries ago, when it was popularly believed that women could be legally, respectably beaten, so long as the stick the husband used was no thicker than the width of his thumb (from which comes the expression "rule of thumb") (Clark, 1992: 191; Dobash and Dobash, 1979: 19).

Infanticide. England's Infanticide Act of 1624 exempted married women, who, if they killed their offspring, were charged with the offence of murder rather than "concealment" of pregnancy or birth, a.k.a. infanticide. It was thought that married women had neither cause nor circumstance for hiding a pregnancy, and it was the offence of concealment which was punished, rather than the actual killing, which was most frequently difficult to prove (Beattie, 1986:

131; Malcolmson, 1977: 192–93). Women convicted of infanticide were commonly young servant girls, impregnated by transient relationships or, under force, by their masters.

As estimated by Spufford, by the early 18th century half of the unmarried women in early England under age twenty-five were chamber maids, cooks, or scullery and dairy workers (Spufford, 1985: 54–57). A child would have resulted in social ostracism and unemployment, and a single woman wouldn't have means to care for a child. Women who concealed their pregnancy and, upon its birth, suffocated or strangled the newborn infant and disposed of its body, could be sentenced to death by hanging. As Beattie discusses, punitive efforts at deterrence were more to discourage sexual immorality than to save infants (Beattie, 1986: 113–14). However, most young women convicted of infanticide were apparently of otherwise good reputation (Spufford, 1985: 54–57).

In the newly emerging age of science and medical discourse, surgeons assisted with determining guilt of the accused. The lungs from the dead infant were put into water: if the lungs "swam," or floated, it was thought the child had breathed and had not been stillborn, in which case guilt was probable. If the lungs sank, the accused was probably innocent (Malcolmson, 1977: 200). Confidence in this test and other evidentiary practices was gradually eroded, and acquittals became commonplace. By the early 18th century juries were increasingly reluctant to send these unfortunate women to the gallows.

Beattie (1986: 123) observes that the mid-18th century establishment in England of charity Foundling Hospitals might have given desperate young women a place to abandon their infant to safe care, instead of killing it. Up to the 18th century, abandonment ("dropping") of babies was not unusual, in the form of leaving the baby in a basket at a church's or a rich family's doorstep. This practice prompted social reformers to campaign for orphanages, the first of which opened in London in 1741.

In Canada, between 1712 and 1759 just four women were accused of infanticide (technically, non-declaration of pregnancy), two of them housemaids, all unmarried (LaChance, 1981: 160). There were likely some cases that went unprosecuted, but the practice seems to have significantly increased in the following century, at the beginning of urbanization. According to Backhouse, "Infanticide was an unsavoury but surprisingly common feature of life in nineteenth-century Canada," and she reports on bodies of newborns discovered in the snow, in rivers and wells, under railway platforms, and in ditches (Backhouse, 1991: 113). Canadian law adopted the British rule against concealment, and women declared guilty could be hanged. As in England, however, courts were lenient and acquittals were not uncommon. Upwards to 10 percent of all infants born in Canada died from "natural" causes, and few social resources existed to care for dependent children outside family arrangements. Canadian society was simply not prepared to take care of orphaned children (Ibid.: 136–37). By 1892 the "crime of concealment provoked a relatively lenient two years' imprisonment" (Ibid.: 330).

PROPERTY CRIMES

In criminology we most commonly mean forms of theft when we refer to property crime. "Common" female criminals in early England were impoverished women engaged in pickpocketing, petty forms of larceny and fraud for small, immediate gain. Such activity took place especially in London and other urbanized regions, where social controls were less direct and less effective. Servant girls in particular were vulnerable to charges of theft, and crimes against masters resulted in hangings. Vagabonds and others lacking community status were likewise at high risk.

In Canada the first person to be officially condemned to death, in 1640, was a French girl, sixteen years old, convicted of theft and executed by a male criminal who was thereby reprieved from his own execution (Cooper, 1987: 128). In 18th century Canada "criminal" women were most often accused of scandal, prostitution, slander/insult and theft; whereas women committed many fewer thefts than men, women were more likely to be charged with theft than with any other offence (LaChance, 1981).

Of eighty-seven persons hanged for theft in one community in England, between 1736 and 1753, six were women. Overall, women charged with theft were more likely than men to be acquitted, to have charges reduced or to be reprieved upon conviction (Beattie, 1986: 237–42). In contrast with the era of the witch hunts, it was now thought by many magistrates, and privileged society at large, that women acted under men's (husbands') influences, and that women were generally less dangerous or threatening to social order. Only rarely did women engage in common "masculine" crimes such as highway robbery on horseback. For example, in a 1735 case, when a robber's female identity was revealed, her male victim was apparently too dumbstruck to respond to her demand to hand over the money. We gather that the robber rode away in feminine exasperation (Sharpe, 1984: 108).

The Black Act. In 18th century England, women were more likely to engage in crimes of social protest than in individual crimes. In the view of the masses of peasants, it was a crime by the state when the laws were changed to allow a privileged class, the gentry, to claim ownership of land that had been previously held as common land. These were the lands that supplied wood and food, basic necessities of life. The gentry revered the law because the laws protected their privilege, and when individuals dissented and violated the laws they were tried in courts controlled by this same gentry class. E.P. Thompson argues that the gentry's control over the people was enhanced by the symbolism of their hegemony, as illustrated by the spectacle of the courts (Thompson, 1975: 262). When the circuit court judge arrived in a town to conduct trials, he and his functionaries formed a dramatic procession, dressed in their scarlet robes and white wigs and greeted by throngs of enthusiastic peasantry. The people defied the gentry but they were at the same time in awe of their power.

England's Black Act of 1723 added fifty offences to crimes punishable by death. The Act was named for people who blackened their faces as disguise and camouflage, hiding in the night on gentry property, formerly common lands, for the purpose of hunting deer, poaching rabbits or fish, or gathering firewood (Jones, 1982: 73; Spufford, 1985; Thompson, 1975). New conceptions of property rights, through inheritance or title, had chased the peasantry from their means of livelihood. It was not usually women who took the dogs hunting, or set the snares. But women guarded the peripheries of the fenced land, waiting to take the goods from the men. The gentry had the power to forbid and to punish poaching, but they couldn't enforce the prohibition. In addition to meeting immediate family needs, poaching could be profitable, and it was the women who took the goods to market. As the gentry became more isolated and institutionalized in their class and professional distinctions (and pretensions), they were increasingly subject to ridicule and contempt.

Women involved with men in various activities in defiance of the Black Act were participants in a significant resistance movement against private property. Over a hundred years later, women in the Scottish Highlands were likewise aggressive in defence of their right to occupy fertile lands. In 1843, constables arrived to serve eviction notices with the following result:

the women met the constables beyond the boundaries, over the river, and seized the hand of the one who held the notices; whilst some held it out by the wrist others held a live coal to the papers and set fire to them. (Richards, 1974: 99)

Richards discusses the crucial role of women in the Highland resistance to losing land, noting that "the women were found at the head, often taking the worst injuries" (Richards, 1974: 106). Women played central roles in family economies, and they were clearly motivated to defend their right to the use of the earth in this necessary enterprise.

The Machine-Smashers. The Luddites are a strong early 19th century example of people organizing to defy both the law and economic injustice. A fictional "General Ned Ludd" was said to have led the people to destruction, but the Luddites represented a spontaneous uprising by people whose jobs were threatened by new technologies (Thompson, 1963: 216–19). Weavers, spinners and others systematically smashed machinery that replaced workers and broke up craft traditions. Technology signified the assembly line and sharp divisions of labour, and these systems displaced many thousands of workers in England, the world's first urbanized, industrialized nation.

Women were among the most aggressively strategic protesters. For example, in 1812, 40,000 weavers in Scotland went on strike for six weeks. In 1826, thousands of Luddites smashed over a thousand looms at twenty-one mills in two days. Mill workers prevented by the state from obtaining minimum wage regulations or job security were organized in their responses. The exploitation, dislocation and unemployment produced by the marriage of technology with capitalism produced desperate people who smashed machines and burned mills, and also organized illegal pacts among themselves and fought for their rights as workers (Thompson, 1963: 216–19).

Factory conditions were brutal and abusive to children, women and men alike, with up to sixteen-hour work days, under the literal whip of the supervisor. Between 1830 and 1832, in protest against growing levels of poverty, over a thousand incidents were recorded of machine-breaking and arson (Ibid.: 253, 366–84). Whereas women were given to peaceful strikes, they did not hold back from more strenuous and illegal encounters. In one case, Luddite women demolished the power system of a mill, a "tangible symbol of middlemen," and, entering town to "the beating of a frying pan," vowed that "they would drown anyone who attempted" to repair it (Stevenson, 1979: 101, 103).

Class differences between bold, roughhewn women demanding their right
to livelihood, and the protected, pale-skinned women who represented the
new bourgeoisie, significantly affected women's gender behaviour. That is,
then as now, "femininity" assumed different meanings according to class and
cultural contexts. It is no surprise that women most often in conflict with the
law (whether for sex/gender crimes or for social crimes involving property)
were women who could not conform to notions of femininity as perpetrated
by the emerging propertied classes. The clamour of unruly women surfaced
from a particular class, who, according to Stevenson, urged their men to violence and "danced and rejoiced in the streets" when an action was a success
(Stevenson, 1979: 103). Reading into the uncomplimentary characterizations
of them as drawn from the perspective of the literate (male) middle and upper
classes who kept the accounts, one can surmise that these women were influential; their resistances apparently caused fear among manufacturers and gave
courage to other job-dependent women and men.

Food Rioters. Among the early English women who couldn't afford the superficial signs of femininity were those who participated in food riots, beginning
in the 16th century and accelerating with the development of a market
economy. Women were especially sensitive to shortages and prices, and those
most affected were not complacent. When threatened with inadequate food
for their families due to increasing intrusion of middlemen and profiteering,
they took direct action. Women went to jail for stealing bread and they
became politicized in this way. As reported by Stevenson:

> Women played a prominent part in English food riots . . . . It was women who had
> to go to market and were faced with the stark imperatives of feeding their family
> and satisfying all the complex demands of preference and status that went into the
> family budget. (Stevenson, 1979: 101)

In early England as few as three individuals in a public demonstration constituted a riot, a criminal offence. Food riots attracted thousands of people,
with forty such incidents recorded between 1585 and 1660 (Stevenson, 1979:
91). By the 18th century such events were even more frequent and pronounced. Groups of protesters would stop movements of grain; they would
seize food in transit from middlemen, or directly from farmers, distribute it
among themselves at a fair price, and pay what was owed on those terms

(Ibid.: 103). In one case in 1629, one hundred and forty women, under the leadership of a butcher's wife, boarded ships and forced the sailors to "fill their aprons and caps with grain" (Walter and Wrightson, 1984: 122). Other women "pelted the teams and their drivers with stones for three miles out of town," and surrounded the house of an official, demanding fair prices for food. "Mixed mobs" were also commonplace, and on the expectation that women would receive more lenient (non-capital) sentences, men would dress as women (Stevenson, 1979: 101–2).

Women and their men held parades, blowing horns and beating drums and frying pans, to call attention to their plight as a hungry nation, and they carried the British flag to show the legitimacy of their protest. It was not the church or monarchy they were protesting but rather the capitalists and their laws. From the perspective of John Locke and other Enlightenment philosophers, private property was the natural outcome of cultivation of land. From the perspective of the food rioters, like the Luddites and offenders of the Black Act, it went against "natural law" to deprive people of sustenance. The rioters, in effect, were politically negotiating the right to survival, at the risk of execution.

• • •

Offenders of the Black Act, food rioters and the Luddites were among significant radical Western social movements that started from the premise of human rights. Women engaged in these illegal activities were not acting from an articulated concern with gender. They were, however, setting precedent for class-based stereotypes of the unfeminine criminal woman, who is contrasted with her innocent, protected, law-abiding and idealized feminine counterpart from the privileged classes.

By the 18th century, even working women were becoming increasingly dependent economically on their father or their husband, and patriarchal relations, codified in law, placed women as property of direct male authority. They could not themselves hold property, or enter into commercial agreements. They were deprived of marital rights, including protection from violence. They were restricted in movement, choice and voice. They were medicalized and their reproductive and parental activities were controlled by their master and by the state. If the husband divorced his wife, she lost custody of her children. In both England and North America, as a means of divorce, men could simply auction off their wives to the highest bidder (Pateman, 1988: 121–25). Every woman had to be submissively controlled by and under a man's care. For the lower classes this was not always an option; men who couldn't afford servants lacked the resources to present their women as helpless dependents, most women would themselves have been incapable of the deception, and, in any case, not all women were attached to men.

Women smuggled poached game for their families and the market, they gathered wood, gleaned corn left by reapers, smashed and burned machines that rendered them impoverished of a livelihood, and rioted and demonstrated for workers' rights and the rights of all citizens to affordable food. Only in retrospect have these crimes been interpreted by scholars as legitimate social activity, ethical phenomena set apart from common criminality because they are driven by basic need and the common good. To steal to feed one's family or community, when other options were removed, was a brave act, and to attack new technologies was to attack the emerging uses of human beings as cogs in or casualties of a faceless machine.

In pre-industrial Canada, with its low population (55,000 non-Aboriginal population in 1759) (LaChance, 1981: 158), women were not participating in such frequent and dramatic uprisings. They did, however, constitute up to 20 percent of those charged with theft and other minor property crimes. Like men, women were vulnerable to severe punishments, including being chained to ship galleys, public whippings, confinement in the pillory and hanging. Canadian judges believed themselves to be exercising leniency when, instead of sending females to the galleys, they ordered them flogged, branded, banished or, for minor offences, subjected to public infamy. However, in the 18th century, it appears that Canadian women were punished more harshly than men, and were hanged in greater proportion than men convicted of similar offences (Ibid.: 168). The 19th century gendered ideology which held women responsible for upholding moral standards similarly resulted in harsher penalties for females, whose public order offences were perceived as symptomatic of the evils of the lower classes (Boritch, 1992: 297). Throughout modern Western history it was primarily women who were burdened with the maintenance of bourgeois morality, and who have paid the price for society's lapses from class-defined gender standards.

CYCLICAL THEORIES OF THE FEMALE CURSE:
BIOLOGY REVISITED

The earliest "theories" of female crime were those transmitted through St. Paul and other Biblical authorities, and St. Augustine, for whom women and wickedness formed an association. As an illustration of the evil significance attached to female sex, consider "benefit of clergy," the ritual by which early Roman clergy were able to exempt themselves from the death penalty for virtually any first offence, including murder. Within ecclesiastical courts, "benefit of clergy" was granted to any religious defendant who could demonstrate his literacy by reading from a pre-selected Biblical passage. If he passed this test he was branded on the thumb and released, during times when anyone else would be hanged for the same crime (Beattie, 1986: 141–46). The connection between this practice and the association of the female body with sin is revealed in the Biblical passages commonly assigned by the court for the literacy test. Consider the following (Green, 1985: 117):

> For I acknowledge my transgressions: and my sin is ever before me. Behold, I was shapen in iniquity; and *in sin did my mother conceive me.* (Psalms 51:3, 5; emphasis added)

Since sex was associated with sin, and procreation required engaging in a sinful act, a newborn was cursed with inevitable sin. The fear and shame attached to sex, the blame attached to females who succumb to male desire, and the condemnation of females who act on their own desires, were transmitted by the church and became firmly embedded in Western law and medicine.

In the 18th century "Enlightenment" period, whereas women were thought to be naturally inferior and perfectly suited to serving men's interests, they were contradictorily understood to need man-made disciplines and controls. These conflicting points of view found explicit expression in the work of Jean-Jacques Rousseau, one of the otherwise great philosophers of the period. In his book *Émile* (or, *On Education,* 1762) he explains why little Sophie doesn't need the same education as her brother:

> The whole education of women ought to relate to men. To please men, to be useful to them, to make herself loved and honoured by them, to raise them when young, to care for them when grown, to counsel them, to console them, to make their lives

agreeable and sweet—these are the duties of women at all times, and [these duties]
ought to be taught from childhood. (Rousseau, 1762/1979: 365)

Rousseau is suggesting that subservience comes naturally to women and,
at the same time, that they have to be instructed in the fine art of service-pro-
viding. The contradiction of having to be taught how to do what comes
naturally is made explicit and negated in Rousseau's *The Social Contract,* also
published in 1762. Rousseau states that "The strongest is never strong enough
to be always master, unless he transforms strength into right and obedience
into duty" (Rousseau, 1762/1973: 184). The sham is revealed: the self-selected
masters in a civilized society must teach certain groups of people that it is their
duty to be submissive inferiors; it doesn't come naturally. Just as men had to
conquer the wildness of Nature, so did women have to be tamed to be useful
to men. This obfuscated recognition is perhaps closer than other Enlightenment thinkers came to acknowledging the potential independence of female
strengths. Rather than viewing woman as inherently evil, Rousseau and his
compatriots conceptualized her as an empty canvas to be filled according to
men's designs in their own interests; this social construction of gender he then
rationalized as women's destiny.

The idealized female bourgeoisie was in stark contrast to the lived experience of vast numbers of women seeking livelihood in Rousseau's own time.
Among those subject to humiliation and degradation in Enlightenment England were young apprentices, male and female, routinely punished by masters
who were entitled to inflict corporal punishment. Smith offers the examples of
"a female apprentice who was stripped naked, hung by her thumbs and lashed
twenty-one times . . . [and another] who was hit with an axe" (Smith, 1984:
222). Thompson reports on later 19th century factory scenes with girls and
boys, eight and nine years old, working fifteen or sixteen hours a day, bleeding
under the whip of a supervisor, often with their parents working alongside
them and slapping them to keep them awake (Thompson, 1963: 366–84).
These practices were incongruous against the historical backdrop of Enlightenment ideals of justice, rationality, free will, equality and the primacy of the
individual which (like democracy, private property and legal rights) were
intended only for men of privilege.

Women in gaols and workhouses fared no better than women in the
emerging manufacturing ghettos. Ignatieff reports on a riot in a mixed gaol
in which the women among the rioters "were particularly unruly, and several

of them had to be gagged, chained, and dragged below to the dark cells" (Ignatieff, 1978: 138). Clearly these women were not destined to be refined English ladies serving the domestic needs of gentlemen.

Increasingly, between the 17th and 19th centuries, male crime was treated as "normal" behaviour of the "dangerous" classes, and female crime was treated as an expression of masculinization and opposition to male authority. Unruly women were women who by choice or necessity refused or were unable to submit, to be silent. Whereas most female crimes, including prostitution and infanticide, were constructed from socio-economic relations, they were nevertheless sexualized. Men's fear of women's reproductive functions, combined with exaggerated presumptions of female lust, reduced women to their sex.

Drawing on the discourses of science, 19th century scholars established deterministic views of females which more than ever denied women the truths of their own experience, and strands of these historical effects are deeply instilled in contemporary life. As a profound illustration, over a century ago, Sigmund Freud, the father of psychoanalysis, heard the testimony of women accusing their fathers of sexually abusing them in their childhoods, but, under professional pressures to conceal such disclosures, he reinterpreted the women's stories to signify female desire for the father and female capacity for masochistic fantasy (Masson, 1984). He suppressed the women's truths rather than face his colleagues with the implications of this revelation about the Western patriarchal nuclear family. It was not until late 20th century that feminists have forced awareness of the (global) pervasiveness and lifetime effects of childhood sexual abuse.

In criminology, as in every discipline, men have traditionally done the research, and men generally study men. Those few male scholars who did study females did not achieve the scientific detachment to which they laid claim. Near the end of the 19th century, Cesare Lombroso, a physician and one of the fathers of both anthropology and criminology, colluded with the authority of science that presented females as lacking human sensibilities of pure emotion or reason, and as being in all ways less advanced than the male of the species. When Lombroso judged women, as in the following excerpts from his work (written with his son-in-law, William Ferrero), he surely exhibited more fear and misogyny than neutrality, objectivity or reason:

. . . the normal woman is naturally less sensitive to pain than a man, and compassion is the offspring of sensitiveness. If the one be wanting, so will the other be. . . . [W]omen have many traits in common with children . . . their moral sense is deficient . . . they are revengeful, jealous, inclined to vengeances of a refined cruelty. . . . [W]omen are big children; their evil tendencies are more numerous and more varied than men's, but generally remain latent. . . . [T]he criminal woman is consequently a monster.

(Lombroso and Ferrero, 1895: 150–52)

Much has been made of Lombroso's misogynist analysis, but he was a man of his times. That such opinions were expressed at the turn of the century is testimony to "malestream" resistances to the suffragist movement and 19th century feminism.

Biological determinism as informed by late-medieval views of women, and as later articulated by Lombroso and others, was the dominant 19th and early 20th century explanation for female deviance. The message was that all women were by nature susceptible to deviancy, and it is up to men to domesticate women and to keep them under control and in service. None of the early criminologists gave women credit for rational human agency: that is, they viewed criminalized women as victims of the normal-pathologized female body. We have lacked contextualized knowledges of women and crime in part because of such time-worn myths, which are revived in every historic period in which women achieve social or political advances or make what are perceived as excessive demands.

Early criminologists who studied women were operating from unadulterated androcentric, patriarchal biases justified by rationales based in biological theory, and their influence has reached into the 20th century. Consider, for example, Otto Pollak's 1950 presentation of women as masked (invisible) and dangerous (deadly) criminals, who learn deception through the processes of hiding menstruation every month, and faking orgasm, and whose cloistered or service-oriented lives allowed for easy concealment of their crimes and encouraged chivalry from men in law enforcement and criminal justice. In his view, wives and nurses, for example, frequently poison men and others and go undetected, recalling the attitudes of fear toward women expressed by witch-hunters Kramer and Sprenger, in the *Malleus Maleficarum* in 1486.

Pollak's exhortation in 1950 to keep women under closer surveillance was consistent with a larger, concerted social commitment to redomesticate North

American women in the years following World War II. The intensification of a renewed Victorian bourgeois familial ideology, idealizing women as confined to the home, "coincided" with renewed "scholarly" pronouncements of women as physiologically prone to be untrustworthy outside the purview of the patriarchal male gaze.

The cycles of recurrent theory continue. In a critique of efforts to make connections between chromosomes and crime, Sarbin and Miller recognized that the "demonic myth has not dissolved in the light of experience but remains a lively fiction; it has taken on many forms and guises . . ." (Sarbin and Miller, 1970: 204). Since 1987, under the pseudonym Late Luteal Phase Dysphoric Disorder, Pre-Menstrual Syndrome (PMS) has been tentatively classified by the American Psychiatric Association, in the *Diagnostic and Statistical Manual of Mental Disorders,* as a scientifically verifiable disease. It is yet one more in a long string of biological explanations of female behavioural disorder, presented by "internal causality" theorists as a way to blame women's crimes on their bodies. As discussed by Kathleen Kendall (1992: 139), medical institutionalization of the syndrome is the last stage of entrenchment of PMS—as yet another indicator of all women's reduction to their unruly bodies and irrational emotions. This is, of course, not a recent development. Lucia Zedner makes reference to the work of Havelock Ellis who argued, in 1904, that "whenever a woman has committed any offence against the law, it is essential that the relation of the act to her monthly cycle should be ascertained as a matter of routine" (Zedner, 1991: 87).

A view of women as biologically unable to control themselves is vividly manifest in the use of Pre-Menstrual Syndrome as a mitigating defence in crimes of violence. Whereas the analysis behind Battered Woman Syndrome is oriented toward social psychology, with feminist-political overtones, the analysis in support of Pre-Menstrual Syndrome is biological and medical, with anti-feminist political undertones. Independently and in collusion, the discourses of law and medicine are grounded in sex/gender power relations, and within a political economy in which women are subordinate. It is in this context that PMS is introduced. Medicine provides the scientific framework within which female subordination is ideologically justified and law supplies the mechanism.

The continuum from which hunts to PMS is broken in the ways by which society responds to female biological "weakness." Whereas witches were hunted down, tortured and executed for their alleged crimes, women who successfully plead PMS can have their sentences reduced. The misogyny of yore is displaced by the essentialist paternalism of a new age, where women are more mad than bad, though the distinction is seldom clear. Claims to truth about female biology and psychology are historical constructs imbued with patriarchal biases, with deep political significance which affects women socially and in the work force. Women's unpredictable "mood swings" served to justify discrimination against and exclusion of women from trades, professions and positions of responsibility through a good part of the twentieth century, despite overwhelming evidence that male angers and mood swings present significantly more danger to other people.

Katharina Dalton (1978) effectively identified the patterns of PMS, which may to varying degrees affect up to 90 percent of all women (Fausto-Sterling, 1985: 94). A fundamental argument against a plea of PMS as a mitigating factor in crime is that most woman, over the course of thirty-five years, experience one or more of the up to 150 physical, emotional and behavioural symptoms attributable to Pre-Menstrual Syndrome (Luckhaus, 1985: 162). This is a condition from which men are presumably exempt, yet men constitute by far the largest share of criminal offenders. Most of the approximately 4 percent of women who suffer extreme monthly hormonal imbalance do not manifest violent symptoms (Ibid.). If radical hormonal changes induce criminal behaviour, one would expect that menopausal women, for example, would dominate our women's prisons; instead they are practically absent from them.

Controversy among feminists over the uses of a PMS defence arose in 1981 when, in separate cases, two women in England received significantly reduced sentences, from murder to manslaughter with probation. They were given medical diversion, on the grounds that their offences were a result of pre-menstrual tension (PMT) resulting in "diminished responsibility" (*R. v. Craddock* [1981] 1 C.L. 49; *R. v. English* [10 November 1981] Norwich Crown Court). Medical testimony supported these decisions and another female disability was honoured by the law.

Of course, this concern with the female menses is not new. Anthropological literature abounds with accounts of females being sent to the "hut" for the duration of their period, taboos against intercourse during this time, men's enculturated fears that they will be contaminated if they get close to women's monthly blood, and so on. But this is perhaps the first time that modern societies have formalized their apprehensions about this natural female cycle.

In Western societies female gynaecological "disorders" have been historically linked with insanity. Osborne cautions that, in the Canadian context,
the PMS defence is situated in the insanity provision of the *Criminal Code* (CC
sec. 16(2), R.S.C. 1985), which "goes to the issue of the accused's mental
capacity to form the requisite *mens rea* for the offence charged." In other
words, the accused, to receive leniency, must be shown to suffer from a "disease of the mind" which prevents aforethought. Insanity is a legal term which
has serious medical implications (Osborne, 1989: 173). As Stoppard warns,
"Women need to understand how PMS functions ideologically to justify sexist
beliefs (and the practices that stem from them) which masquerade as scientific knowledge about women" (1992: 127).

Elizabeth Sheehy expresses concern that "the PMS label supports the cultural belief that womanhood is fundamentally inconsistent with aggressive and
anti-social behaviour" (1987: 24). The Pre-Menstrual Syndrome defence
undercuts a woman's ability to act as an agent in her own life, denying her any
initiative or intention she may have acted upon when she resorted to violence.
The defence sidesteps important questions concerning her relationship with
the victim (such as, for example, whether he is a wife-beater), the conditions
of her life overall, her health, and so on.

The PMS defence, as a medical, psychiatric and now legal construct, dis-
empowers women by reducing them to irrational and helpless victims of
their female nature, echoing the essentialist, deterministic themes of the
early theorists of female crime. Instead of inciting the worst of punishments,
the female out of control due to her hormones is now perceived as having a
partial excuse for even heinous crimes. At the same time, she is denied reliability. In a British Columbia case, a woman was denied custody of her child
because the provincial Supreme Court determined that PMS diminished her
effectiveness as a parent (*Babcock v. Babcock* [5 December 1986] New West-
minster E0010084 [B.C.S.C.]). In the United States a "judge acquitted a
dentist accused of rape and sodomy after the defendant held that the plain-
tiff had reported the incident during a period of premenstrual irrationality"
(Kendall, 1992: 132).

Conversely, as reported by Kendall (1992), in several Canadian cases
women have been acquitted or sentenced to mandatory treatment in assault
and shoplifting cases in which PMS was claimed as the cause of the crime. It
may be in a woman's immediate interests to plead Pre-Menstrual Syndrome
as a mitigating defence, but it is dubious whether becoming the captive of the

medical and psychiatric professions is less punitive than criminal incarceration. Compulsory medical treatment, particularly if it involves (involuntary)
psychiatric incarceration or abusive (prescribed) drugging, may be a more pro-
longed and insidious form of social control than a standard prison sentence,
especially when the PMS-related offences are of a minor nature.

The most significant reason for approaching PMS defences with skepticism
is that the medicalization of female crime obfuscates non-medical social contexts in which women live their lives, and individual reasons for particular
(illegal) behaviours. Clearly, from a feminist perspective, one must be cautious
about attributing serious crime to raging hormones, or otherwise colluding
with historicized myths that women (unlike men) are constitutionally unstable
and can't be held responsible for themselves. Although men commit the vast
majority of violent offences, it is only women who can produce the mayhem
attributed to PMS. It is a paradox of the syndrome that it is produced through
exaggerated Womanliness, but it causes women to behave "like men." If a PMS
defence is valid, then in the interests of gender equity do we not have to accept
the ahistorical internal causation notion that some men can't help raping
women and children? Instead of viewing sex crimes as the extreme end of a
complicated and uneven continuum in sex/gender/age power relations, we
could more simply attribute the crime to hormones and put these men in hospitals, with some variation of Excess Testosterone Syndrome serving as a
mitigating defence.

CONCLUDING REFLECTIONS

It would be irresponsible to uncritically suggest that occasional uses of Pre-
Menstrual Syndrome as a mitigating defence in 20th century criminal trials
is purely analogous to or an inevitable teleological outcome of the episodic
witch-hunt hysteria that afflicted Western societies between the 15th and 17th
centuries. The witch hunts were about female sex/power, the church and the
state, catalyzed or exacerbated by specific political and economic instabilities
in specific historical contexts. The text was imposed by a church-induced
belief in Man's vulnerabilities in the face of supernatural evils, and a concomitant belief that these evils could be eradicated or held at arm's length
through a war on the Devil. On the face of it, PMS is not so explicitly endowed
with mythological weight. It is, after all, a condition that can be scientifically

verified by modern standards and adopted for diagnosis and judgement by the "neutral" modern institutions of medicine and the law. Of course, the same was true of witchcraft up to a century ago.

The PMS woman may be frightening but she is also rendered helpless by the diagnosis. She may be fearsome but she is also pathetic. The accused witches, by contrast, invested with supernatural power, were more plausible scapegoats for ills that plagued Man, and the scapegoaters were both the authority-experts and the common people who accepted their judgements and cheered at executions.

By the 19th century the majority of the English population fell into what the gentry and authorities referred to as "the dangerous classes," because people became unruly in the face of fundamental material inequities. Soon it was women, and then colonized nations, and then women again, who were clamouring for rights, freedoms and compensations. By the mid-1960s, popular protests, rebellions and revolutionary events were globalized, fueled in part by the contagion effects of new developments in mass media. Political minority groups and colonized nations defined themselves and strategized on their own terms, and resisted confinement on every level of existence. Between the 1960s and the 1980s the postmodern movement was born, with the politics and debates of deconstruction, identity, standpoint feminism, radical pluralism and the factor of difference calling for specificity in any social analysis. In this highly charged and rapidly changing configuration of attempts to understand power and social relations, universalizing discourses, doctrines, and grand theories are increasingly challenged on all levels, materially, ideologically and spiritually. There is no longer room for a Master.

Foucault refers to historic breaks in political hegemony as the "insurrection of subjugated voices." In the late 20th century, many of these voices are diversely feminist (Faith, 1993). From a radical feminist perspective sex/gender is the foundational social division in Western history, and sex/gender crimes, in particular, demonstrate pre-modern roots of the sexualization of female crime and the criminalization of female sex. One can readily charge Mankind with continuous misogyny, varying only by degrees and in kind, if one catalogues and privileges, by emphases, the abuses that have been inflicted against women historically. Although the focus here is on women not as victims but as offenders, there is a clear continuum from victimization to offending. The offensive woman, historically and today, is the unruly woman who acts on her own volition or need, both bound by and resistant to the limitations imposed

by social class and fluctuating patriarchal relations according to culture, time
and place.

A socialist-feminist point of view is useful in analyzing the material base of
women's lives as it affects particular criminal offences (see, for example,
Messerschmidt, 1986). Clearly the women who organized against oppressive
profiteers and land-grabbers were not feminine by emerging bourgeois standards. The economic crimes in which women participated as recognizable
political protest are directly invitational to an analysis linking crime with capitalism. And although Marx himself, in the 19th century, dismissed
"criminals" as a part of a lumpenproletariat which had no constructive value
for the revolutionary historical process, one can as readily argue that individual acts of common theft are indeed resistant acts against socially
constructed class-biased inequities.

Socialist-feminist, radical and deconstructive analyses can all be useful in
examining ways by which early sex/gender crimes—witchcraft, prostitution,
scolding, adultery, petit treason and infanticide—are situated in the context
of materially gendered power relations. Western societies, over three centuries,
organized sharp divisions between the world of family and the world of men's
business, and the real action occurred within the intersecting cultural and ideological alleys running between the private and the public, the shadowy places
where sex is invested with social meaning.

NOTE

1. As my friend and colleague Karen Rian pointed out to me in 1970, metaphysical fem-
   inisms which identify women with Mother Earth and Mother Nature are playing right
   into the modernist Enlightenment notions of destiny, that is, fulfillment of natural law.
   Any deterministic or essentialist approach to sex/gender analysis is fiercely rejected by
   "postmodern" 20th century feminist theorists. This anti-essentialist position is elabo-
   rated later in this chapter. Contemporary witches are clearly exercising rituals of
   resistance to the ways by which strict sex/gender dichotomies have served to punish
   and confine women, and shape them according to male desire. The question here is
   the extent to which such resistant strategies, however self-empowering, may or may not
   have an effect on economic and other materially grounded means of maintaining
   female subordination.

REFERENCES

Backhouse, Constance (1991). *Petticoats and Prejudice: Women and Law in Nineteenth Century Canada.* Toronto: Women's Press.

Baroja, Julio Caro (1975). "Witchcraft amongst the German and Slavonic Peoples," in Max Marwick (Ed.), *Witchcraft and Sorcery.* Harmondsworth, Middlesex: Penguin Books, 88–100.

Beattie, J. M. (1986). *Crime and the Courts in England: 1660–1800.* Princeton, N.J.: Princeton University Press.

Boguet, Henri (1929). *An Examen of Witches [Discours Sorciers].* London: John Rodker.

Boritch, Helen (1992). "Gender and Criminal Court Outcomes: An Historical Analysis." *Criminology* 30(3): 293–325.

Browne, Angela (1987). *When Battered Women Kill.* New York: Macmillan.

Capp, Bernard (1984). "English Youth Groups and 'The Pinder of Wakefield,'" in P. Slack (Ed.), *Rebellion, Popular Protest and the Social Order in Early Modern England.* Cambridge: Cambridge University Press, 212–18.

Clark, Anna (1992). "Humanity or Justice? Wifebeating and the Law in the Eighteenth and Nineteenth Centuries," in C. Smart (Ed.), *Regulating Womanhood: Historical Essays on Marriage, Motherhood and Sexuality.* London: Routledge, 187–206.

Cooper, Sheelagh D. (1987). "The Evolution of the Federal Women's Prison," in E. Adelberg and C. Currie (Eds.), *Too Few to Count: Canadian Women in Conflict with the Law.* Vancouver: Press Gang Publishers, 127–44.

Dalton, Katharina (1978). *Once a Month.* London: Fontana.

Davis, Kingsley (1937). "Prostitution." *American Sociological Review* 2(5): 744–56.

Dobash, R. Emerson and Russell P. Dobash (1979). *Violence Against Wives: A Case Against Patriarchy.* New York: Free Press.

Dobash, Russell P., R. Emerson Dobash and Sue Gutteridge (1986). *The Imprisonment of Women.* Oxford: Basil Blackwell.

Ehrenreich, Barbara and Deirdre English (1973). *Witches, Midwives, and Nurses: A History of Women Healers.* Old Westbury: The Feminist Press.

Ehrenreich, Barbara and Deirdre English (1979). *For Her Own Good: 150 Years of Experts' Advice to Women.* Garden City: Anchor Books.

Engels, Friedrich (1976) (original 1884). *The Origin of the Family, Private Property, and the State.* New York: Pathfinder Press.

Faith, Karlene (1993). "Resistance: Lessons from Foucault and Feminism," in L. Radtke and H. N. Stam (Eds.), (1994) Power/Gender: Social Relations in Theory and Practice. London: Sage, 36–66.

Faludi, Susan (1991). *Backlash: The Undeclared War Against American Women.* New York: Anchor Books.

Fausto-Sterling, Anne (1985). *Myths of Gender: Biological Theories About Women and Men.* New York: Basic Books.

Fingard, Judith (1988). "Jailbirds in Mid-Victorian Halifax," in R. C. Macleod (Ed.), *Lawful Authority: Readings on the History of Criminal Justice in Canada.* Toronto: Copp Clark Pitman, 64–81.

Foucault, Michel (1979). *Discipline and Punish: The Birth of the Prison.* New York: Vintage Books.

Gareau, Richard (1992). "An Examination of the Role of Science and Medicine in the Early Modern Witchcraft Trials of Europe and New England." Unpublished manuscript. Burnaby: Simon Fraser University.

Gavigan, Shelley A. M. (1989–90). "Petit Treason in Eighteenth Century England: Women's Inequality Before the Law." *Canadian Journal of Women and the Law/Revue juridique "La femme et le droit"* 3(2): 335–74.

Green, Thomas Andrew (1985). *Verdict According to Conscience: Perspectives on the English Criminal Trial Jury, 1200–1800.* Chicago: University of Chicago Press.

Hansen, Chadwick (1969). *Witchcraft at Salem.* New York: George Braziller.

Hester, Marianne (1992). "The Witch-Craze in Sixteenth- and Seventeenth-Century England," in J. Radford and D. E. H. Russell (Eds.), *Femicide: The Politics of Woman Killing.* New York: Twayne Publishers, 27–39.

Hill, Christopher (1961). *The Century of Revolution, 1603–1714.* London: Thomas Nelson and Sons.

Ignatieff, Michael (1978). *A Just Measure of Pain: The Penitentiary in the Industrial Revolution, 1750–1850.* London: Penguin Books.

Jones, David (1982). *Crime, Protest, Community and Police in Nineteenth-Century Britain.* London: Routledge and Kegan Paul.

Kendall, Kathy (1992). "Sexual Difference and the Law: Premenstrual Syndrome as Legal Defence," in D. H. Currie and V. Raoul (Eds.), *Anatomy of Gender: Women's Struggle for the Body.* Ottawa: Carleton University Press, 130–46.

Klaits, Joseph (1985). *Servants of Satan: The Age of the Witch Hunts.* Bloomington: Indiana University Press.

Klein, Dorie (1973). "The Etiology of Female Crime: A Review of the Literature." *Issues in Criminology* 8(2): 3–30.

Kramer, Heinrich and Jacob Sprenger (1948) (original 1486). *Malleus Maleficarum (The Witches' Hammer).* London: The Pushkin Press.

LaChance, André (1981). "Women and Crime in Canada in the Early Eighteenth Century," in Louis A. Knafla (Ed.), *Crime and Criminal Justice in Europe and Canada.* Waterloo: Wilfrid Laurier University Press, 157–77.

LaChance, André (1988). "Women and Crime in Canada in the Early Eighteenth Century, 1712–1759," in R. C. Macleod (Ed.), *Lawful Authority: Readings on the History of Criminal Justice in Canada.* Toronto: Copp Clark Pitman, 9–21.

Lang, Andrew (1909). *The Maid of France: Being the Story of the Life and Death of Jeanne d'Arc.* London: Longmans, Green & Co.

Lea, Henry Charles (1957). *Materials Toward a History of Witchcraft* (Volumes 1 and 2). New York: Thomas Yoseloff.

Lightbody, Charles W. (1961). *The Judgements of Joan.* Cambridge: Harvard University Press.

Lombroso, Cesare and William Ferrero (1899) (original 1895). *The Female Offender.* New York: D. Appleton.

Lowman, J. (1988). "Street Prostitution," in V. F. Sacco (Ed.), *Deviance: Control and Conformity in Canadian Society.* Scarborough: Prentice-Hall, 54–104.

Luckhaus, Linda (1985). "A Plea for PMT in the Criminal Law," in S. Edwards (Ed.), *Gender, Sex and the Law.* Kent: Croom Helm, 159–82.

MacFarlane, Alan (1970). *Witchcraft in Tudor and Stuart England: A Regional and Comparative Study.* New York: Harper and Row.

MacFarlane, A. D. J. (1977). "Witchcraft in Tudor and Stuart Essex," in J. S. Cockburn (Ed.), *Crime in England, 1550–1800.* Princeton, N.J.: Princeton University Press, 72–89.

Mair, Lucy (1969). *Witchcraft.* New York: McGraw Hill.

Malcolmson, R. W. (1977). "Infanticide in the Eighteenth Century," in J. S. Cockburn (Ed.), *Crime in England, 1550–1800.* Princeton, N.J.: Princeton University Press, 187–209.

Masson, Jeffrey (1984). *The Assault on Truth: Freud's Suppression of the Seduction Theory.* New York: Farrar, Straus, and Giroux.

Matossian, Mary Kilbourne (1989). *Poisons of the Past: Molds, Epidemics and History.* New Haven: Yale University Press.

Messerschmidt, James (1986). *Capitalism, Patriarchy and Crime: Toward a Socialist Feminist Criminology.* Totowa: Rowman and Littlefield.

More, Sir Thomas (1965) (original 1516). *Utopia.* Harmondsworth, Middlesex: Penguin Books.

Murphy, Emily (1922). *The Black Candle.* Toronto: Thomas Allen.

Osborne, Judith A. (1989). "Premenstrual Syndrome: Women, Law and Medicine." *Canadian Journal of Family Law/Revue Canadienne de droit familial* 8(1): 165–84.

Parrinder, Geoffrey (1963). *Witchcraft: European and African.* London: Faber and Faber.

Pateman, Carol (1988). *The Sexual Contract.* Stanford: Stanford University Press.

Pollak, Otto (1950). *The Criminality of Women.* Philadelphia: University of Pennsylvania Press.

Radford, Jill and Diana E. H. Russell (Eds.) (1992). *Femicide: The Politics of Woman Killing.* New York: Twayne Publishers.

Richards, E. (1974). "Patterns of Highland Discontent, 1790–1860," in J. Stevenson and R. Quinault (Eds.), *Popular Protest and Public Order: Six Studies in British History, 1790–1920.* London: George Allen & Unwin, 75–114.

Rousseau, Jean-Jacques (1973) (original 1762). *The Social Contract and Discourses.* London: J. M. Dent and Sons.

Rousseau, Jean-Jacques (1979) (original 1762). *Émile (or, On Education).* A. Bloom (Trans.). New York: Basic Books.

Sackville-West, V. (1936). *Saint Joan of Arc.* London: Cobden-Sanderson.

Sarbin, Theodore R. and Jeffrey E. Miller (1970). "Demonism Revisited: The XYY Chromosomal Anomaly." *Issues in Criminology* 5(2): 195–207.

Sharpe, J. A. (1984). *Crime in Early Modern England, 1550–1750.* New York: Longman Group.

Sheehy, Elizabeth (1987). *Personal Autonomy and the Criminal Law: Emerging Issues for Women.* Ottawa: Canadian Advisory Council on the Status of Women.

Smith, Steven R. (1984). "The London Apprentices as Seventeenth-Century Adolescents," in P. Slack (Ed.), *Rebellion, Popular Protest and the Social Order in Early Modern England.* Cambridge: Cambridge University Press, 219–31.

Spufford, Margaret (1985). "Puritanism and Social Control?" in A. Fletcher and J. Stevenson (Eds.), *Order and Disorder in Early Modern England.* Cambridge: Cambridge University Press, 41–57.

Stevenson, John (1974). "Food Riots in England, 1792–1818," in J. Stevenson and R. Quinault (Eds.), *Popular Protest and Public Order: Six Studies in British History, 1790–1920.* London: George Allen & Unwin, 33–74.

Stevenson, John (1979). *Popular Disturbances in England, 1700–1870.* New York: Longman Group.

Stoppard, Janet (1992). "A Suitable Case for Treatment? Premenstrual Syndrome and the Medicalization of Women's Bodies," in D. H. Currie and V. Raoul (Eds.), *Anatomy of Gender: Women's Struggle for the Body.* Ottawa: Carleton University Press, 119–29.

Summers, Anne (1975). *Damned Whores and God's Police: The Colonization of Women in Australia.* Harmondsworth, Middlesex: Penguin Books.

Summers, Montague (1948). "Introduction," in H. Kramer and J. Sprenger, *Malleus Maleficarum.* London: The Pushkin Press.

Thompson, E. P. (1963). *The Making of the English Working Class.* London: Penguin Books.

Thompson, E. P. (1975). *Whigs and Hunters: The Origins of the Black Act.* London: Allen Lane (Penguin).

Trevor-Roper, H. R. (1975). "The European Witch-Craze," in Max Marwick (Ed.), *Witchcraft and Sorcery.* Harmondsworth, Middlesex: Penguin Books, 121–50.

Underdown, David E. (1985). "The Taming of the Scold: The Enforcement of Patriarchal Authority in Early Modern England," in A. Fletcher and J. Stevenson (Eds.), *Order and Disorder in Early Modern England.* Cambridge: Cambridge University Press, 116–36.

Valverde, Mariana (1991). *The Age of Light, Soap, and Water: Moral Reform in English Canada, 1885–1925.* Toronto: McClelland & Stewart.

Vogel, Ursula (1992). "Whose Property? The Double Standard of Adultery in Nineteenth-Century Law," in C. Smart (Ed.), *Regulating Womanhood: Historical Essays on Marriage, Motherhood and Sexuality.* London: Routledge, 147–65.

Walter, John and Keith Wrightson (1984) (original 1976). "Dearth and the Social Order in Early Modern England," in P. Slack (Ed.), *Rebellion, Popular Protest and the Social Order in Early Modern England.* Cambridge: Cambridge University Press, 108–28.

Williams, Selma R. (1981). *Divine Rebel: The Life of Anne Marbury Hutchinson.* New York: Holt, Rinehart and Winston.

Wilson, Nanci Koser (1993). "Taming Women and Nature: The Criminal Justice System and the Creation of Crime in Salem Village," in R. Muraskin and T. Alleman (Eds.), *It's a Crime: Women and Justice.* Englewood Cliffs, N.J.: Regents/Prentice Hall, 52–73.

Zedner, Lucia (1991). *Women, Crime and Custody in Victorian England.* Oxford: Clarendon Press.

LIVERPOOL JOHN MOORES UNIVERSITY
LEARNING SERVICES

CHAPTER TWO

Contemporary Perspectives: The Crimes and the Theories

ONLY SINCE THE MID-1970s have feminists and other critical scholars engaged in research which demystifies "female offenders," and introduced gender as a social construct with deep significance for crime and punishment. In this chapter I discuss some of the issues that have surfaced between the 1970s and 1990s which illuminate the discipline. That is, just as feminist analyses consider sex and gender in the contexts of law and criminal justice, so do feminist analyses, as presented by both male and female researchers, shed critical light on criminology itself.

At the outset I need to clarify some of the difficulties with contemporary terminology. Women convicted of crime in English-language nations have been labeled "female offenders" by criminal justice agencies, and academics have appropriated and abstracted this designation. The women themselves resist this label, which takes as a given that girls and women are *de facto* offensive in ways that men and boys are not, and vice versa. The empirical evidence does demonstrate that females commit crime less frequently than males, that their crimes are generally less serious, and that their crimes are commonly consistent with "feminine" gender. (For example, young females don't steal cars, they steal clothes and makeup.) But to indiscriminately attach the label "female offender" to all convicted criminal lawbreakers who are female is to deny women's diversity and to promote gender-based objectification and stereotyping. The term "offender" also assumes that convicted lawbreakers' offences are more offensive than those committed by people who either don't ever knowingly break the law or who are never apprehended by the criminal justice system. Certainly many people who never go to court are offensive people, and the greater someone's social power the greater their opportunities to impose their offensiveness on others.

The label "delinquent" has also been applied by academics and agencies to both youth and adults, male and female alike. The word conjures an image of someone in arrears on their payments to society, as well as someone who has violated the law. When applied to youth it bears connotations of serious unruliness, fights, general disobedience and undisciplined sexuality. When applied to adults it suggests a more benign form of lawbreaking than that associated with mad-dog adult criminals. In both cases, it suggests habitual working-class criminal street activity, and it evokes class-based distinctions between "delinquents" and white-collar "offenders" or any other classier breed of criminal. Like the other labels, "delinquent" is not a word a woman would use to describe herself.

In Canada during the 1980s, women's groups succeeded in persuading criminal justice agencies, including Correctional Service Canada, to refer to convicted female lawbreakers as "women in conflict with the law." This comes closer to a non-judgemental description in that it doesn't denigrate or permanently label the woman in question. It doesn't presume that she is a criminal "type," but rather that she is in an adversarial posture vis-à-vis the law. Certainly women do participate in campaigns of civil disobedience; however, women convicted of crime aren't generally committing acts of challenge to the law *per se*. The key problem with the phrase "women in conflict with the law," apart from being cumbersome, is that it denies the fundamental inequality of the relationship, which would be more accurately described as "women in trouble with the law." One cannot be simply "in conflict" with power to which one is subordinate.

The word "criminal" is likewise not useful for most women apprehended by the law. It has a hard edge which suggests that only a certain type of woman would engage in crime, and that she can be characterized by her criminality. The label "criminal" is a tool of danger-stereotyping, invested with the historical meaning of one who is born that way or who acquires the skills and forms a career commitment to The Life. As discussed by Danielle Laberge (1991: 49–50), it also suggests that crime itself is an objective, transhistorical phenomenon; it ignores the shifts in both customary and codified law, according to culture and historically situated hierarchies of authority. It ignores processes of criminalization, namely the ways by which "criminals" are socially constructed and processed by the criminal justice system, within a dynamic of power relations which determine sanctions against specific, selected behaviours and populations. It implies a false and generally class-based dichotomy of good people (non-criminals) and bad people (criminals).

The term that would seem to be the most straightforward of all the descriptive labels is "lawbreaker," since technically only those who break the law can receive any of the other labels. However, the majority of people who break the criminal law are never apprehended by its criminal justice agencies, and even those who are caught are not always "criminalized." One would more accurately refer to lawbreakers-who-get-caught-and-are-punished. By contrast, the term "outlaw" suggests someone who is committed to a free-spirited, illegal lifestyle. One cannot persuasively generalize female lawbreakers as outlaws, given the mythic, romanticized connotations.

Given that labels are culturally invested with ideological significances, and applied with prejudice, it is best to avoid them. Certain women are criminalized, through social processes, and these women are then labeled female offender, delinquent, woman in conflict with the law, criminal or, most courteously, lawbreaker. When we recognize the contextual bases of illegal actions and the discriminatory nature of criminalization processes as applied to either men or women, and when we demystify labeled women by showing their diversities as well as the commonalities they share as women in a gendered power structure, we lose the need for labels, or for gendered stereotypes.

• • •

Leaping a century forward from where we left off in Chapter One, here I discuss the selective criminalization of women in contemporary North America and the evolution of research on women. To begin, I focus on the work of Freda Adler and the circuitous ramifications of her work for the development of feminist research on women and criminal justice, and feminist critique of criminology. The bulk of the chapter focuses on issues, data and theories on women, crime and criminal justice produced primarily in North America and England during the 1970s and 1980s.

The discussion of prostitution which began in Chapter One continues here with contemporary perspectives on the ways by which women's sexuality is commodified and criminalized. Subsequent sections focus on other specific crime categories: theft and fraud, the crimes for which both men and women are most often prosecuted; drug offences, which are relatively common among women but, in Canada, not generally the basis of criminalization except in tandem with other offences, primarily theft; and, acts of violence, the least common but the most dramatic of women's crimes. In the concluding section I consider the conceptualization of "female offenders," "women in conflict with the law," "criminals" and "lawbreakers" as players in a continuum from victimization to criminalization. The women who resist victimization are the truly unruly women.

FREDA ADLER REVISITED

Feminist criminology came into its own in the 1970s, spurred in part by reactions to the publication of Freda Adler's *Sisters in Crime* (1975/1985). This work received extraordinary attention because it was interpreted by the media as a prediction that the women's liberation movement would cause, or already had caused, a dramatic upsurge in female crime.

Adler's study, one of the first works authored by a woman on the subject of women and crime, positioned her among female pioneers in criminology. In 1968, English sociologist Frances Heidensohn critically analyzed reasons why contemporary criminologists ignored women as too insignificant for inclusion in serious crime study. In this work Heidensohn anticipated the feminist analyses which she and other scholars were to introduce within the next decade. The following year, Québécoise criminologist Marie-Andrée Bertrand applied gender role theory to an international study of crime, confirming that young boys in Western societies were permitted a certain amount of masculine delinquency without harming their reputation. By contrast, girls were more closely supervised within the family and were rewarded for conforming attitudes, femininity and socially conservative behaviours, as reflected in their low crime rate (Bertrand, 1969).

In 1973, Dorie Klein presented her now-classic feminist critique of the androcentric theories of the late 19th and early 20th centuries which pathologized the bodies and minds of female offenders, as discussed in Chapter One. Meda Chesney-Lind established her authority in the area of judicial responses to young female offenders with her 1973 study of the ways by which girls in

Hawaii were confined in detention centres, not for crime but for paternalistic "protection" against sexual activity. Also in 1973, the work of journalist Kitsi Burkhart both effectively exposed the unjust conditions of US women's prisons and demystified the women who occupied them. The authenticity of her work was in sharp contrast to the contrived typologies of 1960s academic studies of incarcerated females, which denied their subjects the truths of their own experiences (Giallombardo, 1966; Ward and Kassebaum, 1965).

These and other prescient female authors, who were among the first wave of women to enter the field of criminology, legitimized serious academic inquiry into the neglected areas of female crime and punishment. With Adler's 1975 publication of *Sisters in Crime*, the media, and therefore the lay public, began to turn attention to what she called "a new breed of women criminals" (1975/1985: 7). She did not specifically attribute this perceived change to "liberation," suggesting to the contrary that any increase in female property crime, in particular, would reflect on deteriorating socio-economic conditions of women who embraced traditional gender roles (Ibid.: 7–8). Nevertheless, her linkage of a projected "female crime wave" with the same historical conditions that produced the women's movement gave prominence to that connection and the media reified it by inference. Thus began a mounting, earnest attempt by feminist researchers to counter what was interpreted as an attack on the women's liberation movement.

On the grounds of sociological inquiry, Adler rejected the contradictory biological views of females as either committing less crime than males because they are genetically programmed to be physically and psychologically passive and dependent, in contrast to natural male aggressiveness and independence (Ibid.: 31–37), or as naturally criminogenic but successfully tamed or controlled by men. In accounting for the lesser presence of females in criminal courts she partially accepted Pollak's paternalism thesis (1950), which purported that male chivalry, from initial police contact through every stage of prosecution, showed leniency toward women (Adler, 1975/1985: 49). She also anticipated more rigorous law enforcement against women as gender roles converged. However, later studies offered uneven conclusions concerning leniency. For example, Kruttschnitt found that "respectable" women who are economically dependent on men are treated more leniently than women of less privileged social circumstance (1982).

Mary Eaton in England found that women are granted leniency only to the extent that they can be shown to be "good" mothers to dependent children

(1986). Kathleen Daly's work, researched in the eastern US, confirmed this finding; further, Daly interviewed judges who believed that when male defendants are seen as responsible parents they should similarly benefit from more lenient sentencing (Daly, 1987a, 1987b, 1989a). Karen Masson, in British Columbia, replicated Daly's research and got the same results (Masson, 1992). The state is concerned, then, not with protecting women but rather with upholding a familia ideology, and averting the social costs to society of separating children from parents who meet their caretaker and/or economic responsibilities.

Adler hypothesized that increasing economic pressures on females, due in part to "family breakdown" (1975/1985: 94), would result in diminishing gender gaps in property crime, and that as social disorganization increased in US society, so would more young girls run away to cities where they would engage in prostitution as a means of basic survival (Ibid.: 71). This hypothesis appears valid if one looks at subsequent increases in charges against female youth; however, it's a matter of interpretation. John Lowman observes, based on his 1989 Canadian research, that "an increase of nearly 300%" in prostitution-related charges against youth in Vancouver in one year "appears to reflect an increased emphasis on the prosecution of youths rather than an increase in the proportion of youths on the street" (Lowman, 1989: 195). Further, female street youth prostitution is linked to runaway status induced in significant part by sexual abuse of girls by male adults in the familial home (Ibid.: 146). In this victimization-criminalization continuum, girls leave home to escape abuse, and if they engage in the most conspicuous income-producing activity open to them they are then criminally stigmatized.

Such observations contradict the notion propagated by media that increasing criminalization of young offenders is the consequence of girls exercising newfound freedoms to participate in the social world on terms equal to boys. Indeed, in a persistently unequal world, one effect of the women's movement may have been to justify a more aggressive response by criminal justice personnel to any perceived breach in prescribed gender behaviour, as well as more aggressive prosecution by businesses from which females shoplift—the most common female offence (Steffensmeier, 1978/1981: 63). In the 1970s, however, when the women's movement was gaining momentum, Adler was concerned that gender "role convergence" would result from social instability, and she stated that "there is every reason to anticipate that, as egalitarian forces expand, so too will the crime rate of the female young set" (1975/1985: 94).

Drawing a fine line between women's liberation as a cause of female crime, and socio-economic shifts which forced girls into the world unprepared, Adler conjectured that "the [movement toward] emancipation of women" was influencing girls toward "adoption of male roles." In the absence of awareness of the dangers to girls in the home, a phenomenon that wasn't widely documented until the 1980s, she observed that "departure from the safety of traditional female roles and the testing of uncertain alternative roles coincide with the turmoil of adolescence creating criminogenic risk factors which are bound to create" increases in female "deviancy" (Ibid.: 95).

In support of her role convergence hypothesis Adler noted that, according to the 1972 Department of Justice Uniform Crime Reports, US youth arrests for major crimes between 1960 and 1972 increased 82 percent for boys and 306 percent for girls (Ibid.: 95). This provided ammunition to media opposition to the women's movement; the dramatic percentage increase was cited in connection with the notion that women's liberation was causing radical increases in serious female crime. What the media failed to acknowledge, and the lay public failed to understand, was that the base numbers for females were very low, thus even very small increases caused significant percentage leaps. It was partially on these fallacious grounds that the media backlash against feminism accelerated, as documented by Susan Faludi (1991).

Meda Chesney-Lind draws attention to the more recent media-created "female crime wave," in the 1990s, with a focus on "girl gangs." As she observes from the data, echoing critical responses to the media's treatment of Adler's work, "there is little evidence to support the notion of a new, violent female offender." Instead, Chesney-Lind demonstrates the demonization and criminalization of girls based in part on US media presentations, in which "it is clear that 'gang' has become a code word for race." Images of young African-heritage and Hispanic women banding together "can create a political climate where the victims of racism and sexism can be somehow blamed for their own problems" (Chesney-Lind, 1992: 29, 31).

Adler herself readily acknowledged in 1975 that "a female subculture of violence is still quite limited" (1975/1985: 106), and, indeed, violent crime by females in North America increased very little, with females in Canada constituting from 8 to 11 percent of all crimes of violence between 1965 and 1987 (Hatch and Faith, 1989–90: 436). But it was the inferred image of a rising tide of violent female crime that attracted the media to Adler's work. As this message was reified and incorporated into the conventional wisdom of popular culture, it also entered the criminal justice system and appeared to justify a more aggressive law enforcement stance toward female "deviants." ("Do a crime like a man, do the time like a man.") This media-propelled image also generated public apprehensions, and aggravated aggressive disdain of the women's movement to which the falsely perceived "female crime wave" was attributed.

Adler recognized discriminations, both in the larger society and in the criminal justice system, on the basis of racist stereotypes and economic class position, and a significant portion of her book analyzes the means by which an unequal distribution of resources is reflected in an unequal application of the law. Yet, she writes:

> Stripped of ethical rationalizations and philosophical pretensions, a crime is anything that a group in power chooses to prohibit. Thus when the definitions of crime are extended beyond those deviancies practiced by the lower class to include activities previously countenanced by the upper class, we are witnessing not a discovery of new crimes but the ascension of newly strengthened social segments. (1975/1985: 155)

With the benefit of hindsight, and taking advanced capitalistic trends into account, it is clear that the historical shifts which gave impetus to the women's movement did not produce a strengthening in women's socio-economic circumstances, nor a weakening of racist ideologies. Contrary to the prediction of Adler's colleague, Rita Simon, who expected that females would gain access to more highly paid occupations and therefore to white-collar crime (Simon, 1975), economic shifts instead reinforced social divisions. Through the 1980s, material conditions deteriorated for women lacking the privileges of the middle class. To the extent that women were increasingly being found guilty of property crime, it was not because of newly gained or even newly imposed independence. Rather, an increase in petty thefts by women reflected increasing female dependency on the state, due to increasing "feminization of poverty" specifically as it affects working-class and political minority women (Gimenez, 1990; Pearce, 1978).

Single-parent families are headed primarily by women and the majority of women convicted of crime are from this group (Baunach, 1985). Relegated not only to the lowest-paid occupations, but also, intermittently, to welfare and unemployment lines, their lives are already enmeshed in the state apparatus. These are the women most apt to be criminalized, passed from one state agency to another in processes of "transinstitutionalization" (Davis and Faith,

1987). This relates to questions raised by Pat Carlen, who documents the institutional continuum in Britain, by which women in prison commonly serve time as youth in residential state care for status offences. Three of the major factors she identifies as "prime constituents" of criminalization are poverty, a history of residential "Care" by the state, and addiction (Carlen, 1988: 12).

In Canada, Gloria Geller analyzes how the sites of social control of girls shift from family to criminal justice incarceration to psychiatric intervention (Geller, 1987: 120–21). In their study of psychiatric practices in a Toronto forensic clinic, Dorothy Chunn and Robert Menzies examined how psychiatry supports patriarchal, capitalist relations through moral judgements. They conclude " . . . all criminal defendants stand accused, not just for breaking the law, but also for violating certain norms governing productivity, morality, sexuality and family life. . . . [F]orensic clinicians utilize the same moral and legal criteria as police, prosecutors and judges in their evaluation of female offenders" (Chunn and Menzies, 1990: 50).

Women in the late 20th century who steal, write bad cheques or cheat on their welfare claims—the most common offences for which women in the US and Canada are convicted (Hatch and Faith, 1989–90)—do so not because they have gained independence but because they have not. Women who are dependent on the state are subjected to an infantilizing form of *parens patriae,* as if they were children. For such women, the state takes the place of the absent husband or father as protector and punisher, master of women's lives; society shifts from familial patriarchy to a form of state patriarchy, within an abidingly gendered ideological framework.

North American property crime rates increased faster for women than for men during the 1970s and 1980s, but women did not adopt a "masculine" orientation to criminal offences; rather, they maintained gendered patterns. In Canada (primarily young) males comprise 57 percent of convicted shoplifters; yet, at 43 percent, this offence is the leading female crime (Hatch and Faith, 1989–90: 440). Females primarily commit thefts of value under $1,000, and men dominate in offences exceeding that amount. Females steal household goods, clothing, groceries, makeup and so on. Males steal electronic equipment, tools and other goods of significantly higher value than those taken by females. In other words, in the age of women's liberation, female offenders continue to commit primarily "feminine" offences; they write bad cheques and take items useful to them as homemakers and for feminine appearances. They commit fraud against the government from need and in resistance against the destitution level of welfare allotments for their children's care.

Media interpretations of Adler's work spawned public perceptions of violent, unruly women's liberationists running amuck and signifying a new social danger. It was an invitation to more severe discipline, control and punishment of females who crossed the boundaries of femininity. In effect, it was a return to pre-Enlightenment preoccupations with women as inhabited by the Devil and in need of perpetual surveillance. In the year following her book's release, Adler granted almost three hundred interviews to the press, radio and television in the US and internationally, in which she attempted to clarify the hypothetical basis of her work and to emphasize that the increasing female crimes were non-violent. The media did not accommodate her intentions, and for seventeen years her work has been critiqued by feminists who have seen the effects of her book as a counterforce to liberationist aspirations.

In January 1993, I interviewed Freda Adler in New York. We talked at length about her work in the years since *Sisters in Crime,* including international comparative studies, theoretical texts, issues of deinstitutionalization, research on maritime criminality and, most recently, environmental crime; in particular, we talked about the reactions to her early work on women. Following are excerpts from that exchange (Faith, 1993a):

ADLER It took two years to write *Sisters in Crime.* While I was preparing the book, I never dreamed of its import.

FAITH You didn't anticipate the controversy?

ADLER No. Absolutely not. I couldn't get articles published on disparity in treatment that I found in my research in the '60s, nor did I find much interest in the whole subject of women in drug treatment centres. So why would I assume that a book on female criminality would fare any better? . . . To me, the book said something very different from what the book said to the public. For me, the book asked "why has nothing been done in an area that's so important?" When a woman commits a crime—why does she do it? What does the court do? Does she get a lawyer? How do the police look at women? How do the courts look at women? . . . Women needed a fairer shake. We needed to know why women, as well as men, commit crime. They needed equal treatment in all spheres.

FAITH When you were doing this work, how cognizant were you of the growing women's movement?

ADLER When I'm asked whether I am a feminist, I say that I don't know how you answer because it depends on how you define a feminist. I've read many different definitions of what a feminist is. Did I break with tradition? Yes. Did I get out there into a profession where there were no women? Yes. Did I get out into the field, into the drug abuse centres where no females were working? Yes. Did I try to say "let's look at women in the criminal justice system as practitioners, victims and offenders"? Yes. Did I do my dissertation on women, on disparity [between] black women and white women? Did I write a book about women? Well, am I a feminist? As a United Nations consultant on female criminality, I had the opportunity of making a statement to the nations of the world on the unequal treatment of women [Adler, 1981]. Am I a feminist? I don't know how I can define it better. On the other hand, I am also a scientist. I try to do research that is value free. . . ,

I stated that as female roles change, deviant behaviour may change as well. The statement had nothing to do with whether life would get easier or tougher for women. . . . At the international level I was concerned about transportation of women under 12 for prostitution. I wrote too about class and crime. Did inner-city women commit different kinds of crime because they faced different problems than their more well-off sisters? How did unequal opportunity affect the crime problem?

FAITH Well, there you are at what I think is the crux of much of the criticism that came to you. . . . [T]he last thing the liberated woman does or needs to do is to engage in crime. . . . [I]f we had a society that facilitated liberation, we would have a radical reduction in crime for both males and females.

ADLER I agree . . . that was my point also. I think the problem is this: I used the term opportunity as negative opportunity, not opportunities to be successful legitimately. . . . [W]omen were having a tougher time, especially economically. . . . [M]any of them were single parents who had to go out and fend for themselves. . . . [W]ith the changes that were going on in society, they experienced even harder times. Poverty was growing. I was concerned that crime among women might rise, because I thought their stresses and strains were growing. Moreover, drugs were beginning to be a major problem among women. . . . I talked about disparity in the law . . . about what needed to be changed.

FAITH Probably a lot of us owe you an apology for closing in on those sections that aroused the most visceral reaction from us.

ADLER I thought that particularly women would be very supportive, if I could get this thing published . . . it might help people to realize that there were men *and* women involved in crime. True, there were many more men than women involved, but why shouldn't we ask "what caused those women to commit crime?"

FAITH Aye, there's the rub. That's the crucial moment of interpretation of your
work, from the point of view of someone who is thinking of the feminist movement as something that could ameliorate some of the disparities, as a positive
goal that will enhance the lives of women overall. The counter point of view says,
just as was said by Lombroso in the 19th century, by Freud, by so many by
implication if not explicitly, that the emancipation of women masculinizes
women. The emancipation of women turns women into creatures like the worst
of men. The emancipation of women is a cause of female deviancy and the cause
of female crime. That's the interpretation that was so readily formed from the
early sections of your book. . . . So you're telling me now that there were some
misreadings. . . ? You were not intending to predict that women's liberation itself
would be a causal factor in some projected increase in female crime?

ADLER I never said that "women's lib" caused crime.

FAITH And you never intended to convey that at all?

ADLER No. The women's liberation movement was and is a healthy political movement that has been fighting for equality. . . . I was always very supportive of the
women's liberation movement, and tried to support it by bringing attention to
women offenders.

And that she did, in spades. The attention that came to her work assured a
place for issues on women and crime on the criminological agenda.

FEMINIST REHABILITATION OF CRIMINOLOGY

Like most social sciences which had their origins in the mid-19th century,
criminology has been androcentric and authoritarian in its language,
assumptions, methods and subject matter. Male researchers have studied
male crime most obviously because it is men who dominate both criminology and the criminal justice system, on both sides of the law. Over 80
percent of all enforcers, offenders and theorists of the law and criminal justice are male, yet until recently little attention has been given to the
masculinity factor in considering crime and punishment patterns. Maleness
and masculine gender are taken for granted; they are fundamental to the
enterprise; they are the unarticulated essence of (almost) every criminological paradigm.

To assume that females can simply be added to existing theories of structuralism, functionalism, differential opportunity, social conflict, social control and so on is for females to be perpetually subsumed by the male subjects on whom the theories were constructed. Feminist theory may critique, entertain or borrow from any or all of these approaches, but the sum effect is that the female is recentreed, the male is reexamined, they are studied in relation to one another, and the basic ideologies and intellectual structures upon which the classic theories are founded are held up to question. The implications are serious, as Ngaire Naffine observes:

> Feminist theory is likely to dismantle the longstanding dichotomy of the devilish and daring criminal man and the unappealing and inert conforming woman. The threat it poses to a masculine criminology is therefore considerable. (1987: 133)

Feminists have continued to persuasively critique the theories and methods of criminology as a discipline (see, for example, Cain, 1989; Daly and Chesney-Lind, 1988; Gelsthorpe and Morris, 1990; Smart, 1990). The idea of creating a "feminist criminology" is itself critiqued, because it implicitly perpetuates the reification of "criminality" as a state or condition which can be identified and measured, and which can lead to repressive social control rather than examinations of the social contexts of criminalization processes (Howe, 1990: 7). Further, as Maureen Cain emphasizes, feminists disrupt "the categories of criminology itself" (Cain, 1989: 3).

Pat Carlen insists that feminists have a responsibility to use their knowledges to alter, wherever possible, the material conditions and power relations which entrap some women in both victimization and criminalization processes (Carlen, 1990: 112). Speaking from the perspective of "realist" criminology, Carlen recognizes both crime and responses to it as a real problem for the people who are victims of it as well those who are punished for it, and she is specifically concerned with democratizing policing practices at the local level (Ibid.: 113). The issue, then, is not only to work against unfair laws or criminal justice practices, but also to respond to the needs of those who are harmed by other people's destructive behaviours.

At this juncture, the importance of feminist action research is revealed or underscored. Feminism is, by definition, a political practice. That is, feminist researchers are not only uncovering new information about women and presenting new forms of analysis of gender in the interpretation of both male and female crime. Because feminism *de facto* links theory with practice, "feminist" research, by definition, also promotes political steps toward resolution of power imbalances. The research process itself is politicized to the extent that collectivized and value-explicit methodologies are employed, in the form of both team research by academics, and ways by which community researchers and subjects work in collaboration.

I readily agree with Pat Carlen (1990: 112) that there is no single method appropriate to feminist or, more generally, critical research: that is, quantitative, qualitative, ethnographic and theoretical approaches, among others, can all contribute usefully to our understanding of any given social problem. I likewise agree with Allison Morris and Loraine Gelsthorpe in their insistence that men as well as women can engage in research to the benefit of the feminist enterprise, and that feminist sensibilities do not apply solely to research on women (Morris and Gelsthorpe, 1991: 13–15). Feminism is based on the experiences of women. Men cannot know what it is to *be* a woman, but they certainly can apply feminist analyses to their work.

• • •

In explaining the few numbers of females in the criminal justice system, Mary McIntosh, a British theorist, identified ways by which "women's conformity is achieved with much less criminalisation" than is men's conformity (1977: 396). Females are commonly subject to many more private forms of social control than are males, and the female "deviant" is deemed more deviant than her male equivalent. She suffers greater social stigmatization when she breaches idealized gender standards, and the woman who is successfully passive, submissive and obedient is thought to be an unlikely candidate for nonconformity to the law. This suggests, then, that only women who fail to conform to a femininity model would commit crime, and this is not the case. Indeed, femininity is not a serious factor in who commits crime, as attested by the many very feminine women one meets in prisons.

Taking into account the variables of culture, ethnicity, racial designation and familial responsibility, women of every stereotype are represented at every stage of the criminal justice process, as are women who break every stereotype. One can heartily conform to most social expectations, and be effectively socialized to cooperate with or accept society's norms and sanctions, and nevertheless engage in activity or an event which defies conformity or the law. Allowing for exceptions, we lack evidence to support notions either that females who commit crimes are preponderantly under-socialized (as in engaging in aggressive criminality) or over-socialized (as in following orders from someone in a control position, even when knowing the activity is illegal). In any case, effective socialization to feminine roles will not call forth gendered clones: contextual differences impose varying ideal standards for gender appearances and behaviours, and every standard accommodates individual variation. Deviance from conformity is not a useful concept as we become better aware of the wide ranges of behaviours that constitute normalcy, according to structural context.

With the increasing medicalization of the law in the 20th century, women were tracked not for prisons but for mental hospitals (Allen, 1987). Whereas men who violated social norms and laws were perceived to be bad and dangerous, "deviant" women were deemed mad and pathetic. As Carol Smart says,

> Such a division, however, is arbitrary and reduces rather than clarifies our under-standing of these social phenomena. Given this crude division of labour between the sexes it becomes difficult to account for female criminality and male insanity. That the structure of society may present men with more opportunity and predis-position to become criminal and women with more opportunity and predisposition to become mentally ill is not fundamentally disputed here. What is disputed is that these opportunities and predispositions are inherent in the nature of men and women. (1976: 175)

Smart's now-classic text was explicitly written with the goal of "critically challeng[ing] the emerging moral panic over the relationship of women's emancipation to increasing participation by women in criminal activity" (Smart, 1976: xv). She speculates that apparent increases in female crime in England between 1959 and 1974 signified not more crime by women but more aggressive police and court practices, and that rather than holding the women's movement responsible for these changes one could instead realize that both phenomena were "an outcome of changing social and economic conditions" (1976: 25–26). This view was verified in the United States by the statistical analyses of Darryl Steffensmeier (1978/1981, 1980), who demonstrated that low-income and minority women were most likely to be affected by deteriorating economic conditions and persistence of sex roles in the labour force, and that these same groups were most vulnerable to charges of theft or fraud. He states, in 1978:

The new female criminal is more a social invention than an empirical reality and [the] proposed relationship between the women's movement and crime is indeed tenuous and even vacuous. Women are still typically non-violent, petty property offenders. (Steffensmeier, 1978/1981: 580)

PROSTITUTION

Street prostitution is the gender-specific behaviour, as concerns criminal law, with which women are most closely associated. Although teenage boys have also found a market for their sexual services to men in the late 20th century, it is still primarily a female-identified offence. In Canada it is not a crime to get paid for sex; rather, it is a crime to make a nuisance of oneself by soliciting customers in public, or to set up a brothel, or to have an agent who profits from one's work. That is, although prostitution itself is not a crime, activities often necessary to "doing business," such as running a bawdy house, or "communicating" with customers in public, are illegal. As the bottom line, prostitution symbolizes the time-worn preoccupation with female sexuality as claimed by men at large and as regulated by the state.

Central to Carol Smart's analysis in 1976 was recognition of the sexual "double standard," and, in a chapter on prostitution and rape as linked phenomena in the arena of sexual politics, she identifies how legal practices have historically condemned women who prostitute while, in effect, condoning the criminal behaviours of rapists through half-hearted law enforcement. Historically, penalties for rape have served as "punishment for the defilement of another man's property rather than a form of protection for women or a recognition of women's rights over their own bodies" (Smart, 1976: 78). In the contemporary rape (or, as of 1983, "sexual assault") trial, in Canada as elsewhere (Clark and Lewis, 1977), it has been the victim of the assault rather than the accused perpetrator who has had to defend her virtue. Only the "respectable" girl or woman, who can demonstrate sexual modesty or chastity, can expect a fair adjudication. Courtroom harassment of plaintiffs in sexual assault cases has resulted in significant under-reporting of the crime, and prostitutes, in particular, who are routine victims of male violence, have seldom had grounds for prosecution in practice despite the formal neutrality of law.

Representatives of both church and state, historically, have served the functions of pimps, procurers and clients of prostitutes (Wilson, 1980: 118–20).

The history of prostitution parallels the history of rape, whereby men authorize one another to use and torment the bodies of women who belong to their enemies. Organized prostitution is an invention of the ancient religious orders of Babylonia which placed virginal girls at the service of men, ostensibly as sacrifice to the gods. Mosaic Law did not allow Jewish women to work as prostitutes but Jewish men sought services from women outside their faith. The ancient Greek patriarchs idealized young boys as the most appropriate extramarital sexual companions, but nevertheless established state-run services which stratified female prostitutes according to whether they worked in common brothels or as courtesans. The Romans used rape as a central feature of warfare in expanding their empire but the women of Rome were (theoretically) to be honoured and protected.

In Christian mythology Mary Magdalene has been glorified as the recovered prostitute who is the first mortal being to whom Jesus appears following his resurrection from the tomb. In fact, she is nowhere in the Bible explicitly identified as a prostitute; this inference is drawn from Luke's story of an unnamed female "sinner" who is saved by faith (Luke 7:36–50), and from Luke's account, in the following chapter, of Jesus travelling with his twelve disciples plus a few women. This is his first direct reference to her: ". . . certain women, which had been healed of evil spirits and infirmities, Mary called Magdalene, out of whom went seven devils" (Luke 8:2). An association was formed between "sinner," "prostitute," Mary Magdalene and the possibility of redemption, and thus her reputation as a sexual sinner who could be saved was fixed in Christian lore. The first prisons for women in Spain were called "Magdalen houses" (Perry, 1990), and throughout Europe "fallen" women were ensconced in convents, where they could seek penitence while the good Christian men ravaged the enemy's women with impunity.

No society, historically or in the present, is exempt from the social hypocrisies attendant on persecution of unruly women who "choose" to work in the sex trade. As discussed in Chapter One, the practice of prostitution has been historically tolerated, reviled, made illegal and again made "legal" but under punitive conditions (Layton, 1979; Lowman, 1989; McLaren, 1986).

Prostitutes have been called many names: whore, strumpet, harlot, loose woman, floozy, tart, concubine, courtesan, call girl, slut, painted lady, scarlet woman, fallen woman, street woman, trollop, woman of easy virtue—and Jezebel, after the wicked, whoring witch-wife of King Ahab of northern Israel. According to the Bible, Jezebel painted her face (a sure sign!), and for her evil deeds and treachery she died a horrible death. She was thrown from the tower at Jezreel, stomped by a horse's hooves and eaten by dogs (for the full story, see 1 Kings 16, 18, 19 and 21; and 2 Kings 9).

Among modern myths about prostitutes, as transmitted through literature and film, is the romanticized whore with the "heart of gold" who gives her all to needy men. More negatively, whereas male sexuality is perceived as naturally aggressive and indiscriminate, conventional psychoanalytic wisdom has attributed to females who work as prostitutes an "oedipal fixation" based on incestuous fantasy. Freud's view that female promiscuity signifies displacement of lust for the father dominated causal explanations up to the 1960s. The most common alternative view was that women who work as prostitutes suffer from unnatural lust, or "nymphomania," which they can only satisfy through perpetual sexual encounters. In the literature, this condition seems to affect only women from the lower classes and distinguishes them from wives and other respectable women. (Dale Spender comments that "The difference between prostitutes and wives lies not within the women, but within the men" [1982: 341].)

As reviewed by Jennifer James (1976), scholars have laboured long and hard to explain the motivations that lead to prostitution, with the assumption that something has to be wrong with such women: they are retarded or in other ways genetically unfit; they are "latent homosexuals" attempting to overcome their lack of desire for men and/or deny their feelings for women; they need attention and are not sufficiently attractive to gain it in other ways; they seek adventure; they fall in with the wrong crowd; they are coerced by pimps. The bottom line, and the one explanation confirmed by virtually all prostitutes, is that it is a way to make a living.

Whether or not prostitutes are judged as pathological, they are clearly useful to the hordes of armies and perverts whose sexual needs would be otherwise left unsatisfied, as analyzed by functionalist sociologist Kingsley Davis (1937) who uncritically accepted status quo gendered power relations. The panoply of theories based on patriarchal presumptions have been discredited, since the 1970s, by researchers informed by feminist perspectives which recognize the intersections of economic stratification and sexual exploitation of females. In the words of Nanette Davis, a prominent and pioneer feminist sociologist who has surveyed prostitution practices and policies in sixteen nations (Davis, 1993):

The more attention given to prostitution as a "significant" and "special" social problem requiring extraordinary measures, the less we see the ordinariness of prostitution as a normal response to gender distinctions and market and political inequalities. In a word, there is no rational policy for prostitution as long as gender discrimination persists. (Davis, 1992: 17)

As documented by John Lowman in his 1989 study of Vancouver street prostitutes (primarily adults), 76.5 percent had run away from home in their youth, and 69.7 percent had been sexually victimized by family members or others prior to entering prostitution. The majority began prostituting as youth, having gone no further than Grade 10 in school (Lowman, 1989: 112–13). Over 19 percent were Native women, whereas Natives then constituted just over 3 percent of the provincial population. His research also verified that women who work on the street are from low-income backgrounds as well as the lowest-paid among prostitutes (Ibid.: 200–1). Lowman found that when young prostitutes in Vancouver are picked up by the police they are almost invariably brought to court and "criminalized" so that social services can then intervene. A "substantial proportion of them" will become wards of the state before they turn nineteen (Ibid.: 139–40).

Low-income and minority girls and women who do not work in the sex trade are also persecuted insofar as they are mistaken for prostitutes. A coalition of Aboriginal women in Winnipeg has reported that children as young as eleven have been harassed by "johns" who

> do not discriminate between "working girls" and children on their way to school, or simply outside playing with their friends. Women and children cannot travel anywhere within the neighbourhood without being harassed because the men who frequent the area—as many as 300 cars a night—operate under the racist assumption that if a girl or woman is Aboriginal and on the street, she must be a prostitute and available for sex. (Gordon, 1993: 12)

It is young female prostitutes who are most often targeted for investigation, intervention and the surveillance that accompanies compulsory assistance. Chesney-Lind and Shelden found that "police are more likely to release a girl than a boy suspected of committing a crime, but are more likely to arrest girls suspected of sex offences" (1992: 139). The transinstitutionalization process reinforces the relationship between criminal justice and social services, widening the net of social control agencies and institutions which label people and force them into dependency on the state. Street girls who have been victims of childhood sexual abuse, and who, in effect, are "throwaway" children, are first criminalized and then channeled through the service bureaucracies, which obfuscate the line between punishment and assistance. Such girls have traditionally been seen as bad and lazy more than in need of care. The guardian of girls in the British Columbia Industrial Home for Girls had this to say in 1944, as quoted by Jody Gordon:

> We have the girl who has decided that prostitution is the easiest way of earning an easy living; we have the girl who has turned for affection or protection to some man; and we have the girl who loves the bright lights and accepts sexual relations as part of having a good time. (1992: 37)

In the late 20th century, it is understood through their own testimony (Bell, 1987; Delacoste and Alexander, 1988; Pheterson, 1989) that prostitutes work for the money and they work through many venues, including call-girl services, massage parlours and private clubs. As discussed by English scholar Susan Edwards, many prostitutes are single parents who view prostitution as a financial imperative (1987: 52). It is the street women, who are at the bottom of the pay scale, who are subject to the greatest dangers from "tricks." Because they are the most visible women in the trade, who *de facto* communicate with potential customers in public, they also face the greatest likelihood of criminalization by law enforcement, and are most subject to fines and jail sentences. These are the "damned whores" who arouse societal moral panics which remind other women to keep their sexuality under control, and incite conforming women to condemn those who profit from their sexuality. As Anne Summers put it, "The very fear of being castigated as Damned Whores keeps women in line; most women have no option but to conform to the God's Police stereotype" (Summers, 1975: 154).

Prostitutes are above all stigmatized as a public nuisance, which accounts, in part, for the apparently lackadaisical response of law enforcement to their disappearances and deaths by homicide. In the Seattle area in the early 1980s at least forty-nine women identified as prostitutes were murdered by a serial killer, still at large in 1993, who was dubbed the "Green River Killer" because he dumped the women's bodies near the riverbank. In Vancouver the murders of thirty-nine prostitutes, between the late 1980s and 1992, remain unsolved, and prostitute organizations protest that when they are victims of violence they are not given shelter by transition houses unless they make a commitment to leaving the trade (Mladerovic, 1992). As succinctly stated by Vancouver prostitutes' advocate Marie Arrington (1990), "Women are dying because society doesn't give a damn about what happens to whores—they are disposable." This view is supported by research conducted by Suzanne Hatty on the negligible response of Australian state agencies to violence committed against prostitutes. She concludes that "working as a prostitute disqualifies women from the category of legitimate victim" (1989: 244), which lends support to routine reports by prostitutes of assaults by police officers as well as by clients.

During the early 1970s I was in a conversation about prostitution with a group of imprisoned women, mainly serving time for property and drug-related offences, but including a number of women with prostitution-related offences on their records. As one woman put it, "Why should I break my ass at McDonalds for three dollars an hour, when I can turn a trick in half an hour and make fifty?" A younger woman angrily responded, "Because every time some jerk whistles at me, every time I can't walk down the street without getting hassled, every time some guy figures it's his right to take my body, it's because you're out there telling him that's what women's bodies are for." This exchange stays with me as the crux of early debates between socialist-feminists, who held that women's economic circumstances under capitalism make prostitution an obvious occupational option, and radical feminists, who located female oppression in heterosexuality itself, and viewed the commodification of female bodies, through prostitution and pornography, as reinforcing the objectification and exploitation of all women's bodies.

Every prostitute I've known has a repertoire of stories illustrating the extraordinary hypocrisy in the prosecution of prostitutes. For example, some years ago a friend was paid to serve the sexual interests of a particular judge. Two weeks later she was sentenced on prior charges of solicitation and sent to jail by this same judge, who appeared not even to recognize her. In 1978 a Vancouver prostitute who had consorted with legal officials, and other men in high places, was blamed for the resignation of a Chief Justice of the provincial Supreme Court when a police investigation of her bawdy house threatened to expose him and his colleagues: the court ordered her "little brown book with 800 names" to be sealed (Wilson, 1980: 35). Margot St. James possesses a "tape recording of a telephone conversation in which a San Francisco intelligence-squad detective makes a pitch for her to arrange some 'girls' for him and his friends," and she tells of a brothel madam "falling" from a third-story window while in a physical struggle with a police officer over her "little black book" (Haft, 1976: 207–8).

Prostitutes defy feminist idealism when they "choose," within the parameters of very limited choices, to work in the sex trade. Beginning in the early 1970s they have organized to defend their civil and human rights; the first such group went by the name COYOTE, an acronym for "Call Off Your Old Tired Ethics." Organized in San Francisco by Margot St. James, for many years COYOTE hosted an annual "Hookers' Ball," which was attended by city officials, dignitaries and celebrities as well as by "common" folk. The attendance of the city's elite at these events signified the ambiguities and contradictions attached to society's moral judgements against prostitution as well as the hypocrisy of law enforcement policies.

In England, prostitution organizations have included PUSSI (Prostitutes United for Social and Sexual Integration), PROS (Programme for Reform of the Law on Street Offences), and PLAN (Prostitution Laws are Nonsense), all of which have decried the double standard of law enforcement which prosecutes prostitutes while ignoring the "clients" who are likewise engaged in illegal interactions (Heidensohn, 1985: 136). Prostitutes stress that they are entitled to the same legal rights to safety as any other citizen, and given the unreliability of police protection prostitutes engage in self-help. In Vancouver, a group called POWER (Prostitutes and Other Women for Equal Rights) has lobbied the police to be more vigilant in investigations of murders of prostitutes, and they issue a regular "bad trick" sheet which profiles abusive clients and alerts street women to watch out for men who meet the descriptions. Self-help prostitute groups also include Prostitutes Anonymous, which operates according to the "12-step" recovery program originated by Alcoholics Anonymous. This group takes into account the real grief and tragedy that prostitution can cause, as well as signify. It is designed to facilitate mutual support among women, and also men, who seek to leave the sex industry or who are in processes of recovery from the emotional, physical and stigmatizing effects of the business, including the presumption that prostitutes are fair targets for violence and for outcast status.

Marilyn Haft, in 1976, cites a United Nations study from 1966 which found that "prostitution is not a major factor in the spread of venereal disease in the United States," and from other evidence she concludes that "activities of prostitutes simply do not pose a substantial threat to the health of the community" (Haft, 1976: 217). In 1986, Eleanor Miller documented health problems that gave "street women" incentive to stop prostituting at least temporarily, and she found that the most significant of these were "the bruises, broken bones, cuts, and abrasions that were the result of the ever-present risk of violence" (Miller, 1986: 138).

However, the view that prostitutes carry dangerous disease has been sustained since time immemorial. In 17th century Spain, long before the creation of modern penitentiaries, women's prisons were built to house prostitutes who carried "'a thousand disgusting and contagious diseases'" (Perry, 1990: 10). In 19th century England, prostitutes and vagabond women were persecuted under the Contagious Diseases Acts, as discussed in Chapter One. During the eugenics movement of the 1930s, North American prostitutes were among those classified as "feeble-minded" and therefore deemed by social reformers, such as Sheldon and Eleanor Glueck in the United States (1934/1965), and Helen MacMurchy in Canada, to be appropriate candidates for sterilization and other measures to prevent sexually transmitted disease and to ensure a discontinuance of the genetic line (McClaren, 1990: 40).

In the 1990s, the primary basis for moral panic relative to prostitutes, as rationalized through medical discourse, is the AIDS (acquired immunodeficiency syndrome) epidemic. Given the numbers of gay men who were stricken in North America in the early 1980s, AIDS was initially labeled "a gay disease" and explained by homophobes as a punishment by God and a justification for such proposed measures as quarantine camps. Now that AIDS is a global epidemic affecting primarily heterosexuals, prostitutes have become once again the legitimized scapegoats for social blame translated as the Wrath of God (Plant, 1990; Smith, 1989).

In some parts of the world, including Thailand and India, prostitution is indeed believed to be a key source of transmission of HIV (human immunodeficiency virus), which is generally understood as a precondition of AIDS-related illness. However, in most regions of the world where studies have been conducted, the vast majority of prostitutes have tested negative for HIV, and, where tests have been positive, transmission has been attributed not to sex work but, rather, primarily to the sharing of needles in intravenous drug use and secondarily to unprotected sex with boyfriends who are intravenous drug users (Brock, 1986; Cohen, 1989; Luxenburg and Guild, 1993; Plant, 1990; Voeller, Reinisch and Gottlieb, 1990). In New York, 19 percent of female prisoners in 1991 (compared to 17 percent of male prisoners) were found to be HIV-infected, most of whom contracted the virus through dirty needles (Smith and Jaromir, 1991: 35).

It would be irresponsible to suggest that prostitution is not a potentially high-risk area for sexually transmitted diseases. However, professional prostitutes are more aware than anyone of the occupational hazards, and, from all evidence, most practice "safe sex" with their own interests at heart. As of 1991 "there has yet to be a documented case of a female US prostitute sexually transmitting the virus to a male customer" (Luxenburg and Guild, 1993: 88). The population at large is less cautious, and one of the dangers of targeting prostitutes is that it diverts attention from other sectors of societies in which the risks of HIV and AIDS-related illnesses are rampant.

People who *de facto* regard prostitution as a social threat would be better able to control the practice through legalization than through interminable efforts to eliminate it altogether. However, the national Canadian Organization for the Rights of Prostitutes (CORP), in common with most prostitute groups and advocates for prostitutes' rights (Pheterson, 1989; Shaver, 1985; SCPP, 1985), oppose this option. They take the clear position that whereas prostitution-related activities should be decriminalized, the practice should not be "legalized," because legalization results in the state taking on the function of a controlling pimp, as happened in the state of Nevada. Most fundamentally, prostitutes identify themselves as working women, and believe that "the solution is to decriminalize prostitution, to treat it like any other private, independent and legitimate business. Prostitution would then be subject to the same regulations and restrictions that are the norm for other businesses, including, for example, zoning regulations" (Bernstein, 1990: 39). As workers in a legitimate business, subject to civil laws, prostitutes would also be entitled to the same protections as any other gainfully employed citizen. Frances Shaver notes that feminist defences of decriminalization are "firmly grounded in a criticism of the formulation and enforcement of the law, and an analysis of the underlying social problems that give rise to prostitution" (Shaver, 1988: 87), but she surmises that North American feminists have not yet envisioned a world where egalitarian prostitution would occur as legitimate choice.

Rosa Del Olmo (1979) documents the success of the campaign in post-Batista Cuba to eliminate prostitution in concert with social reforms in education, medicine and the dissolution of a class-based economy. Prostitution, as a symptom of capitalist exploitation, was regarded as degrading both to the women and to the dignity of the nation. However, with the withdrawal of Soviet aid to Cuba and the trade embargo imposed by the US, the Cuban economy in the 1990s has been forced to rely once again on the international tourism industry, and prostitution is once again a visible option. In my own observation while attending meetings in Cuba in 1992, hotel lobbies which are off-limits to most Cuban nationals have become the equivalent of "the street" to very young girls. These teenagers were cuddling up to middle-aged male tourists in the apparent hope of landing a deal which will save them from the island's growing food shortages and embargo-induced social restrictions. I was reminded of a related experience in Australia in 1985 while I attended a predominantly male university conference. On the bedside table in my dormitory room I found a catalogue featuring photos and vital statistics (that is, body measurements) of at least a hundred *very* young women, most of them Southeast Asians, who were available by phone order with a credit card. I felt like a battle-axe about it, but I complained to the conference organizers, who apologized with the explanation that "we don't usually get many women at these meetings." Internationally, prostitution is a bottom-line means for women to earn a living and for women, of all ages, to be exploited.

In North America, prostitution laws have fluctuated historically, or have been enforced erratically, according to political climate and moral crusades. Similarly, in the contemporary context, police have cooperated with neighbourhood vigilante organizations who relocate street prostitutes by literally chasing them and their johns away from one neighbourhood and into another. For example, women were systematically harmed in the Vancouver "Shame the Johns" campaigns in the 1980s—the NIMBY syndrome, "not in my back yard." The contradictory nature of prostitution laws makes it clear that the state cannot or will not attempt to eradicate the service, but nor will it accommodate prostitutes' needs for safe locations and conditions in which to conduct their business (Lowman, 1986).

In 1985 the Fraser Committee, in a major cross-country study sponsored by the Canadian Department of Justice, advocated sensible reform of prostitution-related laws. They recommended decriminalization of prostitution by adult women, prohibition of sex for money with children, and stricter controls over those who exploit prostitutes (SCPP, 1985). Their report emphasized that consideration of economic and social issues were "the most important aspects of reformulating social and political responses to adult prostitution" (Lowman, 1989: 208). The government ignored their analysis, paid minimal heed to their recommendations and, instead, put forth legislation calling for even stricter, more punitive responses to women who "communicate" with potential customers in public.

The issue of pimps is clearly important in those cities where they control the sex trade and, often, work together with syndicates of various vice activities. Gail Pheterson, who has worked with Margot St. James as a codirector of the International Committee for Prostitutes' Rights, writes that "The figure most often blamed for the oppression of whores is the pimp" (Pheterson, 1989: 15). But she clarifies that a pimp can be anyone at all who benefits from a prostitute's earnings, including a male child over age eighteen, and that if prostitutes work together the one handling the business can be charged with pimping. She does not deny that some men "beat women into sexual service and exploit their labour" but she emphasizes that the real issue is economics, and she suggests that the problem has been mythologized to prostitutes' own disadvantage (Ibid.: 16–17).

Pimps are not common in the urban sex trade in Canada, except in Winnipeg and Halifax (Gomme, 1993: 301). A 1993 scandal centreed on two violent men from Nova Scotia who had moved their prostitution ring into Ottawa and Quebec, involving 100 young women and 30 men. The outcome was three- and three-and-a-half-year prison terms for the two ringleaders, and scathing judgement from the sentencing Justice, who called them "parasites" who "abused and exploited young girls in an atmosphere of violence." He also called them "lepers of the underworld and the decent world," echoed by the prosecutor, who is quoted as saying that "These types of crimes tear at the heart of our social structure." Two other men involved in the case received four- and four-and-a-half-year sentences for having injured girls: one had beaten a seventeen-year-old with a wire coat hanger after she was seen talking to a man believed to be another pimp, and while he beat her his partner "fell to the floor laughing." The judge pronouncing their sentences called them "parasites . . . on a level with child molesters" (Cox, 1993: A10). Indeed. In yet another trial involving the Halifax "syndicate," a teenage girl who began prostituting at age fourteen was choked and punched and almost drowned, because she had been spending money on drugs (Sonnichsen, 1993: A6). One doesn't wonder why.

Law enforcement practices have extended to include more arrests of clients (Moore, 1991), but charges are made selectively, most often against men from the lowest economic strata (Lowman, 1990). In some cities in Canada, the names of customers are printed in the newspaper in a variation of "Shame the Johns" campaigns, which doubtless embarrasses and inhibits some men, but probably does little to curb business over all. Similarly, laws against "living off the avails" of prostitution have been enforced against men who could not be properly called "pimps" but rather are the live-in male partners of prostitutes, suggesting that women who prostitute lack the right to establish domestic relationships of their own choosing (Shaver, 1985: 498). Ultimately it is not social morality which the law seeks to regulate, but rather when, where, with whom and for what purpose women can be permitted to exercise their own sexuality.

In the above discussion I have emphasized the factor of qualified "choice" among adult women who work as street prostitutes, with the caveats that adult prostitution is commonly the outcome of childhood sexual abuse, women's objectification and commodification as sex objects, and women's limited economic options. These are all primary factors in "making the decision" to sell sex. In closing this discussion it's important to acknowledge the still inadequately documented phenomenon of international trafficking in human bodies for sexual purposes. For many females all over the world, and especially children, prostitution is not a "choice" by any definition. To the contrary, uncounted girls and women are victims of what Kathleen Barry, in her prescient research (1979), termed "female sexual slavery," and the practices of buying or kidnapping human bodies for purposes of commercial sex include young boys as well.

According to a documentary film produced through the United Nations (*Throwaway Children,* 1989), in a number of impoverished nations, children as young as age three are being sold into brothels, and desperate women who can't feed the children they've already birthed are selling babies from the womb. According to press reports, in 1990 it was possible to buy a child for as little as US $25, with the babies drugged to keep them quiet while being smuggled across borders in shopping bags. The children serve an endless stream of men up to nineteen hours a day, and they are routinely beaten and sold from brothel to brothel with their value decreasing as they grow older, less desirable, and/or contract diseases including AIDS infections (*Vancouver Sun,* 1990). Alan Whitaker, of Britain's Anti-Slavery Society, is quoted as saying that

> There are more slaves than ever in the world today. And millions of them, maybe most, are children . . . owned completely by their masters. The intense competition between . . . desperately poor countries . . . creates a demand for cheap labour, and the cheapest labour is children. However, the growing visibility of large-scale sexual exploitation of children strains belief. (*Vancouver Sun,* 1990)

From a Special Report by *Time* magazine (Hornblower, 1993; Serrill, 1993) I quote the following:

- In Nepal's Himalayan villages, some 7,000 adolescents are sold each year into the sweat-drenched brothels of Bombay.
- In Brazil an estimated 25,000 girls have been forced into prostitution in remote Amazon mining camps.
- A 1991 conference of Southeast Asian women's organizations estimated that 30 million women had been sold worldwide since the mid-1970s.
- In Tel Aviv the number of brothels has skyrocketed in five years from 30 to 150, largely because of an influx of Russians.
- In the past two years, Spanish police have dismantled more than a dozen slave-trafficking rings. In January [1993] a Barcelona police inspector was sentenced to seven years in prison for forcing Guatemalan women into prostitution.
- In Frankfurt [1992], police raiding a bordello discovered that more than half of the 30 Thai seductresses were men who had undergone transsexual surgery [to make money].
- [An] estimated 70,000 Thai "hostesses" [are] now working in Japan as virtual indentured sex slaves in bars usually controlled by *yakuza* gangsters. . . . [T]here are several recorded instances in which police have handed escaping girls back to their abusers.
- In Ho Chi Minh City . . . the number of prostitutes has recently increased from 10,000 to 50,000.
- In Karachi human-rights lawyers are mobilizing opinion against rackets that have kidnapped 200,000 Bangladeshi women into prostitution in Pakistan.
- One of the more tragic reasons for the recent upswing in child prostitution is the mistaken belief that young sex partners are less likely to have AIDS. In fact, the opposite may be true.
- [A French priest and doctor fighting child prostitution says]: "This problem is not just Bangkok's, Colombo's, Manila's. It's Paris', Brussels', Rome's. It's the nice, respectable white man who goes down there [to Thailand] to molest these kids."

And finally, in this compendium of horror stories, we learn that "Technology has created a whole new category of horrific crimes against children." As reported by the "United Nations special investigator on the sale of children," children are being sold or kidnapped so their "organs can be used in transplants, so they can act as surrogate mothers for the baby market, or so they can grow fetal tissues for medical treatments or research." Further, video technology "creates an even larger demand for child pornography" (*Vancouver Sun,* 1993: A2).

Given our current knowledge of the pervasive experience of children as "sexual slaves" to male members of their own families within their own homes, in North America as elsewhere, we should not be surprised that entrepreneurs are capitalizing on men's desires for children's and young women's bodies. Such horrific exploitations deserve our most intense and uncompromising moral judgements and demands for the cessation of this profoundly dirty business. At the same time, these newly surfacing reports behoove us to withhold condemnation of adult women in a gender-stratified world who are electing to take matters concerning their own bodies into their own hands, however they choose to do that.

THEFT AND FRAUD

In Canada in 1990, females were held responsible for 23.4 percent of all property crime, including 33.3 percent of all thefts of property under $1,000.00 in value and 28.7 percent of fraud charges consisting primarily of passing bad cheques, fraudulent use of credit cards, and welfare fraud. Less frequent charges against females included breaking and entering (4.8 percent), theft of a motor vehicle (5.9 percent), robbery (7.5 percent), possession of stolen property (11.9 percent) and theft of property valued at over $1,000.00 (16.7 percent) (CCJS, 1991). The numbers of females involved in Canadian property crime almost doubled between 1974 and 1987, and the rate of increase was almost double that of male property crime. As discussed above in the section on Freda Adler's work, (1) female property crimes are predominately minor in nature and shoplifting is the most common form of female theft; (2) increases are explained in terms of negative effects on women of declining economies (characterized as the "feminization of poverty"); and (3) increases in offences are exacerbated by more aggressive law enforcement against females (based on false presumptions of female emancipation).

The double hypothesis that females would commit more serious property crime as they gained access to better paid positions in the work force was stated in 1975 by Rita Simon as follows:

women's participation in selective crimes will increase as her employment opportunities expand, as her interests, desires, and definitions of
self shift from a more traditional to a more "liberated" view. The crimes
that are considered most salient for this hypothesis are various types of
property, financial, and white-collar offences. (Simon, 1975: 36–37)

This expectation echoed Freda Adler's "role convergence hypothesis," and
it was primarily Adler's hypothesis that researchers tested. In a comprehensive
study conducted in 1986, Timothy Hartnagel and Muhammad Mizanuddin
examined data on female crime from thirty-seven nations. They set forth the
hypothesis that "as gender roles become more similar, female crime should
increase toward the level of male crime" (1986: 1), and they expected that if
such gender role convergences existed, they would occur in tandem with
processes of social modernization. Their findings refuted their hypothesis and
they concluded that straightforward economic explanations were more useful
in explaining increases in female property crime. In their words:

Accompanying international inequality and related to it is a growing marginaliza-
tion of whole segments of the population within both developed and less developed
countries. Thus economic development is accompanied by an increasingly seg-
mented labour market, greater stratification, and a growing inequality in the
distribution of income and other valued resources. . . . This alternative perspective
on economic development casts some doubt on the idea that modernization con-
tributes to gender role convergence and thus to increased female crime. . . . Gender
role convergence resulting from economic development of societies is quite likely
limited to only a small segment of the female population. Thus women in both
developed and underdeveloped countries are disproportionately represented in the
lowest strata. . . (Hartnagel and Mizanuddin, 1986: 11–12)

The fact that female crime increases in Canada and elsewhere are linked to
property offences committed primarily by women lacking material resources
lends substance to Hartnagel and Mizanuddin's conclusions. This position is
strengthened by the research of Kathleen Daly who, in a 1989 study of women
and white-collar crime in the United States, examined cases of bank embezzlement, income tax fraud, postal fraud, credit fraud, false claims and
statements, and bribery. One of her most significant findings was that
although increasing numbers of women had entered managerial bank posi-

tions since 1970, they nevertheless had not engaged in the crime of embezzlement to any noticeable degree. This suggests that even when women have the same opportunities for committing the same crimes as men, they do not act on them.

In Daly's study, women comprised a significant (though still low) percentage in just three of the examined offence categories: false claims and statements (15 percent), credit fraud (15 percent), and postal fraud (18 percent). Postal fraud and false claims were generally related to welfare and unemployment claims. The women indicted were disproportionately non-white, younger than the men in the category of charges, much less likely to have a college degree, and more likely to have dependent children. Most of the women who were employed held jobs as low-paid clerical workers, whose illegal activities supplemented their wages (Daly, 1989b: 775, 778). Though they were officially categorized as "white-collar" criminals, "pink-collar" would be a more appropriate designation.

Within the discipline of criminology, the notion of "opportunity" has been invested with varying meanings. In the now-classic "differential opportunity theory" of Richard Cloward and Lloyd Ohlin (1960), which focused on male crime, those whose social status denies them opportunities to gain material goods through legitimate means will turn to illegitimate means to acquire desired possessions. Even opportunities for illegitimate success are distributed differentially. When applied to females, opportunity theory has suggested that women commit less crime than men because they lack the opportunity to do so, an analysis constructed from class-based, social control presumptions that females are sheltered within the home where they are subject to patriarchal disciplines and protections. In 1986 Darryl Steffensmeier and Robert Terry published evidence that even when women are not confined to the private sphere of the home they are still limited in their crime opportunities due to the sexist attitudes of men who exclude them as accomplices.

Basing their conclusions on interviews with men convicted of serious theft, Steffensmeier and Terry found that when women were involved with men in theft crimes they were assigned to activities which were thought to be suitable to their feminine gender, such as shoplifting, stealing from sex customers, cashing bad cheques or committing credit card forgeries. In the more serious crimes, such as burglary and robbery, women were excluded because the men thought they lacked "particular qualities . . . regarded as important for success as a criminal," including physical strength, emotional stability, reliability and aggression. Following are comments from these interviews (Steffensmeier and Terry, 1986: 307–8):

> I believe the woman, if you put pressure on her, any of them will break.

> I just don't see having woman do crimes. Her place is in bed and in the kitchen I guess.

> [T]he man is the dominant of the two. Women in their subconscious know this.

> I think a man could keep his mouth shut better. [You] can never trust a female.

> I wouldn't trust a woman. I'd say they talk too much.

Comments concerning women's lack of trustworthiness due to their "big mouths" are reminiscent of the historical concerns with silencing women and the punishment of "scolds." As Steffensmeier and Terry observe, "institutionalized sexism within the underworld narrowly restricts the illegitimate opportunities available to females" and "social structure influences sex differences in crime by making options differentially available to males and females for solving economic problems" (Ibid.: 319, 321–22).

One could link this variation on opportunity theory to conventional analysis of gender socialization when considering aggressive thefts such as burglary and robbery. Because they frequently include the use of weapons, as indicators of potential violence, they are "masculine" crimes. Women are consistently underrepresented in these crimes. In Canada, in 1990, just 7.5 percent of robbery charges and 4.8 percent of charges of breaking and entering for purposes of theft were laid against women (CCJS, 1991).

DRUGS

It has been only in the 20th century that traditional elixirs, medicinal tonics, herbs, sedatives and stimulants have been legally categorized, criminalized and transformed into dangerous substances, with moral panics linking them with sin and decadence.

In mainstream Canada, through the late 19th century, opium was marketed in the form of legal, pharmaceutically produced "tonics, elixirs, cough syrups, analgesics, and patent medicines" (Boyd, 1988a: 194). A 1908 statute which prohibited the importation, manufacture and sale of opium coincided with racist campaigns in British Columbia against an "Oriental invasion," fueled by fears of white tradesmen and labourers that influxes of Chinese and Japanese workers would present unfair competition in the job market. The discovery that Chinese opium merchants were profiting substantially from business with young white men and women gave grounds to a moral crusade which was, in effect, a smokescreen. As analyzed by Neil Boyd, "making opiate use illegal was not substantially the product of an ethic of consumer protection. The legislation is better understood as reflecting a fear of socio-economic and socio-cultural assimilation" (Ibid.: 201).

Then followed the Opium and Drug Act of 1911, which added cocaine and morphine to the list of forbidden substances. Subsequent amendments to the Act increased penalties for distribution, to include whipping, imprisonment and deportation of Chinese drug merchants. To the present time, the rhetoric of morality and protection of Canada's youth has obfuscated the economic and political issues which have governed drug regulations in this century. Attempts to criminalize the use of alcohol, the drug of choice of the European population, utterly failed during the Prohibition years of the 1920s, and the negative consequences of alcohol abuse and addiction continue to surpass those of drugs which remain criminalized. The so-called "war on drugs" in North America during the 1970s and 1980s has been a war against people who lack social protections, and anti-drug propaganda has been a prejudicial exercise in reviving notions of a "dangerous class."

In Canada in 1986 females constituted only 11.5 percent of persons charged with drugs/narcotics offences; in the United States the percentage was just 14.4 percent (Hatch and Faith, 1989–90: 445). The low rate of female apprehension for illegal drug offences is based in part on women's limited participation in major drug trafficking, but there may also be a bias at the arrest stage. Chesney-Lind and Shelden cite the 1975 work of L. B. DeFleur, who "discerned a tendency on the part of police to avoid arresting females as often as males if they behaved in stereotypic ways. . . . If, however, female suspects were aggressive or hostile, they were more likely to be arrested and processed" (Chesney-Lind and Shelden, 1992: 129). This perceived paternalistic advantage does not, however, significantly alter the reality that females are less involved than males in illegal substance use.

In keeping with the punitive association between drug abuse and political

minority groups, Native women in Canada are overrepresented in jails and
prisons for alcohol-related offences, as discussed in Chapter Four. In California, women of African or Mexican heritage have been most vulnerable to
incarceration for drug offences. As noted by Coramae Richey Mann, using
1979 California data, "white women drug violators, who represent the primary group arrested for this offence (65.1%), were far less likely to be
imprisoned . . . than any minority female group" (Richey Mann, 1989: 101).

Relative to men, the lower rate of women who use illegal narcotics is
linked in part with women's greater consumption of legal pharmaceuticals,
and the medicalization of female social behaviour (Penfold and Walker,
1983). However, even though most women who are processed through the
criminal justice system are serving time for crimes other than drug-related
offences, many women who enter prison have been or are dependent on
alcohol, prescribed drugs and/or what is generalized as narcotics. In Canada,
71 percent of federally sentenced women in a national survey indicated that
"drugs or alcohol were a factor in their offending" (Shaw et al., 1990: 26).
During this same period, a US survey determined that, depending on the
state, between 44 percent and 88 percent of females arrested tested positive
for illegal substances (Arbiter, 1991: 3). And at the Burnaby Correctional
Centre for Women, in 1993, 38 percent of the women interviewed "abused
or were dependent on alcohol," 30 percent had problems with cocaine, and
slightly more with opium derivatives (primarily heroin); 43 percent of those
interviewed "abused or were dependent on more than one psychoactive substance" (Tien et al., 1993: 12).

Certainly some drugs are worse in their effects or are more addictive than
others. That is, narcotics, legal pharmaceuticals, alcohol and cigarettes are more
addictive and cause significantly greater threats to health than cannabis, for
example. There are also significant variations on street products according to
the level of "purity" and the substances with which the drugs are "cut" to reduce
their strength and increase the dealer's profits. Individual users—according to
weight, age, and chemical, physical, and psychological make-up—vary in their
responses to particular drugs.

Cultural factors and the user's expectations of how the drug will affect her
or him are also important to how the user responds. In 1969 I did research
among rural Ras Tafarians in Jamaica (see Faith, 1990). Many of them smoked
heavy ganja (cannabis) habitually, but they approached it as a sacred ritual, a
spiritual "meditation"; it didn't seem to affect their physical coordination or

strength, their ability to function effectively socially and intellectually in varied life situations, or their ability to interact with complete clarity and coherence. This observation was confirmed by the research of Vera Rubin and Lombros Comitas, who found that rather than inducing lethargy, as they found among marijuana smokers in New York City, the Rastas were industrious, steady and reliable workers even "under the influence" (Rubin and Comitas, 1976). They were also vegetarians and overall had fewer medical problems than other Jamaicans.

In interviews with women in prison I found very contradictory messages about why they used particular drugs and how they reacted to them. Some women used narcotics to calm themselves, others for the energy. Some used pills to kill emotional or physical pain, others to celebrate and have a good time. Some used various substances to escape from bad memories, others to get in touch with their feelings. Some used cocaine to open up their senses, others used it so they wouldn't have to feel anything. Some used speed to get through the work day, and others used it when they got home so they could enjoy it. Some used heroin to help them think more clearly, and others used it to stop themselves from thinking and getting depressed. Some used drugs for sex, and others because they didn't have a sex life. Some wanted to get high, others to get grounded, some to escape reality, others to see reality for what it is. Some used drugs to share their feelings, others to hide them. Some used drugs (especially cocaine) to feel special, others to feel like one of the crowd. Except in the most extreme and rare circumstances, whatever the motivation or effect, there is no evidence that chemical changes, which, with or without drugs, are a routine feature of human physiology, turn people into thieves, much less killers (Brownstein, 1993: 6).

A Native woman I interviewed in California was determined that she wouldn't return to alcohol, and was putting all her energies into relearning the ways of her people and organizing with other Native women.

They have stolen our land, our customs, our means to live. We pay high rent for shacks with back-up sewage. We have 95 percent unemployment. We have illiteracy. Seven-year olds drop out of school. Eleven-year olds are alcoholics. In our time we had a matriarchal extended family. Chiefs were trained from childhood and were tested for discipline and tolerance. We would gather at the Feast Hall to settle disputes. There is no competitive mechanism in our natural way. Each of us belongs to the community. Now we have alcoholics and bingoholics. We need to put liquor aside. We must become self-sufficient again; that is not something we can get through technocracy and bureaucracy. No matter how many people preached to me, I had to find my own way. I had to reach my own bottom. But however long it takes, we must rebuild our lives. We will do it in our own time and in our own way. We are a sad people. But we are not defeated.

Feminist research in the 1990s on the factor of gender in drug use has focused on the criminalization of pregnant women who use alcohol and illegal drugs. The concern is with the uses of law and criminal justice, buttressed by medical discourse, as discriminatory methods of selective social control. Lisa Maher observes of law enforcement in US cities that crack pregnancies, in particular, "provide an ideal opportunity for projecting deep-seated cultural anxieties about the urban poor and about drugging, crime, and female sexuality" (Maher, 1990: 124–25). The legal issues have focused on the question of onset of "personhood." That is, does the fetus have "human rights" that supersede those of the pregnant woman? At what stage does the fetus enter the status of "person"? (Callahan and Knight, 1992).

It is not difficult to achieve consensus that infants in the womb should be protected from the extreme damage that can be caused by a pregnant woman's habitual ingestion of substances that are demonstrably harmful to the fetus. However, given the selectivity of law enforcement, opponents of criminalization of pregnant addicts point to the assaults on civil liberties of women who, due to their social status, are deemed potentially unfit mothers even when their level of alcohol or other drug consumption does not realistically threaten the unborn infant's health. Further, women whose drug use does put their fetus at risk are much less likely to seek medical assistance if they know they may be forced into abortion or lose custody of their child upon its birth (Sagatun, 1993: 126).

In the United States, prosecutors are using "drug trafficking" and "child abuse" laws to lay criminal charges against pregnant women who are known to use illegal drugs or alcohol (Humphries, 1993). Rather than investing in law enforcement against women from political minority groups, and creating draconian and discriminatory welfare policies in the name of "prevention," it would make much more sense to invest in treatment programs (Ibid.: 139–42), as well as "maternal education, health care, and nutrition" (Callahan and Knight, 1992: 25). The overriding need is for economic equity programs to attack the poverty that correlates with both excessive consumption of "bad drugs" and selective criminalization.

Simultaneous with the surveillance of crack-addicted mothers in the United States is the persecution of women in Latin America who have for generations supported their children by harvesting the cocoa plant from which cocaine derives. In Ecuador, Brazil, Bolivia, Columbia, Venezuela and other countries whose economies depend on drug exports, women from the peasant classes, who have been obliviously working away in the lowest echelon of the international drug trade, are now being criminalized and locked in their countries' jails and prisons (Del Olmo, 1990). Women working as couriers are being jailed in the countries in which they are arrested. For example, in 1992, "160 women from countries such as Nigeria, Columbia and Jamaica" were incarcerated in England and Wales for acting as couriers (Shaw et al., 1992: 15).

The pattern is consistent: drug and alcohol dependencies are distributed fairly evenly among women across culture and class, but it is primarily poor women, working-class women and political minority women, across borders, who are criminalized for the use or handling of illegal substances. It is women without material or psychological resources who are in dependency relationships—with drink or drugs, social service agencies and/or unreliable men—who are most likely to be ensconced in total institutions where "inmates" are dependent by definition.

And pity the addicted woman who enters jail or prison, where she will have to withdraw "cold turkey," as discussed in Chapter Three. Some institutions offer sedatives to assist with this process, but more typical is the 1982 policy of Pinegrove Correctional Centre in Saskatchewan, as described by the Deputy Director. (In 1993 this is still the prevalent approach in most Canadian prisons.)

> Withdrawal from heroin is extremely painful; there is vomiting, shaking and feeling cold. The doctor advises going "cold turkey," as the heroin user builds up such a tolerance that she cannot come off it little by little. There is no danger in complete withdrawal. If a woman has been brought in immediately after being arrested and is hallucinating or having convulsions from heroin withdrawal, she is taken to a hospital. Otherwise, she is placed in segregation, where the noise she makes won't bother the other inmates. The Centre is short-staffed and one person screaming disrupts the whole building. (Bouvier, 1982: 23)

The drugs people use depends largely on the drugs that are available to them, which in turn depends on the international market. As cynically stated by a woman I interviewed who had both alcohol and narcotics abuse on her record:

> They want us to drink. A little weed, a little heroin, it messes up their plan. If they legalize marijuana or narcotics, it'll mess with liquor taxes. The country lives off alcoholism. Tobacco and alcohol. People who smoke weed aren't going to drink so much. And they wouldn't be able to put so many people in prison if it were legal to take drugs besides alcohol. As long as everybody can have alcohol, they figure we should be satisfied. But if we have to have one recreational drug, alcohol is definitely not the best one.

During the 1980s, Canadian women were more often in prison on charges of possession of cocaine than of heroin, but according to the staff nurse at the Burnaby Correctional Centre for Women, heroin has made a comeback. Given the physical and psychological pain of withdrawal from narcotics and/or alcohol, in particular, it is no wonder that in almost every prison, male or female, there is a lively underground distribution system. Prisoners commonly use fruit and vegetable scraps to make "brew" or "hootch," which may not taste great but which does the trick. Drugs are brought in by visitors (hence, strip-searches), or by staff in exchange for money or other favours. Or they are hidden at a drop-off point on the institutional perimeter, or smuggled by mail (hence the meticulous searches through letters and packages; stamps may conceal a substance, so these are often removed by authorities).

People who are desperate are often creative, and prison authorities don't expect complete success in eliminating illegal drug use any more than they can entirely prevent sexual relationships within institutions, as discussed in Chapter Four. Indeed, as the Bible admonishes, it may not be a worthy endeavour to try to withhold "chemical relief" from people who crave it, without a concomitant commitment to resolving the social and political problems that contribute to the craving:

> Give strong drink to him who is perishing and wine to those in bitter distress; let them drink and forget their poverty, and remember their misery no more. (Proverbs 31:6–7)

VIOLENCE

Women in Canada, in 1990, were responsible for 14.1 percent of homicide charges and 15.5 percent of attempted murder. (Approximately half of these offences were against family members, primarily spouses, as discussed below.) Women were charged with 11.4 percent of all criminal assaults, 2 percent of sexual assault offences and 7.5 percent of robbery charges, which is officially classified as a crime of violence given the normal presence of a weapon. In sum, in 1990 females were charged with 10.3 percent of all indexed crimes of violence (CCJS, 1991). As observed by Neil Boyd in his appraisal of the significant overrepresentation of men involved in violent offences, "Violence is a learned response and our culture has consistently rewarded men for aggression in a wide range of settings and circumstances." He notes that in Canada between 1867 and 1962 (prior to abolition of the death penalty in 1976) 693 men were executed for murder compared to 13 women, a ratio of over fifty to one (1988b: 3).

On the face of it one could speculate that women are indeed less violent by nature. In this essentialist view, because nature has endowed women with the biological function of child-bearing so are women instilled with a maternal instinct which gives them an innately tender, gentle, nurturing essence. They give life and they sustain it by nursing babies and preparing food for men and children. This idealization holds women as the life force, the harbingers of respect for the sacredness of life, whereas men are the warriors whose biological aggressions prepare them to defend to death their property, their women and children, their honour and their patriotic commitments to their homelands. These messages of gender function are so invasively inculcated, as basic to respectable social identity, that to betray one's gender by taking on the characteristics attributed to the opposite sex is an invitation to persecution.

The Literature. Both academic and journalistic accounts of "women who kill" generally focus on women who can be readily demonized, sending out the conflicting messages that, on the one hand, only a complete psychopath or sociopath could commit these heinous crimes, and, on the other hand, all women are potential killers and society (men) must control them.

Christine Rasche (1990: 48–50) sets forth a typology of models by which females who have murdered their spouses have been explained in the pre-feminist academic literature, including: deadlier species; biological defect;

psychopathology; crime of passion; women's role in society ("domestic" homicides); and self-defence. As Rasche points out, this latter type of murder, self-defence against an abusive mate, has been recognized since Lombroso in 1895, although he considered such events to be anomalous and he was more attentive to "monstrous" women whose crimes were manifestations of unchecked biology (see Chapter One). The 1948 work of Hans Von Hentig, the first specialist in "victimology," attempted to show ways by which victims precipitate their own deaths, but he did not recognize the centrality of wife-battering in cases where women killed their mates (Von Hentig, 1948/1979). A decade later, Marvin Wolfgang's classic study on homicide in North America found that women were significantly more likely to be killed by their husbands than vice versa, but that when women did kill they were commonly "strongly provoked" by the violence of their husband-victims (Wolfgang, 1958).

In an historical account of murders by twelve women in 19th century England and France, Mary Hartman evades the trap of seeking monolithic causal explanation based on "female nature." She observes that "The accused women were not, then, simply freaks or victims or rebels; rather, they were women who were especially vulnerable to the same pressures experienced by the majority of their peers" but who, unlike the majority, "never did manage the adjustments required of them" (Hartman, 1977: 256). Ann Jones (1980), whose study of women who kill is written from an historical, feminist perspective, warns against the limitations of concluding that some people are more dangerous "types" than others. The act of killing is extraordinary, but most often the women who commit this act are in every other way ordinary women, and to focus on the individual psychology of women who kill is to obfuscate the matrix of social conditions which inevitably result in some deaths. As she says, "Whether we become prisoners or guards, wives or mistresses, victims or killers, lies at least as much in our society as in ourselves" (Ibid.: 333).

Jones is criticized by Wilbanks for failing to produce a "systematic theory of why women kill" and instead focusing on "the reaction of a male-dominated society to the women who do kill" (Wilbanks, 1982: 175). But it is precisely through social reactions to such women that we can recognize the historical construction of gender-based presumptions as to when and by whom the act of killing is or is not understood as legitimate. The ordinariness of circumstances leading to murder is reiterated by Lisa Priest, who tells the stories of eleven contemporary "Canadian women who have killed for love, children, money or freedom from abuse" (1992: 6). Several of the women she interviewed intentionally killed abusive husbands. A young, unmarried woman was convicted of infanticide, and an older woman, a devoted Christian, killed her daughter's infant. One woman arranged the death of her estranged husband so as to gain custody of her infant, and an older woman killed her adulterous husband for peace of mind. For money, one woman strangled an ailing cousin, another beat an old man.

Murder stories, when focused on the deed, take on the quality of monster tales, but when the deeds are contextualized and the murderers demystified by the details of their lives, they lose their sensational quality and much of the onus shifts to society's failures to provide relief to women trapped in intolerable situations. This point is made most profoundly by Bonny Walford (1987), who was herself incarcerated for murder. Her stories of women with whom she is serving a life sentence confirm both my own experience with women in prisons and opinions expressed to me by officials in a variety of women's institutions. Namely, women convicted of murder are often the most peaceable women in prison. They are more often middle class than the prison population at large, and the murder is often their first and only criminal offence. Cases like that of the notorious Maggie MacDonald (Gould, 1987), who killed not one but two abusive husbands, and other headline murders by women are so uncommon as to be statistically insignificant and therefore newsworthy.

Hidden Violences. Relative to violence against women, we do not need more panels or research to confirm what frontline shelter workers have been telling us for decades. We have information and laws: what we need immediately is more shelters, comprehensive childcare and education; what we need to be producing is changes in gender relations and in the political economy. At the same time, for social policy purposes there is still a need for research of specific violences committed against, for example, mentally ill women, women in rural areas, immigrant and refugee women, women with physical disabilities, women living on military bases, women in isolated ethnic or religious communities, and First Nation women on and off reserves. Most violence against women is hidden in that it is committed in the home and most incidents are not reported. The victimization of specific groups of women is doubly hidden given the particular isolations of their lives, cultural constraints or minority status which reduces their initiative in contacting law enforcement.

We know less about women as perpetrators than as victims of violence. We don't yet know the full extent of child abuse (Korbin, 1989), research on elder abuse is still in a nascent stage, and the existence of cults which ritually torture and kill children is just beginning to surface. Women are implicated in all these still hidden offences, with both male and female victims.

Violence by women against women is particularly titillating to the porno-graphic imagination, but on more grounded levels it is another unexamined area. Women living with men are much more likely to be assaulted than women living with women. The evidence is clear that gender is a key predictor in the expression of violence, both quantitatively and qualitatively. However, proximity is also a primary factor in the expression of spontaneous violence; neither women nor men who fall into a sudden rage go out looking for a target if one is already available. Among women, lesbian-partner battering has been only recently acknowledged (see Lobell, 1986), just as gay violence has been underreported. Political minority groups in general are reluctant to expose their social problems, knowing it can exacerbate lesbohomophobia, racism, and other oppressions by the dominant culture. The consequence is that the relatively few lesbians who are battered by their partners lack the services and protections that might be avail-able to heterosexual women in the same circumstance. Gay men who are battered are even less likely to find shelter or support.

The equation of lesbianism with masculinity, and the equation of mas-culinity with violence, results in stereotypes which fan lesbophobia and which are exploited as entertainment in women's prison movies (Faith, 1987, and as discussed in Chapter Six). One could hypothesize that greater violence would occur between lesbians or gays who are "into role-playing." It would be con-sistent with the gender notions of masculinity and femininity that one would assume the right to "discipline" the other. However, there is no evidence that "butches" are more likely to be violent than "femmes," just as there's no cor-relation between lesbianism and violence (Brooks, 1981). By all measures, in any context, women are statistically safer with women than with men. The more extreme a woman's adherence to heterosexual scripting, the greater the likelihood of her victimization.

In the United States, between 1979 and 1987, an annual average of 625,800 women were violently injured by male "intimates," primarily ex-spouses at 216,100 (compared to 56,900 by co-habiting spouses); boyfriends inflicted 198,800 serious injuries per year (Harlow, 1991: 1). As confirmed by Browne (1987), women are in more danger from their spouse if they leave than if they stay and "endure." That is, women who are living apart from abusive husbands are most vulnerable to being stalked and killed by them. Battered women who kill do not go chasing after the abuser to kill him; it happens most commonly in the home where she is assaulted.

In Canada, a battered woman is the offender and an abusive husband is the victim in approximately half of all homicides committed by females. Nationally, wife-killing represents less than one-third of homicides committed by males, but men have a higher rate of violent crime overall and males are four times as likely as females to kill their spouse (Daly and Wilson, 1988). In a study of spousal homicide in Montreal in the years 1982–1986, Andrée Coté found that in 43 percent of cases where women were killed, the perpetrator was their spouse or boyfriend; of all male homicide victims, only 3 percent were killed by their spouse or girlfriend (LEAF, 1992: 7). Native women, then officially constituting less than 3 percent of the female population in Canada, committed 21 percent of spousal homicide by females between 1961 and 1983, which may be consistent with a high rate of battery and other violence against Native women. Conversely, Native women are much less likely than European women to harm their children, suggesting that Native women are both more likely to defend themselves against violent men and more protective of their children than are Europeans (Silverman and Kennedy, 1988: 117–19). Jane Ash Poitras, a Native artist, explains it in language that crosses over cultures:

> Many traditional Native people believe that children are specially beloved by the spiritual powers since they have so recently come from mystery. Those same traditions hold that striking a child, punishing a child or treating a child without respect may cause it to return to the mystery from which it came. (Poitras, 1993)

Explanations. As reported by Neil Boyd, in Canada less "than five percent of all murders are committed by men or women legally defined as insane" (Boyd, 1988b: 243). However, individual pathology explanations are expedient when women kill strangers or when they plot the deaths of rivals, as in the headline cases of the Texas Cheerleader (1991) and Amy Fisher (1992). Both cases also, however, reflect on the socially conditioned compulsion to be attractive to and made secure by males, and therefore to be in competition with other females. In the first instance, a woman who wanted her daughter to win the school's cheerleader auditions tried to arrange the murder of the mother of her daughter's competitor. In the second case, a teenage girl shot and seriously injured the wife of her much older lover. In both cases a woman was willing to kill another woman to strengthen her own (or her daughter's) desirability to a man (or men at large), which reflects transparently on the social problem of "pathological" over-conformity to "feminine" gender prescription.

Whereas infanticide was treated as a social crime of single women prior to the 20th century, it is an infrequent offence in the postmodern world, with just two recorded cases in Canada in 1990 (CCJS, 1991); in both cases, both male and female parents were charged. The low numbers relate in part to greater social acceptance of single mothers. As discussed by Ania Wilczynski, prejudices toward women who do kill their infants are at least as great as at any time in the past (Wilczynski, 1991).

Overall, historically and to the present, women who commit criminal acts of violence are an anomaly. However, the recurrent biological debate is whether violent women are compelled by hormonal and psychological irregularities which distance them as sick and anomalous to "normal" women, or whether these women are indicators of a latent, normal female capacity for violence which is held in check by an hierarchical gendered social order.

According to Margo Wilson and Martin Daly (1992), who take a socio-biological approach to the study of spousal homicide, "Men do not easily let women go. They search out women who have left them, to plead and threaten and sometimes to kill" (p. 89). This male problem, in their analysis, is primarily explained by jealousy, which they view as a cross-cultural, transhistorical phenomenon. That is, both wife-battering and wife-killing are motivated by three primary reasons: "adultery, jealousy and male proprietariness" (p. 93). Females are male property; female adultery is serious because it makes paternity uncertain; males compete for and denigrate each other's goods, including their women; jealousy is not wanting another man to take your woman, even if you don't like your woman. Wife-battering and killing is observed globally, but it is not evenly distributed across cultures. Weapons availability and cultural glorification of violence are primary factors. Wilson and Daly note that

Women in the United States today face a statistical risk of being slain by their husbands that is about five to ten times greater than that faced by their European counterparts, and in the most violent American cities, risk is five times higher again. It may be the case that men have proprietary inclinations toward their wives everywhere, but they do not everywhere feel equally entitled to act upon them. (1992: 96)

From a critical perspective, it is not generally useful to look for the causes of crime in the individual. That is, there are many socio-economic, legal, political, cultural and historical factors involved in the construction of both the individual and the crime. In search of an answer to the question "why do people commit crime?", social psychologists look to the defining external as well as internal characteristics and predispositions of the individual, and their relations with intimate others, but they commonly bypass systemic power imbalances. Critical sociologists, by contrast, look to the defining characteristics of the social world that constructs the individual within structured networks of power relations.

Sociological explanations for women's crimes include variations on social control theories, which position women under the watchful authority of father/husband buttressed by state-legitimated and culturally reproduced familial ideology. In the absence of a responsible male, the woman is placed under direct surveillance and regulation by the state. Nuclear family women, in particular, have had less opportunity to enter the public sphere for the purpose of committing crime. Variations on socialization and social learning theories demonstrate that women learn what a woman is supposed to be both through peer dynamics and, sometimes conflictingly, through generations of tradition, transmitted through cultural preachings and teachings by older women's example. A socio-biological theory would maintain that cultural encouragement to females to be passive is society's way of accommodating nature. A feminist analysis of violence, by contrast, places patriarchal relations at the centre of the power dynamic, not only as it can affect male/female relations but as it affects any relationship between unequal partners, from the macro level of class antagonisms to the most intimate of human interactions.

Although sometimes women's harms against women are at the instigation of men to whom they are obeisant accomplices, whatever the compelling motive it is almost invariably "safer" for a woman to hit another woman than to hit a man. Thus, when women are violent they are more likely to assault one another than to assault men. In Canada, 78 percent of female assaults are against other females, and 65 percent of male assaults are against other males (Hatch and Faith, 1989–90: 435). Women do not, however, kill each other. Looking at it historically, in Canada in 1931, 63 women were victims of male homicide, constituting 36.6 percent of victims in that year; in 1988, females constituted 35 percent of homicide victims, with 202 women killed, most of whom were killed by a male "family member" or "close acquaintance" (CCJS, 1991).

Battered Woman Syndrome. Although they are too few in number to constitute a trend, women on trial for violent crimes in Western nations, including Canada, have recently presented courts with unusual pleas for mitigated sentences based on two recently defined syndromes: Pre-Menstrual Syndrome, as discussed in Chapter One, and Battered Woman Syndrome.

Lenore Walker (1984), who coined the term Battered Woman Syndrome, developed a theory of "learned helplessness," referring to the means by which a woman becomes physically and emotionally incapacitated through processes of domination and abuse by her spouse. She can neither defend herself nor escape, nor does she always want to. She just doesn't want to be hit, or worse. The relatively few women who kill abusive spouses have often succumbed to a state of passivity until the triggering moment when opportunity arises for that fateful act. Twenty years ago a woman who killed her husband was almost automatically incarcerated with a long sentence. For example, at the California Institution for Women in 1972, sixteen women were serving life sentences for first-degree homicide (of a total prison population exceeding 600 women). Eight of these women had killed their husband (or common-law partner), and in all eight cases the woman had been habitually battered. However, beginning in the 1980s a number of cases in Western nations employed Walker's theory and gained mitigated sentences.

In Canada the most publicized case was that of Jane Stafford, whose story is told in the book *Life with Billy* (Vallée, 1986). For years, Billy was brutal to his wife in unspeakable ways, and to their child. He had a reputation for brutality within their rural community in Nova Scotia, and he routinely promised his wife that he would kill her and her family if she tried to get away. One afternoon while Billy was sleeping in his truck, Jane shot him with his own rifle. She turned herself in and a jury acquitted her of first degree homicide, with reference to her history as a victim of the deceased as a mitigating factor in the crime. On appeal by the Crown, her acquittal was overturned and she received six months jail time, of which she served only two months with two years probation [*R. v. Whynot (Stafford)* (1983) 37 C.R. (3d) 198]. She subsequently worked with other battered women, but apparently did not recover from her own ordeal. In 1992, she was found dead, and although the circumstances were dubious, the authorities concluded she died by her own hand (Beeby, 1992: A4).

In a major US study of battered women who have killed, Angela Browne (1987) found that of the forty-two women interviewed, almost all had called the police for prior assistance, and most had called many times. Other studies confirm this pattern of repeated, failed efforts to obtain help from the police (see, for example, Sonkin, Martin and Walker, 1985: 1–2). Women also appeal, usually in vain, to family, friends, neighbours and clergy. Shelter space is inadequate. Over a thousand women and their children are turned away from shelters in British Columbia each year (Faith, 1993b), and the picture is grim in all of Canada. It has been generally agreed among those who work with battered women that fewer of these killings would occur if there were more spaces in women's shelters, as borne out by evidence that spousal homicides by women have in fact decreased where shelters have been implemented (BWSS, 1993: 5).

During the 1980s at least four women in Canada received reduced sentences with the aid of evidence that, prior to the killing, the deceased had physically and psychologically brutalized the defendant (Sheehy, 1987: 37). In the landmark *Lavallee* case [*R. v. Lavallee* (1990), 76 C.R. (3d) 329 (S.C.C.)], in 1987 a Winnipeg woman, who had frequently required medical treatment for injuries inflicted by her common-law partner, shot and killed her partner when he handed her a loaded gun with the threat that he would kill her if she didn't shoot him first. A jury found her not guilty of second degree murder but the provincial Appeal Court called for a retrial on the technical grounds that the psychiatrist's testimony of the accused's credibility concerning her history as a battered woman was improper in the absence of admissible evidence. Finally, in 1990, the Supreme Court of Canada ruled that the expert testimony was valid and of assistance to the jury "in assessing the reasonableness of her belief that killing her batterer was the only way to save her life." The acquittal was restored (Comack, 1993: 21–35).

The *Lavallee* decision was considered a victory for women. However, Elizabeth Comack points out that the accused did not testify and the judgement was based on expert testimony of a male psychiatrist. The judgement, then, was a victory for the professional discourse imparted by a professional man who, in this case, interpreted the accused's experience and her "state of mind" to her benefit (Ibid.: 41). Further, her acquittal, supported by the defence of

Battered Woman Syndrome, was based on her feeling of entrapment, help-lessness and powerlessness, all of which suggest her inability to take control of her life and obfuscate the real issue, namely: "the dynamics of male power and control" (Ibid.: 45).

Legal scholar Elizabeth Schneider, cited by Browne (1987: 177), is another feminist critic who is concerned that in order to successfully plead a Battered Woman Syndrome defence, a defendant must be presented as a defeated woman, a passive, helpless victim whose irrational behaviour was the desperate act of a trapped animal. This is, indeed, often the case. However, Schneider suggests that, for many women, that sudden act might be indicative of a capacity for agency, for making a "rational" decision to resist by any means necessary, "in light of the alternatives."

In the United States, beginning in the late 1980s, governors in ten states (Florida, Illinois, Iowa, Kansas, Maryland, Nevada, New Jersey, Ohio, Vir-ginia and Washington) have pardoned or given clemency to dozens of women who were serving time for killing an abusive spouse, and reviews are being sought in other states, including California, Massachusetts and Texas. Indeed, activists are calling 1991, the year in which twenty-six women in Ohio and eight women in Maryland were released, "The Year of Clemency" (Osthoff, 1992: 2). Reviews are similarly being sought in Canada (see Noonan, 1993).

More contentiously among feminists, some activists advocate a tighter con-trol of violent men by police, judges and criminal justice systems at large, with tougher penalties, including incarceration. Other feminists oppose this response as a reinforcement of patriarchal institutions, and re-entrenchment of racist social divisions and belief systems that generate much of the violence (Faith and Currie, 1993). Pushed by grassroots feminist initiatives, in most Western nations the state has in recent years introduced into prisons treatment and education programs for men convicted of assaulting women and children, with mixed results. Given that most such crimes aren't reported, even if such programs were successful in their effect on the participants (a worthy goal in itself), they could not serve as a significant preventive force. Violent "crimi-nals" are isolated physically and in social meaning from the unchecked violators throughout the dominant society, who remain invisible because they are not stigmatized or punished.

Women who are battered present a problem for the courts when they appear as defendants in a homicide case. The traditional plea of self-defence requires that the defendant be faced with imminent threat of death, and that the use of force would be no greater than that of the "reasonable man" (Gillespie, 1989). Women who kill generally do so when the abuser is in some way incapacitated—asleep or drowsy from alcohol, for example—and thus do not qualify for "imminent threat." If the women were to go on attack when the target was fit and in good form, they would most commonly be overcome, beaten up or killed themselves. A woman cannot be a "reasonable man." To address this issue, Elizabeth Comack proposed the idea of a new gender-neutral defence of "self-preservation." Such an approach, she reasons, would introduce "the issue of women's structured inequality into the court's frame of reference" (Comack, 1987: 10). From this perspective one can understand these violences not as individual pathologies as verified by the "psy" professions but rather as manifestations of major social problems that to varying degrees affect countless individuals, and thus must be confronted on the societal level.

Contrary to women's experience, the work of Murray Straus and his colleagues at the New Hampshire Family Violence Center (Straus, Gelles and Steinmetz, 1980) concluded alarmingly that females engaged in violence against spouses to almost the same degree as did males. The work was dismissed by feminists, and effectively critiqued for flawed methodology and decontextualization of wife assault (Schwartz, 1987). The researchers were criticized for use of a "Conflicts Tactics Scale" in which violent events were counted in such a way that a woman throwing kitchen items, one after the other, would be seen as committing more acts of violence than a man who threw just one punch. According to self-report surveys, for each man who is hospitalized due to injuries incurred in "domestic disputes," forty-six women are hospitalized. Moreover, 54 percent of injured men report the violence, compared with 45 percent of injured women, a difference not sufficiently wide to explain the lower serious injury rate of males in terms of lower reporting rates for men (MacLeod, 1989: 52–53).

Differences in force used and injury sustained, the question of who initiated the violence, the issue of whether there's a history of violence, and social traditions, ideologies and power differentials that have made women dependent on men, and condoned male violence while condemning female violence, are all reasons for not placing male and female on an equal footing in the study of what is euphemistically called "domestic violence." Yet, the equality interpretation was revived in a 1992 study at the University of Manitoba, which found that almost 40 percent of married or cohabiting women "engage in some form of abuse tactic as a mode of conflict resolution" and that "the overall rates of violence among females reported in this study are higher than those reported for males in other studies examining the prevalence of abuse between intimate partners." The means of measuring violence levels was, again, to count violent incidents, and they found that the "most common spouse abuse tactic used by female[s]" was "throwing or smashing something (*but not directly at partner*)" (Sommer, Barnes and Murray, 1992: 1318, emphasis added). This would seem a weak basis on which to document or rank female violence, unless, in an attempt at sexist humor, one were to interpret this as proof that women suffer from a poor aim and keep missing their target.

It would be pointless to deny that women are capable of, and engage in, hideously violent behaviours; the evidence is otherwise. Yet there is a crucial line between acknowledging female violence and inferring that either quantitatively or qualitatively male and female are of equal physical threat. Males are homicide victims compared to women at a two to one ratio, but this just underscores "the fact that men kill both men and women, while women tend to kill men only" (Gomme, 1993: 204). In Canada in 1991, 508 men were charged with murder, compared with 47 women (Statistics Canada, quoted in Cobden, 1993).

A commonplace issue among feminist socio-legal theorists in the 1980s was whether one can strive for either a gender-neutral or gender-specific approach to reforming the law. That is, do women plead equality on the grounds of sameness with men, or do women plead for special treatment on the grounds of their differences from men? The introduction of the Battered Woman Syndrome into the courts is only a partial step toward declaring women's common life circumstances as a subordinated group. Despite the contradictions of appealing to patriarchal institutions to validate women's experience, the admission in court of Battered Woman Syndrome opens the door to legal recognition that women's lives, across cultures, generally differ from men's and that equitable justice for women cannot be dispensed on the same terms which define justice for the "reasonable man."

VICTIMIZATION-CRIMINALIZATION CONTINUUM

Poverty and racist discrimination are frequently demonstrated by researchers to be significant factors in criminalization processes. However, since most poor people and most "people of colour" do not engage in crime, neither poverty nor racial designation, alone or in combination, can account for criminal behaviour. Those who are held accountable for criminal behaviours are most often those who are already under the eye of the law and who have little voice.

Females constitute the most impoverished group of every Western society, yet females commit by far the least crime. Theory-makers have increasingly abandoned sexualized, biological and physiological explanations for female crime. Deterministic economic theories are also discredited, in favour of those that stress the broader social environment, or that deconstruct and demystify dominant discourses which define crime and deviance. Gender socialization and stratification may explain why females steal one item rather than another (for example, cosmetics rather than stereo equipment), but other factors must be considered to explain why anyone steals at all, or, more to the point, why so many do not. It is of particular interest when females commit serious crime precisely because it is so rare.

Beginning in the 1970s, documentation of rape, child sexual abuse, wife-battering, sexual harassment and other forms of victimization dominated the interests of feminists working in criminology. Survivors publicly exposed the dark side of confining women to the home to "protect" them. They broke the silence, naming the problem, making public that which had been hidden, uncovering dirty secrets, facing it as a social problem, a problem of male violence and a problem of female inadequacies as well. The speaking out gave impetus to the development of an activist, political movement. The violences were analyzed as "informal methods of social control over women and children" (Hooper, 1992). The documentation validated women's experiences. However, the focus in the literature on the effects of adult male violence on women and children had the sum effect of reifying the female as lacking human agency. Women were no longer so thoroughly objectified as male property, but they were reobjectified as Victim. Competing discourses could accommodate the contradictory and class-based stereotypes of women as both helpless and monstrous. Smart observes how

> legal, medical and early social scientific discourses intertwine to produce woman who is fundamentally a problematic and unruly body; whose sexual and reproductive capacities need constant surveillance and regulation because of the threat that this supposedly "natural" woman would otherwise pose to the moral and social order. (Smart, 1992: 8)

Certainly much crime stems from victimization of every kind, but victimization cannot be named as "the" cause of crime. That is, although most abusers were abused, most victims of childhood sexual abuse do not become abusers. Most victims of racism do not similarly victimize other people. Most poor people do not steal. Most battered women do not kill their abusive mates. Although women who get in trouble with the law have higher rates of prior victimization than women at large, they constitute a very small percentage of the totals of women who have been physically, sexually and psychologically assaulted.

The continuum, then, does not follow deterministically from victimization to criminalization. Rather, social victims en masse serve as the very large pool from which the anomalous woman, who sells sex, steals or hurts people and gets caught, is a candidate for prosecution. These unruly masses are the target of criminal justice as well as the target of other dominant regulatory institutions in bureaucratized societies. The continuum from victimization to criminalization is arbitrarily drawn according to power relations as constructed through racially divided and class-based social structures, in tandem with the authority of law and other dominant discourses such as medicine, social sciences and welfare, which all serve selective law enforcement practices.

The victim characterization conflicts with demands for equality, because if someone *de facto* needs special protections they can't be equal. Feminist resistance is the antithesis of female-victim identity, although privileging of the victim was one of the unintended early outcomes of Second Wave feminist writing and activism. The feisty woman who attacks her abuser is no longer acting out of passive acquiescence to powerlessness, but out of anger, survival instinct and belief that the abuse isn't her own fault. A feminist analysis recalls the factors of agency and choice in examining the ways that girls and women survive, despite structural factors which define the parameters of their choices. It is as survivors, not victims, that women have increasingly characterized themselves. This is the interpretation explored by Meda Chesney-Lind (1989) and Mary Gilfus (1992) who, among others, speak to the ways that girls' and women's survival strategies are criminalized. As Gilfus says,

> Escape from an intolerable home situation may sometimes be the only sane solution for an abused child, and the only way to end the violence. But when children or adolescents run away . . . they become delinquents in the eyes of law enforcement rather than children in need of protection. (1992: 75)

Heidensohn (1985) observed that the machismo of criminological research heroized the male criminal, and Kathleen Daly and Meda Chesney-Lind (1988) suggest that feminist authors might heroize female offenders as well. This is not to romanticize female crime or the women responsible for their offences. Rather, the feminist impulse to decry the harm done to criminalized women is best met with a recognition that women's crimes do not necessarily signify defeat; they may demonstrate women's resilience and capacity for positive action as well as negative reaction against social injustices. As evolving societies, we may or may not tolerate women who go "bad" or "mad." It's less clear why we would tolerate the social and political conditions that produce both symptomatic behaviours and selective criminalization responses by the state.

REFERENCES

Adelberg, Ellen and Claudia Currie (Eds.) (1987). *Too Few to Count: Canadian Women in Conflict with the Law.* Vancouver: Press Gang Publishers.

Adler, Freda (1981). *The Incidence of Female Criminality in the Contemporary World.* New York: New York University Press.

Adler, Freda (1985) (original 1975). *Sisters in Crime: The Rise of the New Female Criminal.* Prospect Heights: Waveland Press. [Original, New York: McGraw-Hill.]

Allen, Hilary (1987). *Justice Unbalanced: Gender, Psychiatry and Judicial Decisions.* Milton Keynes: Open University Press.

Arbiter, Naya (1991). "Women, Children & Drugs: Against Indifference." Washington: US State Department.

Arrington, Marie (1990). "Outrageous: Death of Prostitutes Draws Only Apathy." *The Province* [Vancouver] (April 10): 20.

Barry, Kathleen (1979). *Female Sexual Slavery.* New York: Avon Books.

Battered Women's Support Services (BWSS) (1993). *Newsletter* [Vancouver] (Summer).

Baunach, Phyllis (1985). *Mothers in Prison.* New Brunswick: Transaction, Inc.

Beeby, Dean (1992) "Woman Who Killed Abusive Mate Found Dead." *Vancouver Sun* (February 25): A4.

Bell, Laurie (Ed.) (1987). *Good Girls, Bad Girls: Sex Trade Workers & Feminists Face to Face.* Toronto: Women's Press.

Bernstein, Claire (1990). "Sex, Lies and the Law." *The Province* [Vancouver] (July 15): 39.

Bertrand, Marie-Andrée (1969). "Self-Image and Delinquency: A Contribution to the Study of Female Criminality and Woman's Image." *Acta Criminologica* 2: 71–144.

Bouvier, Vye (1982). "Women in Saskachewan Prisons." *New Breed Journal* 13: 22–25.

Bowker, Lee (1978). *Women, Crime, and the Criminal Justice System.* Lexington: Lexington Books.

Bowker, Lee (Ed.) (1981). *Women and Crime in America.* New York: Macmillan.

Boyd, Neil (1988a). "The Origins of Canadian Narcotics Legislation: The Process of Criminalization in Historical Context," in R. C. Macleod (Ed.), *Lawful Authority: Readings on the History of Criminal Justice in Canada.* Toronto: Copp Clark Pitman, 192–218.

Boyd, Neil (1988b). *The Last Dance: Murder in Canada.* Scarborough: Prentice-Hall Canada.

Boyle, Christine L. M., Marie-Andrée Bertrand, Céline Lacerte-Lamontagne and Rebecca Shamai (1985). *A Feminist Review of Criminal Law* (J. Stuart Russell, Editor). Ottawa: Status of Women Canada.

Brock, Debi (1986). "Prostitutes are Scapegoats in the AIDS Panic." *Resources for Feminist Research/Documentation sur la recherche féministe* 18(2): 13–17.

Brooks, Virginia (1981). *Minority Stress and Lesbian Women.* Toronto: D.C. Heath.

Browne, Angela (1987). *When Battered Women Kill.* New York: Macmillan.

Brownstein, Henry H. (1993). "What Does 'Drug-Related' Mean? Reflections on the Problem of Objectification." *The Criminologist* 18(2): 1, 5–7.

Burkhart, Kathryn W. (1973). *Women in Prison.* Garden City: Doubleday.

Cain, Maureen (1989). "Feminists Transgress Criminology," in M. Cain (Ed.), *Growing Up Good: Policing the Behavior of Girls in Europe.* Newbury Park: Sage.

Callahan, Joan C. and James W. Knight (1992). "Prenatal Harm as Child Abuse?" *Women & Criminal Justice* 3(2): 5–33.

Canadian Centre for Justice Statistics (CCJS) (1991). *Canadian Crime Statistics: Annual Catalog #85–205.* Ottawa: Statistics Canada.

Canadian Council on Social Development (CCSD) (1993). "Choices for Youth: A New Housing and Support Program." *Vis-à-Vis (A National Newsletter on Family Violence)* 10(3): 14–15.

Carlen, Pat (1988). *Women, Crime and Poverty.* Milton Keynes: Open University Press.

Carlen, Pat (1990). "Women, Crime, Feminism, and Realism." *Social Justice* 17(4): 106–23.

Carlen, Pat and Anne Worrall (Eds.) (1987). *Gender, Crime and Justice.* Milton Keynes: Open University Press.

Chapman, Jane Roberts (1980). *Economic Realities and the Female Offender.* Lexington: Lexington Books.

Chesney-Lind, Meda (1973). "Judicial Enforcement of the Female Sex Role: The Family Court and the Female Delinquent." *Issues in Criminology* 8(2): 51–59.

Chesney-Lind, Meda (1989). "Girl's Time and Woman's Place: Toward a Feminist Model of Female Delinquency." *Crime and Delinquency* 35: 5–29.

Chesney-Lind, Meda (1992). "Girls, Gangs and Violence: Anatomy of a Backlash." Paper presented at the Annual Meeting of the American Society of Criminology, New Orleans, November.

Chesney-Lind, Meda and Randall G. Shelden (1992). *Girls: Delinquency and Juvenile Justice.* Belmont: Brooke/Cole Publishing.

Chunn, Dorothy and Robert J. Menzies (1990). "Gender, Madness and Crime: The Reproduction of Patriarchal and Class Relations in a Psychiatric Court Clinic." *The Journal of Human Justice* 1(2): 33–54.

Clark, Lorenne and Debra Lewis (1977). *Rape: The Price of Coercive Sexuality.* Toronto: Women's Press.

Cloward, Richard A. and Lloyd E. Ohlin (1960). *Delinquency and Opportunity.* Glencoe: Free Press.

Cobden, Michael (1993). "Men Ignored, Scorned by Some in Fight against Violence." *Halifax Chronicle-Herald* (July 3): C3.

Cohen, J. B. (1989). "Overstating the Risk of AIDS: Scapegoating Prostitutes." *Focus: A Guide to AIDS Research* 4(2): 1–2.

Comack, Elizabeth (1987). "Women Defendants and the 'Battered Wife Syndrome': A Plea for the Sociological Imagination." *Crown Counsel's Review* 5(11): 6–10, 15–16.

Comack, Elizabeth (1993). *Feminist Engagement with the Law: the legal recognition of the Battered Woman Syndrome.* Ottawa: Canadian Research Institute for the Advancement of Women.

Cox, Wendy (1993). "Pimping 'Parasites' Sentenced to Prison Terms." *The Montreal Gazette* (June 19): A10.

Currie, Dawn (1993). "Battered Women and the State: From the Failure of Theory to a Theory of Failure," in K. Faith and D. Currie, *Seeking Shelter: A State of Battered Women.* Vancouver: Collective Press.

Daly, Kathleen (1987a). "Structure and Practice of Familial-Based Justice in a Criminal Court." *Law & Society Review* 21(2): 267–90.

Daly, Kathleen (1987b). "Discrimination in the Criminal Courts: Family, Gender, and the Problem of Equal Treatment." *Social Forces* 66(1): 152–75.

Daly, Kathleen (1989a). "Rethinking Judicial Paternalism: Gender, Work-Family Relations, and Sentencing." *Gender & Society* 3(1): 9–36.

Daly, Kathleen (1989b). "Gender and Varieties of White-Collar Crime." *Criminology* 27(4): 769–93.

Daly, Kathleen and Meda Chesney-Lind (1988). "Feminism and Criminology." *Justice Quarterly* 5(4): 497–538.

Daly, Martin and Margo Wilson (1988). *Homicide.* New York: Aldine DeGruyter.

Datesman, Susan K. and Frank R. Scarpitti (Eds.) (1980). *Women, Crime & Justice.* Oxford: Oxford University Press.

Davis, Kingsley (1937). "Prostitution." *American Sociological Review* 2(5): 744–56.

Davis, Nanette J. (1992). "Multiperspectivism and the Obscured Problematic of Prostitution: A Comparative Lesson." Paper presented at the Annual Meeting of American Society of Criminology, New Orleans, November.

Davis, Nanette J. (1993). *Prostitution: An International Handbook on Trends, Problems and Policies.* Westport: Greenwood Publishing Group.

Davis, Nanette J. and Karlene Faith (1987). "Women and the State: Changing Models of Social Control," in J. Lowman, R. J. Menzies and T. S. Palys (Eds.), *Transcarceration: Essays in the Sociology of Social Control.* Aldershot: Gower, 170–87.

DeFleur, L. B. (1975). "Biasing Influences on Drug Arrest Records: Implications for Deviance Research." *American Sociological Review* 40: 88–101.

Delacoste, Frédérique and Priscilla Alexander (Eds.) (1988). *Sex Work: Writings by Women in the Sex Industry.* London: Virago Press.

Del Olmo, Rosa (1979). "The Cuban Revolution and the Struggle Against Prostitution." *Crime and Social Justice* 12: 34–43.

Del Olmo, Rosa (1990). "The Economic Crisis and the Criminalization of Latin American Women." *Social Justice* 17(2): 40–53.

Eaton, Mary (1986). *Justice for Women? Family, Court and Social Control.* Milton Keynes: Open University Press.

Edwards, Susan (1985). *Gender, Sex and the Law.* Kent: Croom Helm.

Edwards, Susan (1987). "Prostitutes: Victims of Law, Social Policy and Organized Crime," in P. Carlen and A. Worrall (Eds.), *Gender, Crime and Justice.* Milton Keynes: Open University Press, 43–56.

Eisenstein, Zillah R. (1988). *The Female Body and the Law.* Berkeley: University of California Press.

Faith, Karlene (1987). "Media, Myths and Masculinization: Images of Women in Prison," in E. Adelberg and C. Currie (Eds.), *Too Few to Count: Canadian Women in Conflict with the Law.* Vancouver: Press Gang Publishers, 181–219.

Faith, Karlene (1990). "One Love, One Heart, One Destiny: The Ras Tafarian Movement in Jamaica," in G. W. Trompf (Ed.), *Cargo Cults and Millenarian Movements*. Berlin: Mouton de Gruyter, 295–341.

Faith, Karlene (1993a). "An Interview with Freda Adler." *Critical Criminologist* 5(1): 3–10.

Faith, Karlene (1993b). "State Appropriation of Feminist Initiative: Transition House, Vancouver, 1973–1986," in K. Faith and D. Currie, *Seeking Shelter: A State of Battered Women*. Vancouver: Collective Press, 1–36.

Faith, Karlene and Dawn Currie (1993). *Seeking Shelter: A State of Battered Women*. Vancouver: Collective Press.

Faludi, Susan (1991). *Backlash: The Undeclared War Against American Women*. New York: Anchor Books.

Feinman, Clarice (1980). *Women in the Criminal Justice System*. New York: Praeger Publishers.

Gavigan, Shelley A. M. (1987). "Women's Crime: New Perspectives and Old Theories," in E. Adelberg and C. Currie (Eds.), *Too Few to Count: Canadian Women in Conflict with the Law*. Vancouver: Press Gang Publishers, 47–66.

Geller, Gloria (1987). "Young Women in Conflict with the Law," in E. Adelberg and C. Currie (Eds.), *Too Few to Count: Canadian Women in Conflict with the Law*. Vancouver: Press Gang Publishers, 112–26.

Gelsthorpe, Loraine and Allison Morris (Eds.) (1990). *Feminist Perspectives in Criminology*. Milton Keynes: Open University Press.

Giallombardo, Rose (1966). *Society of Women: A Study of a Women's Prison*. New York: John Wiley & Sons.

Gilfus, Mary E. (1992). "From Victims to Survivors to Offenders: Women's Routes of Entry and Immersion into Street Crime." *Women & Criminal Justice* 4(1): 63–89.

Gillespie, Cynthia K. (1989). *Justifiable Homicide: Battered Women, Self-Defense, and the Law*. Columbus: Ohio State University Press.

Gimenez, Martha E. (1990). "The Feminization of Poverty: Myth or Reality?" *Social Justice* 17(3): 43–69.

Glueck, Sheldon and Eleanor Glueck (1965) (original 1934). *Five Hundred Delinquent Women*. New York: Kraus Reprint.

Gomme, Ian M. (1993). *The Shadow Line: Deviance and Crime in Canada*. Toronto: Harcourt Brace Jovanovich Canada.

Gordon, Jody K. (1992). "The 'Fallen' and the Masculine: A Feminist Historical Analysis of the B.C. Industrial Home for Girls, 1914–1946." Unpublished Honours Thesis. Burnaby: Simon Fraser University.

Gordon, Rhonda (1993). "Coalition Combats Racism, Sexism and Denial." *Vis-à-Vis (A National Newsletter on Family Violence)* 10(4): 12.

Gould, Allan (1987). *The Violent Years of Maggie MacDonald.* Toronto: Seal Books.

Haft, Marilyn G. (1976). "Hustling for Rights," in L. Crites (Ed.), *The Female Offender.* Lexington: Lexington Books.

Harlow, Caroline Wolf (1991). "Female Victims of Violent Crime." US Department of Justice: Bureau of Justice Statistics (NCJ-126826).

Hartman, Mary S. (1977). *Victorian Murderesses: A True History of Thirteen Respectable French and English Women Accused of Unspeakable Crimes.* New York: Schocken Books.

Hartnagel, Timothy F. and Muhammad Mizanuddin (1986). "Modernization, Gender Role Convergence and Female Crime: A Further Test." *International Journal of Comparative Sociology* 27(1–2): 1–14.

Hatch, Alison and Karlene Faith (1989–90). "The Female Offender in Canada: A Statistical Profile." *Canadian Journal of Women and the Law/Revue juridique "La femme et le droit"* 3(2): 433–56.

Hatty, Suzanne (1989). "Violence Against Prostitute Women: Social and Legal Dilemmas." *Australian Journal of Social Issues* 24(4): 235–46.

Heidensohn, Frances (1968). "The Deviance of Women: A Critique and an Enquiry." *British Journal of Sociology* 19(2).

Heidensohn, Frances (1985). *Women & Crime.* London: Macmillan.

Hooper, Carol-Ann (1992). "Child Sexual Abuse and the Regulation of Women: Variations on a Theme," in C. Smart (Ed.) *Regulating Womanhood: Historical Essays on Marriage, Motherhood and Sexuality.* London: Routledge, 53–77.

Hornblower, Margot (1993). "The Skin Trade." *Time* (June 21): 16–27.

Howe, Adrian (1990). "Prologue to a History of Women's Imprisonment: In Search of a Feminist Perspective." *Social Justice* 17(2): 5–22.

Humphries, Drew (1993). "Mothers and Children, Drugs and Crack: Reactions to Maternal Drug Dependency," in R. Muraskin and T. Alleman (Eds.), *It's a Crime: Women and Justice,* 130–45.

Inciardi, James A., Dorothy Lockwood and Anne E. Pottieger (1993). *Women and Crack-Cocaine.* New York: Macmillan.

James, Jennifer (1976). "Motivations for Entrance into Prostitution," in L. Crites (Ed.), *The Female Offender.* Lexington: Lexington Books.

Jones, Ann (1980). *Women Who Kill.* New York: Fawcett Columbine.

Klein, Dorie (1973). "The Etiology of Female Crime: A Review of the Literature." *Issues in Criminology* 8(2): 3–30.

Korbin, J. (1989). "Fatal Maltreatment by Mothers: A Proposed Framework." *Child Abuse and Neglect* 13: 481–88.

Kruttschnitt, Candace (1982). "Women, Crime and Dependency." *Criminology* 9(4): 495–513.

Laberge, Danielle (1991). "Women's Criminality, Criminal Women, Criminalized Women? Questions In and For a Feminist Perspective." *The Journal of Human Justice* 2(2): 37–56.

Layton, Monique (1979). "The Ambiguities of the Law or the Street Walker's Dilemma." *Chitty's Law Journal* 27(4): 109–20.

Legal Education and Action Fund (LEAF) (1992). "Violence." *LEAF Lines* [Toronto]: 7.

Lobell, Kerry (Ed.) (1986). *Naming the Violence: Speaking Out About Lesbian Battering.* Seattle: Seal Press.

Lowman, John (1986). "You Can Do It, But Don't Do It Here: Some Comments on Proposals for the Reform of Canadian Prostitution Law," in J. Lowman, M. A. Jackson, T. S. Palys and S. Gavigan (Eds.), *Regulating Sex: An Anthology of Commentaries on the Badgley and Fraser Reports.* Burnaby: School of Criminology, Simon Fraser University, 193–213.

Lowman, John (1989). *Street Prostitution: Assessing the Impact of the Law (Vancouver).* Ottawa: Ministry of Justice and Attorney General of Canada, Department of Justice.

Lowman, John (1990). "Notions of Formal Equality Before the Law: The Experience of Street Prostitutes and Their Customers." *The Journal of Social Justice* 1(2): 55–76.

Luxenburg, Joan and Thomas E. Guild (1993). "Women, AIDS, and the Criminal Justice System," in R. Muraskin and T. Alleman (Eds.), *It's a Crime: Women and Justice.* Englewood Cliffs: Regents/Prentice Hall, 77–92.

MacKinnon, Catharine A. (1989). *Toward a Feminist Theory of the State.* Cambridge: Harvard University Press.

MacLeod, Linda (1989). "Wife Battering and the Web of Hope: Progress, Dilemmas and Visions of Prevention." Ottawa: National Clearinghouse on Family Violence (Health and Welfare Canada).

Maher, Lisa (1990). "Criminalizing Pregnancy—The Downside of a Kinder, Gentler Nation." *Social Justice* 17(3): 111–35.

Masson, Karen M. (1992). *Familial Ideology in the Courts: The Sentencing of Women.* Unpublished Master's Thesis. Burnaby: Simon Fraser University.

McIntosh, Mary (1977). "Review Symposium: 'Women, Crime and Criminology'." *British Journal of Criminology* 17(4): 395–97.

McLaren, Angus (1990). *Our Own Master Race: Eugenics in Canada, 1885–1945.* Toronto: McClelland & Stewart.

10

Price, Barbara Raffel and Natalie J. Sokoloff (Eds.) (1982). *The Criminal Justice System and Women: Women Offenders, Victims, Workers.* New York: Clark Boardman Company.

Priest, Lisa (1992). *Women Who Killed: Stories of Canadian Female Murderers.* Toronto: McClelland & Stewart.

Rafter, Nicole Hahn and Elizabeth A. Stanko (Eds.) (1982). *Judge, Lawyer, Victim, Thief: Women, Gender Roles and Criminal Justice.* Boston: Northeastern University Press.

Rasche, Christine (1990). "Early Models for Contemporary Thought on Domestic Violence and Women Who Kill Their Mates: A Review of the Literature from 1895 to 1970." *Women & Criminal Justice* 1(2): 31–53.

Richey Mann, Coramae (1989). "Minority and Female: A Criminal Justice Double Bind." *Social Justice* 16(4): 95–114.

Rubin, Vera and Lombros Comitas (1976). *Ganja in Jamaica: The Effects of Marijuana Use.* Garden City: Doubleday.

Sagatun, Inger J. (1993). "Babies Born with Drug Addiction: Background and Legal Responses," in R. Muraskin and T. Alleman (Eds.), *It's a Crime: Women and Justice.* Englewood Cliffs: Regents/Prentice Hall, 118–29.

Schwartz, Martin D. (1987). "Gender and Injury in Spousal Assault." *Sociological Focus,* 20: 61–76.

Serrill, Michael S. (1993). "Defiling the Children." *Time* (June 21): 28–31.

Shaver, Frances (1985). "Prostitution: A Critical Analysis of Three Policy Approaches." *Canadian Public Policy* 11(3): 493–503.

Shaver, Frances M. (1988). "A Critique of the Feminist Charges Against Prostitution." *Atlantis* 14(1): 82–89.

Shaw, Margaret with Karen Rodgers, Johanne Blanchette, Tina Hattem, Lee Seto Thomas and Lada Tamarack (1990). *Survey of Federally Sentenced Women: Report to the Task Force on the Prison Survey.* Ottawa: Ministry of the Solicitor General, Corrections Branch.

Shaw, Margaret with Karen Rodgers, Johanne Blanchette, Tina Hattem, Lee Seto Thomas and Lada Tamarack (1992). *Paying the Price: Federally Sentenced Women in Context.* Ottawa: Ministry of the Solicitor General, Corrections Branch.

Sheehy, Elizabeth (1987). *Personal Autonomy and the Criminal Law: Emerging Issues for Women.* Ottawa: Canadian Advisory Council on the Status of Women.

Silverman, Robert A. and Leslie W. Kennedy (1988). "Women Who Kill Their Children." *Violence and Victims* 3(2): 113–27.

Simon, Rita James (1975). *Women and Crime.* Lexington: Lexington Books.

Smart, Carol (1976). *Women, Crime and Criminology: A Feminist Critique.* London: Routledge & Kegan Paul.

Smart, Carol (1989). *Feminism and the Power of Law.* London: Routledge.

Smart, Carol (1990). "Feminist Approaches to Criminology or Postmodern Woman Meets Atavistic Man," in L. Gelsthorpe and A. Morris (Eds.), *Feminist Perspectives in Criminology.* Milton Keynes: Open University Press, 70–84.

Smart, Carol (Ed.) (1992). *Regulating Womanhood: Historical Essays on Marriage, Motherhood and Sexuality.* London: Routledge.

Smith, G. S. (1989). "Historical Perspectives on AIDS, Society, Culture and STDs." *Queen's Quarterly* 96(2): 244–62.

Smith, Perry F. and Mil Jaromir (1991). "HIV Infection among Women Entering the New York State Correctional System." *American Journal of Public Health* 81.

Sommer, Reena, Gordon E. Barnes and Robert P. Murray (1992). "Alcohol Consumption, Alcohol Abuse, Personality and Female Perpetrated Spouse Abuse." *Personality, Individuality, Difference* 13(12): 1315–23.

Sonkin, Daniel J., Del Martin and Lenore Walker (1985). *The Male Batterer: A Treatment Approach.* New York: Springer Publishing Company.

Sonnichsen, Donna-Marie (1993). "Man Acquitted of Trying to Kill Hooker: Pimp Awaits Sentencing on Other Charges Involving Girl." *Halifax Chronicle-Herald* (June 19): A6.

Special Committee on Pornography and Prostitution (SCPP) [The Fraser Committee] (1985). *Pornography and Prostitution in Canada.* Ottawa: Department of Justice.

Spender, Dale (1982). *Women of Ideas and What Men Have Done to Them: From Aphra Behn to Adrienne Rich.* London: Routledge & Kegan Paul.

Steffensmeier, Darryl (1980). "Sex Differences in Patterns of Adult Crime, 1965–77: A Review and Assessment." *Social Forces* 58(4): 1080–1107.

Steffensmeier, Darryl (1981) (original 1978). "Crime and the Contemporary Woman: An Analysis of Changing Levels of Female Property Crimes, 1960–1975," in L. Bowker (Ed.), *Women and Crime in America.* New York: Macmillan, 39–59. [Original, *Social Forces* 57: 566–584.]

Steffensmeier, Darryl J. and Robert M. Terry (1986). "Institutionalized Sexism in the Underworld: A View From the Inside." *Sociological Inquiry* 56(3): 304–23.

Straus, M. A., R. J. Gelles and S. K. Steinmetz (1980). *Behind Closed Doors: Violence in the American Family.* New York: Anchor.

Summers, Anne (1975). *Damned Whores and God's Police: The Colonization of Women in Australia.* Ringwood: Penguin Books.

Tien, George with Lynda Bond, Diane Lamb, Brenda Gillstrom, Faye Paris and Heidi Worsfold (1993). "Report on The Review of Mental Health Services at Burnaby Correctional Centre for Women." Vancouver: Forensic Psychiatric Services Commission.

Vallée, Brian (1986). *Life with Billy.* Toronto: Seal Books.

Vancouver Sun (1990). [Stories on sexual slavery] (September 26): A3 and (October 1): A3.

Voeller, B., J. M. Reinisch and M. Gottlieb (Eds.) (1990). *AIDS and Sex: An Integrated Biomedical and Biobehavioral Approach*. New York: Oxford University Press.

Von Hentig, Hans (1979) (original 1948). *The Criminal and His Victim*. New York: Schocken Books.

Walford, Bonny (1987). *Lifers: The Stories of Eleven Women Serving Life Sentences for Murder*. Montreal: Eden Press.

Walker, Lenore (1984). *The Battered Woman Syndrome*. New York: Springer.

Ward, David and Gene Kassebaum (1965). *Women's Prison: Sex and Social Structure*. Chicago: Aldine Publishing Co.

Wilbanks, William (1982). "Murdered Women and Women Who Murder: A Critique of the Literature," in N. Rafter and E. Stanko (Eds.), *Judge, Lawyer, Victim, Thief: Women, Gender Roles and Criminal Justice*. Boston: Northeastern University Press.

Wilczynski, Ania (1991). "Images of Women Who Kill Their Infants: The Mad and the Bad." *Women & Criminal Justice* 2(2): 71–88.

Wilson, Margo and Martin Daly (1992). "Till Death Do Us Part," in J. Radford and D. Russell (Eds.), *Femicide: The Politics of Woman Killing*. New York: Twayne Publishers, 83–98.

Wilson, Robert (1980). *The Wendy King Story: The Hooker and the Judge*. Vancouver: Langen Communications Ltd.

Wolfgang, Marvin E. (1958). *Patterns in Criminal Homicide*. New York: John Wiley and Sons.

Wright, C. (1991). *Juristat Service Bulletin: Homicide in Canada, 1990* 11(15). Ottawa: Canadian Centre for Justice Statistics, Statistics Canada.

CHAPTER THREE

The Punishment: Involuntary Confinement

JUST AS THE LABELS placed on women who break the law are laden with ideologically invested social meanings, as discussed in the introduction to Chapter Two, so is the nomenclature of punishment institutions problematic. I begin, then, with a quick review of the terms. The first lock-up arrangements in early England were called *gaols* (that is, jails) and their purpose was short-term incarceration of persons who were awaiting trial or execution, as distinct from modern prisons in which confinement became the punishment, rather than the place of waiting for the punishment. The precursors of prisons were the early *poorhouses, workhouses* and *houses of correction,* established in pre-industrialized England as a way of removing undesirable elements from the streets of new urban centres, and, ostensibly, reforming idle or deviant citizens by teaching them the disciplines and habits of hard work. In practice they served to warehouse people who were stigmatized as unruly, dangerous classes, and who were crowded together in malodorous, filthy and diseased environments, resulting in high death rates.

Early North American prisons were constructed in the 19th century under the influence of Quaker social reformers. They called them *penitentiaries* because it was idealized that the wrong-doers would use their time to seek penance through solitary meditation, religious instruction, discipline and labour. These penitentiaries, a product of emerging capitalist political

economies, were in fact maximum security prisons which confined legally convicted *criminals* who became feared and abused *convicts* as soon as they entered
the institution. The Quakers also established early *reformatories*, which in
theory similarly reflected on the emerging belief, informed by religion and
new medical discourses, that wrong-doers were not "born that way," and could
be trained to overcome their bad habits and attitudes. Women and youth,
because their crimes were generally less frequent and less serious than those of
adult males, were thought to be particularly well-suited to the goals of reformation. However, as exemplified almost a century later by the increased
incarceration of unruly teenagers in 1950s *reform schools* (and *industrial schools*)
these institutions were no less barbaric than early adult prisons. They were
appropriately nicknamed "schools of crime" by critics, who observed that
youth entered these places as anti-social rebels guilty of relatively minor crimes,
but were contaminated by one another and graduated as embittered social outcasts with few life options outside the world of crime.

During the 1950s the fields of psychology and psychiatry were popularized,
and practices of *treatment* interventions were imposed on convicted *offenders* as
a means of *correcting* their behaviours—just as the early *houses of correction* were
intended to do two centuries earlier but now with the "benefit" of *experts* and
professionals. The modern era of *corrections* which began nominally in the 1930s,
gained momentum and definition in the 1950s and has been maintained to the
present time. Women's prisons, specifically, are now most commonly officially
described as *correctional* facilities, centres or institutions, or *treatment* centres,
which house *inmates* (as in mental hospitals), *residents* or *clients* who are under
the watchful eyes of *correctional officers*. Informally, adult women in prison have
been addressed by line staff both as *the girls*, to stress their infantilized status,
and as *ladies*, to underscore the reformist intention of refining these rowdy
offenders. With feminist influences seeping even into *correctional* institutions,
women in prisons are now often referred to as women. When women first arrive
at these institutions they are placed in what is sometimes confoundingly referred
to as the *reception guidance centre*, suggesting a benign welcoming and orientation process, or, more baldly, the *receiving unit*, as in a warehouse.

Progressive prison planners, administrators and staff prefer the soft jargon
to hardline language because it suggests a distinction between the brutal institutions of yore and modern penal philosophies. However, to the women
themselves, the euphemisms are offensive. To the person who is forcibly confined within them, these places are prisons and they are prisoners, and in this

chapter that is how I will refer to them. These words are the most direct means of describing a situation where people are held captive, locked behind bars, walls and fences, under constant surveillance, their every move regulated by guards operating under the authority of the state. I commonly speak of guards rather than *correctional officers* because, whatever other function they might serve, according to institutional philosophy and their own orientation, the bottom line is that they must literally watch and scrutinize these women to maintain the security and custodial functions of any prison.

The most poignant argument against euphemistic language has been reiterated to me from time to time over the years by bewildered women who hadn't realized they were being sent to prison: they were shocked to discover that the *correctional* institution or *treatment* centre to which the judge sentenced them was not a hospital, or a therapeutic environment, or a temporary *assessment* or *reception* facility, but rather a cold, undisguised prison from which they could not escape.

The history of unruly, defiant women is the history of men's efforts to control them (Chesney-Lind, 1980), and this translates into practical terms in the context of criminal justice. "Criminal law has been codified by male legislators, enforced by male police officers and interpreted by male lawyers and judges" (Moyer, 1992: 18). Agreed. It is almost invariably men who put women in prison, but more specifically it has been particular laws, particular men, and particular women who are implicated. And certainly men are much more likely to imprison other men than to imprison women outside the confines of the home.

There are numerous reasons why the crimes of some women may result in some combination of probation, fine, community service or suspended sentence, whereas other women are targeted for prison confinement. Any of the following factors, alone or in some combination, may contribute to whether or not a woman will be incarcerated:

- seriousness of the crime;
- past record;
- persuasiveness of lawyers' arguments for or against the defendant;
- outcome of plea bargaining;
- legal technicalities concerning evidence;
- degree of publicity and public opinion concerning the crime;
- familial status (especially, level of conscientiousness toward dependent children);
- the convicted woman's age and state of physical or mental health;

- regional court biases related to cultural, class and/or racial identity;
- the defendants' conformity to or deviance from mainstream gender role standards;
- sentencing patterns of particular jurisdictions;
- availability of cell space;
- proximity of prisons to the sentencing court;
- known community-based alternatives to institutionalization; and, often most importantly,
- the opinion of the probation officer who writes the pre-sentence report on which judges base their decisions.

Prison philosophies, structures and policies are remarkably similar throughout the Western world. The penal systems which I know most directly, from contact with imprisoned women and men, staff and administrators, over the course of almost twenty-five years as an action-researcher, educator and prisoners' advocate, are those in California (state and federal) and Canada (B.C. provincial and federal). In this extended chapter I make frequent reference to institutions with which I'm familiar, and to women who have been incarcerated in them. For purposes of analysis I also draw from the criminological and sociological literature, particularly that produced by feminist scholars over the past two decades in Canada, Britain and the United States. My own perspectives are those of someone who views modern prisons as monuments to the failures of liberal democracies to meet their promises. I don't assume that I can speak for incarcerated women in all their diversities, just as no single or few individual(s) in prison can speak for all other prisoners. My hope in these pages is to contribute to a more critical appraisal of the uses to which prisons are put. In the two preceding chapters I discussed the structural and discursive processes in the social construction of crime and punishment. In this chapter I describe various features of women's penal institutions which, short of execution, serve as the apex of punishment processes.

PURPOSES OF PRISONS

The traditional rationale for the use of prisons is the glaring imposition of punishment as the "just desserts" means of paying one's debt to a centralized state, which must be compensated for harm done to an impersonal "society." The forgotten individual victim, if there is one, becomes subordinate to the adjudication process. In addition to the necessity of punishment, a belief which has never been discarded, are the purported modern goals of (1) specific deterrence, whereby the individual offender is temporarily incapacitated and expected to refrain from future crime as a result of the incarcerative experience; (2) general deterrence, whereby the threat of incarceration is intended to deter citizens at large from committing criminal offences; (3) crime prevention and/or public safety, which is to say that, at least for the period of incarceration, the guilty person is somewhat refrained from engagement in illegal and actual or potentially dangerous behaviours; and (4) finally, most problematically, the ideal of rehabilitation.

Rehabilitation, as a modern concept, is metaphorically derived from the ancient practice of banishment, whereby the individual lost his dignity by being cast naked into the wilderness to contemplate his anti-social behaviour. Once he (and the mythological figure is a "he") has recovered his sense of social belonging and responsibility, and has attained forgiveness and absolution through appeals to and communion with his god and his conscience, he can regain his right to be part of society. The French word *habiller* means "to dress," or "to wrap up"; to be *re*habilitated is to start life anew, once again fully "clothed" in the garb of respectability with one's dignity restored.

The idea of rehabilitation is most consistent with the belief that criminal behaviours stem from flaws or weaknesses of the individual. Attention shifts from the event of the crime to the person who "falls" from grace due to sin or sickness. Deviation from consensual behavioural norms violates an abstract social contract, whereby each individual has a responsibility to contribute to society in exchange for the state's protections of his or her human rights. In this paradigm such individuals can be "saved," "cured" or otherwise reformed through combinations of religious and moral instruction, psychological treatment and/or vocational training in combination with the behaviour-modifying effects of losing one's freedoms. Early "point" systems, as developed in 19th century Australian prisons under the influence of the reformer Alexander Maconochie, are still practiced in many North American reformatories over a century later. Prisoners could earn back their freedoms by gaining points for good behaviours and moving up the custody classification ladder, from maximum to minimum security, while demonstrating their potential usefulness to society. Such utilitarian reformers have been also concerned with modernizing the conditions of imprisonment so as to make the punitive environment more conducive to rehabilitation. In Canada, the first female Member of Parliament (in 1921), Agnes MacPhail, was a serious critic of the commonplace barbarities of Canadian prisons, such as hanging prisoners from the ceiling for brutal beatings. In 1925, just a few years after her impassioned crusade, construction began on a new women's institution which would finally, in 1934, begin separating federally sentenced females from the horrors of the male penitentiary (NPCFO, 1978: 4). Some women were retained at the men's penitentiary for several years and the new women's prison wasn't put to full use until 1938.

More radical reformers have focused not on individual offenders but rather on both the social conditions which produce anti-social behaviours (some of which are then legislated as crimes against the State, which stands in for any individual victims), and the discriminatory practices of punishment whereby certain populations are more vulnerable than others to the state processes of criminalization. Ultimately, the viability of the notion of rehabilitation is challenged both by the reality that most prisoners will be returned to the same social conditions which generated the undesirable behaviours, and by the indisputably punitive nature of prisons as a measure and expression of power relations within any given society. As characterized by Michel Foucault:

> Prison is the only place where power is manifested in its naked state, in its most excessive form, and where it is justified as moral force. . . . What is fascinating about prisons is that, for once, power doesn't hide or mask itself; it reveals itself as tyranny pursued into the tiniest details; it is cynical and at the same time pure and entirely "justified," because its practice can be totally formulated within the framework of morality. Its brutal tyranny consequently appears as the serene domination of Good over Evil, of order over disorder. (Foucault, 1977: 210)

The straightforward punishment model, which all prisons represent at their foundation, is an outgrowth of a retributive philosophy. The physical routinization, militaristic discipline, and punishment by physical confinement and controls that characterize prisons were designed for male "criminals," and females were stuffed into stifling attic, basement or other isolated quarters of male institutions. Although in Britain "women made up around a quarter of all those sent to local prisons and around an eighth of all those sent to convict prisons up to the 1880s," by the end of the century females constituted just 4 percent of the incarcerated population (Zedner, 1991: 100). A century later this disproportionate ratio has remained fairly constant in Western prisons.

As early as 1813, having observed the shocking conditions of female prisoners in male institutions, the Quaker social crusader Elizabeth Fry set the tone for gender-segregated prisons. Her Victorian, class-biased influence, whereby upper-class "ladies" would strive to improve the morality of lower-class women, has been periodically revived throughout Western nations into the late 20th century. She introduced the notion of matrons and wardresses who, through maternal supervision of prisoners, would instill family values and feminine manners in unruly women by teaching them the value of hard work, personal hygiene, basic literacy and religious instruction (Ibid.: 118–19, 123). These priorities were intact during the late 1970s when I appealed to the Elizabeth Fry group in Los Angeles for assistance for a woman who had spent virtually all her adult life in and out of prison. They informed me that they only worked with women who "showed promise." By this they meant primarily white women with middle-class potential: they didn't work with "ghetto" women or women with histories of drug addiction.

As we approach the 21st century, more women have entered corrections as a career, served on official task forces, and entered academic, legal and other professions which bring focus to "the female offender." Contemporary feminists, in particular, have at least marginally affected policies and endorsed changes which reflect on gender-specific needs of women in prison. To the discussion they bring less moral judgement and more understanding of social problems as they affect women than was true of Elizabeth Fry and other early reformers, who wanted to improve conditions and introduce moral training for women without altering fundamental class, sex, and race discriminations.

HISTORICAL PERSPECTIVES

Prisons were constructed in the 19th century parallel to the gradual reduction in and eventual elimination of capital punishment in all Western nations except the United States. Prisons also replaced public lashings and other public humiliations, and theoretically imprisonment substituted for the punishments of torture. In conventional wisdom, this change signified a humanitarian impulse. However, in Michel Foucault's view (1979), the shift to incarceration occurred in large part due to shifts in the dominant discourses, from centralized power to diffused disciplinary techniques and "normalizing judge-ments" as practiced by emerging professions. He observes a changed focus from punishment of the body to a focus on the human mind and soul. This analysis allows for the complex social and political dynamics behind this sig-nificant historical shift, but it doesn't allow for the fundamental reality that prisoners continued to be subject to physical tortures behind the walls.

Preceding long-term imprisonment as punishment for serious offences was the 18th century British practice of banishing criminals through "transporta-tion," whereby convicted persons could escape the gallows by being sent to the colonies as indentured servants. They were sent first to eastern regions of what became the United States of America until, following the War of Inde-pendence (1775–1783), the new government refused to accept them. They were then sent, in ever greater numbers, to Australia, a colony founded on the backs of Aboriginal peoples by 150,000 of Britain's rejects, of whom less than 25,000 were women—and many of these were sent as "sexual commodities" for both the male convicts and the colony's predominantly male settlers (Dobash, Dobash and Gutteridge, 1986: 33). Transportation, which con-tinued until 1852, was not necessarily a better option than the gallows: assault, starvation, disease and death were rampant on the boats, and for women there was the added burden of sexual exploitation and abuse (Beattie, 1986; Hughes, 1987: 129–57; Zedner, 1991: 174–75). Further, when (or if) they arrived on the shores of the new land, they were immediately subjected to the indignities of being held as servile property.

As noted above, the basic idea of banishment was not an invention of the modern age; ancient and Aboriginal societies similarly had the notion that the best way to instill social responsibility in troublesome individuals was to tem-porarily separate them from their community, so they could reflect in solitude on their misdeeds. The modern version of banishment, however, was not for the purpose of temporarily removing the person so they could return in an improved state, although theoretically a transported person could "do their time" in the colony and, if they had the means, return to their homeland. In fact, transportation was a straightforward means of getting rid of "social garbage," even while producing ever greater supplies on home soil. The modern prison system, from its beginnings to now, has replicated these con-tradictions.

Prior to the development of separate women's institutions, women were confined in cramped quarters within men's prisons. Convicted primarily of drunkenness, theft and prostitution, they were literally hidden away, under cold, abominable conditions including infestations of insects and rodents, filth, inadequate nutrition, disease, total idleness or meaningless labour, harsh punishments for prison infractions, and sexual abuses by male guards and male prisoners. In Canada, female prisoners were kept in the attic of the men's penitentiary in Kingston, Ontario, disdained as lazy and a disgrace to their sex (Calder, 1981: 308–9; Cooper, 1987: 131–33; Morris, 1987: 105). They were not, however, perceived as irredeemable, and together with the men they were put to work on their souls.

> The warden . . . read evening prayers to the convicts while in their cells, and on the Sabbath days have read to them a sermon, with prayers and portions of the Scripture. Morning prayers, and a chapter in the Bible, are daily read in the prison after the breakfast hour by the Deputy Warden. (Beattie, 1977: 115)

In 1836 an inspector observed that "the sentencing of females to the Penitentiary causes some inconvenience," and that same year a matron was hired to oversee them. As a result of the new arrangement, the women became productive: "their labours have been beneficially applied in making and mending the bedding and clothing required for the [male] prisoners" (Ibid.: 106, 116–17). However, all was not well, and in 1849 the warden was charged with failure to rid the women's cells of bugs, neglecting their "moral condition," cruel discipline (including flogging), sixteen charges of "starving" the women, and one charge of driving a woman to insanity with "excessive punishment" (Ibid.: 152–54).

Separate prisons were established out of reformist recognition that male and female prisoners could not be effectively controlled within the same institution and with the same staff, and out of the belief that the relatively few females who go astray could be reformed under proper matronly supervision, hard work and Christian influence (Freedman, 1981; Strange, 1985). The first female-only prisons were developed in early-Victorian England simultaneous with construction in the US of separate buildings for women on the grounds of male institutions. The first entirely separate North American reformatory for females, in the state of Indiana, became fully operational in 1874. Contrary to the reformists' ideal it was not built on the cottage model but rather was a "grim, dark, 'bastille-like' structure" in keeping with the penitentiary model, and initially men remained in charge of female prisoners (Rafter, 1985: 33; Freedman, 1981: 46, 70–71).

In 1879, the first separate prison for women in Canada was opened in Toronto, the provincial Andrew Mercer Ontario Reformatory for Females, which was likewise a fortress-like institution where, under the supervision of an all-female staff, young women did the laundry for male prisoners, the staff and men working on the Canadian Pacific Railway (Strange, 1985: 89). One particularly "uplifting" matron, who described herself as "a mother to all the girls at the Mercer," organized a "Clean Speech Society," which Carolyn Strange describes as "a kind of swearers' anonymous for women with foul mouths. She held weekly meetings and allowed members in good standing to wear a 'clean speech' button" (Strange, 1985–86: 14). "Good girls" could earn points toward early release. A "defiant" woman was one who chewed gum. The best-behaved prisoners earned the privilege of serving the matron (a.k.a. superintendent) as her personal maids (Ibid.).

The cross-oceanic interest in the female reformatory model which grew through the 19th century was stimulated by Elizabeth Fry, of Scotland and England, an early advocate for "fallen" women who, in her view, needed to be tamed and domesticated. Above all, Fry wanted these women to learn feminine manners. Her rules for the women in London's Newgate prison forbade "'begging, swearing, gaming, card playing or immoral conversation' in an attempt to gain some control over 'the ferocious manners and expression of the women towards each other and their abandoned wickedness'" (Forsythe, 1987: 19). Whereas some female convicts were seen as victims of circumstance, pathetic creatures who had been misled, the rowdier women were seen as depraved and "a grotesque perversion of the ideal of feminine chastity, honour, wifely obedience and motherly love" (Ibid.: 128–29). The elusive ideal of the prim, sober middle-class woman was set by reformers as the goal for all destitute, criminalized women.

Although 19th century feminists were concerned more with changing society than changing women fallen from grace, Fry's recommendations for separate prisons were championed by most early North American prison reformers. In the United States and Canada, as in Britain, female prisoners were to be given moral and religious training, taught literacy and domestic skills, and instructed in personal hygiene and femininity. Although US reformers advocated family-style prisons, they did not challenge the strict authoritarianism of prisons, boasting that "Obedience is the first lesson taught each woman" (Freedman, 1981: 97). Women who didn't learn this lesson were physically abused; female staff, who lived in the prison and worked twelve-hour days for very low wages, were no kinder than their male counterparts, and their brutal treatment provoked prisoner uprisings (Rafter, 1985: 75, 77–79).

Women incarcerated in these early prisons were generally perceived as sexual miscreants, thus the ostensible purpose of early women's prisons was to reform the women by training them to serve a family as a proper wife and mother. The social construction of gender was a key factor in the conceptualization of women's reformatories, even though women's prisons were actually constructed on a male, militaristic penitentiary model in which, like men, women often worked either in solitary confinement or in silence on assembly lines in industrial factory-model prisons. As documented by Nicole Rafter (1982, 1985), a few institutions in the United States were actually constructed from a reformatory "open-cottage" design, and this model did introduce new ways of thinking about the potential uses of carceral punishments. However, women convicted of serious crime, and women who, because of their dependent class position and/or racial identity, did not seem redeemable (or worthy of redemption), continued to be placed in conventionally harsh, maximum security institutions, including work camps and industrial farms.

Even the so-called reformatories, according to Estelle Freedman, "increasingly housed those women perceived by the society as the most dangerous, not the most hopeful, cases" (Freedman, 1981: 148). Subsequent attempts to soften or "feminize" female institutions have been consistently subordinate to the issues of custody, order, management, discipline and punishment, which are the fundamental functions of all prisons. The 19th century women perceived as most needful of this discipline, whether in Canada, the United States, or the United Kingdom, were women who didn't conform to gendered ideals, and these women were invariably poor or working class. Dobash et al. suggest that one reason for the significantly greater percentage of women in prison in Scotland than in England was that greater percentages of Scottish women were working in mills and factories, and therefore "lived more independent lives" and had more contact with police than English women, who worked primarily in more protected domestic service (Dobash, Dobash and Gutteridge, 1986: 93–94).

Foreign observers helped to construct the myth of humane North American alternatives to the penitentiary for female felons. For example, in the 1930s a Dutch legal reformer speaks of a Connecticut prison farm as if she were describing a health spa—"attractive" in its rural, lakeside setting with "abundant opportunity for healthy outdoor sports" (Lekkerkerker, 1931: 121).

In keeping with the tendency of "officials" to be enamoured of their ideals, and ignorant of the experiential reality of those subjected to penal disciplines, a British penal administrator earlier declared that the (almost non-existent) US female "cottage" reformatory model

> is teaching the world that a woman's prison is an anomaly, that it is unnecessary and misplaced. If she is to learn a lesson, she can do so in the home life of a cottage more readily than in an amorphous mass behind a wall too high for low skirts. (Morris, 1987: 108)

The history of prisons is the history of failed prison reform. Canada's prisons have been scrutinized and inspected with regularity by many commissions and task forces, at least thirteen of which have conducted investigations of the federal Prison for Women in Kingston. It is remarkable that the Archambault report, released in 1938, recommended the closure of this women's prison in the very same year in which it was fully opened for business. The committee recognized that a centralized institution, designed according to the same surveillance principles applied to 19th century male prison architecture, was not appropriate to females. To radical reformists, tiered rows of cells (each approximately six feet by nine feet) and other features of spartan, militaristic industrial prisons were seen as brutally ineffective for men, as well.

In the U.S.A., from the 1930s to the 1960s, women were commonly racially segregated in either completely separate institutions or on the same grounds. "Negro" women, as a rule, received the harsher treatment, especially in the south, where they worked on chain gangs and in hot fields under brutal masters, in perpetuations of slave traditions. Women of the "favoured race" who were perceived as redeemable were sent out to work as indentured servants under the influence of "good" families. As late as the 1950s, as told to me by a woman who experienced it at the infamous Julia Tutwiler prison in Alabama, when a "Negro" woman and a white woman crossed the colour barrier and formed a close friendship, they were sent to segregated "dungeons" as punishment for "mixing the races."

In California, women were housed with men at San Quentin, in the San Francisco Bay Area, until 1936, when they were moved south to Tehachapi, into what became one of the state's first "correctional" institutions, but which was destroyed by an earthquake in 1952. The women were then moved further south to the present site at Frontera, sixty miles east of Los Angeles, in what is known as "Corrections Valley" due to the proliferation of male, youth, female and co-ed institutions in easy proximity to one another, a peculiar network of last resorts with all roads leading to prison. The California Institution for Women (CIW) is situated on seventy-five acres of reclaimed riverbottom land, a cluster of low buildings in the heart of dairy farm country and grazing land. In the summer the temperatures soar beyond 110 degrees Fahrenheit, the heat unpleasantly exacerbated by the dense smog that settles over the valley and by the foul stench of hot manure that permeates the atmosphere.

California is one of the most carceral jurisdictions in the world, and CIW has been the world's largest prison for women for most of its history. Between the early 1970s and the mid-1980s, during which time indeterminate sentencing was (at least theoretically) replaced with fixed terms, the population of this prison grew from just over 600 to, at one point, almost 2,500 women, with double-bunking and "extra bodies" housed in laundry rooms, the gymnasium, store rooms and every conceivable space, including corridors.

In 1972, the superintendent of the California prison expressed satisfaction with what she perceived to be the progressive steps she had taken to improve the atmosphere of her institution. She spoke of the efforts to beautify what was called "the campus" with fresh paint and landscaping; she identified the new programs she and her staff had introduced; and she expressed a commitment to replacing retiring staff with younger "correctional officers" who, she hoped, could be friends and counselors to the women, as well as being their guards. It disturbed her, however, that, given all these efforts at improvement, so many women were still trying to escape: nine women, of a total then exceeding 600, had managed to "go over the fence" within a period of less than two months. In keeping with an increased statewide security trend, and as a result of the number of escapes, coiled razor wire was placed atop the high, double chain-link fences that surrounded the institution, laser beams were installed, and four armed guard towers were constructed, buttressed by armed guards in a vehicle circling the perimeter of the prison grounds. By now California "correctional" authorities have altogether abandoned the pretense of providing a "rehabilitative" environment: prisons are strictly for punishment.

From the point of view of most people who are locked up, there is no such thing as a good prison. As succinctly stated by Gayle Horii, with the authority gained from seven years inside:

Ours is a cloistered world, one where every minute of our day and night is calculated and where we are forced to conform to inane rules and regulations; one where we are counted over and over and over again, keys smashing our senses as doors crash behind us locking us in coffin-like cages and cells. (1992: i)

Conflicting perceptions of incarceration according to point of view is an old story, as old as the first prison. Women's prison reformers create what they think is a model institution which will at the very least give women a dignified environment in which to serve their prison sentence, and which will at best reform their character. But most prisoners are not asking to be reformed, and are tormented by what they experience as hell holes, whether the furniture, walls and floors are decayed and coated with grime, or brand new and freshly painted and carpeted in "soothing" pastel colours. For a century, the ghosts of disgruntled and despairing women have been climbing the walls of both besoiled and pastel prisons.

> *Listen, the halls are not wide enough*
> *I can touch each side*
> *with my arm outstretched*
> *I tell you there is not enough air in here*
> *Not enough air.*
> (Sin, in Miller, 1974: 3)

CO-ED PRISONS

What effect would women have in our institutions? They would help normalize a fairly abnormal situation, helping to create a more realistic environment. They would also help to reduce tension, lower the level of aggression and improve the hygiene, language and self-image of inmates. (Correctional Service Canada, 1977)

The first prisons in which women were incarcerated were "co-ed" prisons insofar as the few female prisoners were held in "special" sections of male institutions. For example, Helen Gibson writes of the first state prison in Wisconsin, which in 1904 held 566 men and 11 women (Gibson, 1976: 96). This was characteristic of North American prisons, and it was because women were neglected and abused in these prisons that the female reformatory move-

ment gained momentum. In the late 20th century, a number of Western jurisdictions have experimented with a return to "co-ed" prisons with the rationales
that it is unnatural to separate the sexes, and that females have a positive influence on the language, hygiene and appearance of male prisoners. Not
incidentally, identical arguments have been put forth to justify "affirmative
action" policies of hiring women as "correctional officers" in male prisons
(Nicholson, 1985). In Canada this trend began in 1977 with a pilot project in
which teams of females were assigned to male institutions in Saskatchewan,
British Columbia and Quebec.

British Columbia attempted a co-ed prison in Prince George in the 1970s,
to alleviate crowding at the women's provincial jail, the Lakeside Correctional
Facility. The experiment was discontinued due to unfavourable effects on the
females, who, as in all co-ed prisons, constituted a distinct numerical minority.
In Western societies it may be "unnatural" to segregate the sexes, but it is even
more unnatural for men and women to occupy the same space without the
occurrence of sexual intercourse, by mutual choice or otherwise. Speaking for
a 1978 Royal Commission which she chaired, Justice Proudfoot acknowledged
that men were favourably affected by the presence of women but that the
problems outweighed the benefits. In her words,

> Measured against [the benefits] were disadvantages of conflicts and jealousies [8
> women to 140 men at the time of the study]; sexual frustrations; intensified emo-
> tional depression; the detrimental effects of jail romances on outside life; and
> inmate-guard romances. The advantages [to co-corrections] seem superficial and
> are, in the view of the Commission, heavily outweighed by the disadvantages.
> (*Liaison*, 1979: 7)

This view matches my impressions of a US federal co-ed prison in northern
California, the Pleasanton "correctional" facility. Many of the women incarcerated there actively pursued romantic friendships with male prisoners, but
other women were discomfited by the intense gendered dynamics of the institution. And whereas staff commonly observed that the presence of women
had a "civilizing" effect on the male prisoners, others observed that sexual tensions and jealousies exacerbated the normal stresses of the prison environment
for both males and females.

In the context of Hawaii, as reported by Clarice Feinman, "the 1982 experiment [with co-ed prisons] failed because women prisoners were harassed by

male officers and the fear of sexual contact between male and female prisoners led to tighter restrictions and controls for the women" (Feinman, 1985: 31). The frequent occurrences of pregnancy has also caused institutional problems which outweigh the perceived "normalizing" advantages of co-ed prisons. It is telling, in terms of persistent heterosexist presumptions of appropriate gender roles, that advocates of co-ed prisons laud their "normalizing" effects, although Alice Propper observed in 1979 that in mixed youth facilities "homosexual" liaisons between girls were as common as they were in segregated institutions (*Liaison*, 1979: 24).

Despite the bad reports, "co-ed" prisons continue to exist in those jurisdictions in the US and Canada where there are too few women to justify the cost of building separate prisons. In the Yukon Territory the few female prisoners are housed in a section of the male institution. (When I visited there in 1984, all the women were Native, about ten of them, although Natives constitute only about 15 percent of the total Yukon population.) In the Northwest Territories, a 1985 Task Force concerned with incarceration of about fifteen women believed that, due to what was perceived as greater program opportunities in mixed institutions, co-ed prisons could be the most effective answer to the vocational needs of "women in conflict with the law" (DHSS, 1985: 4). However, given that prisons of any size are rarely well-equipped to prepare either men or women for integration in the outside work force, this too is a dubious expectation.

Not unexpectedly, many female prisoners who have never experienced co-ed prisons believe they would prefer to be incarcerated with men (Shaw et al., *Survey*, 1990: 64). However, those with experience point out that women imprisoned with men are doubly exploited as sexual objects and as nurturers. Generally, among critics, there is agreement that co-ed prisons only serve to perpetuate male dominance of dependent women, and that the goal of offering more vocational options to incarcerated women is better met by having the women "commute" to male prisons to participate in their programs, as has been practiced at Canada's Prison for Women since the mid-1980s.

Officials in the United States continue to vacillate as to the viability of co-ed institutions. Allison Morris notes that in the United States in the mid-1970s "there were over 20 co-correctional state and federal institutions," but that by the mid-1980s over half had reverted to segregated institutions (1987: 128). However, Rita Simon and Jean Landis counter that "As of 1989, there were nineteen coed prisons in the state system located in eleven states and seven coed institutions in the federal system" (1991: 88), for a total of twenty-six prisons intentionally designed to tame men with women's feminine influence.

PRISON PLACEMENTS:
CANADA AND THE U.S.A.

There is a difference in the way prisoners are divided in Canada and the U.S.A. according to federal or provincial/state distinctions. In Canada, a federal prisoner is anyone whose crime warrants a sentence greater than two years; women with sentences of less than two years are held in the provincial system. In the United States, apart from short-term city/town jails for "peace disturbants" and those who commit other minor offences, there are three tiers of incarceration: county jails, for sentences of one year or less; state prisons; and federal prisons. Only those crimes specific to exclusively federal law (such as treason) or which involve crossing state lines (as, for example, with drug trafficking, kidnapping or stolen vehicles) constitute federal offences. Women who commit state offences with penalties of greater than one year go to state prison. Thus, both state and federal prisoners serve long sentences, up to life, or indeed, in those states with the option of capital punishment, may be executed.

As of 1990, women constitute less than 3 percent of all federal Canadian prisoners, with sentences of two years to life, and on average women constitute approximately 4 percent of provincial prisoners. As of June 1990, 305 women were serving federal sentences compared to 13,234 men (Statistics Canada, 1990: 1). Additionally, several thousand women went in and out of provincial jails. At any given time, approximately twenty-five women in Canada are serving life sentences, and for half a century most of these women have been housed at the Prison for Women in Kingston. In the much more punitive United States, where the population is only approximately ten times greater than in Canada, there were 580,000 people serving state or federal sentences for "serious" offences in 1987, of whom approximately 29,000 were women (Simon and Landis, 1991: 77).

By way of explaining the low crime and incarceration rate of women, it has become something of a feminist cliché to say that women are controlled privately, in the home, and men are controlled publicly, by the mechanisms of market capitalism, the military, criminal justice and so forth. This has been a foundational analysis, but it is incomplete when it does not take into account social change or differences among women. Consider that almost 25 percent of federally sentenced females in Canada are Native (self-identified and/or as identified by the prosecuting agencies), and the provincial ratio is even higher (Shaw et al., *Survey*, 1990: 4), even though officially registered Indians constitute less than 4 percent of the Canadian population (INAC, 1989:4). Like many other women who have not been successfully confined to the home, Native women have not been restricted to a "private sphere," as discussed in Chapter Four.

In the United States in 1990 there were 56 female-only state and federal prisons, 560 prisons for men, and another 26 prisons which were co-ed (Simon and Landis, 1991: 77). By contrast, Canada has over forty federal prisons for men and just one federal institution for women, the Prison for Women in Kingston, Ontario (P4W). There are, however, plans to construct six new regional women's prisons. This prison was built to hold federal female prisoners from all over Canada, some separated from their families by distances of several thousand miles. Constructed across the road from the men's penitentiary, the grey limestone building is circled by an eighteen-feet-high concrete wall to contain the full range of women considered to be "serious offenders." This includes girls still in their teens who were sexually abused as children, started prostituting in early adolescence and got involved in minor drug trafficking; young mothers with chronic records of theft; and older women who killed abusive spouses. In recent years, of the up to approximately 300 women in Canada serving prison sentences of two years or more, approximately half have been incarcerated at P4W, with the balance serving time in the provinces under Exchange of Services agreements.

FEDERAL PRISON FOR WOMEN
IN CANADA, A.K.A. P4W

At P4Wm, a guard sitting in a wire cage just inside the prison checks the credentials of everyone seeking entry, and on the other side of a metal detector is a maze of staff offices, stairwells, long corridors with stained walls and shiny linoleum-tile floors which lead to and run past the tiny, barred cells in the tiered "range" units, a separate section of dorm-like rooms in the "wing" (to which well-behaved women can graduate after several months), a cafeteria, the isolated segregation and hospital areas, and rooms, upstairs and down, for the limited work, school, recreational, counselling and health programs and services. Between 100 and 150 women will be there for at least two years and often for ten or more, all of them physically and psychologically constrained by life in their prison. In its fifty-five-year history (as of 1993) P4W has had just six wardens, and despite the traditional rhetoric supporting female staff for female prisoners, only two of them have been women.

The issue of centralization has been raised by each of the thirteen reports commissioned by the government since the opening of P4W. The federal government has had dozens of male institutions throughout the country to accommodate prisoners' proximity to family members, to facilitate management of particular offender populations, to accommodate differential custody classifications (minimum, medium and maximum security), and to allow for various kinds of vocational, educational or therapeutic programming. It is a futile and foolish exercise to suggest that women would do better if they were granted a range of "choices" equivalent to those offered to men in the system. Men's prisons are no more constructive experientially or in outcome than women's prisons; programs in men's institutions do not represent real choices for men, and have not proven of any particular use in terms of so-called rehabilitation or post-prison employment. Nevertheless, differences among men are at least theoretically taken into account, whereas women are blatantly denied any recognition as individuals with distinct identities and needs.

At P4W, all prisoners are subject to maximum security custody even though prison officials agree that less than 15 percent of approximately 150 women require surveillance in the interests of public safety (Elliott and Morris, 1987: 150). Given the small numbers of women, a commensurate budget, and the constraints of the physical layout, programs are necessarily limited. This combination of high level security, great distance from families and communities, and few choices for daily activity or movement, together with individual reasons for despair, results in lethargy, claustrophobia, depression, self-injurious behaviour and suicide. From informal tallies it seems that at least twelve women killed themselves at P4W between 1977 and 1991, of whom eight were Native women. Exact statistics are unavailable in part because authorities are reluctant to have suicides blamed on the institution, and they stress that women come in with suicidal tendencies and might well have killed themselves whether or not they had been in the institution. Given the conditions of incarceration, however, one must deduce that women "on the edge" are pushed over by the prison experience.

Seven commissioned reports on P4W were submitted to the federal government in less than a decade, between 1969 and 1978, each of them repeating the time-worn recommendation for the institution to be closed and replaced by small regional facilities. The 1978 report was by the Joint Committee to Study the Alternatives for Housing of the Federal Female Offender, appointed by the Federal Commissioner of Corrections. On the basis of this report, which underscored the recommendations of those that preceded it, in 1979 then-Solicitor General of Canada, Jean-Jacques Blais, prematurely announced at an International Symposium on the Female Offender, in Vancouver, that the Kingston Prison for Women would be phased out (*Liaison*, 1979: 2–5).

Through the 1980s, many women sentenced to a federal term were retained in their home provinces, generally approximately 100 women of a total of 250 federal female prisoners. Through a federal-provincial Exchange of Services agreement which went into effect in the mid-1970s, the provinces hold the women in provincial jail facilities. For example, francophone women constitute more than one-fifth of federal female prisoners, and more than half of these have been held in Quebec at the Maison de Tanguay, under this agreement. In this way, P4W has gradually been dispersing federally sentenced women back to the provinces. However, contrary to the Honourable Jean-Jacques Blais's promise, P4W was not dismantled. In 1981 the Canadian Human Rights Commission ruled that P4W was discriminatory against women, given that it lacked the services and programs available in men's institutions. This resulted in minimal cosmetic and program improvements at the institution and the construction of a "little house" on the grounds for family visits, but little substantive change in the day-to-day prison operations.

CREATING CHOICES: BEYOND P4W

Through the history of P4W, one government report after another recommended that the institution be closed and replaced with regional centres. On April 19, 1990, yet another report on P4W was released. Titled *Creating*

Choices, it was produced by the Task Force on Federally Sentenced Women, a joint venture of a number of government agencies and national organizations including the Canadian Association of Elizabeth Fry Societies and the Native Women's Association of Canada (TFFSW, 1990). In September 1990, on the recommendations of this report, Commissioner Ole Ingstrup announced that immediate changes would be made at the institution, regional institutions would be built, the phase-out of P4W would commence as soon as possible, and the institution would be closed by 1994.

In her summary of this latest report, Kelly Moffat notes that what made this new study different from those that preceded it was that "The research completed for the Task Force was driven by a 'women-centreed approach' and its representatives were from women's groups and others 'whose beliefs stressed that issues such as poverty, racism, wife battering, and sexual abuse are central to women's crime'" (Moffat, 1991: 193). This report was thorough in its condemnation of existing "correctional" services for women. The members of the task force toured Canada and talked to 84 percent of all federally incarcerated females, including those held in the provinces under the Exchange of Services agreement as well as those imprisoned at P4W. Native women did research with Native women, and women in the institution had considerable input, to ensure that the views of the task force were informed by the experiences of prisoners as well as the views of authorities and reform-minded citizens. On the strength of the report, the government made a commitment to alter the face of "female corrections" in Canada.

As discovered by Shaw et al. (*Survey,* 1990: 62), not all women wished to see P4W closed down. When the decision was made, reformers received news of the impending closure with satisfaction, as did many women incarcerated at P4W. Others at P4W, however, have been distressed at the decision. Some women prefer to do their time away from their communities, and find prison visits more unsettling than helpful. Others, especially lifers, have formed a familiar community within the old prison, and are accustomed to one another and to the routines of the institution. Women who are reluctant to be transferred to the home provinces also resist dual mode prisons (merging of federal and provincial), protesting that provincial regulations are significantly more constraining than those at the federal level. It is feared too that given the smaller numbers in regional centres and the transiency of provincially sentenced women, even fewer programs would be available in the provinces than at P4W.

Repeating the recommendations of preceding reports, the 1990 task force proposed small, home-like residences in easy proximity to family and home communities. Emphasis is given to the need for special programs that facilitate mothers' involvements with their children. Given that most women in prison represent no risk to the community, there is no need for an hierarchical, authoritarian, punitive, paramilitary, security-driven staffing model. Women could benefit from self-help cooperative models, and if the report is heeded, staff must be sensitized to cultural differences and needs. In Canada this is especially relevant for Native women, women of African heritage from Nova Scotia, the United States or the Caribbean, and French-language women. For example, almost half of French-speaking female prisoners have been incarcerated outside Quebec, and thus have no access to services in French.

Members of the 1990 task force emphasized the potential role of the community in responding to the social problems that produce crime and criminal offenders. A de-emphasis on institutionalized programming, more individual needs assessment and planning, and full use of community resources could have a positive effect on many women's lives. Vocational training, education, mental and physical health care, and cultural and spiritual communion can all be much better attained outside rather than inside prison. Thus, the proposed function of prison staff would be to facilitate a woman's access to real choices for skill and personal development, as opposed to serving dead time in a punitive and barren prison environment.

The lack of consensus among the women affected is the first problem in closing P4W. A second concern, of proponents of the closure, is whether the recommendations of the task force for "woman-friendly" environments will be actually implemented in the regional institutions. A Healing Lodge for Native women is to be located in Maple Creek, Saskatchewan; as of late 1993, it is still unclear when this facility will be developed and how staffing decisions will be made. Conversations with residents of Maple Creek suggest that there is little support for this initiative, and that even at the early planning stages the proposed facility has generated what can only be interpreted as a racist response.

In addition to the Healing Lodge, five new regional prisons are to be constructed. The first of these regional prisons is a dual mode facility in British Columbia which holds both federally and provincially sentenced women, as discussed in the section "A Brand New Prison." Opened in 1991 in an isolated semi-rural setting, this institution contradicts the task force recommendations both architecturally and in its isolation from community resources, even though many of the administrators and staff are endeavouring to implement policies and programs more conducive to healing and growth than to punishment.

A second new federal women's prison, at the proposal stage, is to be located on the Griesbach military base in Edmonton, Alberta. In Quebec, the Maison de Tanguay is to be replaced with a new institution in Joliette, and a fourth women's prison is to be located in Kitchener, Ontario. Finally, the last of the regional institutions is to be constructed in Truro, Nova Scotia, for women in the Maritimes. In the view of writer and long-term prisoner Jo-Ann Mayhew, the selection of this location is straightforward political patronage. It will provide job opportunities in a depressed Canadian region, but the area is ill-equipped to respond to the needs of incarcerated women: ". . . it is highly unlikely that a community the size of Truro—which by its own submission is sorely lacking in women-centreed programming and almost totally unfamiliar with the issues facing imprisoned women—will be able to do more than provide a warehouse for us" (Mayhew, 1992: 15). Supporters of the new prisons stress economic benefits in terms of new jobs and profits to the regions. Opponents, such as a group in Kitchener calling themselves "People Protecting Children and Homes," stress the drop of housing value in areas in which new prisons are situated, and they also misguidedly argue that women's prisons present dangers to themselves and their children.

The 1990 task force appointed by Correctional Service Canada learned that 90 percent of Aboriginal women and 61 percent of all other women at the Prison for Women during the term of the study had histories of sexual and physical abuse, a point reiterated by more recent Canadian studies of female incarceration (see, for example, Tien et al., 1993). Relatedly, 69 percent reported having been addicted to alcohol and/or illegal drugs, a problem which can be perpetuated by the commonplace uses of prescription drugs within institutions (Shaw, 1982: 264–65), as well as by women's initiatives in gaining access to illegal drugs from outside. In her study of Cornton Vale, the women's prison in Scotland, Pat Carlen was told by prison officers that "*all* the short-term recidivists had a drink problem" (1983: 157), and this most common of pre-prison addictions is manifest in illegal prison activities. In most female institutions, women manage to make homebrew concoctions in their cells which may not taste very good but which bring on the desired effect of ameliorating the stress of incarceration.

The need for counselling and recovery programs relative to sexual abuse, and alcohol addiction, far exceeds the services which institutions can provide, although as Carlen observes in the Scottish context: "Prison officers can justifiably claim that they are the only ones who do anything for the alcoholic women whom nobody else wants" (1983: 172). Given the social dimensions of these problems, community-based services would be critical to any healing process. However, the neighbouring communities of most of the proposed locations of new regional prisons in Canada are unprepared to provide these services.

Kelly Moffat emphasizes that the problems of geographic dislocation cannot be solved by five new regional institutions in the geographically largest country in the world. Most incarcerated women will still not be within visiting proximity to their families. This will particularly affect Native women if they are all sent (by choice or order) to the one Healing Lodge. Also, women will continue to be subject to unreasonable security restrictions, given that women with a minimum custody classification will be housed in institutions designed for women assigned to maximum custody. An even more serious reason identified by Moffat for skepticism about this new plan is that instead of challenging the notion of incarceration as a reasonable response to the crimes of most female "offenders," the new regional institutions will instead reinforce the legitimacy of prisons, and with many more available "beds" will almost certainly result in an increase rather than a reduction in the numbers of women incarcerated (Moffat, 1991: 196–97).

Immediate improvements implemented by Correctional Service Canada following from the task force report included the following: elimination of transfers of women from the provinces to the Prison for Women; recruitment of an Aboriginal elder to meet on a daily basis with Native women and to facilitate sweetgrass and sweatlodge ceremonies; reduction of the policy of placing self-injurious women in solitary confinement; increased paid telephone calls to families from one to two a month; increased efforts to facilitate prisoners' attendance at family funerals; installation of lighting in the exercise yard so it could be used in the evening, and provide more opportunity for fresh air (Ibid.: 8–9). These would seem to be very elementary changes in correctional policy, rather than evidence of substantive and transformative change.

Just prior to the release of the task force report, the Solicitor General opened a new minimum security institution for federally sentenced women in Kingston, situated in a renovated house located across the street from the massive Prison for Women. Accommodating eleven women, the "Minimum House" offers a model for the kind of "homelike atmosphere" recommended by the task force, with the women working cooperatively in the house, working at jobs outside, and participating in programs in the community. As warden Mary Cassidy observed, "The women are more relaxed and there are fewer real or perceived medical problems. That adjustment of the women has been really rewarding . . . I really believe environment changes behaviour. This was a positive move and will have a positive effect on the women's development" (Golligher, 1990: 8). Despite the public relations tone of this pronouncement, perhaps some correctional officials are beginning to recognize in some small measure the futility of lock-up facilities for women who are in trouble with the law.

To the extent that the regional replacements for P4W are simply new prisons, rather than genuine alternatives, the problems that have characterized P4W will be compounded five-fold. Five prisons for women cannot be perceived as an advance over one centralized institution. To underscore Moffat's arguments, and as the history of prisons has demonstrated, if institutions are available judges send people to them, and with increased beds the likelihood is that more women will be imprisoned for lesser offences than is currently the case. And when those beds are filled, advocates of carceral "solutions" will propose the construction of yet more women's facilities. Nothing short of a radical readjustment in "correctional" thinking will break this cycle, and the underlying problems of female "offenders" will remain unaddressed except on the most superficial levels.

A BRAND NEW PRISON

Simultaneous with the research activity of the 1990s Task Force which concluded that P4W should be closed and replaced with small regional facilities, the province of British Columbia was preparing to close the Lakeside Correctional Facility for Women. This decrepit and antiquated institution, situated on the grounds of and adjacent to the Oakalla men's prison, was to be replaced with a new provincial female institution on a semi-rural Burnaby site. In an agreement between the federal and provincial authorities, it was decided that the new Burnaby Correctional Centre for Women (BCCW) would confine women from both jurisdictions and that it would serve as the first of the planned regional prisons for federally sentenced women.

This new institution is an innovative blend of 19th century prison architecture and 21st century advanced technology. Most of the women are

serving short-term sentences and would qualify for minimum security if that
were an institutional option. Technically, the institution is a medium security facility, but for all practical purposes, due to the architectural design and
high-level technological security systems, and because women from every
classification are locked up together, they must all abide by the maximum
custody rules intended for the control of the few women who are perceived
as security risks. The immense rotunda at the centre of the prison recalls and
structurally manifests the Panopticon design, conceived by the English utilitarian prison reformer Jeremy Bentham in 1787 as the ideal architectural
design for (male) penitentiaries or, for that matter, schools or factories. Bentham's historic model, based on the concept of a full view of everything in
the plane of vision, fascinated Michel Foucault (1979) as a metaphor for
modern, strategic social control of unruly bodies, with a guard tower situated
in the centre of tiered individual cells in a circular, rotunda arrangement. In
this "laboratory of power," as Foucault put it, the cells are lighted so as to
ensure that the guard can at any time look into the cell of any prisoner, and
the prisoner can see no one. Aware of the possibility of being observed at any
moment, prisoners internalize the surveillance and each becomes their own
best guard. The guard is likewise supervised and watched by an actual or symbolic superior authority in an anonymous "uninterrupted play of calculated
gazes" (Foucault, 1984: 193).

In the very moment that surveillance is internalized by the person being
watched, the system has accomplished its purpose; behaviours are accordingly
circumscribed and thereby normalized under the authority of dominant discourses and entrenched power relations. Within the frameworks of gender
construction and modern practices of femininity, this process signifies ways
by which females are taught to be acquiescent and obeisant. It is telling, in
this light, that male prisoners complain of being "treated like a woman" (Faith,
1993: 34), just as women in prison complain of being treated like children.
Through what Foucault calls "the infinitely minute web of panoptic techniques" (1984: 213), human beings throughout modern, western societies are
examined, classified, watched, disciplined and "normalized." With the com-
plement of advanced technologies, the new Burnaby women's prison is an
ideal set-up for this process.

In Bentham's model the guards look directly into each cell. The postmodern Burnaby "correctional centre" relies on 114 strategically placed
cameras which are monitored through a "Central Control" unit at the heart of

the rotunda; within this unit the pictures captured by the gaze of the cameras are viewed on banks of television monitors. The surveillance extends through narrow hallways in a spoke pattern leading to six Living Units, each of which has a "common feeding area" in the centre of sixteen or seventeen individual cells. Two smaller units are reserved as "dissociation" or Special Handling Units (super-maximum security) for women on "administrative," "protective" or "closed" custody. Old-fashioned keys are replaced with electronic devices: to enter into or to exit from any of the hallways, or any other part of the institution, one must be screened by video and audio communication with the officers in Central Control, who monitor and control all comings and goings.

Cameras are positioned on the outside of buildings and around the periphery of the prison compound as well as throughout the inside of the building. In addition, high stone walls enclose the tiny "court yards" in which women (and their visitors) can sit outside when the weather is mild. When women breach prison rules and are punished with segregation from the main prison population, or if in the opinion of the staff they are suicide risks or otherwise require "medical observation," they are placed in solitary confinement in top security "strip" cells in isolated locations, where total twenty-four-hour a day surveillance is achieved by both cameras and the direct and constant gaze of guards who sit behind protective glass.

All these elaborate security networks and devices are buttressed by chain link fences, and the total effect is that of an electronic fortress. The institution itself is situated in the countryside at the far edge of a stretch of flatland, four kilometres from the nearest bus stop, with the Fraser River running alongside the front of the buildings. It has been the tradition in North America to situate "reformatories" in what is euphemistically described as a "pastoral setting," which is in fact an isolation imposed by the accurate assumption that people do not wish to have prisons in their neighbourhoods. Given that surrounding communities have expanded through urban and suburban spread, many formerly rural prisons now have housing tracts, manufacturing or business districts in their neighbourhood, but new prisons are still constructed in the boondocks.

The impression imparted by the new Burnaby prison is that this highly secure institution has been constructed for the precise purpose of protecting "the public" from dangerous, unruly criminals, when in reality very few of the women who are sent here represent any threat at all to anyone. Most do not have violence on their records, and women who "act out" within the institu-

tion are put in lock-up and/or calmed with prescribed sedatives or tranquilizers. Thus, the effective function of this phenomenal security system is
fundamentally ideological without any perceptible practical justification. As
reported to me in 1992 by a chief administrator, it cost Can. $37 million (in
1990) to construct this institution to house up to 120 women, with a Can.
$5 million annual prison budget (provincially/federally shared). This averages
out to an expense of $65,000 per annum per prisoner. (In contrast, given the
much greater numbers of male prisoners, it costs $46.000 per annum per male
prisoner.) The mind boggles at the thought of what one woman could do to
improve her life circumstances with $65,000 a year.

Among the provincially employed staff and administrators of this physically intimidating institution are more well-informed and progressive
individuals than I've encountered in any other prison. This is particularly true
of people contracted for special programs and services, but it also applies to
administrators and regular custody staff. In part this move toward less discipline and more practical understanding reflects trends toward more open
penal philosophies on the part of provincial "correctional" directors. While
the prison staff are generally "professional" and conventional in the sense that
their first concern is custody and enforcement of the sometimes incompre-
hensibly petty rules, I have observed an uncommon degree of respect between
many of these individuals (both old-timers who transferred from the old
prison and new, younger staff) and the women under their charge. They
express empathy for the women's circumstances, they recognize that these
women are not for the most part "dangerous criminals," they go out of their
way to facilitate the women's needs both while they're locked up and in preparation for release, and in other ways demonstrate a commitment to the women
which goes well beyond the call of duty.

Increasingly, newly hired staff have attended college or university, which
does not in itself guarantee effectiveness but which does suggest that they have
chosen to do this work rather than having been tracked into it for lack of
options. A number of them identify themselves as feminists and are active in
local women's communities, and some of the most effective and respected staff
are non-closeted lesbians. The vast majority of the staff and administration are
female, but most of the males on staff, such as a particularly insightful and
good-humoured chef, and the coordinator of the expansive gardening project,
have similarly earned the women's respect by recognizing their needs and
worth as human beings.

The above notwithstanding, it's important to interject the caveat that, by my observation and in the opinions of incarcerated women I've interviewed, other staff members are demonstrably committed to the imbalanced power relations that *de facto* define their position within the institution. That is, they exercise their authority without any apparent regard for the women's feelings and they unflinchingly punish women who are "uncooperative." They are prejudicial and demeaning in their attitudes, and they abuse their power in ways that compound the women's grief. These are the classic prison guards whose authoritarian demeanour is consistent with the ideological framework of carceral institutions historically, and which is also consistent with the architecturally imposed security focus of the Burnaby Correctional Centre for Women.

Since the opening of the new prison in April 1991, up to eighty women have been incarcerated at any given time in BCCW, of whom approximately one-third are on remand, awaiting court appearances which may or may not result in incarcerative sentences. Public taxes are thus supporting a mammoth, high security institution for a substantial body of women who are not even yet officially "criminals." In the first year of operation, about 2,000 admissions were processed, including repeaters. Apart from the women on remand, most were serving provincial sentences averaging fourteen days at a stretch. Next door to BCCW is a smaller unfenced building, the independently administered Open Living Unit, which is reserved for twenty-eight women with minimum custody classification. These women are nearing the completion of their sentences, and a number of them are released daily to go to jobs in the "free" world.

According to a report by the B.C. Forensic Psychiatric Services Commission (Tien et al., 1993: 6–9), of the sentenced women at BCCW between May and October 1992, three-fourths were serving provincial sentences of less than two years and the balance were serving federal sentences exceeding two years (including several women serving life terms.) Approximately 40 percent of the women were of full or partial Native heritage, and most of the balance were Canadian "Caucasians." The women averaged thirty years in age. Almost three-fourths had not completed high school and two-thirds were on social assistance prior to their arrest.

According to Tien et al., at the time of arrest, 12 percent of the surveyed women were married, 31 percent were in common-law relationships, 13 percent were divorced and 43 percent had never married. Their own family histories were similarly marginal to the stable nuclear family ideal. As reported by Tien et al. (1993: 7), "Less than half of the inmates interviewed were raised primarily by their biological parents in a stable home." Thirty-one percent were raised by combinations of biological parents, foster parents, relatives or other arrangements, and 24 percent were raised entirely apart from their biological parents, including women who had been institutionalized as children.

This contemporary profile of incarcerated women is reminiscent of the findings of Sheldon and Eleanor Glueck who, in 1934, conducted this century's most detailed study of women in prison. Tracking the lives of 500 women incarcerated in Massachusetts, for crimes of "unlawful sexuality, immorality and stealing, and drunkenness," they characterized the women as "a sorry lot" who left home (or foster homes or institutions) at an early age, who were absorbed in "harmful pursuits," and who did not attend church. They note the women's "illicit sexual indulgence" and "illegitimate pregnancies" and sum them up as a "swarm of defective, diseased, antisocial misfits" who, in the Gluecks' estimation, should be sterilized or kept in prison "until they have passed the period of fertility," given their "lack of control of their sexual impulses" (Glueck and Glueck, 1934). The criminal justice preoccupation with female sexuality begins with youth, and Meda Chesney-Lind pioneered the recognition that whereas boys are incarcerated for actual "criminal offences," girls have most often been incarcerated for "ungovernability" and incarcerated at a significantly higher rate than boys "for their own protection" (Chesney-Lind, 1978; see also Gordon, 1992).

It is generally recognized that whereas sexual abuse does not commonly result in a "life of crime," women who are criminalized have an even higher ratio of abuse in their histories than the female population at large. Thus, Tien et al. found that 47 percent of the women interviewed at the Burnaby Correctional Centre for Women had been sexually abused as children, of whom half had been abused by family members, and the other half by combinations of family members and outsiders. Other forms of childhood physical abuses (such as beatings and burnings), as well as psychological abuses, were also commonplace in the women's histories. As adults they had fared no better, having been victims of rape, having guns pointed at them and various other traumatic events. In their intimate adult relationships, 76 percent reported histories of verbal abuse and 69 percent had been physically (including sexually) abused. Five percent of the women reported that they had themselves been physically abusive towards intimate partners, and 11 percent reported mutual abuse. Predictably, almost half of the interviewed women had attempted suicide, and almost a third had engaged in self-mutilation, a practice which is seriously exacerbated by imprisonment.

Despite the efforts of many caring staff members, most women leave prison with the same problems they had when they entered, and those problems are often deepened by the prison experience. The initial humiliation of being transported to the prison in handcuffs escorted by law enforcement officials, being subjected to yet another "mug shot" and more fingerprinting, being assigned a prison number which in effect delegates the new prisoner to "non-person" status, having all one's personal possessions taken away, the degradations of the body search, being forced to bathe or shower with chemical solutions to kill (usually non-existent) body lice or other vermin, and the series of probing interrogations by intake officers, medical personnel and the officer in the cellblock, are all designed, even if not consciously intended, to break a prisoner's spirit. As discussed by Erving Goffman (1970) in his theory of the "mortification of self" in total institutions, and Michel Foucault (1979), who describes institutionalization as a series of "normalization" processes, these degrading rituals have the effect of breaking down personal identity, confirming that the state has taken ownership of the body/self, which lays the prisoner bare for the processes of "rehabilitation."

> Sometimes late at night I cried. Nobody knew. But you're alone, you and yourself, and maybe you've had a bad day or the letter didn't come or you want your man there, somebody to talk to, to tell you you're all right, you know, that you're still a nice person despite all this. . . . (Kirby, 1983: 17)

Prisons are small totalitarian societies, with rules and regulations affecting every intimate detail of life. The prisoner is reduced to a number, one unit in the vast "correctional" enterprise. Personal testimonies from prisoners produce a jumbled accumulation of agonies:

- the stigma of incarceration;
- the claustrophobia of confinement;
- craving fresh air or the feeling of rain on the face;
- the deadly boredom;
- strict limitations on physical movement and the aggravation of needing an "inmate pass" to move from one part of the institution to another;

- anxiety about one's children (and frequently the devastation of losing them);
- loneliness for close family members, sweethearts and community support systems;
- nervousness from being under constant scrutiny and supervision;
- physical and emotional problems that accompany withdrawal from alcohol and street drugs;
- lack of anyone to serve advocacy for one's needs;
- lack of privacy and the tensions that erupt between people in "total institutions" who haven't chosen to be confined together;
- endless line-ups;
- inability to get straight answers to questions;
- paranoia about breaking what seem like arbitrary, tyrannical or, at best, coercive institutional rules;
- fears of being punitively segregated in isolation for behavioural infractions, or likewise segregated in a prison-within-the-prison for "medical observation" or "protective" or "administrative" custody;
- insensitivities and abuses of power both by staff and other prisoners;
- mail and phone censorship and the risk of losing these "privileges";
- lack of choice in such simple matters as when to eat, sleep or watch television;
- little or no choice of diet;
- weight gain;
- chain-smoking as a coping mechanism;
- having to be locked in one's cell periodically throughout the day and facing the slot in the door for routine "body counts," to ensure no one has escaped;
- the inability to escape from the cacophony of radios, television, people hollering at each other, the rattling of keys and clanging of electronic doors;
- never getting a good night's sleep because of the sounds of the prison, including the snoring, coughing, weeping and wailing of other prisoners, and because for security reasons it's never fully dark, and every night a guard flashes a light in your face. While you are sleeping;
- depressions and mood swings produced by prescribed behaviour-modifying drugs;
- cognitive dissonance from not knowing how or whether to show feelings (if you laugh too much you must be stoned on contraband drugs; if you're too quiet you must be depressed and in need of medicine);

- dependency and infantilization processes that accrue when one is denied the right to make any decision concerning one's own life;
- uncertainty of when you will be released and the realization of very limited choices in the "free" world when the time comes.

These and other conventional features of life in prison can wound the spirit or rupture the already wounded, sometimes irreparably. However, women may also become stronger through sheer anger and their will to survive with their self-respect intact:

> [O]ne thing prison's taught me is to be very strong, and that I am a worthwhile person. Nobody likes to have their freedom taken away from them, but all the abuse and everything they threw at me—it just made me stronger each time. (Padel and Stevenson, 1988: 193)

The clearest need of a majority of incarcerated women is for programs that can address the effects of prior victimization. Most prisons are severely or altogether lacking such services, but BCCW is making some effort. Although the medical doctor is available only ten hours a week, for up to 120 women, the nursing staff offer opportunities to confront eating disorders or other physical health problems endemic to women whose lives are out of control and who, prior to incarceration, have been masking the symptoms with alcohol and other drugs. However, upon entry to the institution, women who have a history of illegal drug use are immediately placed in solitary confinement for "observation," which for those who are physically addicted means "cold turkey" withdrawal without the benefit of transitional sedation.

Upon "settling in," a part-time psychiatrist and three part-time psychologists are available primarily for individual counselling; most women prefer one-on-one counselling to group processes because trust among the women is tenuous, and the prison gossip grapevine is a potent means of losing any semblance of privacy and dignity. Some women testify to the help they've received from these counselling services, but others are skeptical, such as the woman who said to me after she had met with a psychologist, "For all the help she gave me I'd have done better talking to the walls." A drug and alcohol counselor is contracted through the Elizabeth Fry Society, which in some parts of Canada has been in the forefront of progressive women's prison reform and direct support to prisoners. This woman offers both individual and group counselling, and has been a mainstay support for numerous women in recovery in part because she does not have unrealistic expectations, and does not make negative judgements when a woman suffers a relapse. To at least some women's benefit, the Society has also contracted a part-time counselor to work with women in one-on-one personal development and with small focus groups in the areas of life skills, parenting and anger management.

PROGRAMS AND SERVICES

The bulk of prison funding in any jurisdiction is allocated to security: stone walls, fences, steel bars, laser beams, electronic doors and gates, guard towers, surveillance cameras, weaponry, communications technology, and custodial staff whose primary function is to prevent escape. All prisons have certain features in common, and prisoners who are transferred from one institution to another find familiar policies and practices in all of them. However, prisons also vary and have distinguishing characteristics according to many factors, including the following:

- demographic composition of the prison population;
- levels of training or education of the staff;
- philosophies of the head administrators;
- policies enacted by jurisdictional authorities;
- geographic and cultural climates of the prison setting;
- degree to which outside groups participate as volunteers in the day-to-day life of the institution;
- extent to which prisoners are encouraged to interact with family members;
- levels of responsibility granted to prisoners in the running of the institution;
- level of turnover of both staff and prisoners;
- level of security to which prisoners are subjected;
- range of facilities to accommodate programs and services.

State-produced public relations brochures describing most "correctional facilities" focus on the last point, in keeping with the enduring ideal of rehabilitation, even though "correctionalists" themselves have discredited rehabilitation as a realistic goal of penal institutions.

In 1981, the Canadian Human Rights Commission declared the federal Prison for Women in Kingston to be in defiance of human rights standards, insofar as female prisoners suffered from discriminatory conditions vis-à-vis male prisoners. That is, whereas male institutions are both numerous and varied in their construction, locations, custody levels and range of programs and services, federally sentenced females were limited to one decrepit maximum security institution, far from many prisoners' families, with a wholly inadequate infrastructure. Following the ruling, P4W improved the education and recreation programs, expanded vocational choices from basic hairdressing to include woodworking, ceramics, upholstering and word-processing, and began transporting a few women in minimum custody to neighbouring male institutions for training in microfilm, carpentry or auto mechanics. (Conversely, a few male prisoners came to P4W for classes in word-processing.) A few women were given permission to leave the prison by day to attend classes at Queen's University. The administration also arranged for construction of a private cottage on the grounds, which facilitated some women's opportunities for weekend visits with family members, and gave others a place to retreat for solitude.

The Burnaby Correctional Centre for Women has been similarly planned with the apparent intention of giving women more options than has been the tradition in the province. However, this is an almost insurmountable challenge. The majority of the women are not in the institution long enough to complete vocational certificate or diploma requirements. Women serving longer sentences come in with very different needs, orientations and interests from one another, and at no given time could there be sufficient numbers of women enrolled in a variety of programs to justify the costs of a full range of vocational training choices.

It is common to compare the paucity of programs in women's institutions with the greater variety available to men, and in the US in the 1970s, with varying results, women protested this inequity with legal challenges (Pollock-Byrne, 1990: 169–71). In Canada, Gayle Horii successfully defended her right to be the only female incarcerated in a male institution on the partial grounds that the women's institution lacked the university program which was available to the men (Law Society of British Columbia, 1992: 8–46). However, relative to future opportunity this is an almost moot issue, given that very few men leave prisons prepared to successfully engage in the job market as a consequence of vocational training or education in prison. Even if they acquire skills on equipment that is not outmoded, or gain new knowledges, like women they still suffer the common employer distrust of "ex-convicts."

Generally, every woman who enters prison is assigned to a Case Manager who assists her in making decisions concerning her institutional program from arrival to release, and who arranges for her work or school assignment. At BCCW the choices include training with an instructor in the modern prison beauty shop, and a sewing program; both of these vocational programs have been prominent in virtually all modern women's prisons in North America. In a 1977 US survey of women's institutions, Ruth Glick and Virginia Neto found that cosmetology programs—teaching women how to make themselves and other women beautiful—were one of the three most frequently offered vocational choices for women in prison; the others were clerical work and food services (Glick and Neto, 1977: 73). Sewing industries have been the central activity in most factory-type women's prisons since the 19th century. The "tailor shop" at BCCW is better equipped and operated than most, but it nevertheless serves the sexist function of operating primarily as a garment factory in the production of uniforms for men's institutions. (During the years of my work at the California Institution for Women, women from the sewing and cosmetology programs got together to produce popular annual fashion shows. One after another, beautifully made-up prisoner-models paraded gracefully down a runway in the decorated gymnasium to display elaborate hairdos and gorgeous ballgowns, thereby breaking every stereotype of female convicts while at the same time reinforcing every stereotype of proper femininity.)

Work assignments at BCCW also include gardening, advanced training in flower arranging, ceramics, and canine training, with dogs donated by the local pound or brought in by staff or prisoners' families. To the observer, the canine program is weighted with poignant irony: when women are released from their cells, the dogs are released from their cages, and the women are then trained to train the dogs to trust them and follow obedience routines. Such options might sound dubious to anyone concerned with creating choices for meaningful post-prison employment, but the dedicated staff of these programs and the women engaged in them testify to their therapeutic value. (Indeed, there is something breathtaking about a woman gracefully circling a prison courtyard, with her head held high, accompanied by an elegant collie strutting pridefully alongside her.)

Academically, an educational program is provided under contract with Douglas College. The instructors are flexible, versatile and resourceful, and, according to women in the programs, they are among those most trusted by the prisoners of all persons who work at the prison. They have built up a good in-prison library and offer one-on-one tutorials and small-group instruction providing academic upgrading through high school and, among other options, computer skill-training. They face enormous challenges both because of institutional limitations and because of the wide range of abilities and interests of women who enter the prison, including a significant portion who are functionally illiterate. At the other end of the spectrum are the women who are qualified for and who seek higher education, but whose only option is to enrol in a university-level distance education program at their own expense.

Unfortunately, most women at the Burnaby prison do not get involved in full-time education, in part because they can't afford it. Schooling is given status as a paid "work" assignment, but at about Can. $6.00 a day it is the lowest paid of the institutional options. The highest paid work is kitchen duty, which in 1992 paid up to Can. $14.00 per day, and these assignments are therefore the most desired. Although most of the women's basic material needs are supplied by the institution, women must pay for any "frills," which includes phone calls, cigarettes, stationery and greeting cards, postage, snack foods, shampoo and toiletries and any other canteen items, which are sold at a generally higher cost than in the "free" world.

Most women spend time cleaning, doing institutional laundry, or otherwise assisting with the maintenance of the institution. Men in institutions must also do this sort of "women's work" to earn their keep, but without the gender-based ideological pretense that it is a program of rehabilitative value. This premise is an historical constant that has been applied to even the youngest of "female offenders." For example, in 1928 the Matron of the British Columbia Industrial Home for Girls stated that "[s]ince marriage is the greatest trade open to women, household training is her greatest necessity. The successful married life of many of our girls is due largely to this training in domestic efficiency" (quoted in Gordon, 1992: 45–46).

As applied to contemporary adult women,

> The emphasis upon the inculcation of domestic skills and the relative lack of realistic education and training in skills relevant to the job market serves to reinforce the women's own feelings of entrapment as well as their practical dependency upon the welfare state and the men who pass through their lives. (Genders and Player, 1987: 171)

With or without explicit articulation, most contemporary women's prison programs are based on the vestigial bourgeois assumption that women don't need to earn a living. In California, per capita funding to the institution increases according to whether a program or work assignment qualifies as "training." Thus, a woman who pulled weeds day after day, and behaved herself, could be rewarded with a useless certificate in "Landscape Gardening." Or she could spend years mopping floors and scrubbing toilets and in return could receive a certificate in "Vocational Housekeeping." The best she could hope for, upon release, would be a job as a motel maid. The heavy emphasis on sanitation in women's institutions is also symbolic of the historic presumption that all women, but especially "criminal women," are dirty, and need to be purified in body and soul while, at the same time, cleaning up everyone else's dirt.

One of the most "progressive" of modern prison reforms in certain institutions is the implementation of work release programs for prisoners with a minimum custody classification. As noted by Helen Gibson, this idea was initiated historically by female reformers for women: "The Massachusetts Reformatory Prison for Women at Framingham pioneered a work release program as early as 1880" (Gibson, 1976: 97). However, women were soon abandoned; most such programs in North America have been reserved for men. The "open living" units at both P4W and the Burnaby Correctional Centre for Women allow women who undergo careful screening to go to work at a regular job by day, and return to the institution in the evening. Programs elsewhere have been dropped because of escape risks and what are euphemistically described as "administrative problems," meaning that it is not convenient to arrange job placements, facilitate transportation, and keep track of the women who are leaving the institution for work.

Many women who enter BCCW do not engage in any of the optional programs because they are primarily transient provincial prisoners serving short sentences (often only a month's duration, or less), and they have no interest in getting settled into the institution. Even women serving long sentences may remain detached, because they are depressed, suffering from drugged lethargy, or otherwise alienated from the institution in which they find themselves. Such women tend to stay alone in their cells as much as possible, or form one or a few close friendships which become their refuge in what they perceive to be a generally hostile environment. As a way to release tension and also stay fit, some women take advantage of BCCW's well-equipped gymnasium with a weight room or they jog in the early mornings around the finely landscaped outdoor track. Other women seek solace in religion, and a small, beautifully designed chapel is available for solitary meditation as well as organized worship services.

Generally, the most engaging programs in prisons are self-help groups initiated and coordinated by prisoners themselves. At both P4W and BCCW, Native Sisterhood groups, as discussed in Chapter Four, have developed as exemplary models of resistance against institutionalization. Every prison has a core of activists at any given time who assume leadership and become organizational and informational resources for other women with shared interests.

Examples abound, internationally, of women who come into institutions with a high level of critical consciousness, and who have organizing skills. Other times women are politicized by their prison experience and come to recognize the need of women to be self-determining, both in their present circumstance and in preparation for their futures. Judy Clark and Kathy Boudin, political prisoners in the State of New York, document the activities of an AIDS awareness and support group at the maximum security Bedford Hills Correctional Facility. The majority of the prisoners are of African and Latin American heritage, and these groups are also severely overrepresented in AIDS-related illnesses. In the United States generally, heterosexual women are "the fastest-growing population becoming infected with HIV" (Clark and Boudin, 1990: 91; see also Waring and Smith, 1991). One of their key challenges has been to educate the staff as well as prisoners, and to reduce the stigma and prejudice against infected women, who had been ostracized and isolated in a "dark, dirty, roach-infested" unit (Clark and Boudin, 1990: 92). Despite the obstacles posed by an administration reluctant to allow prisoners autonomy in conducting their own affairs, through workshops and other prisoner initiatives the AIDS focus has had the effect of building an understanding of the value of community and collective consciousness as resistance against the oppressiveness of the prison environment.

> Over and over one could see the fear and stigma being overcome by information seeking, caring and nurturing. . . . The same hard, boisterous, selfish "taker" in one situation, when faced with an ill, needy, frightened woman becomes a nurse, a sister, a friend willing to bathe, rub, soothe, sing, and hug. . . . [W]omen from diverse cultures, nationalities, and racial and economic backgrounds find a common bond, as prisoners and as women. (Ibid.: 96, 100, 103)

One reason for an increasingly multicultural composition of prison populations is the result of the US-led international "war on drugs." Women who have been convicted for their work as "mules" in international drug trafficking activity are being held in institutions in countries whose languages and customs are altogether unfamiliar to them. In England, women from Africa, Latin America, Asia and Europe have been held in Cookham Wood, in Kent; when they complete their sentences they are deported to their home countries (Padel and Stevenson, 1988: 194).

Kathleen Kendall (1993: 62) reports that as of November 1992, when approximately 100 women were incarcerated at the Kingston Prison for Women, almost 20 percent were from other nations: half were citizens of the United States, and the balance were from Latin America, the Caribbean/West Indies, West Africa, Poland, France and England. Similarly, several women from outside North America have been incarcerated in the Burnaby prison since its opening in 1991.

This internationalization of both female and male incarceration is a global phenomenon which poses new dilemmas for "correctional" systems. One might say that it is to a convicted woman's distinct advantage to be incarcerated in any "liberal democratic" nation, than to be punished in a country which offers no human rights protections. Clearly, for example, a woman engaged in trafficking would be better off to be convicted and locked up in Canada than to face execution in Thailand or Saudi Arabia. Nevertheless, given the almost complete lack of language translators and other special services for imprisoned women from foreign cultures, the isolation and alienation such women face while doing their time is profound, and for those who face deportation the punishment may have only begun.

WOMEN GUARDING WOMEN

At the new Burnaby Correctional Centre for Women, as of 1992, 103 custodial staff were employed by the province to "serve" both federal and provincial prisoners, then numbering about 70 women. These staff included two Native women and just five men. (By contrast, at various times almost half the staff at the California women's prison have been male.) In addition, a fluctuating contract staff, hired as independent contractors or agency representatives, provide women with special services in such areas as health, education, counselling and vocational training. As in most prisons there are also community volunteers to sponsor projects and special events inside, to assist women with their parole plans, and to lend personal support.

Historically, prison employees have been almost invariably working class and often relatively unskilled. If they were not working in prisons they might well be encountering the troubles that can lead to incarceration. As advanced by the woman who, having worked her way up through the ranks is now the regional director of corrections (Vancouver Metropolitan Region), and as evidenced by the composition of new staff at BCCW, a concerted effort has been made to recruit young women, often college-educated, who aren't likely to make a "career" of corrections. In the prison they can gain life experience before proceeding to law, graduate studies, criminal justice or social assistance administration, or some other work that requires knowledge of social problems. It will be interesting to see how this hiring philosophy pans out in Canada, given that prisons are a growth industry which may be headed toward privatization, as is already happening in England and the US

For those who are critical of prison systems it is easy to lapse into prejudice toward people who work in them, and to unfairly stereotype them on the presumption that no healthy person with choices would want to make their living locking up other people for the state, with all the dirty work this entails. In the United States, during the 1950s, male military veterans were given preference in law enforcement and criminal justice hiring, given the paramilitary nature of these agencies. To the present, prison guards in both male and female institutions in the United States are ranked as sergeants, lieutenants and captains, and many exercise their authority as controlling and intimidating militarists.

Older women who have made a career of corrections often try to be "motherly" toward the "girls," but they find that many of these "girls" don't want or need to be mothered. A feminist dictionary defines a female prison guard in a women's prison as a "model of permissible female behaviour who acts on behalf of Male Supremacy to keep women in their place" (Kramarae and Treichler, 1985: 358). More accurately, these jobs are a means by which working-class men and women serve the patriarchal state by keeping unemployed outcasts in their place. Even in the relatively benign day-to-day routines of maintaining order, prison guards have traditionally exercised virtually unchecked power against the "social lepers" in their charge. The exercise can make them cynical and abusive, and it can make them sick: administrators complain about the high rate of sick leave taken by their employees, and high staff turnover; prisoners complain about guards coming to work with alcohol on their breath. A young woman who was formerly a guard in a midwestern

US women's prison explains why her troubled conscience had led her to alcoholism after a few years in the business:

> We controlled every moment of the lives of the women we guarded. We told them
> when and where they could go, when they could eat, shower, sleep, when and with
> whom they could talk. We strip-searched them after an afternoon visit with their
> children. We made them work to acquire skills, but told them they were capable
> only of sewing, mopping floors, or preparing food. We confiscated their personal
> belongings. We read their mail. We threw them in the "quiet room" for punish-
> ment. We were the ones who took away their dignity. . . . [W]e were disempowering
> them and setting them up for failure once back on the street. (Bordt, 1992: 31)

A variation on this point of view is reiterated by women employed as guards
at England's Holloway Women's Prison, which has 300 officers guarding 500
prisoners, as young as age seventeen, of whom half are on remand. In a documentary film, staff speak of the reasons for a high turnover despite relatively
high pay and subsidized housing on the prison grounds. As one woman states,
"You cut a woman down [from an attempted suicide-by-hanging] or you've
seen a woman who has cut her wrists . . . and that's when you get your alcoholics in the job . . . or you get staff who commit suicide because they just
haven't got anybody to turn to" (First Tuesday Unit, 1992). Another comments:

> I don't think prison solves anybody's problems. [The problems] are still out there
> when they go back out, and they're going to end up committing a crime again to
> solve exactly the same problems they've already spent time in prisons for. (Ibid.)

Women who make a career of "corrections" will spend much more of their
life in prison than most of the women they guard. They become fixed in their
role as the authority who can't be challenged, as do those teachers, office man-
agers, bureaucrats, factory supervisors and other frontline workers who
internalize policies made by people higher up. Those who cling to their ideals
may attempt to implement "reforms" in the system, without seeming to grasp
the structural niche played by penal institutions in the larger society. They
may "bend the rules" to show their care or concern for particular prisoners.
They may become close to certain women, including recidivists who come in
and out over the years, or long-termers for whom the prison is home, and
when women who become their friends are released they may go out of their

way to help them get resettled. Some women are repaid with gratitude from the women they assist, but it is still a top-down relationship dependent on altruism and appreciation.

In terms of institutional structure, some prisons are built on a "normalizing" philosophy which tries to diminish the distance between inside and outside: they look more like a "campus" than a prison, the guards wear street clothes and eat with the prisoners, and in other matters of physical design, penal philosophy and management policy they strive to replicate normal life and relationships. But at no time can guards enjoy a relationship of equality with women in their custody, as poignantly understated by a woman who had a crush on her guard (who was also a part-time student):

> She is an English major, so I wish she could write this for me. She was only six units from graduating, she said, but went off hitchhiking instead. She came down to where I was [in the cell block] and I believed that we were almost the same in many ways—except that she locked me in my room at night, and later asked me to turn my radio down. (Frances, in Miller, 1974: 16)

The early notion that women rather than men should guard other women, because women understand one another, and because "matrons" are in a better position to teach wifely and maternal values to young, wayward women, is problematic for reasons beyond the tyranny of imposed gender roles. On the fundamental level of security and custody, one can't generalize that prisoners are better off with either female or male guards. Any guard-prisoner dyad is fraught with the complications inherent in imbalanced power relations, and women are perceived to be as competent as their male colleagues in maintaining discipline in male institutions. This may relate in part to the fact that a female officer in a male institution will be backed up by her male counterparts, but the bottom line is the status differential between prisoner and guard: it is the authority of the position which exacts cooperation, rather than the gender of the officer.

One reason for arguing for female staff in female institutions is the privacy issue. It's discomfiting to have people of the opposite sex who are in a position of authority intrude on what little personal space one can create within a prison, and this is problematic for both men and women. In terms of women's specific needs, given power relations in the world at large, but especially within prisons, a predominance of female guards in female institutions provides a check against potential sexual abuse of incarcerated women. The common history of sexual abuse in the lives of incarcerated women can evoke particular vulnerability and sense of threat in the presence of male officers. Women who have been abused don't commonly feel safe with men who have institutionalized power over them (Solicitor General, 1992: 34). The argument that women who have been abused can benefit from interaction with men who are respectful toward them may hold some weight, but in the institutional setting women are "much more likely to benefit from exposure to women who have been where she has been and who have subsequently learned to forgive, honour and love themselves" (Mills, 1992: 4).

Joanne Belknap (1991), in a US study of female "correctional officers" who work with both male and female "inmates" in jail, found that 34 percent preferred working with males but only 14 percent preferred working with females (the balance had no preference). She cites another study (Pollock, 1986) which indicates that 72 percent of female officers preferred male "inmates" while only 11 percent preferred working with females (and the balance had no preference). In both studies, the female officers reported that "male inmates treated them with more respect than did women inmates" (Belknap, 1991: 101–2). One of the reasons offered by both male and female staff for stating a preference for working with men is that female prisoners are perceived by them as "more manipulative." However, as Belknap notes, women have specific needs which men don't have, and "what appear to be differences between male and female inmates' behaviour may in fact be sexist perceptions on the part of [the guards]" (Ibid.: 103). For example, female prisoners often have gynaecological complaints, and, on the most mundane level, in many jails (and in prison segregation units) they are put in the position of having to ask for a tampon every time they need a clean one. Female prisoners are also more likely than males to badger staff to let them use a telephone to contact their children or other family members.

In the 19th century, it was accepted as a truism that female prisoners were "temperamentally unstable, less likely to submit to prison discipline, and more prone [than men] to riotous behaviour which only confirmed suspicions of their moral degeneration" (Zedner, 1991: 184). Staff in contemporary prisons who have worked with both male and female prisoners also often say that females are more resistant than males to incarceration, and are harder to handle because they're "more emotional"—which is to say they are more expressive of their feelings. However, as discussed in Chapter Five, it is men who cause by far the most destructive disruptions, including riots and acts of violence against both one another and the staff.

In my observation, there is a particular pattern that occurs among new prison staff who bring with them a social-worker orientation, especially those assigned to youth or female institutions. They enter with a high degree of idealism and they want to "help" the prisoners, especially those for whom they feel great sympathy. They bend the rules, such as allowing unauthorized telephone calls or allowing extra portions of food. However, when a prisoner fails to show gratitude or betrays their trust they are disillusioned. If their leniency results in an infraction which has professional consequences for the guard, they curse their naïveté and decide that all the prisoners are "con artists" who have "chosen a criminal way of life" and who will exploit them if they don't hold their ground. In time, these staff become distrustful and authoritarian. In contrast are those guards and vocational staff who have a realistic understanding of the problems that for most prisoners precede incarceration, and who respond to the women neither with "saviour behaviour" nor punitive judgement, but rather with practical assistance and informational support. Such individuals are not so likely to be disillusioned by the women, but they do often become disillusioned with "the system."

One commonly observed limitation of prison staffing is the cultural disparity between the guards and the prisoners. Whereas a disproportionate number of prisoners in Canada, the US, Australia, and England are women of colour, most guards are white. The global racism that infects societies as a whole is not only reflected within the microcosm of prison societies but is given greater opportunity for expression through discriminatory handling of prisoners. Depending on regional context, African-American, and First Nations women and Latinas, complain that "whities" get all the privileges; white women complain that the white staff, out of fear of being labeled racist, give extra privileges to women of colour. Staff from political minority groups may be harsher toward women of their own culture, so as not to be accused of favouritism toward their own people, and often because they are angry at them for bringing dishonour to their communities. Others may relish the opportunity to exercise control over women from the oppressive dominant culture. Even staff who conscientiously avoid racist actions may be too ignorant of cultures other than their own to show sensitivity toward or respect for difference. Even if they think they are disciplining everyone by the same, fair standard, they will be perceived differently. Only rarely is cross-cultural training a feature of preparation for "corrections" work.

Ultimately, the success of an institutional staff in maintaining order and discipline depends in large part on the stability, philosophy and management practices of the administration. If the administration is overly authoritarian, morale breaks down, and unless unions are very strong there is little recourse for abuses against staff, who find it difficult to lodge complaints on their own behalf (or on behalf of prisoners who are being mistreated). Grievances are buried, job stewards are shut out of administrative decision-making, and staff are intimidated with the threat of job loss to prevent them from testifying: "you open your mouth and you see what happens to you. If you don't like it, hit the road" (ASCC, 1977: 63–64, 70–71). Prison staff, just like prisoners, can be subjected to institutional rituals, like skin searches, which reinforce their subordination, as discussed in an internal document (Ibid.) concerning a period of havoc at the California Institution for Women (see Chapter Seven).

A newly appointed warden (a.k.a. "superintendent") of the California women's state prison, where four wardens before her had quit or been fired in the span of just sixteen months, observed that "the staff was shattered, apathetic, and in many instances had lost all sense of professionalism. They were uncertain of their roles, areas of responsibility and authority, and because of so many conflicting instructions were uncertain of when and how to conduct the business of running an institution" (Ibid.: 3). It is an ongoing problem that the need to be "in control" is both the essential mandate and the nemesis of the prison business. Enlightened administrators and high level officials may issue progressive policy changes but they're not on the front line from day to day to ensure their implementation. Enlightened staff usually lack the authority or influence to "buck the system."

From the point of view of prisoners, the question of how best to staff a prison is often a moot issue because their support comes primarily from one another. As Ruth Glick and Virginia Neto found, in a national survey of ninety-eight prisons, jails and community-based programs in fourteen states, only 2.8 percent of the prisoners put a high value on staff as significant to their incarceration experience. By contrast, 66.6 percent ranked educational opportunities (or lack thereof) as the most important factor in terms of the effect of imprisonment on their post-prison life (Glick and Neto, 1977: 176–77).

GETTING OUT

time passes slowly
when surprises are removed,
when everything expected
falls in smoothly,
when every hour is planned
and all the places are manned
by people that are chosen
and placed far in advance,
oh my, but how the time goes by so slowly.
(Diane, in Faith, 1972: 6)

For most women, the most miserable feature of the prison experience is the plodding, structured repetition and routinization of day-to-day life where, in an ordered, herdlike atmosphere, the freedom to think for oneself is put on hold. The clock and the calendar mark the deadly monotony while at the same time promising release. Eventually, for most, the time will run out.

The first challenge a woman faces in preparing for parole is getting her paperwork in order and getting the information she needs to proceed. Many delays occur because of the bureaucratic maze a woman must maneuver before her case can be heard (Shaw, Rodgers and Hattem, 1990: 7). Even relatively small institutions with a conscientious Case Management policy, as exists at the Burnaby Correctional Centre for Women, cannot in every case provide the detailed attention without which women must rely on their own resources. Then follows the tremendous anxiety that precedes the appearance at the parole hearing, especially for women who have received "write-ups" for prison infractions, who have been serving time for serious crimes, or who have been unable to make solid plans for their immediate future.

Most jurisdictions in the United States and Canada no longer have "indeterminate sentencing" which, on the decision of the parole board, can prolong imprisonment indefinitely for relatively minor offences. (In California this could include a woman's having a "bad attitude" or having not accepted or declared Jesus Christ as her personal Saviour.) However, there are still many grounds on which boards can deny release at the expected or hoped-for time. The applicant sits facing a panel of representatives of the parole board (a.k.a. the Community Release Board or Board of Prison Terms), generally com-

prising three or more people, who grill "the defendant." In some cases she may
have an advocate with her, or even an attorney, but it is her own "performance"
and record, and the particular biases of the board members, that will determine the outcome. Because she is often compelled to rehash the details of the
crime(s), the interrogation can be akin to a re-trial and once again the verdict
might be "guilty!" In California, board members have typically been retired
law enforcement officers and, more recently, unemployed politicians who have
a vested interest in not showing leniency toward prisoners. If the woman is a
member of a minority group, as she often is, she can be intimidated by real or
perceived racist as well as class biases against her.

   I think of the experience of an African-American woman who, when I met
her, was forty-one years old and had spent most of her adult life in and out of
prison for heroin possession and chronic theft in support of her habit. Josie,
as I'll call her, had finally overcome her addiction and had "cleaned up her
act." In anticipation of parole, and with the support of many recommendation letters, she had been interviewed and had obtained the promise of a job
as a counselor in a rehab centre. Her mother and her five children were
looking forward to her release, and had an apartment waiting for her. She had
an excellent behaviour record within the prison, where she had engaged in virtually every program available to her, and she had gained the trust and respect
of both prisoners and staff. She was, everyone thought, a perfect example of a
"rehabilitated" woman and a likely candidate for a "gold seal," which would
have given her a complete discharge instead of supervised parole.

   On the day of her hearing Josie dressed up in a new, tailored dress and carried a new purse over her arm. She went into the board room walking tall
with self-confidence, and came out a short time later to report that the
"panel" (two men and a woman, all white) had asked just a few questions and
seemed satisfied that she had reformed her ways. Told to wait outside in the
hallway while they deliberated, less than fifteen minutes had passed when
they called her name and she went back in for the verdict. Just a few seconds
had passed when suddenly her voice tore through the building—piercing,
terrible screams trailing into a long crying wail. She burst from the room, all
the while moaning "No-no-no-no-no . . . ," choking on her grief, tears
streaming down her cheeks, and then she collapsed and her new purse fell
open onto the floor. It was empty, a futile effort at dignity. The board had
"shot her down" and given her "her top," which meant she still had twenty-
seven more months to serve. Their justification was based on the prison

psychiatrist's evaluation, which I thought when I read it bore no resemblance to the woman I knew:

> She resents all authority. Until she realizes that she cannot blame her problems on being black or on authorities she will fail in her life experiments. She is acting out aggressions toward her father and she needs extensive therapy to develop self-esteem. (Faith, 1973)

Josie did get out after twenty-seven more months. The job and her family were still waiting for her and she managed to stay out for eight years before getting a new charge. She ended up growing old in prison.

Some women become so institutionalized that they cannot function effectively on the outside. Although there are never any guarantees, the most important factors in achieving a successful parole are employment and family support: most women, upon release, do not have these advantages. Another older woman of my acquaintance, who had spent over ten years in prison for chronic theft, was still unable to find employment after six months on parole. Feeling defeated and lonely, she deliberately stole goods from a department store, in full view, purposefully breaking the law (and thereby violating parole) with the hope of being returned to prison where she could count on "three hots and a cot." In this she succeeded.

Few women are so consciously deliberate in their resolve to return to prison when the going gets rough, but the odds of surviving inevitable obstacles in the outside world are slender. In 1989, just 36 percent of Canadian federal female prisoners were serving time for a first conviction (Shaw et al., 1992: 7). Following the first term of incarceration, an ex-prisoner has a high probability of returning either from a new offence or from breaching the terms of parole—which can include such infractions as going to a bar, failing to show up (or being late) for an appointment with the parole officer, or even associating with other ex-prisoners. This latter point is especially problematic. Former-prisoners often don't have many friends or acquaintances who have not themselves served time, and often the best support comes from people who understand one's predicament. The "no contact" rule is premised on the assumption that if two or more "criminals" are allowed to associate with one another they are bound to get into trouble. And, often, they do, not because of their association with one another but because of their mutually limited options. Prisons are said to have "revolving doors" because once someone has been in prison the chances of returning are so great.

It's a bitter commentary on society at large when a woman released from prison is so unwelcome in the community that she would regard prison as a refuge. More remarkable is the following case, from a brief and (to me) amazing news story:

> Dewi Sukarno, former first lady of Indonesia, says she had a great stay in Aspen [Colorado], even though most of it was spent in jail. Sukarno, sentenced to 60 days for slashing the face of a fellow jet-setter at a party last year . . . described her time behind bars as "a precious experience. I will treasure it the rest of my life. I liked it immediately from the first day. . . . I'm going to miss my life in jail. It was great."
> (*Vancouver Sun*, 1993: C1)

One can only guess at the reasons for Sukarno's ecstasy, and perhaps the moral of her story is that women who break the law should do it in Colorado. More typical are the feelings expressed by a woman who, on the eve of her parole, likened her anticipation to the process of birthing herself:

> *the contractions are coming harder now*
> *all my efforts are more concentrated*
> *i feel the wall thinning*
> *more endeavour goes into my efforts*
> *the pushing the straining the pain*
> *bearing down from everywhere*
> *will end*
> *blessed relief the emergence of me*
> *when i finally walk out those gates*
> (Stafford, 1975: 43)

For almost any woman, the relief of *getting* out of prison is quickly replaced by the anxiety of *being* out. Parole officers are often well-respected (Shaw, Rodgers and Hattem, 1990: 14), but with heavy caseloads there are limits to how helpful they can be. Also, it's up to the P.O. to turn a woman in if she breaches the conditions of her parole. The dual responsibility of friend and guide on the one hand, and pseudo-cop on the other, often makes for an untenable relationship. Halfway houses can be useful but there are too few of them. In Canada, women from remote regions where halfway houses are non-existent may have the choice of entering a house in an urban area. Such arrangements may facilitate early conditional release from prison, but they prolong the woman's separation from family and community.

As Margaret Shaw, Karen Rodgers and Tina Hattem (1990) learned from interviews with women paroled to Canadian halfway houses, depending on the house the experience can be as distressing for some women as that of prison itself. Poor management (too structured, or no structure); a whole new set of rules; being treated like a child in such matters as money management; unhygienic conditions; distrust of other residents; unrealistic expectations by staff for a woman's quick adjustment; the diverse needs of residents due to age differences, varying cultural backgrounds, "criminal" histories and so on; the mixing of men with women and attendant lack of privacy; religious indoctrination; the imposition of middle-class values and manners; lack of counselling for personal problems, including those related to an impulse to return to alcohol or other drug use; and, lack of transitional support services (especially related to help with finding employment and housing, or assistance in regaining access to children) were among the frustrations expressed by these women. A woman in British Columbia described to me the pain of trying to explain to her young child, who lived in the neighbourhood of the halfway house to which she was assigned, why she still couldn't live at home, and had to leave him with a caretaker at a strict hour every evening to go sleep in a house with a bunch of strangers. Others have spoken of being treated with distrust by neighbours and by potential employers when it is learned that they are residing in a house for people on parole from prison.

Some correctional systems attempt to alleviate the shock of re-entry by allowing Escorted Temporary Absences for special events, Unescorted Temporary Absences for those nearing parole, and Day Parole for prisoners to go to jobs by day and return to the prison at night, or to stay in a halfway house if space is available. Although many women do not benefit from these programs, and must face release "cold turkey," the very existence of the programs testifies to the awareness of correctional policymakers of the difficulties faced by every long-term prisoner during her (or his) transition back to normal society in the "free" world.

In the words of a woman who did time in both a brutally hardline prison and a modern "correctional" facility in the United States, "When you're in prison you might as well as be dead." She was referring specifically to the ways by which women locked up feel rejected and forgotten by their communities, but her words also describe the subjective constraints of incarceration itself.

Christina Jose-Kampfner, among others, uses this analogy of death to analyze the experience of women serving life sentences, and she builds a model based on the work of Elizabeth Kubler-Ross with terminally ill medical patients in describing how women "grieve for the loss of themselves and their outside world" (Jose-Kampfner, 1990: 112; see also Axon, 1989: 82–85). As with the stages of grief experienced by persons who learn they are dying, the woman sentenced to life in prison first undergoes shock which then translates into denial, the first stage of grieving ("You cannot allow yourself to believe it") (Jose-Kampfner, 1990: 113). When denial becomes a futile exercise, anger takes over and is expressed as assertive rebellion against the institution, the staff and other prisoners, and as bitterness toward God, family, and the outside world.

The effect of assertive anger is to underscore the woman's actual power-lessness. This translates into the third stage, depression, and it is at this stage that women may attempt suicide, for which the usual punishment is solitary confinement, which only increases the sense of isolation and depression. Women who survive this stage enter into mourning for the loss of themselves and the life they'll never live. At this stage they also mourn for the victims of their crimes and the effects of their actions on their children and families: "I feel sorry for my husband's family. I did not mean to kill him. I just didn't know how to seek help" (Ibid.: 120).

Eventually most women enter the stage of acceptance, a numbing empti-ness in the void of existential death, where "Nothing seems to matter anymore." For some, acceptance "coexists with hope," which means seeking court appeals and striving "to find a way out of the prison." For others, accept-ance results in an understanding that "existence in the outside world is no longer possible" (Ibid.: 121–22), and these are the women who resign them-selves to the prison as their home, and who come to accept other prisoners as the community to which they belong and in which they must redefine their identity. When a woman does succeed in settling into prison, she is then jolted by the challenges and obstacles she faces when it's time to leave.

Having adapted to prison, most people who are incarcerated, including those serving "life" sentences, will be one day released, hundreds of thousands of them every year in North America alone. The United States, in particular, with the highest per capita rate of incarceration in the world, produces an inordinate number of parolees every year. In 1989, 3.5 million persons in that country, 2 percent of the adult population, were in jail, in prison, on proba-tion or on parole (Rogers, 1992: 132). Between 1980 and 1990, the number of women in US jails and prisons nearly tripled, to approximately 75,000, though the seriousness of their offences has not changed; they still commit non-violent property crimes and "deportment" offences, such as drug possession (Immarigeon and Chesney-Lind, 1993: 242–44).

The American Correctional Association found in 1990 that over half of all women exiting from US prisons are from political minority groups, primarily African-American (36 percent). Sixty-two percent of women starting parole in the US have dependent children and 59 percent have not completed high school. Fifty percent of them have at least one other family member in prison, most commonly a sibling, and almost a third of them have attempted suicide more than once. A majority of criminalized women have a history of physical/sexual abuse, no material resources, lack of marketable (legal) job skills, history of substance abuse, and problems in keeping their families intact. An increasing number, especially in the northeastern US, are infected with HIV or have already contracted AIDS-related illness (ACA, 1990: 6–7, 33, 47). None of these problems will have been diminished during the time of incarceration, and most will have been exacerbated.

Because parole is a state of suspended freedom during which the parolee continues to be scrutinized, and is an easy mark for over-zealous parole officers or police, who are often already acquainted with the (ex-)offender, some women choose to bypass the process altogether and wait until qualifying for a full release (Shaw, Rodgers and Hattem, 1990: 8). But this does not solve the problems. As described by a woman who was "cut loose" in California after three years of incarceration with good behaviour:

Psychologically you feel like you have a sign on your forehead saying "Ex-Con." When you walk up the aisle of the supermarket you feel like everyone knows where you've been. Your new neighbours ask you where you come from and when you tell them they withdraw from you. They want to protect themselves from you because they're afraid of anyone who has been in prison. I can understand why they would be. People are afraid of anyone who is different from them. A prison record is just one more way to make someone different—to make you seem like a scary person.

You want to make a good impression on a prospective employer but if you admit that you have been in prison you probably won't be hired, and it's against the law to not admit it. Your children look at you as a stranger. When my son's grandma left him with me he started crying because he didn't know me and he felt he was being

deserted by the only mother he knew. My little girl was older. She remembered me
a little, but she has never been able to live with me because she and my sister had
grown so attached to each other that it would be unfair of me to snatch her up.
(Diane, in Faith, 1972: 5–6)

Although more members of political minority groups are being appointed
to parole boards in the US and Canada, the boards are still dominated by
"respectable" members of society, which is to say middle-class people who are
generally from the dominant culture.

The parole ritual is seldom an easy one for any woman (or man), and even
if she is granted release she will live on the outside under continued surveillance, social restrictions and reporting systems which remind her that the state
is still her guardian. Seldom can an ex-prisoner relax in her regained partial
freedom. As Mary Eaton comments, in the British context:

She is a prisoner and she brings this knowledge, this identity, out into the world.
The prison experience will affect her response to the outside world, the prison
record will affect the response of others to her. When she comes out she brings
something of the prison with her. As [one woman] put it [in a paraphrase of a statement by Paul Hill, falsely convicted as an IRA bomber]: "You can never leave prison,
because prison never leaves you." (Eaton, 1993: 56)

A Canadian woman similarly expressed the effects of incarceration upon
her release from Canada's Prison for Women:

> They open wide the door
> "You've done your time, you're free"
> But I still feel locked and chained
> deep down inside of me.
> (Anon., 1982: 27)

RESTORATIVE JUSTICE

Headlines of sensational cases to the contrary, even most women who have
killed do not represent a danger to society (see Walford, 1987), and there is
no concrete benefit at all to be derived from incarcerating people unless there

is empirical reason to judge them as dangerous. Generally, the benefits of prisons to society are entirely symbolic, and an exercise in scapegoating. As Dobash et al. conclude, "Historical and contemporary evidence suggests . . . that imprisonment *per se* is both an irrelevant and a damaging response to women's crime" (Dobash, Dobash and Gutteridge, 1986: 214). Incarceration imposes criminal identity on people whose mistakes are often less serious than the unpunished "crimes" of those who judge them. Prisons breed bitterness and may stimulate more serious criminality. Through what Foucault refers to as "dividing practices," exemplified by early leper colonies, imprisonment further stigmatizes the individuals locked up while placating an unknowing public with the myth that dangerous people are behind bars under the care of professionals who claim special knowledges.

Prison as punishment reinforces the legitimization of an institution that is inherently destructive, and because prisons are omnipresent as a legal option they displace efforts toward more practical solutions to both the problems presented to society by criminal actions and the problems of people who are criminalized. The focus of penal philosophies is on the medicalized and criminalized individual instead of the relational social causes of most illegal actions. The practices of incarceration, and the hegemonic authority of discourses to which prison planners are obeisant, stifle the imagination of policy makers.

Prison abolitionists, or those who call for community centres as a replacement for centralized institutions, have existed since the beginnings of prisons. The Archambault Commission in Canada recommended that the Kingston Prison for Women should be closed in the very year, 1938, that it was fully operational. In 1972, in England, critics who opposed expansion of the Holloway Prison for women argued that its primary function was to hold women on remand who had not even been sentenced (Heidensohn, 1985: 62). The movement by social critics toward advocacy of "alternatives to prison" is accelerating even as more institutions are being constructed and greater numbers of women and men are being sent to them (Immarigeon, 1987; see also Bureau of Justice Statistics, 1990: 4).

The Law Society of British Columbia states that "The onus should be on the Crown to show why the exceptional sanction of imprisonment should be imposed in a particular case" (1992: 8–26). In 1983, in the British context, Pat Carlen stated that "I myself do not support the view that all prisons should be abolished" (Carlen, 1983: 218). But in 1990 she discussed strategies for "the abolition of women's imprisonment" for all but those relatively few abnormal cases where women are convicted of crimes of serious harm against others. Noting that the majority of prisoners are poor women who cannot pay fines, she supports education projects and greater use of community service orders "combined with supportive probation-run women-only groups." The choice is to continue to squander billions of pounds and dollars on imprisonment or to take "bold steps to stop legislators and sentencers" from regarding prison as "the ultimate panacea for all political, social and penal ills" (Carlen, 1990: 123–25).

> Take away the women's prisons from the judges and the magistrates, deal with each abnormally serious crime as it comes along, and for the rest of the women work at feasible sentences combining denunciation of the crime with interventionary work on its causes (whether those causes be personal or social or both). (Ibid.: 123)

Retributive justice is "eye for eye" justice which exacts punishment. Restitution models demand that the offender replace stolen goods or their value, or otherwise compensate for the offence. That is, one returns harm in equivalent portion to the harm done, which only perpetuates the cycles of violence and conflict, and the other requires "paying one's debt" without consideration of the causes of the offence. Neither retribution nor restitution accomplish the healing that is inherent to models of restorative justice, where the pains of the victims are acknowledged and where the community is the mediator. It makes no sense to place the state at the centre of human conflict resolution, given that the state produces and protects the causes of conflicts.

Aboriginal justice attempts to achieve restoration of harmony by involving the whole community in a healing process. The call by Native people in Canada for self-determination is motivated, in part, by the wish to overcome the harm done to their communities by the state, which imposes revengeful punishment on those whom it prejudicially judges as offensive. The self-determination model is problematic in the context of the Canadian system of justice, but with the cooperation of some jurisdictions it is already being tried with some success in a number of Native communities. One can hope (since there's little empirical evidence of a trend) that the principles that guide the restorative model will one day contribute to and be reflected in transformations in Canadian cultural values and social policies.

In my view it is an error to think about "alternatives to prison" if what we mean by that is "electronic bracelets," through which people are subject to computer-monitored house arrest, or granting fuller surveillance and disciplinary powers and technologies to other state agencies, such as welfare and mental health, through "transcarceration" policies. An advocate of greater use of community resources, as a way of reducing reliance on prisons for relatively minor offences, states that "we can no longer simply imprison everybody we are *angry* with; we have to save those beds for the ones we are *afraid* of" (Reynolds, 1993: 17). I would argue further that we need to reconsider the validity of our fears.

We need to decrease, not increase, the means by which the state, in its multifarious networks of authority, controls human lives and selectively incapacitates people who, no less than others, have the potential to contribute to the improvement of the human condition. To the degree that such transformational vision could be collectively realized, together with essential concomitant changes in the larger political economy and dominant discourses, women, men and children who have been heretofore scapegoated for society's problems would emerge as beneficiaries of a radically new social order. To cultivate a commitment to such a world would be to see most prisons, along with the inequities they represent, disappear from the social landscape. As it is, if we reserved prisons for truly dangerous offenders, few women would qualify.

REFERENCES

American Correctional Association (ACA) (1990). *The Female Offender: What Does the Future Hold?* Washington, D.C.

Anonymous (1982). "Free?" *Tightwire* [Kingston: Prison for Women]: 27.

Assembly Special Committee on Corrections (ASCC) (1977). "Follow-Up Report: California Institution for Women." Sacramento: California State Legislature.

Axon, Lee (1989). *Model and Exemplary Programs for Female Inmates: An International Review*, I. Ottawa: Ministry of the Solicitor General.

Beattie, J. M. (1977). *Attitudes towards Crime and Punishment in Upper Canada, 1830–1850: A Documentary Study.* Toronto: University of Toronto, Centre of Criminology.

Beattie, J. M. (1986). *Crime and the Courts in England: 1660–1800.* Princeton: Princeton University Press.

Belknap, Joanne (1991). "Women in Conflict: An Analysis of Women Correctional Officers." *Women & Criminal Justice* 2(2): 89–115.

Bordt, Rebecca L. (1992) "What Prisons Do to Those at the Bottom: Reflections of a Former Prison Guard." *Odyssey: Creative Alternative in Criminal Justice* (Spring): 29–32.

Bureau of Justice Statistics (1990). *Prisoners in 1989.* Washington, D.C.: Department of Justice.

Burkhart, Kathryn Watterson (1973). *Women in Prison.* Garden City: Doubleday & Company.

Calder, W. A. (1981). "Convict Life in Canadian Federal Penitentiaries, 1867–1900," in L. A. Knafla (Ed.), *Crime and Criminal Justice in Europe and Canada.* Waterloo: Wilfrid Laurier University Press, 297–318.

Carlen, Pat (1983). *Women's Imprisonment: A Study in Social Control.* London: Routledge & Kegan Paul.

Carlen, Pat (1990). *Alternatives to Women's Imprisonment.* Milton Keynes: Open University Press.

Chandler, Edna Walker (1973). *Women in Prison.* New York: Bobbs-Merrill.

Chesney-Lind, Meda (1978). "Young Women in the Arms of the Law," in L. Bowker (Ed.), *Women, Crime, and the Criminal Justice System.* Lexington: Lexington Books, 171–96.

Chesney-Lind, Meda (1980). "Re-Discovering Lilith: Misogyny and the 'New' Female Criminal," in C. Griffiths and M. Nance (Eds.), *The Female Offender: Selected Papers from an International Symposium.* Burnaby: Simon Fraser University Criminology Research Centre.

Clark, Judy and Kathy Boudin (1990). "Community of Women Organize Themselves to Cope with the AIDS Crisis: A Case Study from Bedford Hills Correctional Facility." *Social Justice* 17(2): 90–109.

Cooper, Sheelagh D. (1987). "The Evolution of the Federal Women's Prison," in E. Adelberg and C. Currie (Eds.), *Too Few to Count: Canadian Women in Conflict with the Law.* Vancouver: Press Gang Publishers, 127–44.

Department of Health and Social Services (DHSS) (Corrections Division) (1985). "Report to the Minister: Female Offender Study Committee." Northwest Territories.

Dobash, Russell P., R. Emerson Dobash and Sue Gutteridge (1986). *The Imprisonment of Women.* Oxford: Basil Blackwell.

Eaton, Mary (1993). *Women After Prison.* Buckingham: Open University Press.

Elliott, Liz and Ruth Morris (1987). "Behind Prison Doors," in E. Adelberg and C. Currie (Eds.), *Too Few to Count: Canadian Women in Conflict with the Law.* Vancouver: Press Gang Publishers, 145–62.

Faith, Karlene (1972). "Interview with Diane." Unpublished mimeograph, Santa Cruz.

Faith, Karlene (1973). Unpublished research notes, University of California, Santa Cruz.

Faith, Karlene (1993). "Resistance: Lessons from Foucault and Feminism," in L. Radtke and H. N. Stam (Eds.), *Power and Gender.* London: Sage.

Feinman, Clarice (1985). "A Statement on the Issues: United States View," in S. Hatty (Ed.), *Women in the Prison System.* Canberra: Australian Institute of Criminology, 27–32.

First Tuesday Unit (1992). *Locking Up Women.* Yorkshire Television.

Forsythe, William J. (1987). *The Reform of Prisoners, 1830–1900.* London: Croom Helm.

Foucault, Michel (1977). *Language, Counter-Memory, Practice* (Ed. Donald F. Bouchard). Ithaca: Cornell University Press.

Foucault, Michel (1979). *Discipline and Punish.* New York: Vintage Books.

Foucault, Michel (1984). *The Foucault Reader* (Ed. Paul Rabinow). New York: Pantheon Books.

Freedman, Estelle B. (1981). *Their Sisters' Keepers: Women's Prison Reform in America, 1830–1930.* Ann Arbor: University of Michigan Press.

Genders, Elaine and Elaine Player (1987). "Women in Prison: The Treatment, the Control and the Experience," in P. Carlen and A. Worrall (Eds.), *Gender, Crime and Justice.* Milton Keynes: Open University Press, 161–75.

Gibson, Helen E. (1976). "Women's Prisons: Laboratories for Penal Reform," in L. Crites (Ed.), *The Female Offender.* Lexington: Lexington Books, 93–119.

Glick, Ruth and Virginia Neto (1977). *National Study of Women's Correctional Programs.* Washington, D.C.: National Institute of Law Enforcement and Criminal Justice.

Glueck, Sheldon and Eleanor Glueck (1934). *Five Hundred Delinquent Women.* New York: Alfred A. Knopf.

Goffman, Erving (1970). *Asylums: Essays on the Social Situation of Mental Patients and Other Inmates.* Harmondworth: Pelican.

Golligher, Gabriella (1990). "Task Force on Federally Sentenced Women Released." *Let's Talk/Entre nous* [Ottawa: Correctional Service Canada] 15(6): 4–10.

Gordon, Jody K. (1992). "The 'Fallen' and the Masculine: A Feminist Historical Analysis of the B.C. Industrial Home for Girls, 1914–1946." Unpublished Honours Thesis. Burnaby: Simon Fraser University.

Heidensohn, Frances (1985). *Women & Crime.* London: Macmillan.

Horii, Gayle K. (1992). "The Art In/Of Survival." *Matriart: A Canadian Feminist Art Journal* 3(1): i.

Hughes, Robert (1987). *The Fatal Shore: The Epic of Australia's Founding.* New York: Alfred A. Knopf.

Immarigeon, Russ (1987). "Women in Prison." *The Journal of the National Prison Project* [Washington, D.C.: American Civil Liberties Union Foundation, Inc.] 11: 2–5.

Immarigeon, Russ and Meda Chesney-Lind (1993). "Women's Prisons: Overcrowded and Overused," in R. Muraskin and T. Alleman (Eds.), *It's a Crime: Women and Justice.* Englewood Cliffs: Prentice Hall, 242–59.

Indian and Northern Affairs Canada (INAC) (1989). "Basic Departmental Data, 1989." Ottawa: Ministry of Supply and Services Canada.

Jose-Kampfner, Christina (1990). "Coming to Terms with Existential Death: An Analysis of Women's Adaptation to Life in Prison." *Social Justice* 17(2): 110–25.

Kendall, Kathleen (1993). "Literature Review of Therapeutic Services for Women in Prison." Ottawa: Ministry of the Solicitor General, Corrections Branch.

Kirby, Teri (1983). "Daily Fear Was World of Convict: Call Girl Con Spends 11 Months in Prison." *Tightwire* [Kingston: Prison for Women]: 16–18.

Kramarae, Cheris and Paula A. Treichler (1985). *A Feminist Dictionary.* London: Pandora Press.

Law Society of British Columbia (1992). *Gender Equality in the Justice System,* Volume 2. Vancouver: Gender Bias Committee.

Lekkerkerker, E. C. (1931). *Reformatories for Women in the US* Gronigen: J. B. Wolters.

Liaison (1979). "The Female Offender/La délinquante." *Liaison: Monthly Journal for the Criminal Justice System.* 5(2): 2–36. [Ottawa: Ministry of the Solicitor General.]

Mayhew, Jo-Ann (1992). "Truro: Women Delivered to a Pork Barrel Decision." *Matriart: A Canadian Feminist Art Journal* 3(1): 15.

Miller, Debra and 22 women in the California Institution for Women (1974). *no title at all is better than a title like that!* Santa Cruz: Women's Prison Project.

Mills, Judith A. (1993). "Gender of Physicians and Therapists and the Health Worker-Client Relationship." *Blueprint for Change: Report of the Solicitor General's Special Committee on Provincially Incarcerated Women.* Halifax: Province of Nova Scotia. Appendix D: 1–4.

Moffat, Kelly (Hannah) (1991). "Creating Choices or Repeating History: Canadian Female Offenders and Correctional Reform." *Social Justice* 18(3): 184–203.

Morris, Allison (1987). *Women, Crime and Criminal Justice.* Oxford: Basil Blackwell.

Moyer, Imogene L. (1992). "Crime, Conflict Theory, and the Patriarchal Society," in I. Moyer (Ed.), *The Changing Role of Women in the Criminal Justice System: Offenders, Victims, and Professionals.* Prospect Heights: Waveland Press, 1–29.

Muraskin, Roslyn (1993). "Disparate Treatment in Correctional Facilities," in R. Muraskin and T. Alleman (Eds.), *It's a Crime: Women and Justice.* Englewood Cliffs: Prentice Hall, 211–25.

Muraskin, Roslyn and Ted Alleman (Eds.) (1993). *It's a Crime: Women and Justice.* Englewood Cliffs: Prentice Hall.

National Planning Committee on the Female Offender (NPCFO) (1978). "The Female Offender." Ottawa: Solicitor General Canada.

Nicholson, Rita (1985). "Women's Function in N.S.W. Male Prisons," in S. Hatty (Ed.), *Women in the Prison System.* Canberra: Australian Institute of Criminology, 193–97.

Padel, Una and Prue Stevenson (1988). *Insiders: Women's Experience of Prison.* London: Virago Press.

Pollock, Joycelyn M. (1986). *Sex and Supervision: Guarding Male and Female Inmates.* New York: Greenwood.

Pollock-Byrne, Joycelyn M. (1990). *Women, Prison & Crime.* Pacific Grove: Brooks/Cole Publishing Company.

Rafter, Nicole Hahn (1982). "Hard Times: Custodial Prisons for Women," in N. Rafter and E. Stanko (Eds.), *Judge, Lawyer, Victim, Thief: Women, Gender Roles, and Criminal Justice.* Boston: Northeastern University Press, 237–60.

Rafter, Nicole Hahn (1985). *Partial Justice: Women in State Prisons, 1800–1935.* Boston: Northeastern University Press.

Reynolds, Carl (1993). "Texas Commission Proposes Corrections Overhaul." *Overcrowded Times: Solving the Prison Problem* 4(2): 1, 16–17.

Rogers, Joseph W. (1992). "Probation, Parole, Power, and Women Offenders: From Patriarchal Parameters to Participatory Empowerment," in I. Moyer (Ed.), *The Changing Role of Women in the Criminal Justice System: Offenders, Victims, and Professionals.* Prospect Heights: Waveland Press, 131–42.

Shaw, Margaret (1990). *The Federal Female Offender: Report on a Preliminary Study.* Ottawa: Ministry of the Solicitor General, Corrections Branch.

Shaw, Margaret, Karen Rodgers and Tina Hattem (1990). *The Release Study: Survey of Federally Sentenced Women in the Community.* Ottawa: Ministry of the Solicitor General, Corrections Branch.

Shaw, Margaret, with Karen Rodgers, Johanne Blanchette, Lee Seto Thomas, Tina Hattem, and Lada Tamarack (1990). *Survey of Federally Sentenced Women.* Ottawa: Ministry of the Solicitor General, Corrections Branch.

Shaw, Margaret, with Karen Rodgers, Johanne Blanchette, Lee Seto Thomas, Tina Hattem, and Lada Tamarack (1992). *Paying the Price: Federally Sentenced Women in Canada.* Ottawa: Ministry of the Solicitor General, Corrections Branch.

Shaw, Nancy Stoller (1982). "Female Patients and the Medical Profession in Jails and Prisons: A Case of Quintuple Jeopardy," in N. Rafter and E. Stanko (Eds.), *Judge, Lawyer, Victim, Thief: Women, Gender Roles, and Criminal Justice.* Boston: Northeastern University Press, 261–73.

Simon, Rita J. and Jean Landis (1991). *The Crimes Women Commit, the Punishments They Receive.* Lexington: Lexington Books.

Solicitor General (1992). *Blueprint for Change: Report of the Solicitor General's Special Committee on Provincially Incarcerated Women.* Halifax: Province of Nova Scotia.

Stafford, Norma (1975). *Dear Somebody: The Prison Poetry of Norma Stafford.* San Francisco: Unitarian-Universalist Service Committee.

Statistics Canada (1990). *Juristat Service Bulletin: Women and Crime* 10(20). Ottawa: Ministry of Industry, Science and Technology.

Strange, Carolyn (1985). "'The Criminal and Fallen of Their Sex': The Establishment of Canada's First Women's Prison, 1874–1901." *Canadian Journal of Women and the Law/Revue juridique "La femme et le droit"* 1(1): 79–92.

Strange, Carolyn (1985–86). "Unlocking the Doors on Women's Prison History." *Resources for Feminist Research/Documentation sur la recherche féministe* 13(4): 13–15.

Task Force on Federally Sentenced Women (TFFSW) (1990). *Creating Choices.* Ottawa: Ministry of the Solicitor General, Corrections Branch.

Tien, George, Lynda Bond, Diane Lamb, Brenda Gillstrom, Faye Paris and Heidi Worsfold (1993). "Report on the Review of Mental Health Services at Burnaby Correctional Centre for Women." Vancouver: B.C. Forensic Psychiatric Services Commission.

Vancouver Sun (1993). "Wonderful time . . . wish you . . . ," (March 4): C1.

Walford, Bonny (1987). *Lifers: The Stories of Eleven Women Serving Life Sentences for Murder.* Montreal: Eden Press.

Waring, Nancy and Betsey Smith (1991). "The AIDS Epidemic: Impact on Women Prisoners in Massachusetts: An Assessment with Recommendations." *Women & Criminal Justice* 2(2): 117–43.

Zedner, Lucia (1991). *Women, Crime, and Custody in Victorian England.* Oxford: Clarendon Press.

CHAPTER FOUR

Women Confined

IN THIS CHAPTER I discuss categories of women whose prison experience has set them apart from other women with whom they are confined, or for whom the prison experience has included discriminatory treatment, due to their cultural heritage, family circumstances, or sexual identity.

One of the starkest indicators that criminal justice systems do not issue fair and equal justice is that, in virtually every nation-state in the world, people who are identified with oppressed political minority groups are radically overrepresented in prison populations. From a positivist perspective this can be interpreted as evidence that people from the dominant group(s) have superior moral character and therefore commit less crime. However, given the pervasiveness of white-collar and other hidden crimes among the controlling classes, this argument does not hold up. From a neo-Marxist perspective, one can say that, given major inequities in political economies, people from minority groups are more vulnerable to poverty and social breakdown, and that these factors induce the kinds of visible "street crimes" for which people are most often labeled "criminal" and incarcerated. Adding to this analysis from a more contemporary critical perspective, one can observe that both poverty and cultural disparities limit the resources of the accused in putting forth a strong defence, and that it is not just the factors of crime commission or police surveillance which result in incarceration, but also such factors as discrimination in prosecution and sentencing patterns. In societies founded on racist assumptions that some groups are inferior to others, even judges who are intent on legal fairness are vulnerable to decision-making which finds support in negative stereotypes. It is most specifically those dissident groups which resist assimilation (that is, which do not acquiesce or "adapt" to the dominant culture) who are most seriously overrepresented in criminal justice systems.

In the United States, men and women of African heritage, in particular, and increasingly other political minorities as well. have been subject to racist injustice. The imprisonment rate of people of Latin American heritage increased 64 percent between 1983 and 1986 (Headley, 1989: 5). Among adult female prisoners in the United States in 1990, 36 percent were "Black," and 15.3 percent were of "Hispanic" origin (of whom 5.5 percent were categorized as "Black Hispanics"). Native women constituted just 1.9 percent of incarcerated women in the United States, Asians less than 1 percent, and those categorized as "Other Races," 2.8 percent (ACA, 1990: 47). According to the 1990 census, the United States had a total population of 248,710 million people, 80.3 percent of whom were of European (not including Hispanic) heritage (US Department of Commerce, 1992: 17), but "White" women constituted just 43.4 percent of adult female prisoners (and most of them were from impoverished or working-class backgrounds). In other words, women whose cultures comprise less than 20 percent of the national adult female population constitute almost 60 percent of incarcerated females, and African-heritage women are notable in this overrepresentation.

Canada, given border-shifting political realignments over the globe this century, is geographically now the largest country of the world and one of the most sparsely populated, with just over 27 million total population in 1993 (almost equivalent to the population of the state of California). Approximately 25 percent are Québécois, or French-Canadians dispersed through the provinces (Statistics Canada, 1989: 1–2), and there are additional political minority groups, including immigrants, refugees and second and third generation Canadians, from every continent and dozens of national origins. In Canada, including the Yukon and Northwest territories, less than 4 percent of the total population claims First Nations heritage, but it is Native women who are disproportionately represented in criminal justice systems. It should be noted that increasing numbers of women of African heritage, from the US and the Caribbean, are serving time at the Prison for Women (P4W) on importing and trafficking convictions. Also, in the province of Nova Scotia, women of African heritage are the dominant political minority group and these women constitute the majority of the approximately twenty women in the provincial prison. (Solicitor General, 1992: 5, 13) This is an issue that calls for research. Nevertheless, in Canada overall it is Native women who are the most consistently overrepresented in prison populations, as discussed in the first section of this chapter.

The second section of this chapter is focused on issues that concern incarcerated women who are the mothers of dependent children. The majority of women who go to prison are parents and most commonly they are single parents. Some jurisdictions have taken care to acknowledge and, to a limited degree, to respond to the special problems faced by mothers in prison. The more enlightened administrations of women's institutions have also facilitated the work of outside groups which attempt to protect imprisoned women's legal rights as parents, and to support their visitation rights. Given the nature of prisons, however, children whose mothers are incarcerated are among the most vulnerable victims of criminal justice traditions.

For reasons discussed in the third section of this chapter, it is probable that lesbians are underrepresented in prison. And given the lesbophobic (and homophobic) attitudes toward lesbians (and gay men) that have prevailed for a century throughout Western cultures, and that specifically have resulted in persecution of same-sex relationships in prisons, most women, if asked by authorities, would deny that they are lesbians. Nevertheless, most women who go to prison, whether or not they are self-identified as lesbians, voluntarily engage in variations on the lesbian experience during their period(s) of incarceration. Thus, the issue here is only partially "How many lesbians are incarcerated?" or "Are women incarcerated because they are lesbians?" The primary questions are "How do authorities and academic observers respond to women loving women in prison?" and "What is the reaction of the women themselves to this experience?"

Most women sent to prison in Canada fall into one or more of these three categories. That is, the majority of incarcerated women are mothers and in Canada many of these women are also Native women. Whereas relatively few incarcerated women are self-identified as lesbians, a majority of women in most North American prisons engage in intimate friendships which may include sexual desire or a sensual and romantic involvement. Opportunities for actual sexual contact are very limited within prison environments, and involve serious disciplinary risks to the participants. Nevertheless, for many women, it is these friendships which make the prison experience endurable.

ABORIGINAL WOMEN

Do you know the story about the Indians on the moon? When the Americans first landed on the moon they saw two Indians sitting on a log. The Americans hailed them through a loudspeaker and the Indians said to each other, "Oh, no. Not again." (a Cree woman in Saskatchewan, in Goodwill, 1975: 43)

Through all the centuries of war and death and cultural and psychic destruction have endured the women who raise the children and tend the fires, who pass along the tales and the traditions, who weep and bury the dead, who are the dead, and who never forget. (Paula Gunn Allen, 1986: 50)

I use several terms, not precisely interchangeably, in reference to Native women in Canada. The word "Native" has been popularly adopted by Native peoples themselves, as well as by Europeans, to signify people who are indigenous to North American soil (or, more precisely, were the first to enter the continent—through what is now known as the Bering Strait, which, since the Ice Age, has bridged Asia and North America, and connects the Bering Sea with the Arctic Ocean). The Canadian legal system uses the term Aboriginal to designate people who were on what became Canadian land at the time of first contact (invasion) by European explorers and settlers, and this term has also been adopted by the reference group to signify their fundamental rights concerning, for example, the uses of the land, with such phrases as "Aboriginal entitlement."

The word "Aboriginal" is used synonymously with "Indigenous," which Webster defines as "living naturally in a particular region or environment." The current struggles of Native people in Canada to overcome the effects of European practices of cultural genocide are occurring simultaneously with revivals and resistance movements of Aboriginal peoples across the globe, and the United Nations has declared 1993 the Year of Indigenous Peoples. Resistant Native people in Canada do not consider themselves Native "Canadians" because the borders established by the Europeans are meaningless to their heritage. Some of my ancestors are Métis and Cree, and in my own life on the prairies I experienced the US-Canadian border as just one more political tool for dividing and separating people of shared cultural roots.

It was the European colonizers who applied the generic label "Indian" to the people they encountered on this continent. The word became common parlance among the peoples of reference and it served to consolidate their diversely distinct identities amidst attempted assimilation processes imposed by state agencies. However, since the inception of contemporary "Red Power" activism beginning in the late 1960s, fewer Native people have acquiesced to this "white man's label." By the 1990s the term has become more generally problematic in Canada, given the steady and significant influx of immigrants from the Republic of India in South Asia, and although Indians from Asia living in Canada often refer to themselves as "Indo-Canadians," the confusions underscore the cultural distinctions between the two groups.

The more formal term, "First Nations" (sometimes used synonymously, with the purposefully pluralized term "First Peoples"), fleshes out the racism inherent in the Anglo concept of "tribes." The term signifies the literal truth that many diverse cultures shared this continent as its original occupants, and that they constituted separate societies, literally nations, each with its own laws, governing bodies and jurisdictions, means of livelihood, cultural traditions, belief systems, kinship patterns and so on. It is the term which most vividly expresses a growing respect for the inherent rights of peoples who were not only here before anyone else, but who have had to struggle and endure for centuries the indignities imposed by the colonists. The term "First Nations" most fully and forcefully encompasses the rich historical, political and cultural dimensions of what is more loosely generalized as Native or Aboriginal identity within Canada.

There is yet another important cultural group in Canada, the Métis, who have also periodically resurfaced in their resistance to assimilation by either the dominant culture or "Indian" societies as defined by the federal government. Métis peoples (literally, "half-breeds") are those whose ancestry combines the heritages of First Nations peoples and Europeans. French, Norwegian and other settlers of what became Canadian soil frequently married "Indian" women. They and their progeny were important to the hunting and trapping activities upon which European traders were dependent and they have also been important to Canada's rich agricultural and fishing traditions. Métis social traditions, including story-telling and fiddle-playing, have added vital dimensions to Canada's cultural history. They have been generally excluded from negotiations between the European colonizers and people with "Indian" status as determined by the Indian Act of 1876, and although they claim rights as a "distinct people," their interests have been almost entirely ignored by the government (Hamilton and Sinclair, 1991a: 194–99).

The prominent 19th century Métis leader Louis Riel was incarcerated as a "crazy" person—a man offensive to white people in part, no doubt, because he was brilliant and highly educated. He was executed in Regina, Saskatchewan in 1885 on the charge of high treason; his crime was to have been chosen as leader of a rebellion on the prairies against the federal government's reneging on treaties with the inhabitants of what was then the Northwest Territories, and against the intimidating presence of soldiers and police to keep order (Miller, 1991: 74–82). A century later Riel has been acclaimed as one of Canada's most significant resistance heroes. A politically astute community, the Métis remain economically disenfranchised, and despite certain separations their interests are often joined with the ongoing struggles of Native peoples (see, for example, Campbell, 1973, and Adams, 1975/1989). In this section I make few specific references to Métis women because as a group they are not identifiable within criminal justice systems, but Métis women are among the "Native" women who are overrepresented in Canadian prisons.

The romantic image of the "Indian Princess" and the derogatory image of the "Ugly Squaw" are being put to rest by all but the most delusional, ignorant and/or sexist racists of contemporary society. In place of these stereotypes are the more realistic images of Native women in all their diversities, from culturally displaced streetwalkers to the much greater number who work at every kind of job, manage households and raise their families, to the publicly visible First Nations women who are assuming their places as influential artists, politicians and community leaders throughout Canada, including those such as Jean Folster (Swampy Cree), Wendy Grant (Musqueam) and Charlene Belleau (Alkali Lake) who have been elected as Chiefs of their bands. There is much work to be done to overcome the effects of colonization, and, following Aboriginal traditions, the women are doing much of this work.

Due to a gender-discriminatory section of the Canadian Indian Act of 1876 [s.12(1)(b)], Native women who married non-Indians were banned from their heritage. When registered "Indian" men married white women, their wives and children became "Indians," but when Native women married non-Indians, they and their children lost their band membership, their property and their inheritance; they could no longer live on their home reserves, participate in Native ceremonies, nor be buried with their ancestors. For all legal, social and cultural purposes they became "non-Indians," and even if they were widowed or divorced, they remained excluded from their communities

(Jamieson, 1978: 1). As observed by Donna Greschner, "For both church and state, patriarchy was the necessary ingredient of the assimilation and 'civilization' of the Aboriginal populations" (Greschner, 1992: 347).

> When I got married [to a "non-Indian"] I was told to sign a piece of paper, so I did. Then I got a blue card saying I was no longer a band member nor recognized as an Indian by the Government of Canada. That really shakes you up. I am more aware of my Indianness today than when I was a registered Indian simply because I understand the situation more. That blue card! If I could tear it up and burn it I would. (Goodwill, 1975: 13)

A long and ultimately successful resistance campaign led by a group of women from the Tobique reserve in Quebec, with eventual support from the United Nations, resulted in a partial victory in 1985 (Silman, 1987). The offending sections of the Indian Act were amended by Bill C-31 (passed by Parliament to take effect April 17, 1985), and the more glaring features of the double standard were eliminated. However, among other challenges, formerly excluded Native women are still struggling to regain Aboriginal identity for their children (Faith et al., 1990; Holmes, 1987).

The reinstatement to "Indian" status of tens of thousands of Native women, combined with a major decline in the infant mortality rate and a rapidly increasing birth rate among very young Native women, has had the result of increasing the officially registered Native population from just over 2 percent of Canada's total in 1984 to just under 4 percent in 1989 (INAC, 1989: 4, 26). Half-again as many Native people do not figure in this percentage because they are not registered as "Indian" with the government. Almost one-third of Native families are headed by a single female parent, compared to 10 percent for Canada as a whole (Hagey, Larocque and McBride, 1989: 12). The technical issue of legal marriage would be insignificant if all these women had the support of extended families, but the majority of them are struggling on their own.

As the most consistently and systematically oppressed political minority group in Canadian history, First Nations women and men are the most seriously overrepresented groups in contemporary prison populations. Most incarcerated Native people enter the criminal justice system at a very young age. In 1982 the Ontario Native Women's Association found that 37 percent of the Native women in Ontario institutions were younger than twenty years of age. More than half had first been arrested between the ages of fourteen and seventeen, and almost 20 percent had first been arrested when aged thirteen or younger (CSC, 1983: 4).

In 1990, while comprising less than 4 percent of the national female population (not including Métis), Native women constituted almost 25 percent of federally sentenced female prisoners (Shaw et al., 1990: 4). The disproportionality is significantly greater in provincial and territorial institutions, where, depending on the region, between 20 and 90 percent of women in jails are Native women, who are incarcerated for often inconsequential, class-based offences such as public disorder and non-payment of fines for minor offences. In a 1983 study in Ontario, it was found that 98 percent of jailed fine defaulters were Native (Jolly and Seymour, 1983: 22). In 1985, 80 percent of the women in provincial jails in Manitoba were Native women, and over 50 percent of these women were incarcerated for non-payment of fines (Hnatiuk, 1985: 1).

Native women are also overrepresented in prison because so many of them lack the will, or legal or cultural resources, to defend themselves in court.

> Since they felt powerless and had no trust in or understanding of the process, some acquiesced. They accepted an unfavourable plea bargain, or remained silent, refusing to offer evidence that either exonerated them or implicated others. . . . They endured being sent to prison in the same silence with which they had greeted past victimization. (Sugar and Fox, 1989–90: 476)

Patricia Monture, a Mohawk law professor, protests the silencing process that accrues to any group which is subordinated through the social structure, and which is humiliated through assumptions of its inadequacies and "disadvantages."

> We are only disadvantaged if you are using a White middle class yardstick. I quite frequently find that the White middle class yardstick is a yardstick of materialism. . . . Disadvantage is a nice, soft, comfortable word to describe dispossession, to describe a situation of force whereby our very existence, our histories, are erased continuously right before our eyes. Words like disadvantage conceal racism. (Monture, 1986: 161–62)

Aboriginal people in Canada attribute their overrepresentation in prisons in part to aggressive policing practices against them. Indeed, a woman from the Carrier band points out that "In my language, the name of the RCMP translates into 'those who grab us'" (Goodwill, 1975: 23). Fran Sugar and Lana Fox, in their survey of Native women at P4W, found that over half of the thirty-nine women they interviewed stressed "negative" experiences with the police, who are described together with government Indian Agents as "administrators of oppressive regimes whose authority we resent and deny" (Sugar and Fox, 1989–90: 475). The perception of unfair policing is widely shared, and confirmed by the United Nations in a guide to human rights in countries throughout the world. Whereas the Canadian government had a very high (94 percent) rating in protecting the human rights of Canadians as a whole, on the issue of "torture or coercion by the state" the government fell short due to "occasional abuses by police, usually as violence against non-whites" (Humana, 1992: 67).

The Manitoba "Aboriginal Justice Inquiry" Commissioners are emphatic as to the problems of both over-policing and under-policing of Native peoples.

> We heard of Aboriginal people being stopped on the street or in cars for no reason. Those arrested were afraid of the police and many reported being beaten by police officers. . . . [This is] a problem of considerable magnitude. . . . They may also be charged with a multiplicity of offences arising out of the same incident. Many such charges are never proceeded with, and appear to be harassment. We believe that many Aboriginal people are arrested and held in custody when a white person in the same circumstances either might not be arrested at all, or might not be held. . . . [At the same time] police were not present on a day-to-day basis to prevent crime or to provide other services to the [Native] community. (Hamilton and Sinclair, 1991a: 593–96)

Among the most dramatic examples of racism in policing practices in contemporary Canada, as supported by an indifferent or actively racist (and sexist) society, is the case of nineteen-year-old Helen Betty Osborne. In 1971 she was abducted by four young white men whose sexual advances she had rebuffed, in The Pas, a small town in Manitoba. They brutally beat her beyond recognition, and finally murdered her with over fifty stabs to her body with a screwdriver. Her body was found in the bushes outside town the next day, and the Royal Canadian Mounted Police proceeded to round up and question her friends, all Aboriginals. Over time, through informal confessions, virtually everyone in town knew the identities of the four men who had committed the atrocity. Evidence was plentiful. But it wasn't until 1987, sixteen years later, that charges were finally laid, thanks to the determination of a Constable who was unwilling to see the file on the case put to rest. Only three of the four men were charged. Of these, one was granted immunity from prosecution in exchange for his testimony. A second was acquitted. Just one was convicted and sentenced to imprisonment, for ten years (Hamilton and Sinclair, 1991b; Priest, 1989). If four Aboriginal men had killed a white woman, punishment would have been swift and sure. If the cynicism of Aboriginal people toward Canadian criminal justice practices is to be assuaged, policing, prosecution and sentencing patterns will need to be completely overhauled, which would require a major reduction in racist attitudes in society as a whole.

In her research in British Columbia, Karen Masson (1992: 59) found a "correlation between severity of sentence and racial designation," with Native women more likely to receive a custodial sentence (at 41.2 percent) than white women (25.7 percent). Conversely, 74.3 percent of white women received a fine or probation compared to 58.8 percent of Native women. The discrepancy is clearly tinged with the suggestion of racism, which is exacerbated by the correlation of Native crime with alcohol consumption. As discussed by Michael Jackson,

> Put at its baldest, there is an equation of being drunk, Indian and in prison. Like many stereotypes, this one has a dark underside. It reflects a view of Native people as uncivilized and without a coherent social or moral order. The stereotype prevents us from seeing Native people as equals. The fact that the stereotypical view of Native people is no longer reflected in official government policy does not negate its power in the popular imagination and its influence in shaping decisions of the police, prosecutors, judges and prison officials. (Law Society of British Columbia, 1992: 8–20)

The racism factor is also compounded by the fact that women who have their children living with them are more likely to receive lenient sentences than women whose children are not under the mother's direct care. In Native communities children may be integrated into an extended family, and the fact that the birth mother is not always under the same roof is not indicative of bad parenting but rather of the communitarian values of Aboriginal traditions (Monture, 1989: 6). The courts, however, do not take this into account in sentencing practices.

Because of the racism that is endemic to Canadian society, when Native women are sent to prison they experience a continuation of white authority.

> For Aboriginal women, prison is an extension of life on the outside, and because of this it is impossible for us to heal there. . . . For us, prison rules have the same illegitimacy as the oppressive rules under which we grew up. . . . Physicians, psychiatrists, and psychologists are typically white and male. How can we be healed by those who symbolize the worst experiences of our past? (Sugar and Fox, 1989–90: 476–77)

Although their crimes are seldom politically motivated, given their histories of political oppression one can readily characterize Native people in prison as political prisoners. One of the ironies of the Native prison experience in recent decades, both male and female, is that through self-help organizations they have reclaimed their cultural identities within the very environment that has intensified their oppression. This process has met with considerable resistance from some prison officials (Jackson, 1989: 289–90), but through perseverance they have prevailed. The first Native Brotherhood organization was formed in 1958 at the Stony Mountain penitentiary in Manitoba. By the end of the 1960s, chapters were formed throughout the prairies and in west coast institutions, and in 1971 the first Native Sisterhood group was organized at P4W (Anon., 1976: 4). The level of activity has waxed and waned according to the energies of women inside at any given time and fluctuating administrative support, but since 1979 it has been for the most part a thriving group. For example, in most years, the Sisterhood has sponsored powwows to reinforce cultural ties and to sustain contact with Native communities outside. In 1981 the first Native Studies course was taught inside the prison. Through the initiative of Art Solomon, a respected Elder, Fran Sugar, an effective inside organizer, and others, a sweat lodge was constructed on the grounds in 1982.

In 1989 Fran Sugar and Lana Fox, both of whom were then imprisoned at P4W, conducted a study as part of the Task Force on female prisons in Canada (Sugar and Fox, 1990). As a result of their work the voices of incarcerated First Nations women were heard across Canada. The thirty-nine women they interviewed articulated anger at the ways by which Native women have been abused and silenced both outside and inside institutions. Speaking their own truths, and with the support of Elders such as Joan Lavallee and Art Solomon,

Native female activists in prison have developed creative means by which they can come together to learn about, experience and collectively honour Aboriginal traditions. The self-directed transformations that are occurring among Native peoples behind bars, despite institutional obstacles, reflect movements toward recovery and self-determination occurring in First Nations communities across North America (Fordham, 1993).

> It is racism, past in our memories and present in our surroundings, that negates non-Native attempts to reconstruct our lives. Existing programs cannot reach us, cannot surmount the barriers of mistrust that racism has built. It is only Aboriginal people who can design and deliver programs that will address our needs and that we can trust. It is only Aboriginal people who can truly know and understand our experience. It is only Aboriginal people who can instill pride and self-esteem lost through the destructive experiences of racism. We cry out for a meaningful healing process that will have real impact on our lives, but the objectives and implementation of this healing process must be premised on our need, the need to heal and walk in balance. (Sugar and Fox, 1990: 16)

At both P4W and at the new Burnaby Correctional Centre for Women (BCCW), Native women have formed healing circles and have revived such practices as fasting, potlatches, burning sweetgrass, sage and cedar, and holding to medicine bundles. These practices have an antidotal effect against the negative ambience of prisons. As one woman put it, "I wanted life after going to Native Sisterhood, it meant everything to me" (Sugar and Fox, 1989–90: 479). The "right" to these practices was not granted without a struggle. One woman "spent about eight months in solitary [confinement] because she insisted upon having access to the spiritual teachers and the prison staff refused her" (Faith et al., 1990: 185). Problems have arisen with prison staff laying their hands on medicine bundles with the rationale that they had to be "searched," without regard for their sacred value; the tradition holds that if anyone handles someone else's medicine bundle, it is desecrated and loses its spiritual power. Fran Sugar describes how she recovered herself while in prison, despite these antagonisms borne from ignorance and unchecked power.

> At times when I'd burn my medicines, when we had sweetgrass smuggled in to us because sometimes it was seen as contraband, the sweet smell of the earth would

create a safe feeling, a feeling of being alive even though the cage represented a coffin, the prison a gravestone, and my sisters walking dead people. These medicines were what connected me as a spirit child. One time when I was close to suicide I was told by [a spiritual adviser] that my spirit was alive and it was housed in my physical shell. And from that hard time I learnt that my spirit was more important than my body because my body was controlled by the routine of life in prison. It was then the connectedness to being an Aboriginal Woman began. I began feeling good about myself even though I had only a few reasons to feel good. I understood there was a spirit within me that had the will to live. (Sugar and Fox, 1989–90: 467)

Until recently, the "right" to practice First Nations ceremonies in prison has been dependent on the goodwill of each institution's administrative staff. Correctional Service of Canada has now endorsed this fundamental prisoners' right for all federal institutions, and if challenged it is likely that these ceremonies would be upheld as a protected human right under the Canadian *Charter of Rights and Freedoms.* Native ceremonies and circles are no less an exercise in "religious" faith than the Christian practices which have been obligatory in the history of Western prisons, or than the Jewish, Islamic or Buddhist services which have been permitted in many North American male and female institutions in more recent times. The value of Native spirituality is clear to those learning to understand its core purpose.

The circle of chairs we sat in represented the cycle of life from birth to death, and that circle did not exclude anyone. . . . [W]e forgive and accept each person as an individual, as an individual who has made mistakes on their path of learning and teaching, and who can strive to reach a place where their spirit is healed. (Sugar and Fox, 1989–90: 481)

Although there are over 600 different Native bands across Canada, with 52 extant Aboriginal languages and 2,234 reserves and Crown lands (INAC, 1989: 4), certain fundamental beliefs are common to many of them, as discovered by women from different traditions who meet in prison. At BCCW the Native Sisterhood gathers for a weekly circle, sharing a self-prepared meal of "homemade" soup and bannock. The Elizabeth Fry Society has contracted with a Native advisor who is effectively serving as a liaison between the Sisterhood and the Native Brotherhood of a nearby male institution. These men have sent hand-crafted drums and artwork to the women, and although the two groups do not have physical contact, a spiritual connection has evolved between them.

At BCCW, as at P4W, First Nations women, together with elders and other supporters, have constructed a sweatlodge in which they gather for healing and purification. In addition to their spiritual value to Native women, the symbolism of the sweatlodge and other rituals has not been lost on women from the dominant culture. Some white women still protest that Native women receive special treatment, but others have participated in powwows and other events and express respect for First Nations peoples and their rituals, in this most unlikely of cross-cultural circumstances.

One cannot be complacent about the rise of Native consciousness in Canadian prisons and the validation of First Nations cultures. At P4W just one counselor was of Native heritage but she left the institution and as of April 1993 she had not been replaced (Pollack, 1993: 68). Native women stress the need for culturally appropriate methods of addressing such problems as prior sexual and physical abuse. Clearly it will require ongoing vigilance to ensure that the effort toward greater support for incarcerated Native women is not thwarted by institutional indifference.

Not all Native women are leaving prisons better prepared than when they entered to cope with a prejudicial society, whose competitive and individualistic values contradict revived First Nations ideals of cooperation and community. Many of these women have been severed from their cultures since childhood; 64 percent of registered Indians no longer live on reserves (Statistics Canada, 1993). Most older women were confined as children and youth in compulsory, horrifically abusive residential schools, operated primarily by the Catholic church. Although these schools gradually fell into disuse, they were not completely shut down until 1988. Children from the age of six were forced from their families, locked in dormitories where many of them were physically and sexually abused, and denied the right to use their own language or otherwise retain their own cultural practices (Haig-Brown, 1988). The children were segregated by sex, and brothers and sisters were not permitted contact with one another. As stated by the Commissioners of the 1991 Manitoba "Aboriginal Justice Inquiry,"

> The early missionaries condemned Aboriginal child-rearing methods as being negligent, irresponsible and "uncivilized." . . . Aboriginal people were reduced to being "wards of the state." [The missionaries were convinced that] the only way to "civi-

lize" Aboriginal people was to remove [the children] from the disruptive influences of the parents and the community. . . . The federal government delegated the job of "civilizing" and "educating" Aboriginal people in Canada to religious organizations and churches. . . . Their uncivilized and pagan ways would be replaced by good Christian values. The residential school system was a conscious, deliberate and often brutal attempt to force Aboriginal people to assimilate into mainstream society . . . by forcing the children away from their languages, cultures and societies. . . . That experience was marked by emotional, physical and sexual abuse, social and spiritual deprivation, and substandard education. Aboriginal communities have not yet recovered from the damage caused by the residential schools. (Hamilton and Sinclair, 1991a: 513–15)

In the words of a woman who was sent to one of these schools:

They strapped you. . . . They'd make fun of how you looked. . . . You didn't want to look in the mirror anymore, you didn't want to know what you looked like. . . . [I]f you got 100 straps and didn't cry, they'd give you more, just to try to break you . . . [About the sexual abuse . . .] How are these little children, at six or seven, going to know this is wrong? That they could speak up? . . . If you were quiet, that's the ones they picked on. Those were the ones that suffered. . . . They degraded you terribly. And then you'd look at how the people at home fared, when all the kids were taken. They have nothing to do, nothing to work for, nothing. This is how alcohol came in real strong [to fill that void]. (Faith et al., 1990: 182)

The torments inflicted against the children and, by extension, their parents, were literally unspeakable. Celia Haig-Brown documents such abuses as the "needle tortures," whereby children who made the mistake of speaking in their own languages had sewing needles forced through their tongues, described as "a routine punishment" (Haig-Brown, 1988: 1–2). We should not be surprised, then, that so many Aboriginal cultures "abandoned" their original languages. Nor is it any wonder that Native peoples became habituated (if not resigned) to family breakups and institutionalization:

If a young girl fought back in residential school—that's the thing that she knew protected her there. When she comes out on the streets, she comes in conflict with the law, she fights back. The correctional system, going into the Prison for Women, is a lot like going to residential school. From one institution to another. A lot of those kids grew up lacking parenting skills. They were in an institution all the time. (Faith et al., 1990: 182)

Many younger Native women in Canada's jails and prisons have been raised in foster or adoptive homes which, in effect, have been an extension of the residential school policies. Aboriginal peoples have been generally judged by child welfare officials as ineligible to serve as foster or adoptive families for Aboriginal children who have been taken from their birth families. Between 1971 and 1981, up to 80 percent of adopted Native children from Manitoba were taken into non-Aboriginal homes, and "38% of 'Indian' adoptions and 17% of Métis adoptions in 1981 were placements in the United States" (Hamilton and Sinclair, 1991a: 523). These children lost their families, were wrenched from their homelands, and their very names have been taken from them—just as Africans transported to slavery in the United States were forbidden to use their own names.

Among Native women in institutions a common alternative to being literally stolen and, in effect, "sold" to "good" white families was to be raised on colonized, impoverished reserves, often with inadequate utility services and polluted water sources. Many of these communities have been plagued by pervasive violence and diseases including virtual epidemics of cancer, diabetes and tuberculosis (Faith et al., 1990: 172). Illnesses related to alcohol abuse have been endemic on some reserves, and the frequency of babies born with "fetal alcohol syndrome" has long been identified as a serious social and medical problem in Native communities (Asante, 1981). The myth of "the drunken Indian" who has a greater physiological susceptibility to alcoholism than white people has been broken by contemporary research (Leland, 1978; Yerbury, 1992), but the conditions that produce alcohol abuse are abundant on reserves. The suicide rate among Natives (with a particular concentration among young males) is 34 per 100,000, more than double that of Canada as a whole (Hagey, Larocque and McBride, 1989: 25). Whether they remain on the reserves or migrate to the cities, many Native women are wholly without resources, beyond inadequate welfare payments, to care for themselves and their children. A Native family support worker describes a typical case:

She has two children, and two grandchildren she's raising. The money she gets is absolutely nothing. They can't go to the show, they can't do anything. No ways or means of going out and getting a job, because they're not qualified, they don't have any skills. So of course they'll try something else. A lot of them shoplift—"My kid needs that, by God he's gonna get it." (Faith et al., 1990: 182)

Through cultural genocide campaigns to Christianize "the natives" in the 19th century, the Canadian government forbade potlatches, powwows and all traditional ceremonies (Fisher, 1977). Although "assimilation" was the purported goal, Natives were in fact excluded from participation in Canadian society; thus, they were condemned to a political void. Not until 1960 were "Indians" granted the vote in federal elections. But the times are indeed changing, and First Nations peoples are vehemently resisting the perpetuation of injustices against themselves and organizing to reclaim their lands, recover their languages, and protect their land- and water-based livelihoods. Within their communities they are forming sharing circles based on the medicine wheel, and reviving holistic healing practices to, address the silencing effects of violences. Through this resurgence of Aboriginal cultures young people are being taught the traditional arts of carving, dance, songwriting and beadwork. Nationally there are many inspiring examples of successful efforts by First Nations groups to recover physically, emotionally, spiritually, culturally, economically and politically from the internalized effects of official attempts to eradicate "Indians" from Canadian society through "assimilation" policies (Faith et al., 1990). At the same time, Natives are staking their claims to full citizens' rights in contemporary society. Increasingly, Native women are working as courtworkers, community health workers and youth counselors, circumventing the cycles of being abused and "getting lost" that have been experienced by so many of the young people who have ended up on the streets. The commitments and activities of Native Sisterhood organizations in prisons, then, are developing in the context of this widespread recovery process.

In the view of Native activists, many Aboriginal men, in particular, have "lost their ways" through dislocations imposed by the dominant European cultures, and women and children have suffered their losses (Faith et al., 1990). In most traditional Native cultures women's powers were fully recognized and honoured; many First Nations societies were matrilineal, tracing descent through the female line, and in these societies it was the women who selected the chiefs (Kirkness, 1987–88: 410–11). Given that not all Aboriginal peoples were respectful of women, and given the global pervasiveness of male dominance, traditionally as well as in modern times, white feminists have been skeptical of Native women's claims that their cultures have been historically free from patriarchal oppressions. However, as Donna Greschner has pointed out, to question Native women's accounts of their own histories is "a refusal to accept Aboriginal women's understandings and truths on their own terms. It is another manifestation of cultural arrogance to suppose that the problems of one culture are replicated in another" (Greschner, 1992: 340; see also Gunn Allen, 1986: 213). In any case, traditions which showed respect for women have been corrupted by official provisions of the Indian Act which, in keeping with English common law, held men to be dominant over women in all matters of property, contract, marriage and decision-making in band affairs. The result is that Native women are now subject to the same abuses that European patriarchal traditions have inflicted on women and children (Hamilton and Sinclair, 1991a: 480–81; see also Singer, 1992). Emma LaRocque, a Métis professor of Women's Studies, is unequivocal in her analysis of the transference effects of patriarchal values into Native cultures:

> sexual violence is best explained by sexism and misogyny which is nurtured and inherent in patriarchy. Rape in any culture and by any standards is warfare against women. (Hamilton and Sinclair, 1991a: 482)

Aboriginal women have been reluctant to expose violence against themselves both because it disrupts their relationships within their communities, and because it exacerbates racist stereotypes against Native people (Courtrille, 1991: 13–14). However, this is changing as white women are more forthcoming about the abuses they, too, have suffered, and as Native communities come to clearer understandings of the effects of abuses by colonizers and learn to resist self-blame. Some Native women insist that Aboriginal men, including and even especially Chiefs and Elders, must be held accountable through the Canadian legal system for their harm to women and children lest the cycle continue. Others, with support from men who are acknowledging their own violences, emphasize that perpetrators have themselves been the victims of abuse, in a continuum from residential schools through contemporary criminal justice systems. They point to the failures of the European-imposed adversarial system to restore balance, and they put their trust in Native traditions of non-confrontational, non-punitive and non-coercive means of facilitating conciliation and renewed harmony, with the family as the foundation of the healing process.

This debate is echoed among white feminists who work against violences against women and children (see Faith and Currie, 1993), but it assumes a different quality in the context of First Nations discussions where gender complementarity rather than equality is at issue. In 1993, Canada's first Native person to be elected as a Member of Parliament, Ethel Blondin-Andrew from Yellowknife, set a nationally publicized example for compromise. She laid charges of assault against her husband and obliged him to accept his responsibility. However, in response to queries by television reporters, she also publicly declared her unbroken love for him and, in a spirit of healing rather than blame, she articulated her understanding of the angers which produced the violence. Finally, with support and counsel from their families and home community, upon his release from jail they were reconciled with their mutual dignity intact.

The leadership of the Native Women's Association of Canada has challenged campaigns for First Nations self-government on the grounds both that the majority of Aboriginal peoples are now dispersed in urban centres across Canada, and, more seriously, that women and children would be unprotected to the extent that local Chiefs and national leaders failed to address the common violences within their communities (Hamilton and Sinclair, 1991a: 485). Shelters for women, such as the Helping Spirit Lodge in British Columbia, the Eagle's Nest Shelter in Alberta, and Gignoo House in New Brunswick, are generating understanding of the needs for Native women to create healing centres separate not only from the dominant culture but from the contexts in which the violences against them occur.

Sharon McIvor, a lawyer and activist from the Lower Nicola Band in British Columbia, who has given voice to the concerns of First Nations women across Canada, emphasizes the flaws in stereotypes of Native peoples as having a greater propensity for violence than other peoples in Canada. She identifies four categories of Native people:

> The first category is the traditional people. They're out doing what they traditionally did, what their forefathers did, and they're quite happy. They may be out hunting and trapping and having very, very little contact with the non-Native society. No problems there.

At the other end of the scale, the fourth category includes the people who are completely assimilated. They live in the city, work in the city, and have a lot of
non-Native friends. They're content with their life.

The third category . . . is when you're both. You jump back and forth. You're quite
comfortable in the non-Native society, and you can also go back into your traditional society, and you're quite comfortable there.

The remaining category is the people who have come out of the traditional society
and don't fit in with the non-Native society. This last category is the one having the
conflict. They haven't had their values solidly in place. When they get into the non-
Native society they get mixed up, and they're having a lot of conflict. . . . They are
the people that end up not only in the prisons, but also end up with social problems. . . . They're the ones that all of the conflict comes from. . . . It's just this one
group. (They have one foot in each culture and) they're not settled in either, or comfortable in either. (Faith et al., 1990: 177)

Confirming McIvor's perception, the women most often sent to prisons are
those who have left their rural reserves for cities where they land on the streets
and drift further away from their cultures through the exigencies of survival
struggles. Most have never known their native language or experienced familial
continuity. They may identify as Aboriginal women but they lack a context
for expressing that identity. Growing numbers of very young Native women
are single parents responsible for dependent children, and they are among the
76 percent of Native women in Canada who are unemployed (Law Society of
British Columbia, 1992: 8–45). As of 1991 at least eight Native women had
committed suicide in P4W since the late 1970s. The challenge for Native communities is to prevent these tragedies, and "white man's justice" is not a likely
source of aid in facing this challenge.

First Nations women in North America are reclaiming their heritage,
resisting the oppressions that have claimed their sisters' and brothers' lives, and
forging visions of a future in which harmony is restored in their communities. Their initiatives are indicative of a rejection of state mechanisms which
have entrenched structural obstacles to Native self-determination. Their work
illuminates the futility of promoting assimilationist approaches to problem-
solving in their communities, and is both reflective of and distinct from other
movements toward self-reliance in the larger society. The process begins with

demystification, as articulated nearly two decades ago by Maria Campbell, a prominent Métis storyteller from Saskatchewan:

> [T]here is the ancient Indian belief that women have special powers. The mission-aries who came exploited this sacred belief by impressing on us that women were a source of evil. The oppression of native people will never end until these myths are recognized and destroyed. (cited in Goodwill, 1975: 61)

A holistic focus on healing signifies a genuinely transformative model of jus-tice based on renewal. In the words of Paula Gunn Allen:

> [W]e acknowledge that the violation of the Mothers' and Grandmothers' laws of kinship, respect, balance, and harmony brings about social, planetary, and personal illness and that healing is a matter of restoring the balance within ourselves and our communities. To this restoration of balance, of health, and wellness (wealth) we contribute our energies. For we are engaged in the work of reclaiming our minds, our gods, and our traditions. The sacred hoop cannot be restored unless and until its sacred center is recognized. (Gunn Allen, 1986: 208)

MOTHERS

> Signed up for phone call home after a month of waiting—the watch commander didn't have time so I couldn't talk to my mother and baby. One day later I asked the Catholic Father and he let me call and my baby said hi. My mother said she'd be able to come so I can see my baby on her second birthday. (Claudia, in Miller et al., 1974: 12)

It's inspiring and energizing to see how people in prison face adversity with resilience and courage, but prison work can also be heartbreaking. For example, Kathy was a quiet twenty-five-year-old single mother who was in her second year in the California prison, serving an indeterminate sentence for repeated theft. Her six-year-old child had been placed with a foster family who lived only sixty miles from the institution, but they refused to bring her child for visits. Nor would they accept phone calls or, she later learned, give the child the cards and handcrafted gifts Kathy mailed on a regular basis. Kathy appealed to prison officials, who mumbled half-promises to "look into it" but who did not pursue it. She wrote to the probation officer who had reviewed her case at the time of her offence, and to the legal aid lawyer who had unsuccessfully defended her. Neither replied nor took any initiative to resolve the situation. Then Kathy received a court order to appear at a custody hearing two weeks hence. In a panic she sought help from a counselor who, despite a case load of 120 women, assured her that he would arrange for an escorted temporary absence from the prison so that she could attend the hearing.

One day passed without any word from the counselor, and then another and another. I attempted to intervene, as did a sympathetic guard. We were both rebuffed with the commonplace explanation that there were literally dozens of women within the institution in similar circumstances, and the administrative staff could do only so much. For Kathy they did nothing. The court date came and went, and because Kathy was not in attendance at the hearing, she lost her child to the foster/adoptive family on the grounds of "abandonment," defeated by bureaucracy and her status as a prisoner.

In sociological jargon, the "master status" of a mother in prison is not her mother identity but her criminal identity. Women's parental credentials are called into question on the grounds that no woman who has used drugs, worked as a prostitute or otherwise shown "deviant" or criminal tendencies can be a "good" mother (Zalba, 1964: 38–41). As of 1992, US courts have not yet ruled conclusively on questions of whether incarceration can be considered "evidence of parental unfitness" or whether the state can charge mothers with "abandonment" when institutionalization separates them from their children (Boudouris, 1985: 25–27; see also Beckerman, 1991; Knight, 1992: 100). In Canada, a woman may lose civil rights if she is incarcerated outside the province or territory in which action is being taken in custody matters (NPCFO, 1978: Appendix B). This issue has been identified as significant to Native women in particular, as articulated by the Manitoba "Aboriginal Justice Inquiry" Commissioners:

> Many of the women [who were interviewed] were concerned particularly that their children had been taken away from them and that their criminal involvement had led to questions being raised about their competency as parents. Many of them stated that it was in order to feed and provide for their children that they had committed their crimes in the first place, and they felt particularly wronged for having had their love and concern for their children questioned because of what they had done. (Hamilton and Sinclair, 1991a: 499)

Considerable attention has for some time been given to the effects on families of the incarceration of husbands and fathers, and support services available to them (Fishman and Cassin, 1981). However, women who are incarcerated are more likely to be parents than incarcerated men, and most incarcerated mothers are single parents. In a Canadian study which interviewed twenty-three imprisoned mothers, only one had a partner caring for her child (Solicitor General, 1992: 22). In a survey in the U.S.A. in 1989, more than three-fourths of all incarcerated women had children compared to 60 percent of the men (Greenfeld and Minor-Harper, 1991: 6).

In an examination of 1983 data on Canadian mothers in prison, Linda MacLeod estimated that approximately 2,700 women admitted to provincial jails for short-term sentences and to prisons for longer terms were separated from their children, affecting at least 5,400 children and an additional 360 newborn infants. In the early 1980s, just under half of all federal female prisoners were active mothers at the time of arrest (MacLeod, 1986: 11–12), which reflected not on greater leniency toward mothers, which has been an historical constant, but rather indicates a higher proportion of younger women in the courts. Also, more young mothers are losing their children to the state prior to arrest. For example, 69 percent of the women interviewed at the new prison in British Columbia in 1992 had at least one child, and the children of 42 percent of these women had been apprehended by authorities prior to the difficulties which led to incarceration. Women who were single mothers were most likely to lose their children: two-thirds of the single parents had lost their children, whereas one-third of the women who had been married (even if they were now divorced) or who lived common law suffered the same outcome in their parenting (Tien et al., 1993: 7).

Reformers of early British prisons attempted to separate children from their mothers because, from an administrative point of view, "a baby disorganizes the entire female prison" and, from a moralist perspective, "a child born or raised in the dismal surroundings of the prison and who remained under the influence of its criminal mother was inevitably doomed to a life of criminality itself" (Zedner, 1991: 147–48). In 1972, the first year of my research at the California Institution for Women (then holding 600 women) twenty-five babies were born to mothers in the (now closed) prison hospital. If relatives didn't come for them they were taken by the state and placed in foster homes. Most prisons for women are not large enough to have hospital facilities, so the women are transported to public hospitals to give birth, often in handcuffs and shackles. A woman at P4W is taken to the Kingston General Hospital, accompanied by matrons who stand guard throughout her labour even though the possibility of a woman escaping while in labour is nil. The baby is taken immediately upon its birth to be placed with the family or a state agency.

It is considered reasonable in several prisons in the United Kingdom for imprisoned women, particularly those who give birth in prison, to keep their infants with them (Dobash, Dobash and Gutteridge, 1986: 198; Morris, 1987: 117–19). Of eight institutions in England which hold women for more than very short terms, three accommodate babies (Padel and Stevenson, 1988: 194–96). Very few women's institutions in the United States or Canada have allowed this practice. One of the ostensible purposes of the Open Living Unit (OLU), adjacent to the Burnaby Correctional Centre for Women (BCCW), is to enable up to four women at a time to keep their infants with them up to age two, continuing the tradition established in B.C. at the now-closed Twin Maples facility which was one of just two such programs in all of Canada (the other being the Manitoba prison in Portage La Prairie).

Although it is commonly accepted that infants should be kept with their incarcerated mothers whenever possible (Hatty, 1985), in practice very few women have been able to take advantage of this option. During the several months of 1992 when I conducted interviews with women at BCCW, only one child was in residence at the Open Living Unit. A fragile token of an open parenting policy, she was lavished with affection and many women assisted with her care. Ironically, some of these same women worked in the prison child care centre which was set up for the staff; women who cannot have their children with them instead take care of the children of their guards. A similar program, often touted as a "model" day care centre, has been in place for many years at the Purdy Treatment Center for Women in Washington state (Boudouris, 1985: 14), which some observers consider to be one of the most progressive women's prisons in the United States (Glick and Neto, 1977: 218). The women who choose this work get paid prison wages, and the work itself is meaningful for them, but to the critical observer it is reminiscent of the old indenture system, whereby female prisoners were sent to "good homes" to toil as servants.

In the planned small residential facilities for women serving provincial sentences in Nova Scotia it is intended that women will have their children with them, complete with generous living quarters, a garden and ample recreation space (Solicitor General, 1992: 49–50). It is not reasonable to separate children from mothers who cannot be shown to be unfit parents, whatever crimes they may have committed. Immediate separation upon birth is at least as great a trauma for the caring mother as is her separation from older children. And to let a mother keep her child up to age two, and then take the child away, would be a serious, long-term trauma for both of them. This is a relatively moot issue in North America given the infrequency with which the policy is put into practice. The tendency of courts to show relative leniency to women who are perceived to be responsible parents is rationalized in terms of the "social costs" to the state (Bickle and Peterson, 1991; Daly, 1989; Eaton, 1986; Masson, 1992). In terms of human costs to mothers and children, alternatives to incarceration are by far the most progressive options within existing criminal justice systems.

In every women's prison, photos of their children decorate mothers' prison cells, and each letter or new drawing they receive is both a cause for celebration and a poignant reminder of their separation. As a self-help activity organized by a prisoner at P4W in the early 1980s, mothers were able to video-tape messages to their children—most of whom resided too far from the institution to visit their mothers. This could serve the important purposes of keeping the children alert to their mothers' existence and her concerns for them, and enabled the mothers to send direct expressions of their love, but such one-way, indirect communication could as easily exacerbate the pains of separation as alleviate them.

As was done at the Prison for Women, with the construction of a "little house" for weekend visits, BCCW installed a tastefully decorated and well-equipped two-bedroom apartment, complete with crib, toys and other evidence that the institution recognizes women's needs for private, homelike time with their children and/or other family members. However, many women's families are unable to come to the prison for these visits: as has been the case at P4W, women at the Burnaby Correctional Centre for Women come from very distant locations, including other provinces and the territories through Exchange of Services agreements. Given the relatively few prisons for women, the problem of distance imposes limits on children's visits with imprisoned mothers throughout North America.

James Boudouris has identified a number of variations on child-visitation programs around the world, including a program in South Dakota

where children spend one week of every month with their mother, and
"penal colonies" in developing countries on a number of continents in
which families remain together during the husband's or wife's prison sentence (Boudouris, 1985: 22). One among a number of notable North
American examples of prisoner-initiated efforts to encourage mother-child
interaction has been generated at the Bedford Hills Correctional Facility in
New York state, which has had for almost seventy years a nursery which
permits up to twelve mothers to keep their babies to age one (Ibid.: 7).
While serving time at Bedford Hills, Jean Harris, a former private school
headmistress convicted of killing her lover, Dr. Herman Tarnower (of Scars-
dale Diet fame), is credited with setting up a model Children's Centre,
including a nursery and a lively children's program, both operated by prisoners, as well as daily open visiting and a family visit trailer on the prison
grounds (Harris, 1988).

Virtually every parent-child program in penal institutions has been centreed on incarcerated mothers and their families. However, women are not
always eager to have their children locked up with them. It is not that they
don't love their children, but rather that they do not want them in a degrading
environment. Some of the women who are most concerned for their children
are wracked by guilt because, upon reflection inside the prison, they see the
ways that they neglected their children prior to their incarceration. They may
also be seeking social approval from staff and other prisoners (Hatty, 1985:
125). When mothers feel guilt it is compounded by mother-blaming ideological presumptions of women's primary maternal duty and purpose in life;
this essentialist view of women deeply affects almost all women's self-image,
given that so few women can be "perfect" mothers and that many women
cannot be or choose not to be mothers at all.

To the detriment of many good mothers and their children, the anti-feminist "fathers' rights" movement has capitalized on the recognition that
maternal custody is not always "in the best interests of the child." If this argument were carried to its logical conclusion, and if housing children in prisons
with their mothers became standard policy, we would soon see some men in
institutions demanding that their children be incarcerated with them, a
prospect fraught with disturbing possibilities. The focus on mothers reflects
the lived reality of separate spheres for men and women, which places responsibility for children on women, but just as custody of children automatically
went to fathers until late in the 19th century (Backhouse, 1991) so could

"postmodern" men assert their "fathers' rights" privileges in a way that would challenge mothers' own basic rights.

At the same time, it is a mistake to assume that every separation between mother and child is damaging to the child. To reiterate the point, to assume a private, incomparable bond between every mother and her children is to mystify motherhood as every woman's essential and highest calling. Margaret Mead (1954) was one of the first to recognize that children most benefit from extended families; if the mother isn't up to the task there are other loving people, albeit usually other women, to help with her children's care. All children need love and care, but it is not only the mother who can provide it. The Victorian nuclear family model of the absent father, and the mother in isolated domestic confinement with her children, has not proven to be healthy for families. Given the biological relationship, mothers commonly experience an instinctual bond with their children, but good parenting is an acquired art, as many "new age" fathers are discovering. Some women's prisons now offer classes in parenting skills, and this practice could extend to men's institutions.

Women who give birth in North American prisons have been commonly advised to give the child up for adoption (Haley, 1980: 347). It's a serious question as to whether prison can be an appropriate environment for children, but women serving prison time are no less likely to be loving mothers than women in any representative group on the outside. Because mothers in prison have generally had primary care for dependent children prior to incarceration (Baunach, 1985: 32; Henriques, 1981; Stanton, 1980), they face many special problems, such as: guilt about their crimes and the almost inevitably negative effects of their incarceration on their children's lives; feelings of anger and powerlessness, which are common to imprisoned women, but which are compounded when they lose custody of their children; and, anxiety about their children's care by relatives or foster families who may be unwilling or unable to facilitate communication between the children and their mother.

In one of the earliest studies of prison mothers, Brenda McGowan and Karen Blumenthal found that mothers were most satisfied when their children were with grandparents, and most stressed when they were in foster care (McGowan and Blumenthal, 1976: 126). When children are with foster families the mothers are not always informed of their whereabouts. They worry both about whether the children are being cared for, and about the children transferring their affection to their caretakers. The stereotype of "criminals" would suggest that women in prison lack a strong value system or parenting skills, but this is by no means an accurate generalization, and many women have reasonable worries that the children's caretakers will be a bad influence on them.

The mother often has no way of controlling the messages her child is receiving concerning her incarceration. The children may be told that their mother is a bad person; that's she's gone away to school or to take a holiday; that she's sick and in a hospital; that she has run away and isn't coming home; or even that she's dead (Baunach, 1985: 35). Even the relatively truthful explanation that "mummy made a mistake and must be punished" can have devastating effects on a child. Children may blame themselves for their mother's absence; they may be terrified that they'll never see her again, or angry at what they experience as abandonment. Even children who are with loving family members commonly show symptoms of being troubled as a consequence of their mother's incarceration, especially if they are stigmatized and ridiculed by peers. If the father is also in prison the problem is severely exacerbated, perhaps especially for boys (Boudouris, 1985: 4–5).

If a mother is considered a security risk, or if she has broken any of the rules applied to visitation or other institutional policies, she may be either denied visits altogether or she will have to "visit" with her children in a booth through glass and phones, with no physical contact. Some women would prefer not to see their children at all during their incarceration rather than expose them to the tensions and humiliations that accompany the usually brief and infrequent visits within a hostile prison environment. When preparing for release, women express chronic concern about both regaining their parental rights and finding a means of supporting their children. As discussed by Phyllis Baunach, this concern is exacerbated by the patterns of dependency created by incarceration which render women uncertain of their ability to assume or resume familial responsibilities, combined with fear that their children will reject them. Nevertheless, 88 percent of the mothers she interviewed intended to have their children with them upon release (Baunach, 1985: 8, 44–45). One of the key contradictions of women's prisons is the value placed on a woman's parenting skills and the inevitable disruptions to family life caused by prison itself.

> My baby was three months old
> Three years ago.
> He calls his Grandma "Mommy."
> My daughter just turned six.

She calls Aunt Marilyn
"Mommy."
My children do not know me.
I haven't seen my husband's face
Or heard his voice
In these three years.
I don't know when
I stopped loving him.
I can't love a stranger.
(Diane, in Faith, 1972: 7)

As emphasized by the 1990 Task Force in Canada, any effective strategy to address the problems of mothers who are labeled "offenders" as a result of criminal action must be enacted "within the social context and allow the problem-solving to develop in the realistic climate of the community, friends, and family" (Haley, 1980: 349). The attitude of authorities and unsympathetic agencies has been that "If she didn't want to cause all these problems for herself and her children, she should have thought of this before she did her crime." Dismissive attitudes, which implicitly deny the complexities of (gendered) power relations that result in selective criminalization and incarceration, are a way for society to not have to pay attention to yet one more serious social problem that affects truly helpless children, often for the duration of their lives.

WOMEN LOVING WOMEN

Kinsey estimated in the early 1950s that 28 percent of the female population (in the United States) had experienced a "homosexual response" with another woman and that 13 percent had been actively involved in a lesbian relationship (Kinsey et al., 1953: 474–75). We have no way of knowing how many lesbians exist in any given society, since lesbians have no identifiable physical or personality characteristics and are easily rendered invisible. The stereotypes are breaking down, and in the 1990s sexuality can be understood as a continuum of desire which is informed by socialization processes and sexual politics. Yet, many girls and women who engage in and/or desire same-sex relationships remain in the closet out of fear of ostracism or persecution, and remain invisible through assimilation within both dominant and minority cultures. Many closeted lesbians are currently or formerly married women who don't come out due to the well-founded fear of losing their children. Only recently have some courts begun to concede that lesbians can be good mothers.

The evidence is not in as to how many women have a biological orientation toward sexual preference for other women, and who feel they were "born that way." What is clear is that in the quarter century since the almost simultaneous emergence of both the Second Wave feminist movement and the lesbian and gay liberation movements, hundreds of thousands of women in Western nations have made the choice to be in lesbian relationships. They have gained visibility as a political movement and they have organized dynamic cultural communities whose headliners, activists and mass demonstrations are now receiving increasing "malestream" media attention. On the one hand, lesbianism is "in" in the 1990s. On the other hand, it is still a major cause of suicide among young girls who fear ostracism, and "old dykes" still bear the scars from generations of persecution and "treatments" for mental illness and social deviance. Prior to the 1970s, "gay bars" were one of the few places lesbians could gather to socialize, and alcohol abuse became a pervasive symptom of alienation from the dominant culture. By the 1980s, in many communities 12-step programs had become key locations for meeting other lesbians and forming "clean and sober" relationships.

Virginia Brooks found in her 1981 research that North American lesbians as a whole are healthier than other women. They are less likely than other women to be infected with sexually transmitted diseases, for example, and they rarely fall victim to cervical cancer or other illnesses related to heterosex. Since they only get pregnant when they want a child, they don't have to cope with the problems associated with birth control or abortion. They are also, in Brooks' findings, apt to be more highly educated and in better-paying jobs, and to have greater self-esteem than women at large. This latter generalization could not have been made prior to the development of the contemporary women's movement in the late 1960s and early 1970s, and it does not adequately account for continuing class divisions within the movement. Indeed, in many communities it was working-class lesbians who took the most radically feminist initiatives on behalf of women's rights. In the absence of verifiable statistics, and given the "feminine-dependence" factor in the bulk of female crime, one could readily deduce that lesbians have a low representation in women's prisons, contrary to sensationalized media-inflicted stereotypes of imprisoned women as dangerous "bull dykes."

Media projections of "lesbian" dominance in women's prisons have been fueled by academics, such as Ward and Kassebaum (1965) (discussed below), who have themselves relied on the unsupported opinions of prison administrators. Authorities at the California Institution for Women during the 1960s and 1970s estimated that between 15 and 20 percent of the prisoners were "true lesbians" at the time of admission. Their means of making this determination, however, was highly prejudicial. That is, intake staff decided whether a new prisoner was lesbian on the basis of (1) a woman's appearance, (2) whether she showed a "normal interest in the opposite sex," or (3) rumours conveyed through the paperwork of criminal justice offices and jails that handled the woman prior to long-term incarceration (Faith, 1991: 163). The determination of whether or not a new prisoner was a lesbian was usually made without asking the woman, who, in any case, given the climate of homophobia both in and out of prison, would probably have denied it.

Homophobia has been constructed through three primary discursive models which have justified persecution of gay men and lesbians in all segments of Western societies, but which have been particularly devastating for those who are institutionalized and therefore subject to professional scrutiny and discipline (Faith, 1987: 214–15; 1991: 167–68). Religious discourse has condemned "homosexuality" as sinfulness, which suggests that the evil person can be forgiven through processes of salvation and acts of repentance which include, at the very least, a commitment to celibacy. The discourses of psychologists and sociologists have relied on the paradigm of deviance to explain "homosexuality," with the presumption that those afflicted with this "social disease" are choosing their condition and can be rehabilitated through behaviour modification and counselling. Finally, medicine has labeled "homosexuality" as a diagnosable illness or disease from which one can be cured through proper treatment, including psychoanalysis, aversion therapy involving pharmaceuticals and/or electroconvulsive treatments, or, as a last resort, psychosurgery (a.k.a. lobotomies).

On the one hand, the notion that same-sex preference is a biological or genetic phenomenon can be a defence for regarding it as "natural" and therefore appropriately exempt from social control mechanisms. On the other hand, if same-sex preference is regarded as a biological "accident of nature," the afflicted person can be more vulnerable to the oppression of medical "cures." All three discourses–religion, social science, and medicine–which collectively identify same-sex activity as sin, deviance or sickness, have been applied interactively in setting policies for persons who are locked up for legal infractions which have no relevance to their sexual preference. What all these discourses have in common is a foundation of fear toward anyone who rejects the gender norms of conventional social order, and a shared (as well as competitive) propensity to underscore the controlling authority of professional judgement against the lived experience of human subjects. Within the prison environment, to be saved, rehabilitated or cured is singularly experienced as punishment.

It is a misnomer to generalize women who love women in prison as "lesbians." While in prison, however, many women learn to love one another and often, in the process, learn to love themselves, as described by a woman in the California prison:

> I never really liked women until I came here, I guess because I didn't like myself. We have so much time together, to really know each other. It's really something to have friends who know everything about you, and still like you. Until I came here, I was very ashamed of my body, but now I'm pretty damned proud of it. And I know now that there's nothing wrong with "homosexuality." I'm a woman and now I'm proud of it. It's time we all started listening to our own souls, instead of to all the perverted rules other people make up for us. (Quoted in Faith, 1991: 164)

Whatever their personal preferences and habits on the outside, and depending on the levels of institutional controls and disciplinary risks, women in prison not uncommonly learn to give and receive intimacy with one another (Faith, 1987, 1991). Imprisoned women don't turn to one another because they feel deprived in the absence of men and use other women as a substitute, which borrows from theoretical presumptions based on studies of "homosexuality" in male prisons. Rather, in an atmosphere where women are not competing for male attentions, previously heterosexual women discover that they are attracted to women in their own right.

> In here a friendship can turn to love, even though outside it would just be a good, strong friendship. And after you get love, sex is just another step. You don't have to say "C'mon, let's try it. . . ." It just happens. I learned that I don't need men. A lot of women are with men because it's all they know. (Faith, 1991: 164)

Prisons tend to intensify every emotion, and when women fall in love it can become a consuming passion even if the circumstances prevent sexual contact. As is the case with many lesbians in the "free" world, for women in prison sexual passion is often subordinate to the shared emotional comfort, social camaraderie, spiritual communion and political connectedness that can be achieved in balanced relationships.

> Sex is a very important part of a relationship—when all the barriers are gone, and you're really exposed to another person. But what is more primary is the friendship, how you share dealing with the world. Somebody to face this madness with. (Quoted in Faith, 1991: 169)

In her examination of 19th century documents, Zedner found that concern about intimacy between female "warders" (that is, guards) and female prisoners was at least as great as concern about relationships between two female prisoners. The warders who lived at the prison, and seldom ventured out, were expected to exert a positive, reforming influence on the women in their charge, which required close contact and communication. Although they were warned against "undue familiarity," cases of a warder "tampering" with a prisoner were not uncommon: "cut off from human contact with the outside world [the warders and prisoners] found sanctuary in one another from the cold hostility of prison life" (Zedner, 1991: 162). By the 20th century, vigilance against lesbianism in women's prisons had turned almost entirely to that between prisoners, as the functions of "matrons" became almost exclusively custodial and authoritarian.

Morris (1987: 126) cites a 1978 British report which claimed that, "'homosexuality' runs through the whole female 'criminal' population," but this is countered by research which emphasizes the slim evidence of lesbian activity in British prisons due to the strict prison controls which forbid and punish same-sex relationships (Dobash, Dobash and Gutteridge, 1986: 186; Genders and Player, 1986). This does not mean that women in British prisons do not find ways to achieve closeness. Take the following testimony of a woman named Margy, speaking of her prison experience in England in the early 1980s:

> I was terrified because I had never been in a proper prison before. . . . I had heard that the lasses used to beat you up when you first got in and that the lesbians used

to grab hold of you and that there was loads of violence and everything. I was really scared. . . . The lesbians didn't bother me. You can easily get done [punished] for lesbian activities. People used to lose a lot of time for that. If you've got a mate, a best mate, and she's on a different house, you'll write her a note because you hardly ever see her, and if you get caught for that you lose a couple of weeks. I got done for that. I don't know why they are so strict, because a lot of the screws [guards] are lesbians. If they knew you were friendly with someone, they would try their hardest to separate you. (Quoted in Padel and Stevenson, 1988: 53)

In the California state prison, when the admitting staff decided on the basis of appearance, demeanour or rumour that a woman was a "homosexual," this information was placed in her file (signifying "an 'H' on her jacket"), and this affected disciplinary actions during her incarceration as well as her applications for parole. The Los Angeles Sybil Brand Institute, the immense county jail in which women are incarcerated for "minor" offences with sentences of up to one year, and where many women are held prior to being sent to state prison, had a "Daddy Tank" in which "butches" were segregated from the rest of the population to avoid contamination (Faith, 1991: 168). Other US women's prisons have required women to wear differently coloured uniforms to indicate their sexual label (Burkhart, 1973: 375). In most women's prisons, anyone caught engaging in "Personal Contact" can still be punished with segregation, a threat which has the effect of causing some women to withdraw into themselves.

It magnified the loneliness to be in such a crowd and not be close to anyone, but it was dangerous to form close friendships. When two women did become close they were subject to suspicion and harassment. If two women were caught having "Personal Contact"—hugging or touching one another—they were sent directly to the hole, that is, to separate holes. (Quoted in O'Dwyer, Wilson and Carlen, 1987: 180)

In the British context, as elsewhere, "any show of affection between women in prison is in danger of being reported as a 'lesbian activity.' Discouraged thus from any form of mutual self-help, already distraught women" are further isolated from one another (Ibid.).

By contrast, Judy Clark and Kathy Boudin (1990: 95) describe the common contemporary experience of imprisoned women in many North

American institutions when they say that "There is less homophobia and denial of [intimate] relations within a women's prison" than is true of men's prisons. This is not to say that prejudices don't exist, or that close relationships are encouraged, but in some institutions special friendships between women can discreetly mature into deep love without interference. In North America the gay and lesbian liberation movements of the almost twenty-five years since the Stonewall rebellion have begun to dispel fears of "abnormality," not only relative to relationships between women locked up but also relative to the personal lives of women who work in women's institutions.

Shoshana Pollack, who conducted research on peer counselling in Canada's federal Prison for Women, confirms this advance in recognition of women's choices in forming intimate partnerships:

> Lesbian partnerships are common and fairly accepted at p4w. Many prisoners, whether or not they were lesbian identified on the street, find comfort and support in relationships with other incarcerated women. Often these partnerships are their first experiences of "unconditional love" and play a significant role in helping ease the isolation of imprisonment. (Pollack, 1993: 57)

Studies of US women's prisons in the 1960s were functionalist accounts which confuse issues of "pseudo-families" and lesbianism—although they do not use the term "lesbian" except to refer to the "perverted" women who are "homosexuals" even when they are not in prison. Rose Giallombardo studied prison "role-playing" in the US federal prison in Alderson, West Virginia, as a replication of male/female cultural roles in society at large. She described an elaborate "kinship system" whereby "homosexual alliances" constitute a "marriage unit" between "studs" and "femmes"; anyone who doesn't "turn out" is a "cherry" (Giallombardo, 1966: 128). She describes conventional husband-wife relationships where the stud has to protect "his" woman, open the door for her and perform "all the courtesies expected of gentlemen" (Ibid.: 149). The femme-wife, in turn, does the stud's laundry and housekeeping. If things don't work out, they get a divorce, at which point the femme-wife might decide to take on the stud role with yet another femme. The parodic quality of these descriptions, delivered with straight-faced academic seriousness, extends to detailed accounts of elaborate kinship links with siblings and in-laws, including avoidance of "incestuous" relationships—although Giallombardo did think she had identified one case of "incest," "between an uncle and niece" (Ibid.: 160–61, 172).

Variations on Giallombardo's analysis have been reiterated by gender-role oriented researchers trying to get a handle on intimacy between women in institutions. Barbara Carter, for example, reproduces racial stereotypes within a butch/femme model: "Whether black girls become butches because they have been socialized to be more aggressive than white girls, or are more aggressive because they have become butches, is unclear." Although groups of women both inside and outside prisons form close friendships which give them a sense of being "like a family," they do not commonly adopt strict roles which replicate actual kinship systems. Yet, with no intentional nuance of farce in her analysis of role-playing among girls in reform school, Carter states that "*Parents* assume some responsibility for socializing their *children* into the informal culture of the institution" (Carter, 1981: 422, 430, emphasis added).

David Ward and Gene Kassebaum similarly observed, following the "importation" model of analysis, that in the California state prison "Women bring to prison with them identities and self-conceptions which are based principally on familial roles as wives, mothers and daughters" (Ward and Kassebaum, 1965: 70). Since women, in contrast to men, have a need for "affectional relationships," as a "mode of adaptation" to institutional life, they turn to "homosexuality [sic] as the predominant compensatory response to the pains of imprisonment" (Ibid.: 76). They see the women's relationships as efforts to duplicate family life, with the women adopting masculine or femi- nine roles, and they note that the "unattractive" women who take on the "butch" or "stud broad" role are most vulnerable to institutional discipline, and specifically punitive segregation (Ibid.: 110). As interpreted through the gaze of these male researchers, femmes, for their part, "respond positively to the overtures of the butches and continue to be the object of love and atten- tion that they were in the heterosexual world" to which they will return (Ibid.: 115). Among other policies designed to impose feminine conformity, women "playing the masculine homosexual role were required to allow their hair to grow to a certain length" (Ibid.: 83). They were also, as women told me, required to shave their legs. As a gesture of solidarity, women identified as "femmes" also stopped shaving their legs. Most imprisoned women would have to be described as "femmes" if the stereotypes were valid, and, when tested, women prisoners do in fact score high on "femininity" scales (Morris, 1987: 39).

A number of the women with whom I conducted life history interviews in the California prison in 1972 had been "subjects" in the Ward and Kasse-baum study. Although most of these women did not identify as lesbians on the outside, most had had relationships with women in the prison and had long since overcome their own homophobias. When I showed them the published Ward and Kassebaum text, and they saw how they had been char-acterized, they responded with hilarity in some cases and chagrin and anger in others. None of them recognized themselves in the heterosexist models by which they had been categorized according to the tiresome academic par-adigms of "deprivation," "importation" and "subculture" theories, and they did not recognize the "surrogate," "make-believe" or "pseudo-" families by which their relationships were characterized. They hadn't been told that it was a study of "prison homosexuality." They critically described being inter-viewed in the administration building, where the interviewers were "protected from the real life" of the prison. They did not think of their close friendships as role-playing or as temporary "modes of adaptation," and they found the jargon ridiculous. Rather, most of these women talked freely and sometimes joyfully about how in prison they had learned to overcome their fears of loving women, and how even though most of them (particularly those with children) would probably return to men when they returned to the "free world," they didn't want their "special friendships" with women to be denigrated.

The stereotypes of lesbians presented by social "scientists" have been the fodder for ludicrous depictions of lesbians in Hollywood women's prison films, as discussed in Chapter Six. They have also, however, found their way into "respectable" accounts of women in prison, such as the work of Edna Chan-dler (1973), a California housewife, mother of five and children's fiction writer who was socially introduced to an administrator of the women's prison, became fascinated with the subject, and decided to write her first "nonfiction" book about it. Here is her fantasy, presented as fact, of a prison "stud-broad" whom she names "Jo," and Jo's encounter with a new prisoner. In a corruption of the very real phenomenon of "jailhouse turnouts" (JTOs), whereby young women have their first same-sex encounters within a prison environment, she unabashedly relies on the media myth of imprisoned lesbians as masculine and violent (Chandler, 1973: 26–30).

Jo's mannish looks, low-slung belt and masculine-style vest told only part of the story. The rest was in her strong, well-built body, her iron-muscled arms that could beat with a towel-wrapped bar of soap until her victim was unconscious, with never a bruise on her entire body.

As an attractive, high-grade butch she could have any "turned-out" woman she wanted as her homosexual partner. . . . Now she was about to pave the way for trying out another "fish" as she had tried out dozens of others.

The tension heightens in Chandler's tale when the new woman, Mary, is tested to (successfully) prove that she's not a snitch, which results in her having to spend ten days in "rack" (segregation). Soon after, Jo makes her big move—unsuccessfully, but with a "happy" ending bound to please the heterosexist reader.

"You're a doll," Jo said. "You're my people. You know?" She smiled knowingly and put her hands on Mary's breasts caressingly. Her touch was warm, affectionate. "You turned on, honey?" she asked. "No—never tried it, with a woman that is." "I could turn you on. I'm good at it! In here it's the best we got, you know. No kids gonna come from it, either."

Mary shook her head, afraid to say no but determined not to say yes. "I'm married," she answered, hoping the lie would excuse her. "So are most of the broads in here. Or have been one time or another. That don't matter."

Still Mary shook her head. "You've been good to me, Jo, and if I could be a femme for anybody it would be for you. But I can't. You see I love that guy I'm married to. . . . If I let you have me I'd be thinking of him all the time, and it just wouldn't be any good. Not for you—not for me."

It was the most talking Mary had done since she'd been there, and she was scared. No one said no to Jo on anything! And now she, Mary, a fish, had dared to say it. (Mary goes on talking.) "I'll tell you what. I won't let any other broad have me. When I've been here a long time I may change my mind. If I do, I'll let you know. OK?" Lovingly she laid her head against Jo's shoulder. Jo hugged her, kissing her affectionately, without passion. The crisis had passed.

At this point in the story the yard supervisor (guard) comes along and sternly questions the women about what they're talking about.

Jo walked away, her face a sullen mask, her hips twisting in the most sensual way she could manage.

There are enormous differences between "homosexual" relationships in men's prisons, whereby heterosexual men rape and otherwise control men perceived as effeminate (surrogate females), and women's prisons, where partnerships more often satisfy needs for intimacy. As Lee Bowker expressed with serious understatement, "Women are more likely to experience rape on the street, but it is men who are more likely to be raped while incarcerated," and he makes reference to his own and other research which gave "evidence on the prevalence and severity of homosexual rape in male correctional institutions" (Bowker, 1981: 416). It is inaccurate to refer to rape of men in prison as "homosexual" rape since it is "heterosexual" men who commit it, a point conceded in 1977 by Norman Carlson, then the federal director of US prisons, at the urging of the US National Gay Task Force. But Bowker's point is well-taken. He also observes that "Most homosexual [sic] behaviour in women's prisons occurs in a context of a loving relationship so that it is integrated into a total interpersonal experience. For men, there is little love, and the experience of overt sexuality tends to be segregated from the caring relationships that they may have with their friends" (Ibid.: 414).

Doug Chinnery, while the warden at P4W in 1979, similarly states "The women are discreet and that's why I can be tolerant." Noting that "female sexuality has none of the aggressive brutality common in men's institutions," he observes

I see warmth in women's relationships. Homosexual relationships in men's institutions are a totally different thing. . . . I suspect this issue will eventually be resolved through the use of inmate rights whereby we will finally decide whether or not inmates have the right to relieve their sexual tensions while serving very long terms. (Liaison, 1979: 23)

Chinnery's progressive attitude was in keeping with the decision in 1973 by the American Psychiatric Association that "homosexuality" is not a mental or affective disorder requiring psychiatric classification in the *Diagnostic and Statistical Manual of Mental Diseases* (DSM). However, psychiatrists at the Prison for Women in this era were not so enlightened. Kathleen Kendall (1993: 67) observes, from examination of psychiatric reports at the institution, that one psychiatrist, in 1979, listed "'gender uncertainty' and 'in-prison lesbian behaviour' among her descriptors of disordered behaviour." Another, in 1982, referred to "homosexuality" as a prevalent "vice" at P4W. Thus, the notion of women loving women as illness and perversion was sustained into the 1980s and is by no means eradicated a decade later.

In 1993, a Canadian committee examining issues related to AIDS and prisons advocates that "prison sex" should be legalized, if only for the reason that prisoners are acquiring HIV infections from clandestine liaisons within institutions. The focus of the study is on male institutions, given that men having unprotected sex with men are particularly vulnerable to sexually trans-mitted disease. As quoted in the press, "Allowing consensual sex 'should not be seen as encouraging sexual activity, but rather as discouraging unsafe behav-iour'" (*Vancouver Sun,* 1993: A9). Clearly if the arguments for supporting "safe sex" in male prisons were to affect "correctional" policy, the implications would extend to women's institutions and would serve to further reduce ves-tigial judgements against same-sex relationships between incarcerated women.

Despite greater levels of "tolerance," in 1993 gay and lesbian liberation struggles are still in the nascent stages in Western nations, including Canada and the United States, and this is reflected in prison disciplinary policies. In some Canadian provincial prisons, for example, there are "strict rules about kissing, holding hands, or being in someone else's cell" (Shaw et al., 1992: 25). Even in relatively enlightened jurisdictions, such as British Columbia, lesbians in prison are still subject to discrimination. For example, lesbians at the Burnaby Correctional Centre for Women are not generally harassed or pun-ished on the grounds of sexual preference; however, all women in the prison are restricted in their private contact with other women. Lesbians, in partic-ular, encounter difficulty in arranging visits with their partners from the outside and/or their shared children, and unlike other women they are not entitled to private family visits with their partners (Law Society of British Columbia, 1992: 8–40).

Among women who discover the benefits of same-sex partnerships within prison, those who have been least likely to remain with women upon release have been young mothers. In custody disputes, the combination of lesbianism and a criminal record has been almost a guarantee that a woman will lose her children on the grounds that she is "unfit" (Haley, 1980: 343). But despite this negative prognosis in the short term, we can celebrate recent, positive atti-tudinal changes not only among prison administrations and staff but also among incarcerated women whose discoveries ameliorate the effects of lesbo-phobic socialization.

> I admit I had my own funny ideas about [lesbians] before I went to jail that first time. I had to learn the hard way that it's not [lesbians] who are sick and hung up around sex; it's the ignorant people who are out to get them. (Quoted in Faith, 1991: 168)

Women who form long-term, stable relationships in prison help each other through every adversity, and the sadness is mutual when one or the other is released on parole.

> *you left me*
> *on a sunday night,*
> *it wouldn't be*
> *so bad, if i didn't*
> *have to face*
> *monday alone.*
> (Rose, in Miller, 1974: 13)

REFERENCES

Adams, Howard (1989) (original 1975). *Prison of Grass: Canada from a Native Point of View* (2nd edition). Saskatoon: Fifth House Publishers.

American Correctional Association (ACA) (1990). *The Female Offender: What Does the Future Hold?* Washington, D.C.

Anonymous (1976). "The Formation of the Native Brotherhood." Unpublished essay. Vancouver: University of British Columbia Archives, 1–4.

Asante, K. O. (1981). "Fetal Alcohol Syndrome in Northwest B.C. and the Yukon." *B.C. Medical Journal* 23(7): 331–35.

Backhouse, Constance (1991). *Petticoats & Prejudice: Women and Law in Nineteenth-Century Canada.* Toronto: Women's Press.

Baunach, Phyllis (1985). *Mothers in Prison.* New Brunswick: Transaction, Inc.

Beckerman, Adela (1991). "Women in Prison: The Conflict between Confinement and Parental Rights." *Social Justice* 18(3): 171–83.

Bickle, G. S. and R. D. Peterson (1991). "The Impact of Gender-Based Family Roles in Criminal Sentencing." *Social Problems* 38(3).

Boudouris, James (1985). *Prisons and Kids: Programs for Inmate Parents.* Maryland: American Correctional Association.

Bowker, Lee H. (1981). "Gender Differences in Prisoner Subcultures," in L. Bowker (Ed.), *Women and Crime in America.* New York: Macmillan, 409–19.

Brooks, Virginia (1981). *Minority Stress and Lesbian Women.* Lexington: Lexington Books.

Burkhart, Kathryn Watterson (1973). *Women in Prison.* Garden City: Doubleday & Company.

Campbell, Maria (1973). *Half-Breed.* Toronto: McClelland & Stewart.

Carter, Barbara (1981). "Reform School Families," in L. Bowker (Ed.), *Women and Crime in America.* New York: Macmillan, 419–31.

Chandler, Edna Walker (1973). *Women in Prison.* New York: Bobbs-Merrill.

Clark, Judy and Kathy Boudin (1990). "Community of Women Organize Themselves to Cope with the AIDS Crisis: A Case Study from Bedford Hills Correctional Facility." *Social Justice* 17(2): 90–109.

Correctional Services of Canada (CSC) (1983). "Native Women." *Liaison* 9(4): 2–8.

Courtrille, Lorraine (1991). *Abused Aboriginal Women in Alberta: The Story of Two Types of Victimization.* Edmonton: Misener-Margetts Women's Research Centre.

Daly, Kathleen (1989). "Rethinking Judicial Paternalism: Gender, Work-Family Relations, and Sentencing." *Gender and Society* 3(1): 9–36.

Dobash, Russell P., R. Emerson Dobash and Sue Gutteridge (1986). *The Imprisonment of Women.* Oxford: Basil Blackwell.

Eaton, Mary (1986). *Justice for Women? Family, Court and Social Control.* Milton Keynes: Open University Press.

Faith, Karlene (1972). "Interview with Diane." Unpublished mimeo, Santa Cruz.

Faith, Karlene (1982). "Love Between Women in Prison," in M. Cruikshank (Ed.), *Lesbian Studies: Present and Future.* Old Westbury: The Feminist Press, 187–93.

Faith, Karlene (1987). "Media, Myths and Masculinization: Images of Women in Prison," in E. Adelberg and C. Currie, *Too Few to Count: Canadian Women in Conflict with the Law.* Vancouver: Press Gang Publishers, 181–219.

Faith, Karlene (1991). "Sex is Always the Headliner." *Sinister Wisdom* 43–44: 160–70.

Faith, Karlene and Dawn Currie (1993). *Seeking Shelter: A State of Battered Women.* Vancouver: Collective Press.

Faith, Karlene, with Mary Gottfriedson, Cherry Joe, Wendy Leonard and Sharon McIvor (1990). "Native Women in Canada: A Quest for Justice." *Social Justice* 17(3): 167–88.

Fisher, Robin (1977). *Contact and Conflict: Indian-European Relations in British Columbia, 1774–1890.* Vancouver: University of British Columbia Press.

Fishman, Susan H. and Candace J. M. Cassin (1981). "Services for Families of Offenders: An Overview." Washington, D.C.: US Department of Justice.

Fordham, Monique (1993). "Within the Iron Houses: The Struggle for Native American Religious Freedom in American Prisons." *Social Justice* 20(1–2): 165–71.

Genders, Elaine and Elaine Player (1986). "Women's Imprisonment." *British Journal of Criminology* 26: 357–71.

Giallombardo, Rose (1966). *Society of Women: A Study of a Women's Prison.* New York: John Wiley & Sons.

Glick, Ruth M. and Virginia V. Neto (1977). *National Study of Women's Correctional Programs.* Washington, D.C.: US Department of Justice.

Goodwill, Jean (1975). *Speaking Together: Canada's Native Women.* Ottawa: Secretary of State.

Greenfeld, Lawrence A. and Stephanie Minor-Harper (1991). "Women in Prison." Washington, D.C.: US Department of Justice, Bureau of Justice Statistics.

Greschner, Donna (1992). "Aboriginal Women, the Constitution and Criminal Justice." *University of British Columbia Law Review: Special Edition on Aboriginal Justice.* 338–59.

Gunn Allen, Paula (1986). *The Sacred Hoop: Recovering the Feminine in American Indian Traditions.* Boston: Beacon Press.

Hagey, N. Janet, Gilles Larocque and Catherine McBride (1989). "Highlights of Aboriginal Conditions, 1981–2001. Part 2: Social Conditions." Ottawa: Indian and Northern Affairs Canada.

Haig-Brown, Celia (1988). *Resistance and Renewal: Surviving the Indian Residential School.* Vancouver: Tillacum Library.

Hamilton, A. C. and C. M. Sinclair (1991a). *The Justice System and Aboriginal People. Report of the Aboriginal Justice Inquiry of Manitoba*, volume 1. Winnipeg: Queen's Printer.

Hamilton, A. C. and C. M. Sinclair (1991b). *The Deaths of Helen Betty Osborne and John Joseph Harper. Report of the Aboriginal Justice Inquiry of Manitoba*, volume 2. Winnipeg: Queen's Printer.

Harris, Jean (1988). *They Always Call Us Ladies: Stories from Prison.* New York: Scribners.

Hatty, Suzanne (1985). "Maternal-Infant Incarceration: Sociological and Psychological Perspectives," in S. Hatty (Ed.), *Women in the Prison System.* Canberra: Australian Institute of Criminology, 115–58.

Headley, Bernard D. (1989). "Introduction: Crime, Justice, and Powerless Racial Groups." *Social Justice* 16(4): 1–9.

Henriques, Zelma Weston (1981). *Imprisoned Mothers and Their Children.* Washington, D.C.: University Press of America.

Hnatiuk, Rosemary (1985). "Treatment of Native and Other Visible Minorities in the Judicial System." Unpublished essay. Manitoba: Hand-to-Hand Distribution.

Holmes, Joan (1987). "Bill C-31: Equality or Disparity? The Effects of the New *Indian Act* on Native Women." Ottawa: Canadian Advisory Council on the Status of Women.

Humana, Charles (1992). *World Human Rights Guide.* New York: Oxford University Press.

Indian and Northern Affairs Canada (INAC) (1989). "Basic Departmental Data, 1989." Ottawa: Minister of Supply and Services Canada.

Jackson, Michael (1989). "Locking Up Natives in Canada." *University of British Columbia Law Review* 23(2): 215–300.

Jamieson, Kathleen (1978). *Indian Women and the Law in Canada: Citizens Minus.* Ottawa: Minister of Supply and Services Canada.

Jolly, Stan and Joseph Peter Seymour (1983). "Anicinabe Debtors' Prison." Toronto: Ontario Native Council on Justice.

Kendall, Kathleen (1993). "Literature Review of Therapeutic Services for Women in Prison." Ottawa: Ministry of the Solicitor General, Corrections Branch.

Kinsey, A., W. Pomeroy, C. Martin and P. Gebhard (1953). *Sexual Behavior in the Human Female.* Philadelphia: W. B. Saunders Company.

Kirkness, Verna (1987–88). "Emerging Native Woman." *Canadian Journal of Women and the Law/Revue juridique "La femme et le droit"* 2(2): 408–15.

Knight, Barbara B. (1992). "Women in Prison as Litigants: Prospects for Post-Prison Futures." *Women & Criminal Justice* 4(1): 91–116.

Law Society of British Columbia (1992). *Gender Equality in the Justice System,* volume 2. Vancouver: Gender Bias Committee.

Leland, Joy (1978). "Women and Alcohol in an Indian Settlement." *Medical Anthropology* 2(4): 85–119.

Liaison (1979). "The Female Offender/La délinquante." *Liaison: Monthly Journal for the Criminal Justice System* 5(2): 2–36. [Ottawa: Ministry of the Solicitor General.]

MacLeod, Linda (1986). *Sentenced to Separation: An Exploration of the Needs and Problems of Mothers Who Are Offenders and Their Children.* Ottawa: Solicitor General of Canada.

Masson, Karen (1992). "Familial Ideology in the Courts: The Sentencing of Women." Unpublished Master's Thesis. Burnaby: Simon Fraser University.

McGowan, Brenda G. and Karen L. Blumenthal (1976). "Children of Women Prisoners: A Forgotten Minority," in L. Crites (Ed.), *The Female Offender.* Lexington: Lexington Books, 121–35.

Mead, Margaret (1954). "Some Theoretical Considerations on the Problem of Mother-Child Separation." *American Journal of Orthopsychiatry* 24.

Miller, Debra and twenty-two women in the California Institution for Women (1974). *no title at all is better than a title like that!* Santa Cruz: Women's Prison Project.

Miller, J. R. (1991). "The Northwest Rebellion of 1885," in J. R. Miller (Ed.), *Sweet Promises: A Reader on Indian-White Relations in Canada.* Toronto: University of Toronto Press.

Monture, Patricia (1986). "Ka-Nin-Geh-Heh-Gah-E-Sa-Nonh-Yah-Gah." *Canadian Journal of Women and the Law/Revue juridique "La femme et le droit"* 2(1): 159–71.

Monture, Patricia (1989). "A Vicious Circle: Child Welfare and the First Nations." *Canadian Journal of Women and the Law/Revue juridique "La femme et le droit"* 3(1): 1–17.

Morris, Allison (1987). *Women, Crime and Criminal Justice.* Oxford: Basil Blackwell.

National Planning Committee on the Female Offender (NPCFO) (1978). "The Female Offender." Ottawa: Solicitor General of Canada.

O'Dwyer, Josie, Judi Wilson and Pat Carlen (1987). "Women's Imprisonment in England, Wales and Scotland: Recurring Issues," in P. Carlen and A. Worrall (Eds.), *Gender, Crime and Justice.* Milton Keynes: Open University Press, 176–90.

Padel, Una and Prue Stevenson (1988). *Insiders: Women's Experience of Prison.* London: Virago Press.

Pollack, Shoshana (1993). "Opening the Window on a Very Dark Day: A Program Evaluation of the Peer Support Team at the Kingston Prison for Women." Unpublished Master's Thesis. Ottawa: Carleton University.

Priest, Lisa (1989). *Conspiracy of Silence.* Toronto: McClelland & Stewart.

Shaw, Margaret, with Karen Rodgers, Johanne Blanchette, Lee Seto Thomas, Tina Hattem, and Lada Tamarack (1990). "Survey of Federally Sentenced Women." Ottawa: Ministry of the Solicitor General, Corrections Branch.

Shaw, Margaret with Karen Rodgers, Johanne Blanchette, Tina Hattem, Lee Seto Thomas and Lada Tamarack (1992). *Paying the Price: Federally Sentenced Women in Context.* Ottawa: Ministry of the Solicitor General, Corrections Branch.

Silman, Janet (as told to) (1987). *Enough is Enough: Aboriginal Women Speak Out.* Toronto: Women's Press.

Singer, Beverly (1992). "American Indian Women Killing: A Tewa Native Woman's Perspective," in J. Radford and D. E. H. Russell (Eds.), *Femicide: The Politics of Woman Killing.* New York: Twayne Publishers.

Solicitor General (1992). *Blueprint for Change: Report of the Solicitor General's Special Committee on Provincially Incarcerated Women.* Halifax: Province of Nova Scotia.

Stanton, Ann M. (1980). *When Mothers Go to Jail.* Lexington: Lexington Books.

Statistics Canada (1989). "Profile of Ethnic Groups." Document 93–154.

Statistics Canada (1993). *Aboriginal Peoples Survey.* Ottawa: Ministry of Supply and Services Canada.

Sugar, Fran and Lana Fox (1989–90). "Nistum Peyako Séht'wawin Iskwewak: Breaking Chains." *Canadian Journal of Women and the Law/Revue juridique "La femme et le droit"* 3(2): 465–82.

Sugar, Fran and Lana Fox (1990). "Survey of Federally Sentenced Aboriginal Women in the Community." Ottawa: Native Women's Association of Canada.

Tien, George, Lynda Bond, Diane Lamb, Brenda Gillstrom, Faye Paris and Heidi Worsfold (1993). "Report on the Review of Mental Health Services at Burnaby Correctional Centre for Women." Vancouver: B.C. Forensic Psychiatric Services Commission.

US Department of Commerce (1992). "Resident Population by Race and Hispanic Origin." *Statistical Abstract.* Washington, D.C.: Bureau of the Census.

Vancouver Sun (1993). "AIDS Fight: Report Urges Legalizing of Prison Sex" (July 24): A9.

Ward, David and Gene Kassebaum (1965). *Women's Prison: Sex and Social Structure.* Chicago: Aldine Publishing Company.

Yerbury, Colin (1992). "Native North Americans and Alcohol Studies," in C. Yerbury and K. Faith, *Minorities and the Criminal Justice System.* Burnaby: Simon Fraser University, School of Criminology and Centre for Distance Education, 89–121.

Zalba, Serapio R. (1964). *Women Prisoners and Their Families.* Sacramento: Departments of Social Welfare and Corrections.

Zedner, Lucia (1991). *Women, Crime, and Custody in Victorian England.* Oxford: Clarendon Press.

CHAPTER FIVE

Institutionalized
Violence

ELSEWHERE I have discussed media exaggerations of violence by prisoners in North American women's prisons (Faith, 1987; also see Chapter Six). In this chapter I begin with that theme in the context of male/female comparisons. It is not only the media that capitalize on the myth that an innate, generalizable female propensity for violence is let loose inside women's prisons. This view is similarly put forth, by inference or explicitly, by academics, by prison authorities and sometimes by prisoners who have themselves internalized fears of other women. My interest in the first section of this chapter is to put that view to rest.

Whereas women entering prison do not generally have to fear other women, there are forms of violence in women's institutions which require vigilance, and medical practices are among them. Although we can assume that most health practitioners strive to meet the ethical obligations of their professional commitments, given the nature of institutions certain practices by doctors and psychiatrists who work in prisons are more akin to the coercion of punishment and the dehumanization of prisoners than to healing wounded bodies, minds and spirits. Prisons serve a primarily custodial function; thus, in this chapter, I also discuss institutionalized assaults by line staff on prisoner's bodies which are conducted in the name of security.

Although women do not commonly endanger one another within institutions many do cause harm to themselves through the need to find an outlet for their intense frustrations and griefs. "Slashing," or self-mutilation, is one manifestation of this inability to direct anger at more appropriate targets, and the women who engage in this form of self-injury commonly have histories of childhood sexual abuse. Particular attention is given to Marlene Moore who, in Canada, has become a symbol of the tragedy of childhood victimization resulting in self-destruction. The final two sections of this chapter focus on sexual assault of incarcerated girls and women by staff, an uncommon occurrence but an important indicator of the corruption of power within penal institutions.

COMPARING MEN AND WOMEN

Historically, in England, imprisoned women were characterized as fundamentally disorderly and were described by officials as resisting confinement by breaking out in a frenzy, which involved throwing things, breaking windows, tearing up clothes, and "yelling, shouting or singing as if they were maniacs" (Zedner, 1991: 208). In the 19th century one official declared that it was "a well-established fact in prison logistics that the women are far worse than the men. When given to misconduct they are far more persistent in their evil ways, more outrageously violent, less amenable to reason or reproof" (Ibid.: 210).

This view persists. Observers of contemporary British women's prisons likewise characterize female prisoners as having "By far the highest rates of offences against prison discipline" (Heidensohn, 1985: 73), and insist that "There is much violence in the adult women's closed prisons at Holloway and Styal" (O'Dwyer, Wilson and Carlen, 1987: 178). Most seriously, respected scholars have issued such statements as "Violence and disturbance seem more prevalent in female institutions" (Heidensohn, 1985: 82). The issue is worthy of serious context-specific debate, because the notion that women are more violent than men promotes essentialist views of women's evil "nature" and supports stereotypes of "criminal" women as dangerous and therefore appropriately imprisoned even for minor offences. The promotion of the idea that women in prison are more violent than men is analogous to arguments that women in the home assault their husbands as often as the reverse, as discussed in Chapter Two. In both cases, the evidence is spurious and the effect is to obfuscate the pervasiveness and significant effects of male violence as a socially constructed gendered phenomenon.

It is in the interests of penal authorities to characterize imprisoned women as violent. Perpetrating that image not only justifies the women's incarceration, it also invests the job of guarding them with special risk and importance. It is in the interests of prison critics to focus on prison violence insofar as that image illuminates the barbarity inherent in lock-up institutions—a barbarity which in women's institutions is more psychological than physical, and imposed not by prisoners but by the institution. Certainly for commercial entertainment value it is in the interests of the media to play up whatever violence does occur, and to use fictional devices to present women as monsters.

Women who are locked up may themselves exaggerate the threat of violence, speaking not from measured reality but from their own fears. The very idea of it adds a component of negative excitement to the normally boring prison experience, and many enter prison with media-induced paranoia that they will be attacked. First-term prisoners who are homophobic, and who harbour images of masculine "bull dykes" using Coke bottles to rape "normal" women (see Chapter Six), would seem to be the most paranoid of all during the initial months of their incarceration. This phenomenon echoes concerns of elderly women in the larger society; they have the highest level of fear of street crime of any social group because they are so vulnerable, but in terms of random offences by strangers they have the lowest victimization rate, due primarily to their cautious and restricted lifestyles (Fattah and Sacco, 1989; Hanrahan, 1993). But mythologies aside, apart from exceptional events between women and less exceptional but still unusual abuses by authorities, women's prisons are truly placid environments compared to most male institutions, where neither one-on-one incidents nor group rebellions are uncommon. Advocates of co-ed prisons (as well as advocates of female staff in male institutions), who see that women have a "civilizing" effect on men, understand this very well.

"Common sense" might suggest that women serving sentences for crimes of violence would be responsible for whatever violence does occur in women's prisons, but as a woman serving life for murder in Canada has written.

> Short-termers are usually the ones who get into fights. . . . In fact most of the trouble-makers and segregation occupants are the prisoners doing short time. The warden will tell you that the lifers are the most agreeable, stable and well-behaved group in the prison. (Walford, 1987: 15, 98)

Observation and opinions expressed to me by prison officials and staff confirm that women doing long sentences for murder are their most peaceful "inmates." However, even in jails, where women tend to be younger, more transient (such as serving weekends for public drunkenness or disorder), and generally rowdier than older women serving long-term prison sentences, one could not say that they are more disruptive than their male counterparts. Even the problem of "snitching," whereby a prisoner reports another prisoner's breach of prison rules in the hope of earning some favour, a problem which often leads to violence, is frequently endemic in men's institutions and usually very rare among women. Certainly, in every women's prison, there are some aggressively angry women (usually young and new to the institution, but not always), or normally stable women who lose their cool, who push, slap, punch or, much more rarely, stab, burn or otherwise seriously assault other prisoners or staff (see Faith, 1987). However, confined women much more commonly present danger to themselves than to others, and I will return to this theme below. As one woman said, after five years in P4W, "Stabbing [or the equivalent] is so rare that I can only remember one in two and a half years. . . . There are no big bad bullies that go around beating up people—when a fight happens there is usually a cause and there is seldom an actual physical fight. Usually it's a lot of screaming and threatening" (Anon., 1983: 19).

Although it strains credulity, defies gender analysis and challenges empirical evidence to say that women are more violent than men, reliable research does show that women who are imprisoned in Britain are "twice as likely [as men] to be punished for 'disobedience or disrespect'" (Sim, 1991: 121). This is predictable given the social expectations that women should be better behaved than men even if "reasonableness" is not in their "nature." Researchers who emphasize that "violent" incidents are more frequently noted on the prison records of women than of men observe that "women prisoners get nicked for trivial offences which would be overlooked in the men's prisons" (O'Dwyer, Wilson and Carlen, 1987: 179).

If men in prison beat up and rape each other it receives little attention because it is so commonplace. Exaggerated perceptions of female violence are formed because when two women get into a serious physical fight it is a noteworthy event. Take the example of a woman who was assaulted for "snitching" in 1972 in the California prison which, at the time, held over 600 women, including many young and rambunctious first-timers. It was rumoured throughout the institution that the woman was stabbed and that in the process of the disturbance a number of other "residents" and staff had been hurt. The rumours were false, but the facts of the case were deemed by the administration to be sufficiently serious to warrant front page "headlines" in the prison "Daily Bulletin." This mimeographed newsletter was distributed to everyone incarcerated in or employed by the prison and the story underscored the extraordinary quality of the incident. After assuring the population that no one had been stabbed, and that only the woman in question had been injured, the administration continued:

> One rumour is not unfounded, and that is the fact that both the staff and residents are outraged over the beating made upon our resident, a beating which has miraculously led to only a few contusions and bruises incurred by our resident, but which has made us all victims and has left deep wounds. . . . Many of us—both residents and staff—are now ready to admit our collective guilt over this incident. . . . Like many of you, we too are afraid. But you can be assured that we will not let fear stand in our way to attempt to find solutions which will maximize everyone's physical safety. Suggestions on how to reach this goal will be appreciated and are encouraged. (ciw, 1972: 3)

Following the story, by way of emphasizing the issue of "collective guilt" and seeking to inspire a collective solution, the administration postscripted the article with the 17th century poetry of John Donne: "No man Is an island . . . any man's death diminishes me/ because I am involved in mankind/ and therefore never send to know/ for whom the bell tolls/ it tolls for thee." Two decades later the population of this prison has tripled and the tensions have increased. Conflicts are commonplace, including physical confrontations among an increasingly younger population. But it is still the undercurrent of fear and petty, arbitrary and "catch-22" disciplinary policies that dominate the atmosphere, not violence by women against other women.

In Canada women are most often "disciplined" for such infractions as "using a radio without headphones; sitting in the cell of another inmate; having extra clothes in the cell; possession of 'contraband' (e.g., having a tomato or lemonade mix in the cell) . . . using bad language" and so on. The women who receive the most disciplinary charges are most commonly younger women with previous convictions, and Native women (Shaw et al., 1992: 25–26). One can concur with most critics that "prison regimes and management practices themselves play a significant part in [the] production" of what are considered disciplinary problems in women's institutions (Ibid.: 32).

Joe Sim found that staff in women's prisons in Britain are not only quick to "write up" institutional infractions, but also that women are strip-searched more often than men, they are given more drugs as a means of controlling unruly behaviour, and they are much more likely to receive psychiatric labels (Sim, 1991: 120–21). Because women are generalized and stereotyped as inherently unstable emotionally, those who commit crime in some jurisdictions never make it to prison, but are instead diverted into mental treatment programs. Indeed, as Hilary Allen found in Britain, women who appear in court are "about twice as likely as a man to be dealt with by psychiatric rather than penal means" (Allen, 1987: xi), and at the sentencing stage this is interpreted as leniency. It has been the tradition in California since the 1950s that those who are sent to prison are treated contradictorily as both bad and mad: they must be punished for their law-breaking and because, in the words of a prison psychiatrist "females have more mental problems than males" (ASCC, 1977: 159), they must be disciplined through treatment to acquire the habits of emotional stability.

Given the extreme repressiveness of all prisons, and given the ways by which men are socially encouraged to aggressively defend themselves against real or perceived indignities, male prisons are by their very nature explosive environments. In my work with incarcerated men (Faith, 1975), I have been witness to the raw, physical violence against others (to the point of death) which critics agree is structurally inherent to maximum security prisons occupied by men. Organized acts of aggression in male prisons are commonly a protest against actual injustices, but they often result in violent chaos and it is relevant that it is men who "act out" in this way. It is expected of them and they oblige. Women's institutions have received much less attention than men's in part because there are so many fewer women in prison and because their offences are of a relatively minor nature. But women have also been "the forgotten minority" because they haven't called attention to themselves with the kind of disruptions that have been common to men's prisons.

When a woman acts up in prison she's singled out as a trouble-maker and given behaviour-modifying drugs; when men act up it may be the prelude to a prison war. Riots in male prisons are significant as political events, usually culminating in a set of demands for reforms which are seldom implemented. Highly publicized examples for which there is no female equivalent include a 1967 riot at San Quentin in California which involved nearly 2,000 prisoners. A subsequent string of major uprisings at US and Canadian men's prisons began in 1971 with a four-day uprising at the Attica prison in New York, which resulted in the deaths of thirty-two prisoners and eleven guards and civilians, most as a consequence of lethal firing by state forces (NYSSCA, 1972). This event was "book-ended" in 1980 with a riot at the New Mexico men's penitentiary in which thirty-three prisoners were killed by other prisoners (Weiss, 1991: 1–3).

During 1975 and 1976, peak years of prisoners' rights activism, there were sixty-nine major "disturbances" in male prisons in Canada alone, and thirty-nine of these involved hostage-taking (Lowman and MacLean, 1991: 138). All of these "incidents" involved risk to or actual loss of human life. Men in prison not uncommonly have shivs (self-crafted knives) hidden in their cells. If a paring knife goes missing from the kitchen of a women's prison the whole institution goes into an emergency lock-up until it is located (ASCC, 1977: 28–29). Women in the California prison had a Christmas "riot" in 1975 when, for unexplained "security" reasons, the administration cancelled family holiday visits and decided that the women couldn't receive packages. Christmas is the most emotionally laden time of the year in prisons, and the women protested by gathering together in the yard, breaking a number of windows, making a lot of noise, and burning their Christmas trees in a "solidarity" bonfire. No one threatened physical violence and no one was hurt. When men riot they destroy the prison and often human life in the process.

By way of anecdotal contrast, in 1972, while doing research in the California women's prison, I was "taken" as a "friendly hostage" in a solidarity attempt by approximately fifty racially mixed women, who gathered in a dayroom to plot negotiations with the administration over what were perceived to be "cruel and unusual" cell and body searches. Among other grievances, guards had flushed pet fish down the toilet, and had confiscated personal items of sentimental value, including letters and photographs. The women were particularly angry because several women had been sent to "rack" on suspicion of harbouring contraband drugs, though there was no evidence this was the case. During the several hours that I was "held" by the women, during which time no one touched me, I was permitted by the organizers to continue with my interviews in a private corner. Everyone else continued to discuss their strategies and to entertain each other with music and polemics. In the end, the female "superintendent" (a.k.a. warden) agreed to schedule a meeting to hear their complaints, the women under suspicion were released from solitary confinement, and the women cheerfully thanked me for my cooperation before armed male guards escorted me out of the institution. When I returned the following day to continue with interviews everything was back to normal.

At P4W in 1991, forty-three women engaged in a highly publicized three-hour "riot," which was the most serious disruption in that prison in many years. Yet another Native woman, twenty-three years old, had committed suicide by hanging herself in her cell. Serving a two-year sentence for robbery, she was the fourth Native woman to kill herself in a sixteen-month period. Of the forty-three women who refused to carry on with their normal prison routine, twenty expressed their angry grief by barricading themselves in the recreation room, and the state responded by sending in prison guards with tear gas and attack dogs. The prisoners had no weapons and were not threatening violence against anyone. No one was injured in the melée. But because the prison officials called their action a "riot," which, by the terms of the *Criminal Code,* constitutes an offence warranting two years' imprisonment, all the "offenders" were placed in lock-up and were liable to time added to their original sentence (Faith, 1991: 190–91).

The recent rash of suicides by Native women incarcerated in Canada's Prison for Women is a commentary on imprisonment just as it is indicative of the oppressions against Native peoples in Canadian society at large. It is also, however, directly related to the history of personal physical and sexual abuse which has been inflicted on these women. Whereas male-dominant discourses commonly treat violence against women as an individualized problem of disturbed or pathological men, many men have themselves begun to recognize the systemic nature of these common (usually unprosecuted) crimes of power imbalance. A male guard who, after over twelve years working with men in prisons in England was transferred to the Holloway Women's Prison, was distressed to discover that most of the women in his charge had been abused, and that a history of abuse was often the precipitator of self-mutilation. In a documentary film in which he laments the thirty-six suicide attempts which had occurred in the prison in the preceding year, he comments: "Sometimes I feel ashamed for my gender because it's men who have done this to women" (First Tuesday Unit, 1992).

In terms of day-to-day prison disruptions, Lee Bowker reviewed selected 1970s US prison studies and concluded that male prisoners, compared to females, "were characterized by a problem with authority." He notes "a steady increase in the percentage of violent crimes committed by men as a prelude to incarceration and a parallel increase in violent crimes committed by men against fellow prisoners and staff." He summarily observed that "victimization rates of all types (physical, psychological, economic and social) seemed to be higher in male than in female correctional institutions" (Bowker, 1981: 410, 414, 417).

Men who enter prison enter an active combat zone. Women who enter prison are usually physically safer than they are on the outside. As we approach a new era toward understanding the abuses that are committed against male as well as female children, we will perhaps come closer to recognizing that adult male-on-male violence requires no less sensitivity or commitment to healing than the violences imposed by adult males against females and children, and that these are not separate issues. In Canada, as discussed in Chapter Two, men are responsible for approximately 90 percent of all reported violent offences, against women, children and other men; over 98 percent of all sexual assaults are committed by men; and so on (CCJS, 1991). If we want to prevent violence against women and children, which is facilitated by power relations rooted in patriarchal ideologies, men must learn the unacceptability of violence against one another. Prison environments are not conducive to learning that lesson.

MEDICAL PRACTICES

Medical "care" has been both deficient and abusive in women's institutions (see, for example, Shaw, 1982), and many (certainly not all) psychiatrists have been among the worst offenders. When beginning my research in the California prison, in the early 1970s, I discovered that the psychiatrist there creatively blended Freudian symbolism with literal interpretations of Lombrosian biological determinism to explain "female deviance": from his perspective virtually any crime committed by a woman had a sexual origin. He was specifically obsessed with Freud's theory of "penis envy," as illustrated by his diagnoses of two particular women's problems as recorded in their official institutional files. A young woman convicted of possession of heroin was clearly, in his view, a victim of penis envy: the needle she used to inject heroin into her body was her penis substitute. In the case of a woman convicted of writing bad cheques, the pen she used for this purpose was her phallic symbol, and proof of her desire to be in possession of the male power tool. Such anachronistic and sexist diagnoses were clearly not useful to women who could have used some help.

Because prisons are the dead-ends of society it is unreasonable to expect the people who run them to be able to address all the problems that lead to them. At the same time, it's not reasonable that both male and female (but especially female) prisoners who need counselling or psychiatric care (in part due to their

incarceration) have been silenced with tranquilizers and psychotropic drugs
(Resnik and Shaw, 1983), and that physicians and psychiatrists have been yet
another coercive arm of the custodial staff (Glick and Neto, 1977: 67–69). There
is a fundamental contradiction between the authoritarian and punitive functions
of prisons and the non-judgemental basis of a therapeutic environment. Psychiatrists cannot respond to women's psychological needs when they are required to
report rule infractions to the higher authorities, undermining any possibility of a
"patient's" right to confidentiality. Prisoners, for their part, resist staff efforts to
gain their confidence because they realize there can be no reciprocity of trust.

Many women are grateful for any magic chemical prescription (or smuggled street drugs) that can help them cope. Often women who have had to go
"cold turkey" from street addictions aggressively ask for medication, and are
assisted by medical personnel into pharmaceutical addictions, which in turn
supports an underground in-prison drug market (ASCC, 1977: 110, 160–71).
In the California prison just one extra mind-altering pill could be bartered for
as much as three packages of cigarettes. Increased understanding over the past
decade and a half of the harmful effects of prescription drugs has made medical personnel in many institutions, including the health staff of the new
Burnaby Correctional Centre for Women, more cautious. But given the institutional order that can be achieved through chemical pacification of the
prisoners, this is not a problem that will just go away.

Jessica Mitford's muckraking exposé of medical experiments on prisoners
(1973) documented the widespread convergence of medical and penal discourses in US prisons, where pharmaceutical companies tested drugs on
incarcerated men and women with highly detrimental effects. At the California prison, I interviewed a long-term prisoner who had volunteered for an
experimental program, sponsored by the federal Food and Drug Administration, which combined hypnotic suggestion with the drug Anectine. The
hoped-for result was to free people from illegal drug addictions (in yet another
form of Alice-in-Wonderland logic, as in "methadone maintenance" programs
in the "free" world for heroin addicts). She signed up because she was paid for
her participation, she admired the researcher, she wanted to rid herself of crav-
ings for her illegal "drugs of choice," and she was convinced that it was a way
to aid humanity and therefore to offer restitution to the society she had
offended as a dealer of (illegal) pharmaceutical drugs. However, she didn't
know what she was getting into. The effect of the Anectine was to cause temporary (ninety-second) cessation of breathing and paralysis, and several years

after the (failed) experiment she still awoke in the night with breathing problems, in terror that she was dying.

Medical intervention extends to many facets of prison life. Take tattoos, for example. By the 1990s, decorative tattoos (which originated in the South Pacific and were popular among sailors) have become fashionable throughout the Western world. Traditionally, they have been a key means by which Western "deviants" in general, and prisoners in particular, could lay claim to their own bodies, as well as signify their identification with outcast culture. Among criminologists from the time of Lombroso, who took a great interest in tattoos, they have signified criminal stigmata. In 1971, 300 women in the California prison (then half the prison population) underwent procedures to remove tattoos and moles, having been convinced that this would make them appear more attractive and feminine (Chandler, 1973: 92). The men wielding the knife were students from the medical school of the nearby University of California at Los Angeles, who were learning fundamental techniques of cosmetic surgery and needed human guinea pigs.

More seriously, at this same prison in 1970, fifty-four women, almost all of them white, were given "nose jobs" by the UCLA medical students (Ibid.). They, too, were persuaded by the authorities that it would make them more attractive, in keeping with the hegemonic "feminine" appearance imperative. Unfortunately, from my own observation, the medical students must have been operating from a single pattern. That is, all fifty-four women came out with pretty much the same nose: it suited some, it didn't suit others. It was a running joke among women at the institution that you could always recognize "the CIW nose." In one pathetic case, the woman's nose became infected and the tip of her nose literally dropped right off. She not only looked strange, she also had constant nasal irritation, and nothing was done to correct it.

Inadequate medical care has been a chronic issue among critics of prisons, and abuses have been commonplace. For example, in California during the 1970s, hysterectomies (the surgical removal of the source of "female hysteria") were indiscriminately performed on women by general practitioners in retirement from military careers who had virtually no experience in gynecology (ASCC, 1977: 9, 110). The prison hospital in which these surgeries were performed was finally closed for lack of accreditation.

As an anecdotal example of how medical abuse (or, more accurately in this case, neglect) becomes a component of the punishment system, a woman I interviewed who had a serious "club-foot" limp explained that some years previous she was trying to escape by climbing the high perimeter fence but was foiled in her attempt, and when she dropped to the ground she broke several bones in her foot. Screaming for help, she was picked up by the guards, put into segregation, and her pleas for medical attention were dismissed with "You made your bed, now lie in it," a frequent retort when women protested perceived injustice (another being "You did the crime, now do the time—and don't complain about it"). She consequently lived with her interminable punishment: a permanent limp and chronic pain.

IN THE NAME OF SECURITY

When I speak of "institutionalized violence" I am concerned with institutional dangers presented to prisoners by the unchecked "authority" of abusive employees who are themselves over-institutionalized. Exceptionally abusive people are a distinct minority among "correctional officers" but those who are guilty can cause incalculable harm. Examples abound of systematic abuse against people confined to institutions, and in prisons the most frequent and insidious of these harms are those justified in the name of security and punishment for institutional infractions. In a major understatement, a member of an investigative committee said of strip-searching in the California prison, "the undressing of women in the 'quiet room' by male guards is demeaning" (ASCC, 1977: 191).

In male prisons, convicted child molesters and rapists are the pariahs among the more respectable lawbreakers. Among female prisoners, those convicted of any form of sexual assault are a tiny minority, if they are present at all. The rare, anomalous women who are convicted of killing, molesting or otherwise harming children and young people are not commonly physically attacked, but they may be ostracized by other prisoners or placed in "protective" custody, which usually means solitary confinement.

Ordinarily there's no relationship between the nature of one's crime and the punishment of super-maximum security segregation units, the prison within the prison (a.k.a. "dissociation unit," "protective-" or "administrative-custody," "adjustment cell," "quiet room" or "isolation," or, in prisoner vernacular, "seg," "hole," "digger," "dungeon" or "rack"). Women who have harmed children may be "protected" by isolation, as may women who have "ratted" to the staff on other prisoners' institutional infractions. But any disorderly or uncooperative prisoner might gain direct knowledge of the inhumanity of foul segregation units in which prisoners are strip-searched; kept in virtual cages under bright lights and camera surveillance; have food pushed through a slot at the bottom of the bars; are denied privacy for toilet activity; are harassed, ridiculed and humiliated by uncaring guards; are denied visits with their children and other family members; and are otherwise subjected to the indignities of extraordinary powerlessness within already-disempowering circumstances.

In their experience of the pains and degradations of segregation, and in other features of incarceration, women share almost everything in common with men in prison. During the 1970s male prisoners in North America took the first initiatives in filing one court case after another, to protest the inhumane conditions of the institutions in which they were incarcerated. Paradoxically, in this same era, female prisoners began to file gender discrimination appeals in the courts, pleading for reforms on the grounds that they lacked equal rights with incarcerated men relative to, for example, classification; vocational, educational and recreational programs; condition and diversity of facilities; visitation rights; and health care (see, for example, Muraskin, 1993). Given that women cannot be seen as "similarly situated" with men in the larger society, given their special needs as an historically oppressed group and, especially, as primary caretakers of children, there has been considerable merit to the spirit of these legal challenges. However, if we view prisons in their concrete totality and recognize the sustained conditions of dehumanization in men's institutions, one can only conclude that imprisonment is one arena in which it is foolhardy to plead for gender equality. Equal misery cannot be perceived as a social advance for women or anyone.

Elie Wiesel, the renowned author and survivor of the mid-20th century Holocaust (in which an estimated 6 million Jews and uncounted homosexuals, gypsies, mentally ill and physically disabled people were tortured, burned, slaughtered and starved to death), speaks of how, in order to detach themselves from the horror, people learned to hold their spirit separate from their body. In the preceding chapter I quote Fran Sugar, who speaks likewise of keeping her spirit alive in her "physical shell." Therapists working with survivors of childhood sexual abuse also attest to the pervasiveness of this ability to "dissociate" as a psychic survival strategy. Indeed, it is a familiar adage in prison communities that "they can take my body but they can't take my mind [or soul]." But this is often more a battle cry than a statement of fact. Despite the prevalence of such testimony, for many women the body/mind/soul can't be separated, and for such women one of the most devastating aspects of imprisonment is indeed losing control over one's own body. A woman in California in the first year of a five-years-to-life sentence for selling marijuana, for whom incarceration was intolerable, was unsuccessful in a suicide attempt. The response of the authorities was to teach her just how complete was her loss. As she recounted to me in an interview:

> As soon as the hospital released me, I was sent before the Disciplinary Board. It's against the rules to attempt to kill yourself, and the Board sentenced me to 30 days in solitary detention—a very long, lonely thirty days. The only human being I saw in that time was the matron who brought the food around. By the time I was released from the "quiet room" I was so withdrawn I couldn't communicate with other people, so my closed custody status, where I could only leave my cell to go to work and to the Central Feeding Unit, was extended by six months.

The claiming of the prisoner's body begins with admission and is unremitting for the duration of imprisonment. As Jose-Kampfner noted from interviews with women serving life sentences in the United States, "cavity searches" cause a "humiliation that they never get used to" (1990: 112). Russell Dobash, Rebecca Dobash and Sue Gutteridge similarly note that women imprisoned in the United Kingdom "found body searches increasingly hard to bear" (1986: 204). For the women who experience it, a forced vaginal exam is tantamount to state-authorized rape, and torturing and shaming women in this way seems clearly intended to reinforce their dehumanized, prisoner status. The following excerpted text, by Lyn Mac-Donald, accompanied "a collaborative sculptural installation" by Vancouver artist Persimmon Blackbridge:

> When I was transferred from one jail to another, they gave me a vaginal "exam"— whole hand style. . . . The full exam went like this—vaginal (speculum and bi-manually) and checks through all your body hair; nose; mouth; ears; between toes; bottoms of feet. We had lice shampoo squirted into our hands and had to rub it into our pubic hair and shampoo with it while one or two guards watched. We stood naked and spread-eagled while these guards circled us with clipboards noting our various scars, birthmarks and tattoos. I flipped out when the nurse stuck her hand in me and stated, "You've been pregnant." I COULDN'T STAND her having that knowledge without me telling her. I felt like they could start peeling me in

layers, down to my raw nerves. . . . I started screaming at her/them, backing into the wall, hugging myself, threatening them. Fortunately, another nurse quickly covered me with a robe and led me to a chair. I got myself together . . . these outbursts are usually punished with isolation or worse. (Blackbridge et al., 1992: 23)

SELF-INJURY

At P4W as in most women's prisons in this century, women who "slash" or "carve" themselves (a.k.a. "letting"), or otherwise demonstrate that they've reached their limit of endurance, including those who attempt suicide, have been most commonly sent to "dissociation" (a.k.a. segregation units). The rationale is to observe them for potential suicide attempts. But the women perceive the policy as punishment for tampering with state property, namely their own bodies, and paradoxically women are more apt to slash while in segregation than within the general population (Heney, 1990: 15).

Slashing has been an aggravation to the P4W prison administration for at least three reasons: (1) if the injury is serious enough to require ambulance transportation to a hospital it can cost the institution hundreds of dollars; (2) when one woman slashes herself, other women who are on the edge follow suit in a domino reaction which is burdensome to staff; and (3) more generally, a slashing "disrupts the discipline and order of the institution," in the words of a senior guard supervisor (recounted in Kershaw and Lasovich, 1991: 98). In other words, administrative expense and inconvenience is at issue, not the profound pain, or the reasons for it, which induce and follow from a woman's self-injurious actions.

It is not only women who slash themselves; men in prison are also vulnerable to this practice (Jackson, 1983: 80). But the greater reported frequency with which it occurs among women is consistent with theories that men are conditioned to turn anger, blame or frustration against others, whereas women turn such feelings against themselves. Estimates of women who slash vary from one institution to another, and according to time periods. A 1979 study of Ontario female provincial prisoners found that 86 percent had engaged in self-mutilation (Ross and McKay, 1979). From interviews with forty-four federal female prisoners in Canada a decade later, Jan Heney found that 59 percent had engaged in self-injurious behaviour, primarily slashing (92 percent) but also head banging (8 percent) or "head banging, starvation, burning and/or tattooing in addition to slashing" (Heney, 1990: 8). It is Heney's view that "self-injurious behaviour is a *coping strategy* that manifests itself as a result of childhood abuse (usually sexual)" (Ibid.: 4).

> The woman may cope with feelings of powerlessness by dissociating, or psycholog-ically separating herself from her body, a tactic often used to survive the actual abuse during childhood. Self-injury may be a desire to reconnect with one's own body—a desire to ensure that one can feel. In this sense it is a life-preserving measure. (Pollack, 1993: 59)

Whereas the prison experience is not usually the underlying cause of slashing, a lack of support systems for incarcerated women and a sense of absolute powerlessness exacerbate the impulse. Although slashing and attempted suicide are not at all synonymous, the suicide of a prisoner triggers a slashing response from other women, and slashing itself has a domino effect. Overall, "prison tension" is cited as the impetus for slashing by over half the women interviewed by Heney. As a prisoner says

> Friendships are intensified in the prison. When someone you care about slashes, it upsets you because you are already upset about the same shit she is. When your friend slashes it tilts you because of her distress. (Heney, 1990: 10)

Heney emphasizes that "self-injurious behaviour is a mental health issue as opposed to a security issue," citing the women's repeated insistence that they slash when they lack someone to talk with about their problems. Almost half indicated the need for more counselors but others suggested that a friend, including another prisoner, would be just as useful. Heney emphasizes that treating slashing as a security issue compounds the problem, and she encour-ages greater attention to mental health services which would include giving prisoners more opportunities to develop structured peer support systems. She also emphasizes the need to take seriously the pervasiveness of childhood sexual abuse among women who self-injure, which is experienced as "loss of control [and] determination over the fundamental right to their bodies" (Ibid.: 24–29, 38).

As a direct result of Jan Heney's research, a Peer Support Team (PST) was implemented at P4W in 1990. Heney had observed the importance of an "informal network of counselling and support among women who self-injure"

(Pollack, 1993: 2). Her vision was to legitimize this network with a team of eight to ten volunteers, prisoners of diverse background (Caribbean, Native, East Indian, Italian, Jewish, African-American) (Ibid.: 32), who were trained in feminist (woman-centreed) peer counselling skills, with focus on racism, classism, homophobia, self-injury, women's anger, sexual assault, self-care, gender stereotypes and substance abuse (Ibid.: 4). Upon completion of six weeks of training these women were available for crisis intervention with other prisoners within the institution.

This experimental program suffered certain limitations imposed by the prisoners' dependency on the institutional bureaucracy, issues of confidentiality, and potential for co-optation (whereby the prisoner-counselors could become "a tool to maintain the status quo" [Ibid.: 8]). Further, there were no French-speaking counselors (Ibid.: 48). However, of the women interviewed by Pollack (more than half the women in the institution), 32 percent had used a peer counselor (Ibid.: 45), seeking assistance primarily for depression and the urge to self-harm. Over 80 percent of these women felt significantly assisted by the counselling: they felt "less alone," "less depressed," "more optimistic," and "less angry" (Ibid.: 47). The peer counselors were themselves assisted by their involvement in the program:

> The group training experience provided an opportunity for prisoners "with a lot of scars" to "let down our guards" and discover the goodness in one another. Trainees arrived to the program with a genuine desire to help but, in the process, they began also to heal their own scars. (Pollack, 1993: 67)

P4W saw an epidemic of suicide, predominantly by Native women, between 1988 and 1991. (At the same time, healing circles, sweat lodges and other ceremonies, as discussed in Chapter Four, as well as the participation of Native women in the Peer Support Team, have probably had the effect of circumventing some Native suicides.) However, it was the 1988 suicide by hanging of Marlene Moore, a white woman, which has been most extensively documented. She became a symbol of the negative effects of institutionalization when her story was published by two Kingston *Whig-Standard* reporters, Anne Kershaw and Mary Lasovich, and later expanded as a book-length document (1991). Marlene, or "Shaggie" (a.k.a. "Shaggy") as she was known to her many friends, had been officially labeled Canada's "most dangerous [female] offender" at a court hearing after a virtual lifetime of trouble with the law, aggravated by alcohol abuse. Marlene was indeed a very troubled young woman, and slashing was the only way she found to release her unremitting pain.

Marlene never killed anyone but she was assaultive and for a time she robbed women of their purses at knifepoint. Such crimes are very serious, requiring incarceration, but certainly not as serious as those of countless men who have never been officially designated as "dangerous offenders." Above all she was angry and verbally aggressive toward authorities, and her lawyers and supporters believed she was judged by a double standard. As one of her friends observed, "The system isn't used to women who mouth off. It's abnormal, unnatural, threatening, dangerous, scary" (Kershaw and Lasovich, 1991: 151).

A victim of repeated childhood sexual and physical abuse at home and rape by a stranger as a teenager, Marlene's history of victimization was at least as intense as the harms she committed. Her internal scars were clearly as deep as those that covered her arms from self-inflicted injuries. For all the chaos of her life, Marlene was an appealing woman who, during a visit with her at P4W in the mid-1980s, won my heart with her soft-spoken demeanour which belied her rowdy reputation. June Callwood was notable among social activists who tried in vain to help Marlene turn her life around, and in 1990 filmmaker Janis Cole produced a brief film (*Shaggie*) on Marlene's life for Canadian Tele-Vision. Most girls who suffer the indignities that plagued Marlene's life remain anonymous to a generally indifferent society, but given the peculiarly affection-glossed notoriety she achieved, her death came to symbolize the stupid futility of criminalizing girls who "act out" in response to abuse.

ONTARIO GRANDVIEW SCHOOL FOR GIRLS

As a young teenager in 1970, Marlene Moore was sent to the maximum security Grandview School for Girls in Cambridge, Ontario, not for a crime but as "a child in need of care and protection." Perhaps no human environment is as potentially deadly or abusive to stigmatized populations as are total institutions which are supported by social ideologies that blame victims. Not until the 1990s has it been publicly known, from survivors' testimony, that systemic violences were committed in the 1960s and 1970s against teenagers incarcerated in the Grandview School. Repeatedly and routinely, the girls were assaulted by staff and exploited for sexual purposes. Finally, at the initiative of survivors, the press is documenting how prisoners of this institution, who were incarcerated primarily for "unmanageability," were abused by staff from at least the mid-1960s until 1976 (*Province,* 1992: A15).

In 1976 the "School" was closed in the midst of a Ministry of Corrections investigation of allegations of improper behaviours by staff. The findings, which were covered up until 1990, included rape, "savage" beatings, and other brutalities against the girls, ages twelve to seventeen, who were locked naked in solitary confinement "cages" as punishment for misbehaviours. (Among other indignities the survivors report having been denied toilet facilities, and having to clean up their own excrement from the floor.) Self-mutilation was such a commonplace reaction to the cruelties that at one point 86 percent of the girls had slashed themselves, 117 out of the 136 girls then incarcerated. It was their way of releasing the "feelings of rage and sorrow, a way to feel alive," given their powerlessness to direct their angers at their persecutors (Yates, 1992: 25). It is now understood that there are direct correlations between slashing and unresolved childhood sexual abuse (Heney, 1990).

In 1992, following a two-year investigation, the provincial and Waterloo Region police laid twenty-one criminal charges against a former chief psychologist who is among those implicated in the abuses at Grandview. Survivors testify that "sexual favours" were exchanged with male staff for privileges such as cigarettes or being taken out on shopping trips (*Toronto Star,* 1992: A18). One survivor reports having been assaulted by six different male guards, who observed one another's actions in a form of ritual abuse. Another woman reports that at least two female guards facilitated the assaults: in one instance a female guard took her to an isolation cell (officially known as a "dissociation unit"), stripped her, and left her there with a male guard who "had sex" with her. She was fourteen years old (*Toronto Star,* 1991: A8). This clearly contradicted the ostensible purpose of having both male and female staff at the institution, which was to provide the girls with "housemothers" and "housefathers," surrogate "good parents" whose job was "to get to know the girls and create a healthy and happy environment" (Phillips, 1973: B1; see also Amor, 1973: B3).

An internal memorandum obtained through the provincial Freedom of Information Commission confirms that "officials at the highest level of the Corrections Ministry were aware of very serious allegations" of criminal wrongdoing (Thompson, 1992: A1, A2). Sixty-four former "inmates" have alleged that they were abused. According to a group calling for an inquiry, consisting of about fifty former prisoners who call themselves the "Grandview Survivors Support Group," the wrongdoing includes unexplained deaths of five girls (D'Amato, 1992: A3). One of the survivors alleges that a guard boasted of having killed one of the girls while threatening to kill another. Most bewilderingly, the survivors' group claims that, between 1967 and 1975, 229 girls went missing from the institution and that no one has ever investigated these disappearances.

The fundamental horror of this story is that under Canada's Juvenile Delinquents Act, which was in force until 1982, the "crimes" for which most of the young girls in this "secure" institution were being punished with indeterminate sentences consisted of such status offences as "incorrigibility," "unmanageability," "potential for sexual immorality," "living in unsuitable homes" and "running away" (often from abusers). It is not surprising that, as reported by Kathleen Kendall (1993: 24), "a number of inmates once held in detention at Grandview, later became incarcerated at the Prison for Women."

SEXUAL ABUSE

Romantic sex between prisoners and guards generally remains on the level of rumour or accusation without follow-up. In numerous instances in California where male staff were accused of forming relationships with female prisoners, the men were suddenly transferred to male institutions without explanation. I know firsthand of a long-term, intimate and mutually desired relationship between a prisoner and a professional employee. I have also frequently witnessed young women flirting aggressively with male staff, sometimes reciprocally, sometimes to the men's apparent discomfort. Sexual dynamics are inevitable in any prison environment (whether the participants are both male, both female or mixed), but flirtation, romance and love need to be distinguished from the sexual harassment or abuse by guards to which incarcerated women can be uniquely vulnerable. This is especially true in those institutions in which male officers are assigned to female living units, or carry out security duties such as "frisking" the women for contraband, supervising showers, or "escorting" resistant women to segregation or other isolated sections of the institution.

Given their already discredited status, girls and women who have claimed sexual abuse at the hands of "authorities" have not been heard or believed, they have been perceived as fair game, and they have been persecuted in the name of "discipline" for reporting offences against themselves. In one documented case at the California prison a woman was impregnated by a guard: he was fired and she was sent to the psychiatric unit (ASCC, 1977: 106). In several undocumented cases of which I am aware, the guards were transferred to men's institutions and the women were paroled. In a Florida case, a woman fought unsuccessfully for her right to keep a baby fathered by a guard (Boudouris, 1985: 9).

In 1992, a sexual harassment counselor in the state of New York testified that in fifteen years she had "represented about twenty-five female inmates who claimed they were sexually assaulted by male corrections staff," of whom three women had been impregnated. In one case, this counselor had to aggressively defend the prisoner against being placed in solitary confinement for the duration of the pregnancy (over six months), which the authorities believed would be the appropriate action until such time as blood tests could determine the veracity of her accusation against the guard. She adds that reported instances of "verbal sexual harassment by male guards is really too large to count." She emphasizes that given the power relationship between prisoners and guards, an element of coercion is present "even if it is alleged that the sexual relationships are consensual and the sexually flavored banter is appreciated" (Cassell, 1992: 2–5).

Commercial television is generally more likely to generate myth than fact. However, on the issue of violence against incarcerated women, investigative reportage on the Oprah Winfrey show, like the Grandview print media coverage, has accomplished what academic researchers have been unable to do given the exigencies of "scientific" inquiry and the hidden nature of the phenomenon. The program (NBC, March 31, 1993) opened with a clandestine videotape produced by a guard at the Georgia Women's Correctional Institution Main Unit (with a population exceeding 900 women). We see male and female guards struggle with resistant women, strip them naked, place them in restraining jackets, and leave them hogtied (ankles and wrists bound at their backs) *and* chained in dark isolation cells. According to the report, this form of "discipline" had been applied to sixty-four women, some of whom had been diagnosed as mentally ill.

Winfrey noted, by way of introduction to the live talk portion of the show, that charges of sexual and other abuses are being laid against officials in jails and prisons in Georgia, California, Hawaii, Ohio, Tennessee and New York. Her guests, interviewed both in the studio and by satellite, included four survivors of abuse in Georgia, a still-incarcerated California victim, a former

Georgia guard charged with sexual offences (who said he was "just following orders") and four other former prison employees from Georgia and California. Following are encapsulations of just a few of the charges. It should be emphasized that although the abuses described below are not representative of most women's prison experience, it is important that we be conscious of the ways that the isolation of prisons can facilitate violence against women.

- A woman held at the Georgia "Colony Farm" was taken to nearby secluded woods where she was raped and forced to perform oral sex on male guards on twenty separate occasions in the course of two years. After she had repeatedly reported the offences she was transferred to another facility where she was again raped, and she became convinced that this was part of the routine of being incarcerated.
- A prison chaplain raped a woman on his desk. She subsequently became the victim of a "correctional officer" who took her away from the prison to his home and raped her there while his wife was at work; this happened "almost every other day" for several months.
- In a loft in the prison, officers "who would watch out for each other" kept mattresses and ropes for the purposes of rape rituals, following which the women were put in the "cages" (segregation). Having been taken to an outside hospital for a hysterectomy, one of these women believed she would no longer have the same "appeal" as a rape victim, but two weeks following her return to prison, while still recovering from the surgery, she was raped yet again.
- A prisoner who was serving a life sentence at the California Institution for Women reports that for three years during the 1980s she was repeatedly raped by two officers in the shower room and elsewhere in the institution, and that officials ignored her pleas for help. One of the accused was the son of a former warden (a.k.a. superintendent). When she laid criminal charges she was put into solitary confinement and was kept there the entire two years of the court proceedings. Since 1987, when the case was settled, at least twenty-one guards and other staff have been disciplined or fired for intimacy with the prisoners. She was transferred to a federal facility for her protection but she still fears for her life.

A former counselor at the Georgia prison, who verified the women's reports of serious abuses, explains why guards and officials expect impunity for their crimes against women in prison: "Because the inmates are criminals . . . their credibility is going to be in question from the very beginning. [The perpetrators of the violences] counted on a cloak of silence, that the inmates were going to keep quiet." It does, of course, require enormous courage for women in prison to speak out. In explaining why she had decided to come forward, one of the victims of repeated assault said, "I was sentenced to prison, I wasn't sentenced to be raped."

By way of commenting on the testimony of the women who have been victimized, a woman employed as a North Carolina correctional official offered important perspective. Whereas she agrees that society should be alert to these abuses and work to prevent them, she emphasizes that women who are not incarcerated are also vulnerable to sexual and other abuses. She points out that "women in prison mirror the same issues of women outside: victimization; dependency on men; and low self-esteem." One caveat to this last point is that it's an error to generalize women in prison as having low self-esteem. Ruth Glick and Virginia Neto, in a US national survey, found that "the majority of incarcerated women felt relatively good about themselves" (1977: 171–72).

The prevailing, time-worn assumption that female prisoners have low self-esteem may well be a blaming or condescending projection by class-biased people who can't imagine that women with so many problems could think well of themselves. My experience with many women inside is that they do not take on judgements against themselves offered by people whose authority or personal character they do not respect. This perception is consistent with the findings of Marion Earnest who, in 1978, concluded that prisoners adopted a self-conception of themselves as "criminals" only if their most "significant others" viewed them as criminal (Earnest, 1978: 79).

Certainly a history of abuse can have the effect of producing torment, including shame, self-blame and self-injury, but it can also produce anger and the sense that "I'm okay, it's the world that's messed up." It's a safe assumption that lack of self-confidence is not more prevalent among women inside than outside prisons. Given that most incarcerated women have had to hustle in some way to survive, many of these women might well have a greater sense of their resourcefulness than is the norm among women, even when their means of survival appears self-destructive to others.

REFERENCES

Allen, Hilary (1987). *Justice Unbalanced: Gender, Psychiatry and Judicial Decision.* Milton Keynes: Open University Press.

Amor, Dave (1973). "Accentuating the Positive, Eliminating the Negative." *Cambridge Daily Reporter* (March 27): B3.

Anonymous (1983). "Response to 'Daily Fear'." *Tightwire* [Kingston: Prison for Women]: 19.

Assembly Special Committee on Corrections (ASCC) (1977). *Report on Incarcerated Women.* Sacramento: California State Legislature.

Blackbridge, Persimmon with Geri Ferguson, Michelle Kanashiro-Christensen, Lyn MacDonald and Bea Walkus (1992). "A Collaborative Sculptural Installation: Doing Time." *Matriart: A Canadian Feminist Art Journal* 3(1): 23–25.

Boudouris, James (1985). *Prisons and Kids: Programs for Inmate Parents.* Maryland: American Correctional Association.

Bowker, Lee H. (1981). "Gender Differences in Prisoner Subcultures," in L. Bowker (Ed.), *Women and Crime in America.* New York: Macmillan, 409–19.

California Institution for Women (CIW) (1972). "Daily Bulletin" (August 1).

Canadian Centre for Justice Statistics (CCJS) (1991). *Canadian Crime Statistics: Annual Catalog #85–205.* Ottawa: Statistics Canada.

Cassell, Ruth (1992). "Testimony Before the Governor's Task Force on Sexual Harassment." New York: Prisoners' Legal Services.

Chandler, Edna Walker (1973). *Women in Prison.* New York: Bobbs-Merrill.

D'Amato, Luisa (1992). "Rae Rules Out Grandview Inquiry: Ontario Awaiting End of Police Probe." *Kitchener-Waterloo Record* (June 22): A3.

Dobash, Russell P., R. Emerson Dobash and Sue Gutteridge (1986). *The Imprisonment of Women.* London: Basil Blackwell.

Earnest, Marion R. (1978). *Criminal Self-Conceptions in the Penal Community of Female Offenders: An Empirical Study.* San Francisco: R & E Associates, Inc.

Faith, Karlene (Ed.) (1975). *Soledad Prison: University of the Poor.* Palo Alto: Science and Behavior Books, Inc.

Faith, Karlene (1987). "Media, Myths and Masculinization: Images of Women in Prison," in E. Adelberg and C. Currie (Eds.), *Too Few to Count: Canadian Women in Conflict with the Law.* Vancouver: Press Gang Publishers, 181–219.

Faith, Karlene (1991). *The Female Offender.* Burnaby: Simon Fraser University, Centre for Distance Education and School of Criminology.

Fattah, E. A. and V. S. Sacco (1989). *Crime and Victimization of the Elderly.* New York: Springer-Verlag.

First Tuesday Unit (1992). *Locking Up Women.* Yorkshire Television.

Glick, Ruth M. and Virginia V. Neto (1977). *National Study of Women's Correctional Programs.* Washington, D.C.: US Department of Justice.

Hanrahan, Kathleen J. (1993). "Fear of Crime among Elderly Urban Women," in R. Muraskin and T. Alleman (Eds.), *It's a Crime: Women and Justice.* Englewood Cliffs: Prentice Hall, 374–95.

Heidensohn, Frances (1985). *Women & Crime.* London: Macmillan.

Heney, Jan (1990). "Report on Self-Injurious Behaviour in the Kingston Prison for Women." Ottawa: Ministry of the Solicitor General, Corrections Branch.

Jackson, Michael (1983). *Prisoners of Isolation: Solitary Confinement in Canada.* Toronto: University of Toronto Press.

Jose-Kampfner, Christina (1990). "Coming to Terms with Existential Death: An Analysis of Women's Adaptation to Life in Prison." *Social Justice* 17(2): 110–25.

Kendall, Kathleen (1993). "Literature Review of Therapeutic Services for Women in Prison." Ottawa: Ministry of the Solicitor General, Corrections Branch.

Kershaw, Anne and Mary Lasovich (1991). *Rock-a-Bye Baby: A Death Behind Bars.* Toronto: McClelland & Stewart.

Lowman, John and Brian MacLean (1991). "Prisons and Protest in Canada." *Social Justice* 18(3): 130–54.

Mitford, Jessica (1973). *Kind and Usual Punishment.* New York: Alfred A. Knopf.

Muraskin, Roslyn (1993). "Disparate Treatment in Correctional Facilities," in R. Muraskin and T. Alleman (Eds.), *It's a Crime: Women and Justice.* Englewood Cliffs: Prentice Hall, 211–25.

New York State Special Commission on Attica (NYSSCA) (1972). *Attica: Official Report.* New York: Bantam Books.

O'Dwyer, Josie, Judi Wilson and Pat Carlen (1987). "Women's Imprisonment in England, Wales and Scotland: Recurring Issues," in P. Carlen and A. Worrall (Eds.), *Gender, Crime and Justice.* Milton Keynes: Open University Press, 176–90.

Phillips, Jim (1973). "Grand View School: 'A Holding Tank for Society's Outcasts'." *The Cambridge Times* (March 28): B1.

Pollack, Shoshana (1993). "Opening the Window on a Very Dark Day: A Program Evaluation of the Peer Support Team at the Kingston Prison for Women." Unpublished Master's Thesis. Ottawa: Carleton University.

Province [Vancouver] (1992). "School was 'Nightmare'" (February 18): A15.

Resnik, Judith and Nancy Shaw (1983). "Prisoners of Their Sex: Health Problems of Incarcerated Women," in I. Robbins (Ed.) *Prisoners' Rights Source Book: Theory, Litigation and Practice,* volume 2. New York: Clark Boardman.

Ross, R. and H. McKay (1979). *Self-Mutilation.* Toronto: Lexington Books.

Shaw, Margaret with Karen Rodgers, Johanne Blanchette, Tina Hattem, Lee Seto Thomas and Lada Tamarack (1992). *Paying the Price: Federally Sentenced Women in Context.* Ottawa: Ministry of the Solicitor General, Corrections Branch.

Shaw, Nancy Stoller (1982). "Female Patients and the Medical Profession in Jails and Prisons: A Case of Quintuple Jeopardy," in N. Rafter and E. Stanko (Eds.), *Judge, Lawyer, Victim, Thief: Women, Gender Roles, and Criminal Justice.* Boston: Northeastern University Press, 261–73.

Sim, Joe (1991). "'We Are Not Animals, We Are Human Beings': Prisons, Protest, and Politics in England and Wales, 1969–1990." *Social Justice* 18(3): 107–29.

Thompson, Catherine (1992). "Ontario Releases Memo on '76 Grandview Probe." *Kitchener-Waterloo Record* (June 18): A1, A2.

Toronto Star (1991). "Sex Abuse Alleged at Girls' School" (June 15): A8.

Toronto Star (1992). "Keeping It Secret" (May 12): A18.

Walford, Bonny (1987). *Lifers: The Stories of Eleven Women Serving Life Sentences for Murder.* Montreal: Eden Press.

Weiss, Robert P. (1991). "Attica: The 'Bitter Lessons' Forgotten?" *Social Justice* 18(3): 1–12.

Yates, Elizabeth (1992). "Women Angrily Recall Beatings, Sexual Abuse at Training School." *Niagara Falls Review* (April 4): 25.

Zedner, Lucia (1991). *Women, Crime, and Custody in Victorian England.* Oxford: Clarendon Press.

CHAPTER SIX

Going to the Movies[1]

[A]s a teacher I am constantly in search of ethnographic materials which will provide insight to my students and will help to combat the "monster" stereotypes of the criminalized and incarcerated which dominate public and academic discourse. (Gaucher, 1988: 54)

M Y PRIMARY FOCUS in this chapter is on contemporary film representations of "criminal" and other unruly women, and on the issue of gender in these media stereotypes. Examples are drawn mainly from Hollywood movie productions (the primary North American medium for generating "bad girl" images), and secondarily from international and independent film productions and television. Since the late 1960s, film theorists have increasingly recognized the significance of gender to every aspect of the craft. There is by now a rich body of feminist analyses of the social meanings and constructions of femaleness and femininity in cinematic representation (see, for example, de Lauretis, 1987; Doane, Mellencamp and Williams, 1984; Kuhn, 1982; Pribram, 1988; Todd, 1988). As stated in an introductory film theory text,

> During the past decade the politics of gender has effectively displaced the politics of class within film theory. . . . [C]inema, concerned as it is with representation and identity, has been seen as playing a vital role in maintaining the oppression of women. . . . At all points, then, within the institution of cinema—production, consumption, criticism—women's voices [are] beginning to be heard. (Lapsley and Westlake, 1988: 23)

Authentic women's voices are rarely heard in Hollywood films depicting women outside the law, and in the worst of these films the characters are metamorphosed into masculinized monsters. I identify films of this and related genres with the aim of demystifying fallacies perpetrated by bad-girl stereotypes. In particular, I point to images of demonized women, lesbians as villains, teenage predators in reform school, and pathologized killer beauties. I end by acknowledging notable exceptions to the bad-girl movie stereotypes, and comment more generally on media constructions of gender.

MEDIA MASCULINIZATION OF STRONG WOMEN

As discussed in Chapter Two, in the mid-1970s Western media raised the blood pressure of feminists internationally with the revived Lombrosian message that women's liberation would have the effect of producing a new class of female criminals. It was a regurgitation of the age-old fear that emancipation will make women more like men, a myth that has historically suppressed goddess-worship and other expressions of female power. Merlin Stone, for example, documents how female prophets in ancient Babylonia have been interpreted by historians as "temple prostitutes" (Stone, 1976: 210–11) or witches. In the Old Testament, the Levitican priests condemned the matriarchal Semitic divinity Astarte, a.k.a. Ashtoreth (the Great Mother), and shamed her by addressing her as a man. The history of the social control of women has supported the notion that women need to be dependent on and answerable to their father or husband, lest they go mad or wild. Spurred by the media, contemporary antifeminists invoked fears of wild Amazons tearing through respectable neighbourhoods and hiding in dark alleys, presenting a physical danger to all good citizens. Just as moral panics have been produced by the press relative to male youth gangs (Cohen, 1972), so did the spectre of female gangs ring an alarm and arouse public excitement and unease.

A cinematic arena in which gender stereotypes are entrenched without relief is that of low-budget women's prison movies. Prison movies have been predominantly about men, and the stock characters in female prison films are borrowed from the male genre. The female prison, like the male, is presented as a violent, totalitarian, closed dungeon in which force is the rule. Because the female in prison is a criminal, and because criminals in the public mind are more appropriately male and masculine, she is deemed to be like a man, absolved of any feminine attribute (Faith, 1987).

In speaking of films which demonize male characters, Surette observes that "Psychotic supermales generally possess an evil, cunning intelligence, and superior strength, endurance, and stealth" (1992: 36). Strong and heroic female characters are imbued with "masculine" courage and physical bravery in confronting He-Monsters, such as Jodie Foster's character in *Silence of the Lambs* (1991). In that film, the adversaries, Evil Man and Good Woman, raise the genre to a rationalistic, intellectual level of horror. Mass audiences relish terror and violence as long as the Hero defeats the Beast in the end.

In recent decades, about one-fourth of prime time television has been devoted to crime themes (Surette, 1992: 32). Crime and punishment motifs have been disproportionately prominent historically and across cultures—in mythology, ballads, the early press, literature, theatre and opera. In most Western cultures, the arts, places of worship, psychoanalysis and many other forms of discourse have perpetrated and reified Good and Evil dualisms, which in modern culture extend from crime to sci-fi horror.

People apparently are aroused by, and clearly will pay for, appeals to dark fears of or vicarious identification with masculinized power. Through media-inducing fantasy, if we are or wish to be masculine (strong, brave) we can identify with the hero's seemingly inviolable powers, and if we are feminine (weak, dependent) we can feel protected (though not usually until we have been already victimized). Contemporary media exploit these fears and fantasies with high-tech special effect ammunition that adds superficial horror value, as in brute-force Arnold Schwarzenegger spectacles, but which obliterate the classic elements of tragedy common to, for example, Shakespeare's crime stories.

Those who cheered for or recoiled from *Thelma and Louise* (1991), played by Geena Davis and Susan Sarandon, included many women who understood the fantasy of two women on the run (after one shoots the man who raped the other), who go robbing and gun-slinging in defiance of men and the law. Given the widespread enthusiasm of women for this film one might ask: Do such characters represent an actual trend in female crime? The answer is "No." Do they resonate with the fantasies of victims of (male) violence? Probably. Do they arouse fears among men which stimulate backlash against women's struggles for safety and independence? Perhaps.

FORMULAIC HOLLYWOOD
WOMEN-IN-PRISON FILMS

Beginning in 1950 with *Caged,* and continuing for over four decades, there is a genre of crude women-in-prison films with a standard plot: a pretty and mostly innocent (usually blonde) young woman is thrown into a cage or den of raving, masculinized, lesbian, predatory criminal maniacs, run by sadistic matrons. With explicit pornographic overtones, these films very expediently dichotomize women as good or evil, compliant or dangerous, madonna or whore. They produce images of monster women bearing no resemblance to the ordinariness of the relatively few women who are actually locked up. With sleight of hand, media producers characterize offending women as "like men." Both genders are denigrated and women are denied their sex, designated as other than Woman.

The monster-criminal woman of fifties movies was the anonymous woman, the shadow woman, a killer so primitive as to lack an individual identity. The first such characterization was in *Caged,* the prototype which is now a classic, with Agnes Moorehead as warden, Eleanor Parker as innocent protagonist and Hope Emerson as brutal matron. The characters of the imprisoned women, except for Parker's character, are grotesque. Dozens of them are crowded into a dingy, claustrophic prison-dorm setting where they are collectively charged with violent energy. They and the psychotic lesbian matron are evil and terrifying, especially to the predictably white, pretty goody-goody who got there by mistake, the only character with whom the intended audience can identify. The others are evil by nature.

Caged and similar films demonstrate conflicts between old-line guards and custodians who want to treat the women "like the animals they are," and wardens and superintendents with newfangled ideas from psychologists and social workers. Such assembly-line films end pessimistically and leave the audience with a full set of meaningful gendered messages about crime and about penal institutions and the women who inhabit them.

Since incarcerated women are already designated Bad, no holds are barred in movie depictions of how women treat one another when there are no men around to serve as protective buffers. They are punched in the face (by each other and by the female guards), tied to a chair while all their hair is shaved off, and locked in narrow, dark, dank concrete holes (*Caged*). They are stalked by lesbian predators, raped with a knife (by a woman), beaten to a pulp by a female mob in the shower, and thrown into segregation next to women who have already gone mad (*Turning to Stone,* 1986, see below). Films of this ilk exploit racism just as they exploit homophobia and classism; the darker a woman's skin colour, the more dangerous she is. Mass media have consistently articulated racist stereotypes which reflect, reify, construct and perpetuate base prejudice and institutionalized discrimination. The media, of course, operate in a social context. As Dates and Barlow observe, ". . . to be effective a stereotype must be anticipated by conditioned perceptions of the beholder as well as existent in the imagination of the image maker" (1990: 2–3).

The same depravities as appear in women's prison stories also show up in films of women in mental hospitals. The classic film depiction of mental illness hellholes is *Snake Pit* (1948), in which a beautiful but badly disturbed woman, played by Olivia de Havilland, is witness to and victim of unspeakable atrocities committed by other inmates and line staff. In the end she is saved by a psychiatrist, and through his masculine authority and strength she is restored to a potentially fulfilling life as a normal, feminine woman. As was true of Eleanor Parker's prison character in *Caged* (until she hardened), it is only because the patient or prisoner is desirable to men in her feminine figure and social demeanour that she is accorded a chance at salvation. She has this chance because she is different from the repulsive, dangerous women with whom she has been locked up. The stereotypes of the madwoman or the criminal woman are not challenged, but, rather, are grossly exploited so as to highlight and promote the image of a good, desirable woman. The monsters serve as the sick/bad backdrop for her potential normalcy.

DEVIL WOMEN

One of the most frightening Hollywood film depictions of the devil inhabiting the female body was that of Mia Farrow's character in the Roman Polanski film *Rosemary's Baby* (1968). As a young, winsome bride, she is forbearing in her pretty innocence, even after having been sexually assaulted and impregnated by Lucifer in cult ritual abuse. Evil child films, such as *The Bad Seed* (1956) with Patty McCormack, and *The Exorcist* (1973), with Linda Blair, similarly capitalize on the notion that Satan plants Himself in female bodies and makes of them agents of Evil.

In every medium and in many eras, men of certain authority have codified their fear of women through law, medicine and religion, and have attributed them with supernatural powers. As discussed at length in Chapter One, between the 15th and 18th centuries, under Biblical authority ("Thou shalt not suffer a witch to live"; Exodus 22:18), untold numbers of women were executed on grounds of witchcraft resultant from copulation with the Devil (Klaits, 1985; Macfarlane, 1977). The caricatured images which survived that holocaust, via fairy tales, produced enduring stereotypes of ugly, fearsome, evil witchy women.

One great exception to the ugly hag stereotype is *The Witches of Eastwick* (1987), with the tantalizing, comedic trio of Cher, Michelle Pfeiffer and Susan Sarandon romping in a ménage-à-quatre with devilish Jack Nicholson. Another tongue-in-cheek witch film, *The Witches* (1990), was introduced to me by my eight-year-old grandson, a fan of the writing of children's author Roald Dahl upon whose story the script was based. Produced by Muppets creator Jim Henson and starring Anjelica Huston as the Grand High Witch, special effects are exploited to transform a coven of ordinary suburban housewife-types into a mob of indescribably ugly women who terrorize children and turn them into mice. Like most fairy tales, this story has a happy ending, thanks to the heroics of a clever nine-year-old boy-turned-mouse. But the insidious message, that behind the most innocent-appearing female countenance lies an unspeakable monster, is as misogynist as any made-for-adults rendition of this theme. The theme is repeated in 1993 with *Hocus Pocus,* starring Bette Midler, Sarah Jessica Parker and Kathy Najimy; contemporary, self-identified "witches" complain that once again the message is that powerful women cause evil havoc.

LESBIANS AS VILLAINS

The presentation of lesbianism as an alien state of being emerged . . . in the Fifties
in hard female characters who were seen as bitter reminders of the fate of women
who tried to perform male roles. (Russo, 1987: 99)

Common messages gleaned from female prison films, none of which are supported by observations of actual women in institutions, include:

- Innocents are corrupted by the wicked;
- Brutal on-line staff have more power than wardens;

- In segregated institutions women (both prisoners and guards) behave like monster men;
- Women locked up are masculine, and do routine physical damage to one another, including predatory rape with knives, bottles and other horrifying and life-threatening weapons;
- A disproportionate number of women in prison are lesbians, and they in particular control other women and commit horrific acts of violence.

The effect of characterizing female prisoners as sex-crazed monsters is to invite hostility toward both prisoners and lesbians at large. That is, whereas few prisoners are lesbians and few lesbians are sex-crazed, the stereotypes are otherwise, and film has the cultural power to reify images which run altogether counter to reality.

In a discussion of female impersonators in the movies, Russo observes, "Rendering the idea of actual lesbianism all but invisible, the identification of such women in exclusively male terms serves only to reinforce the idea that sexuality is the proper domain of men" (Russo, 1987: 13). It follows that sexualized females are masculinized via lesbianism, or as bisexual vampires such as portrayed by Catherine Deneuve in *The Hunger* (1983); exquisitely handsome, she played to Susan Sarandon's and David Bowie's characters with equal passion.

Elsewhere I've analyzed the equation of female criminality with masculinity, violence and lesbianism (Faith, 1987). This theme is best illustrated by the film *Turning to Stone,* a 1986 Canadian television production which took the pornographic possibilities of the women-in-prison genre to new lows.

Aired in prime time on CBC, *Turning to Stone,* like the formulaic Hollywood films it imitates, equates masculinity with violence. Hideous women inflict unspeakable brutalities upon one another, demonized within the masculinized ambience of the prison. Moreover, these unnatural lesbians in the guise of men are not caricatured as homosexual men, but rather as macho heterosexual men. In fact, the same men who are predators against women on the outside attack "feminine" men (straight or gay) in prison, and cinematic representations of lesbians in prison are modeled after these brutal men.

In *Turning to Stone,* as in many films, the camera serves the function of the guard in the rotunda of a Panopticon. The camera, signifying surveillance, holds a steady (male) gaze on the body of the prisoner. The camera closes in on the twisted faces and hands of unruly women who are wielding weapons and it then shifts to the bloody damage done to their victims. The predators are portrayed as "lesbians," women who are "like men" and who therefore force violent sex upon women to achieve the desired end, namely having power and control over another human being. Sadistic, homophobic fantasy is a consistent feature of prison films, male or female, and this Canadian government-sponsored television version outdid even Hollywood in constructing women in prison as masculinized monsters.

In real life, public attitudes toward any woman convicted of serious ("masculine") crime range from unsympathetic to hostile. When a woman commits a crime that is normally committed only by men she is guaranteed headlines. The public is fascinated with such women, and their crimes are profitable to media producers. In the case of the first female "serial killer," Aileen Carol "Lee" Wuornos (1991), a self-identified lesbian hitchhiker (in the US) who was accused of seducing, assaulting, robbing from and murdering six random men in Florida who had given her a ride, the media maximized every hideous detail. A television docudrama starring Jean Smart (1992) allowed for some ambiguity as to her motives, but in tabloid television her "lesbianism" was played out as perverted, man-hating rage, a determining feature of her character. The Wuornos trial was a media spectacle. Her person and her crimes stirred up fear and revulsion, and her self-proclaimed lesbianism allowed for simplistic and homophobic explanations for why she had killed these strangers. One woman's evil deeds—or acts of self-defence, depending on her believability (Chesler, 1993)—translated into indelible visual and audio images. As Ericson et al. explained in their study of crime and justice in the news media,

> Television is not compelled to speak in the figurative language of, say, the witness in court or before a royal commission, for whom questions of evidence, contradiction, lying, and the basis of truth claims are omnipresent. It deals in tropes that do not simply assert that "things look this way," but rather urge one to "look at things this way." (Ericson, Baranek and Chan, 1991: 227)

TEENAGE PREDATORS

The early reform school and She-Monster films of director Sam Arkoff, in the 1950s, foretold the rapid decline of girlish innocence in cinema. As a reaction to the development of the contemporary women's movement, females were increasingly portrayed through the sixties and seventies as devoid of old-fashioned virtue. By the 1980s no one was innocent, certainly not girls in fantasized reform schools. A rash of movies depicted young women as capable of violences and cruelties to compete with the worst actions of brutal young men.

Between the 1950s and the 1980s, films about "bad girls" simultaneously exploited female sexuality and extolled the values of professional treatment of delinquents, and the benefits to girls of strong male influences. Such films as *So Young, So Bad* (1953), where reform school girls were attacked with power water hoses, delivered the clear message that girls who fail to walk the feminine line risk horrendous fates. In *Girls in Prison* (1956), a good chaplain takes the pretty young protagonist under his protective wing. The hero of *Reform School Girl* (1957) is a kindly male teacher who can justify his otherwise futile efforts in the prison classroom if he can "just save this one girl."

The innocent heroine in prison, teenager or adult, who gets into trouble by associating with the wrong people, provides the object lesson in female prison films. She only rarely escapes with her virtue intact. The mobs of witch-like s/he-monsters (both prisoners and guards) who corrupt the innocents—by assaulting them with power hoses, beating them up, and mutilating them with sharp weapons—are all stereotypically deranged. In *Chain Gang Women* (1977) it is grown-up women who are out to destroy the weak among them. In *Chained Heat* (1983), starring Linda Blair, the kids take it to the limit, with young women raped, beaten, cut with razors and under constant risk of being killed by other girls.

The Queen of Camp in youth films, in my view, is Wendy O. Williams in *The Reform School Girls* (1985). This film features Williams as a nearly naked Amazon predator in a sadistic world which runs rampant with bloody beatings, shootings, and sexual and other tortures. It steals plot gimmicks, frame by frame, from *Caged*: the brutal-dyke matron kills a contraband kitten; in a riot-escape scene, mobs of crazed female convicts advance on the matron, chanting in unison, "Kill Her! Kill Her!"—and they do. The film goes over the top with a blonde, dominatrix fascist warden who wears a military uniform and carries a whip. The toughest girls, in a gang controlled by Williams' character, pose in string bikinis when they aren't showering in the nude. They all have Playboy bodies and the film is glaring in its pornographic intent. As in *So Young, So Bad* three decades earlier, the transparently conspicuous phallus is a huge, gushing power hose with which the girls are assaulted. The film is sufficiently bad to be laughable.

Given that teenage girls are seldom involved in actual killings, the media have aggressively exploited such events when they have occurred. The first of these, in North America, was the case of Caril Ann Fugate who, at age fourteen, went on a killing rampage with her nineteen-year-old boyfriend, Charlie Starkweather. The Hollywood version, *The Badlands* (1973), was decidedly unsympathetic. This story was reprised in a 1993 television miniseries which characterized the young teenager as a mindless moll, lacking evil intent but nevertheless guilty in her amorality.

An even more striking example of media overkill was the coverage of the 1969 Manson case. A communal group of young women and men, affected by massive doses of psychedelic drugs under the mesmerizing, totalitarian control of Charles Manson, killed seven affluent people in two Beverly Hills homes on successive nights. Three young women, not yet or barely out of their teens, were sentenced to death with Manson and other male collaborators, but all their sentences were commuted to life in prison by a 1972 US Supreme Court ruling against capital punishment as "cruel and unusual." (The ruling was revoked in 1976.)

From a feminist perspective the Manson case signified the extent to which well-socialized, chemically charged girls and women will go to gain the approval of the master in whom they believe and on whom they are dependent. However, gender analysis of the crime was lost to Satanic symbolism gleaned from the media's focus on the "X" that all three female defendants carved into their foreheads, their shaven heads and the unanimity of their responses in court, which echoed Manson's own words. The young women were presented by the media, in all forms, as She-Devils in cahoots with Manson, the Devil incarnate who claimed to be the Son of God.

The publicity that attended the Manson case has scarcely receded in the almost twenty-five years since the case broke. The book *Helter Skelter* (1974), written by flambuoyant prosecutor Vincent Bugliosi, is still in print, and the movie by the same name (1976) is shown *ad nauseum* on late night television. The three women were thoroughly objectified as personifications of evil who, like witches of yore, should have been burned. Public attitudes toward the women involved in the case may have been very different had Bugliosi's characterizations not been infused into mass consciousness.

SUPER-BITCH KILLER BEAUTIES

A rash of anti-feminist feature films about pathologically manipulative, violent females who threaten (or take) the lives of men and other women, but whose beauty and charms mask their evil natures, has surfaced in the late 1980s and early 1990s. Like most women-hating-women films, the characters are depicted as appropriating "male" power (threat, force, violence) as a means of investigating and experimenting with "female" power. *Fatal Attraction* (1987), starring Glenn Close, takes the lead as the prototype of the postmodern failed-woman film. Close's character is a woman whose rage at "not having it all" takes nasty turns against a family that seems idyllically happy (except for the husband's secret adultery). She is the image of the beautiful, solitary, ominous, male-identified, childless, pathologically obsessive woman, "liberated" in anti-feminist terms, who would take what she wants at any cost. In the end, she pays with her life at the hand of the injured wife.

Other contemporary examples of the evil woman behind the sweet and/or sexy and tantalizing demeanour (which serve as warnings to women-who-want-it-all), include *The Hand That Rocks the Cradle* (1991), with Rebecca DeMornay's viciously deceptive character seeking to destroy the family (this one truly perfect) who entrust her with their child's care; and *Single White Female* (1992), starring Bridget Fonda as an innocent woman under siege from her sex-pervert soul-robber roommate, played by Jennifer Jason Leigh, who kills good men and a dog and then goes after Fonda's character, who retaliates with an ice pick. The same weapon figures in *Basic Instinct* (1992), yet another terrifying and masterfully homophobic sex saga. It features a stunning, brilliantly manipulative bisexual, played by Sharon Stone, whose past and present female lovers are killers who mess with men's minds and bodies, but who get their comeuppance. Such characters combine traditional misogynist notions of female madness and contemporary anti-feminist notions of women becoming criminal and aggressive like men.

The director of *Single White Female*, Barbet Schroeder, admits he has "kind of a weakness for monsters" (Brantley, 1992: 162). As Peter Travers said about the film,

> Forget the fancy subtext about trading identities; this is just another woman-killing-woman flick wallowing in the muck with "Fatal Attraction" and "The Hand That Rocks the Cradle." . . . It's dispiriting that more and more thrillers show

women turning on each other for empowerment rather than to each other. (Travers, 1992: 72)

The myth of the liberated woman gives media producers both the incentive and the rationale to present independent women as emasculating monsters who hate normal men *and* women. Such films, wittingly or not, are transparent expressions and perpetrators of backlash against feminism.

MEDIA COUNTER-IMAGES TO GENDER STEREOTYPES

Counter to the monstrous female felons which dominate Hollywood's portrayals of "criminal" women are some more realistic or sympathetic media representations of girls and women involved in criminal actions. The most believable of these characters are often based on legendary women, and at the head of the list of such films is *I Want to Live!* (1958), the story of convicted killer Barbara Graham passionately portrayed by Susan Hayward (whose performance won her an Oscar). Other examples include the 1932 film *Mata Hari,* with Greta Garbo as Margaretha Zelle MacLeod, an "exotic" spy and nude dancer who was executed by the French in 1917. The 1937 film *You Only Live Once,* featuring Sylvia Sidney and Henry Fonda, is the story of attractive, enigmatic outlaws who shot and stole their way to notoriety and died in a burst of lawman gunfire (a story which was reprised in 1967 as *Bonnie and Clyde,* with Warren Beatty and Faye Dunaway).

Decades later, three Hollywood comedies effectively conveyed the notions that crimes and the women who commit them can be a lot of fun: *Fun with Dick and Jane* (1977), with Jane Fonda; *How to Beat the High Cost of Living* (1980), with Jessica Lange, Jane Curtin and Susan Saint James; and, *Burglar* (1986), with Whoopi Goldberg. All these films presented likeable characters who found ingeniously comical ways of bilking people without hurting anyone the audience might care about, as was also true of Marianne Sagebrecht's character in the Percy Adlon film *Rosalie Goes Shopping* (1990). They all showed women as gutsy, resourceful, clever and funny, and although this characterization is a far cry from the painful circumstances that lead most female "offenders" into lawbreaking, it allows for the reality that some female "criminals" are indeed free-spirited women.

More serious female outlaw films widely viewed in North America during the 1980s and early 1990s, including several produced outside Hollywood, have in common appealing female characters who betray gender stereotypes by virtue of their acts of resistance:

- *A Question of Silence* (1983), a film by Marleen Gorris of Holland, in which three ordinary women, strangers to one another, kill the proprietor of a store when one of them is caught shoplifting;
- *Marianne and Julianne* (1984), a docudrama about the hearts and minds of political prisoners in Germany;
- The Lizzie Borden film, *Working Girls* (1986), a documentary-style story of bawdy house prostitution in New York City;
- *Crimes of the Heart* (1986), the dark comedy of three southern sisters, one of whom shoots her contemptible husband, starring Sissy Spacek, Diane Keaton, and Jessica Lange;
- *Running on Empty* (1988), starring Christine Lahti, the tale of a family in hiding from the FBI in the 1980s for crimes committed as war protesters in the sixties;
- The French film *Story of Women* (1988), starring Isabelle Huppert as the family woman who risks everything to perform abortions;
- *Married To the Mob* (1988), in which Michelle Pfeiffer plays the captivating wife of a criminal, making her complicit in The Life;
- *The Grifters* (1990), featuring Anjelica Huston as an outlaw involved with mob crime, who, through force of character, gains the audience's respect (and an Oscar nomination for Huston);
- *Fried Green Tomatoes* (1991), with Mary-Louise Parker and Mary Stuart Masterson as endearing young women in the deep South, who have deep love for one another and who team up in righteous combat against racism, wife-beating and cancer;
- *Bugsy* (1991), in which Annette Bening plays sexy love object and resourceful business partner to the crook Bugsy Siegel.

Traditionally, "feel-good" female outlaw characters have been cheerfully maternal prostitutes in westerns and gangster movies. This stereotype is broken by more complex celluloid prostitutes such as played by Elizabeth Taylor in *Butterfield 8* (1960); Shirley MacLaine in *Sweet Charity* (1969); Jane Fonda in *Klute* (1971); and Theresa Russell in *Whore* (1991). Julia Roberts's happy prostitute in *Pretty Woman* (1990) set the tone for a revived Cinderella genre, where the wealthy Prince simply purchases the object of his desire. Variations on this theme were repeated in *Honeymoon in Vegas* (1992), with Sarah Jessica Parker; *Mad Dog and Glory* (1993), with Uma Thurman; and, *Indecent Proposal* (1993), with Demi Moore.

Since the 1970s the media have responded in certain respects to liberal feminist critiques (see, for example, Janus, 1977 and Tuchman, 1979), and feminist producers, writers, directors and editors, though relatively few in number, have inserted authentic and diverse female voices that can be empowering to other women. While there have always been some male directors and writers who have shown respect for individualized female characters, with rare exception it's the character's exceptional beauty, intrigue or charm which defines her identity; she is represented not as the common woman but rather as the exception.

In the crime genre it is not only female lawbreakers who are appearing in a positive light; intelligent women are also featured as idealized detectives, cops and lawyers. For example in *V. I. Warshawski* (1991), Kathleen Turner plays the role of a female private detective who doesn't flinch in the face of danger. Cop shows such as *Blue Steel* (1990), with Jamie Lee Curtis, the 1980s TV series "Cagney and Lacey," and "Sirens" in the 1990s have likewise supported the idea that women (especially if they are white and attractive) can be both tough and sensitive; so have such courtroom dramas as "L.A. Law," "Civil Rights," and, in Canada, "Street Legal."

The most useful counter-images to the female prisoner stereotypes are a number of documentaries. Produced internationally, these offer honest representations of women in prison, and raise gender issues in the context of debates concerning the viability of incarceration.

In Canada, prison documentaries include P4W (1981), produced by Holly Dale and Janis Cole at the federal Prison for Women in Kingston. Interviews with an assortment of women give weight to the problems they encounter in their lives and in the institution. (This film includes an interview with Marlene Moore, whose life is discussed in Chapter Five.) Another Canadian film, *C'est pas parce que c'est un chateau qu'on est des princesses [Castle/No Princess]* (1986), documents life at Maison Gomin in Quebec, and effectively exudes the lethargy, weariness, deadly tedium and monotony, and perpetual waiting which, for many women, is the most difficult aspect of incarceration. Yet another documentary, *Prison Mother, Prison Daughter* (1987) was produced by John Kastner (who was also, contradictorily, responsible for the horrific *Turning to Stone,* discussed above). Without sensationalism, he interviews a hard-drinking mother who loses her infant son due to her incarceration, and a young middle-class woman whose parents are determined to get her out of prison and away from the "real criminals" in Canada's Prison for Women.

Also in Canada, Juliet Belmas, after six years as a prisoner, produced *A Year Whose Days Are Long* (1992), a prize-winning short film which artfully and metaphorically draws on her experiences in jail and prison. Using images drawn from her memories, every impression is magnified and invested with meaning. The jail setting is juxtaposed against the wedding of Princess Diana on television, thrusting both postmodern irreverence and reification of icons onto the refracted, visceral harshness of a spartan, locked environment. Belmas' lens manages to capture both the confining artifice of modern life and the all too real loss of liberty experienced by women in prison.

Two feature films, directed by women, which break away from the women-in-prison formula had limited distribution in North America, one as a "foreign" film and the other as a US Home Box Office (HBO) television special. The first of these, a landmark, is *The Scrubbers* (1982), a British film directed by Mai Zetterling of Sweden, which employs conventional stereotypes to tell a different kind of story. The film is comedic and poignant; for example, at night when the dormitory lights are turned off, we hear the girls and women calling out and singing to one another. The film is evocative throughout in its careful revelations of ways that institutionalized women are intimate with one another. The inevitable, physically stereotypical "butch" character—a tall lanky girl with a ducktail haircut, tight jeans and leather jacket—is level-headed and admired by the other women.

The HBO production, *Prison Stories: Women Inside* (1990), is a trilogy which presents the stories of three imprisoned women who are single mothers. Directed by Joan Micklin Silver, Penelope Spheeris and Donna Dietch, each segment exploits certain conventional devices, such as fist-fights among "the girls." Nevertheless, the stories convey authentic multicultural representations of women longing to be with their children; more generally, they demystify "criminal" women, and bring woman-identified substance and realism to the entertainment potential of incarcerated women.

CONCLUDING REFLECTIONS

Film and other media have been primary conduits both for the transmission of status quo values, and for the refraction of changes in values. The tension between respect for tradition and the constancy of change is what holds our attention. The media reflect and create mythologies which support dominant value systems, and reproduce time-worn stereotypes in keeping with status quo representations. At the same time, the media generate deviant, conflicting images against which the standard of normality can be set. The media also serve as sites of resistance, as reflected in cultural shifts and emergings of counter-identities.

In commercial films in the nineties, when women who can think, choose and act are represented in film or on television more often than in previous decades, most characters still have in common an unexamined devotion to the heterosexual imperative. As observed by David Altheide in speaking of television news, any challenge to the status quo must be incorporated "within the prevailing symbolic system" (Altheide, 1991: 9; see also Jaddou and Williams, 1981: 121). That hegemonic system is distinctly heterosexist, and gender-fixed notions of sexual identity are still prevalent in the media, despite clear shifts toward sizeable counter-cultures. With a focus on late 1980s TV rock videos as an opening site of cultural resistance, Ann Kaplan discusses the gender ambiguities in some music videos, which correspond with empirical shifts in sexual identities and gender relations amongst counter-culture youth:

> The plethora of gender positions on the [music] channel is arguably linked to the heterogeneity of current sex roles . . . all traditional categories, boundaries and institutions are being questioned. The androgynous surface of many star images indicates the blurring of clear lines between genders. . . . [O]ne often cannot tell whether a male or a female discourse dominates. (Kaplan, 1987: 90)

Unlike some avant garde rock video imagery, the "androgyny" of characters in low-budget female prison films is not a gender-bending technique reflective of contemporary shifts in the social construction of gender. Far from blending the strengths of "masculinity" and "femininity," or illustrating identity choices or points of view, the female characters are presented as surrogate male monsters. With simple-minded non-plots and gratuitous "sex" and violence, they have been popular as high camp pornography but cannot be viewed as serious portrayals of girls or women convicted of crime. Even when these films aspire beyond the low standards of B-movies, the female characters invariably constitute time-warped caricatures of men. Portrayals of women's prisons are reiterated over the decades by use of the same formulaic stereotypes.

Most women's prison movies are predictable and therefore, ultimately, boring. The unidimensional monster characters who repeatedly explode into violent rages appear more foolish than threatening. The characters lack the complexity of contemporary life. They are not to be believed. They do, however, viscerally influence how people think about and feel toward women convicted of crime. The cultivated fear of unruly women such as those depicted in most women-in-prison movies helps justify the construction of new maximum security prisons for women across North America. At any given time no more than 10 percent of women confined could be accurately perceived as representing a threat to other human beings or to the social order. Media-supported notions of she-monsters have contributed to public acceptance of monetary and social costs of imprisoning women who are not dangerous. To demystify the criminal woman would be to rob the entertainment industry of one of its cherished misogynist stereotypes.

NOTE

1. An earlier version of this chapter, under the title "Gendered Imaginations: Female Crime and Prison Movies," was prepared for Richard R. E. Kania (Ed.), *The Justice Professional* (Special Issue: Media, Crime and Criminal Justice) (1993).

REFERENCES

Altheide, David L. (1991). "The Impact of Television News Formats on Social Policy." *Journal of Broadcasting & Electronic Media,* 35(1): 3–21.

Black, M. (1979). "More about Metaphor," in A. Ortony (Ed.), *Metaphor and Thought.* Cambridge: Cambridge University Press, 19–43.

Brantley, Ben (1992). "Barbet's Feast." *Vanity Fair* (September): 162.

Bugliosi, Vincent with Curt Gentry (1974). *Helter Skelter* New York: W.W. Norton & Company.

Chesler, Phyllis (1993). "On Aileen Wuornos." *Off Our Backs* (June): 8–9, 22.

Cohen, Stanley (1972). *Folk Devils and Moral Panics.* London: MacGibbon & Kee.

Dates, Jannette L. and William Barlow (1990). *Split Image: African Americans in the Mass Media.* Washington, D.C.: Howard University Press.

de Lauretis, Teresa (1987). *Technologies of Gender: Essays on Theory, Film, and Fiction.* Bloomington: Indiana University Press.

Doane, Mary Ann, Patricia Mellencamp and Linda Williams (Eds.) (1984). *Revision: Essays in Feminist Film Criticism.* Los Angeles: University Publications of America, Inc.

Ericson, Richard V., Patricia M. Baranek and Janet B. J. Chan (1991). *Representing Order: Crime, Law and Justice in the News Media.* Toronto: University of Toronto Press.

Faith, Karlene (1987) "Media, Myths and Masculinization: Images of Women in Prison," in E. Adelberg and C. Currie (Eds.) *Too Few to Count: Canadian Women in Conflict with the Law.* Vancouver: Press Gang Publishers, 181–219.

Gaucher, Robert (1988). "The Prisoner as Ethnographer." *The Journal of Prisoners on Prisons* 1(1): 49–62.

Jaddou, Liliane and Jon Williams (1981). "A Theoretical Contribution to the Struggle against the Dominant Representation of Women." *Media, Culture and Society* 3(2): 105–24.

Janus, Noreene Z. (1977). "Research on Sex-Roles in the Mass Media: Toward a Critical Approach." *The Insurgent Sociologist* 7(3): 19–31.

Kaplan, E. Ann (1987). *Rocking Around the Clock: Music Television, Postmodernism and Consumer Culture.* London: Methuen & Co.

Klaits, Joseph (1985). *Servants of Satan: The Age of the Witch Hunts.* Bloomington: Indiana University Press.

Kuhn, Annette (1982). *Women's Pictures: Feminism and Cinema.* London: Routledge & Kegan Paul.

Lapsley, Robert and Michael Westlake (1988). *Film Theory: An Introduction.* New York: Manchester University Press.

Macfarlane, A. D. J. (1977). "Witchcraft in Tudor and Stuart Essex," in J. S. Cockburn (Ed.), *Crime in England, 1550–1800.* Princeton, N.J.: Princeton University Press, 72–89.

Pribram, E. Deidre (Ed.) (1988). *Female Spectators: Looking at Film and Television.* London: Verso.

Russo, Vito (1987). *The Celluloid Closet: Homosexuality in the Movies* (Revised Edition). New York: Harper & Row.

Stone, Merlin (1976). *When God Was a Woman.* New York: Harcourt Brace Jovanovich.

Surette, Ray (1992). *Media, Crime, and Criminal Justice: Images and Realities.* Pacific Grove: Brooks/Cole Publishing Company.

Todd, Janet (Ed.) (1988). *Women and Film.* London: Holmes & Meier.

Travers, Peter (1992). "Review: Single White Female." *Rolling Stone* (September 3): 72.

Tuchman, Gaye (1979). "Women's Depiction by the Mass Media," *Signs: Journal of Women in Culture and Society* 4(3): 528–42.

CHAPTER SEVEN

Education for Empowerment: California, 1972–1976[1]

O N WEEKENDS during the years 1972 to 1976, carloads of grad-uate student instructors, professors, law students, artists, performers and community activists, from throughout the state, converged at the California Institution for Women (CIW). Situated in what was called "cor-rections valley," a cluster of prisons amidst fertile fields, orchards and cow pastures in rural Riverside County sixty miles east of Los Angeles, it was the world's largest prison for women, then filled to capacity with over 600 pris-oners.[2] The purpose of these prison gatherings was to offer university courses, cultural workshops and artistic performances to imprisoned women. With the sponsorship of the History of Consciousness graduate program and Commu-nity Studies at the University of California, the Santa Cruz Women's Prison Project (SCWPP), from a distance of almost 500 miles, organized and coordi-nated this regular weekend activity.

Hundreds of people engaged in this work and each would have their own memories and stories to tell. I am confident as I begin that I will leave out important details that have escaped my memory. And I regret that, after twenty years, I do not have complete memory or records of all the individuals who participated, so that I could acknowledge everyone's vital contributions. As it is, I am including names of at least some of the instructors and other vol-unteers within the text, both to emphasize the collective nature of the work and to begin at least a partial recognition of individuals involved in this work. One day the complete history can be written, but for now this is the story as I remember it.

• • •

Radical and Black Power politics in the US in the late 1960s and early 1970s, and a series of uprisings in men's prisons across the continent, resulted in critical analyses of prisons, the creation of prisoners' rights organizations and unions, and new communications between prisoners, academics and community activists. By the early 1970s, prisoners' writings were required reading in numerous university courses, and some universities began teaching courses inside prisons. In California, almost all of this activity was centreed on African-American male prisoners, who were (and are) seriously overrepresented in the imprisoned population. African-American women were similarly overrepresented at 40 percent of the California female prison population, while constituting only 10 percent of the female population in the state. Yet women in prison had received virtually no attention from activists: they constituted less than 4 percent of all state prisoners, they were not generally as politicized as the men, and they did not engage in the kinds of protest actions which attracted media attention.

In 1970, while teaching a political science course with prisoner-students at the Soledad maximum security men's institution (Faith, 1975), I was startled to discover that even they knew nothing at all of women in prison, not even the location of the one state facility for women. These men knew all about the dozens of state and federal male prisons which dotted the state, and among them they had served time in many of these institutions, but female prisoners were as invisible to them as they were to the broader public.

Out of frustration that there was so little community knowledge of incarcerated women (and so few library references), I turned my focus to "women behind bars." Beginning in the spring of 1972 I virtually lived at the California Institution for Women during most weekdays for a five-month period, doing participant-observation research up to fourteen hours a day. I also gathered data from prison files, administered questionnaires and did life history interviews with 100 women. Dozens more participated in small-group interviews on the experience of incarceration. A recurrent complaint among the women was the lack of programs with relevance to their own life experience, and some wanted to know specifically about "women's lib," then a hot topic in the media. Thus began the work of organizing the first university-level course to be taught in a women's prison, on the topic of "Women in Society."

Publishers and Santa Cruz bookstores donated texts. The university Community Studies department, chaired by Bill Friedland, agreed to provide credit on a Pass/No Record basis[3] through arrangements with Carl Tjerandsen, Director of the Extended Studies Division. Although most of the women in prison would not have qualified for university admission by normal criteria, they could enter this special program as "mature students." The prison administration and education director agreed to allow up to fifty women to enrol in the course, in two sections which met on alternate evenings in the school building. The fifty spaces were filled, first come first served, in the first day of sign-up. A friend, Jean Gallick, offered to work with me as co-instructor and she also offered to individually tutor women who lacked particular academic skills.

The women who signed up for the class were representative of the heterogeneity of the prison population at large: they were aged eighteen to over sixty, with the majority in their early thirties. Most were mothers, a few were "old dykes." They were serving sentences of lengths varying from two years to life, primarily for theft, fraud and drug-related offences. A few were serving their first prison sentence; others had been in and out of state prison since their youth. About half the students were white, almost half were African-Americans, and a few were Latina (primarily Chicana), Asian and Native. Most had grown up with poverty, and had not completed high school, but all were prepared to work hard to prove they could do university level work. And they did.

The course made use of reading materials from anthropology, literature, law, psychology, sociology and history, and virtually everything that had been published by Second Wave feminists to that time. The discussions, readings and written assignments all stimulated the women to consult their life-histories to form their analysis. The course topics centreed on the family, schooling, racism, women and the law, and "'myself' as woman." Many of the women were critical of the "white middle-class" perspectives of some of the assigned literature, but almost to a woman they believed in the importance of "women's liberation" as they came to understand it on their own terms. They also participated in rigorous discussions of how prejudicial attitudes based on racial identity worked to divide them within the prison and to obscure their commonalities as women. The response to this class was overwhelmingly positive, as indicated by a sampling of excerpts from the evaluations:

Through this class I have seen something happen. I've done so much time and I've never seen a group of convicts hang in with each other in so much unity. It's been beautiful, a spiritual experience really. You walk past people every day in the institution and you don't know they've got all this in their head or in their heart and we came together in this classroom and there it all was.

All the reading and writing taught me things I hadn't known before—about the world and about myself. It gave me hope.

I saw sisterhood in action for the first time. I was in with a group of women of all different types and we all became one. It's the first time I have ever been with a group of people where I felt completely free to say whatever I thought or felt. It was something very beautiful.

The class was one of the most meaningful experiences I've ever had. I learned a lot of respect for myself as a woman, as your teachings showed me I have a right to be proud of myself. The writing assignments made me sit down and take a really good look at myself as a person and as a woman and, hey! I learned to like myself.

I appreciated getting credit but I would have kept coming to class anyway because I found myself learning so much.

Since starting the class I have given much thought to what I want to do with my life as a vocation. I would really like to learn how to write. [This woman became a published poet before being paroled.]

The outcome of the class was unbelievable. This is what we need. I certainly hope that this first college class at ciw will give an example to bring in more classes for the benefit of the women who are willing to further their education. I am very proud to have been one of your students this summer.

We need more such courses here to help us get ready to go back into society. This is definitely something we must carry over into the future.

As is common in Women's Studies courses, everyone involved in the class (including Jean and myself) had their consciousness raised through this first class experience. We were all satisfied that the experiment was a success and that we should carry on with an expanded program. Both the university and prison administrations agreed. Jean and I talked it up in Santa Cruz and through the women's movement grapevine. Our interest was contagious, buttressed by the sponsorship of the avant garde History of Consciousness graduate program at the University of California at Santa Cruz, a campus which has had a reputation for innovative initiatives in outreach education and community alliances. Many women and some men from all over the state, including other community activists, performers, graduate and law students, and university faculty (mostly from Santa Cruz, but from other universities as well, including Stanford, San Jose and UCLA), let us know they would like to participate. The Santa Cruz Women's Prison Project evolved rapidly from an interdisciplinary academic initiative to a statewide educational, political, cultural, artistic, spiritual and entertainment network which converged on weekends at the women's prison. From the beginning, the volunteers included many feminists and other revolutionaries on the cutting edge of post-1960s cultural and political resistance movements. Some had spent time in jail, or would in the future, for actions against the Vietnam war and against investment in South Africa, and for their support of other radical causes including civil rights campaigns.

The work of the Santa Cruz project was coordinated by a fluctuating number of women, generally between seven and ten of us, located in Santa Cruz, Los Angeles and San Francisco. As unpaid but often full-time coordinators, working with dozens of other volunteers at any given time, our activities included: liaising with the university and the prison; working with women inside in designing accredited arts, humanities and social science curricula; recruiting university professors, graduate students and community activists as volunteer instructors; providing academic advice to prisoners enrolling in the program; arranging classrooms and other basic logistics; setting up poetry readings, concerts, dances and other cultural events in the prison according to the women's interests, and doing the same on the outside to introduce people to the work of the project; setting up outside art shows of work done by women in the institution; working on projects with in-prison groups such as a three-day Black Culture Marathon co-sponsored by the African-American Sisterhood; providing sponsorships for new self-help groups such as the Long-Termers Organization which, in our third year, sponsored an historic in-prison public forum on "alternatives to incarceration" attended by over 200 guests from the outside; supporting projects such as "family days" and the construction of a playground through the mothers' support group; soliciting donations of textbooks from publishers; writing small-grant proposals for modest funding from progressive social change foundations such as Vanguard and Liberty Hill; organizing prisoners' rights benefits on the outside in collaboration with diverse community groups, such as the Vietnam Veterans Against the War, Women Against Rape and the Women's Health Center; maintaining contact and coalition work with a myriad of political activist groups around the state, and with graduate students and dissident faculty from the School of Criminology at the University of California at Berkeley, which was shut down by then-Governor Ronald Reagan as a result of social justice work and student/faculty protest activity; assisting prisoner-students when they were released on parole (which over time became increasingly time-consuming, involving a statewide network of support contacts); writing admission recommendation letters and arranging transfer credit for parolees enrolling in other colleges and universities; an enormous amount of public speaking, writing articles, and radio, television and film work to raise and maintain statewide interest in and support for the project; and, generally, balancing our goals for the program with the demands of the university, those of the prison authorities, and the prisoners' own priorities.

The coordinators, in their respective locations, organized local support groups that made collective decisions concerning the specific work of their own group, and, through phone consultations, made decisions on issues that affected the group as a whole. Primary organizational and scheduling responsibilities, curriculum planning and liaison with the university rested with the Santa Cruz group, with primary leadership from Catherine Cusic (Angell), Jean Gallick, Debra Miller, Nancy Stoller (Shaw) and myself working with a core group of approximately forty people. The San Francisco group was organized by women then in law school, among them Tanya Neiman, Abigail Ginsberg, Marilyn Waller and Ann Grogan, who engaged the energies of over thirty women and a number of men, and they handled the legal education component for the four-year duration of the program. The Los Angeles group, with the closest proximity to the prison, organized special events, an on-going art workshop, and, under the leadership of Frances Reid, and later Mary K. Blackmon, Ruth Maraner and Marilyn Stamos, was closely involved with the Santa Cruz group in planning and logistics. The Los Angeles group also sponsored a major public forum on women in prison and organized a group called the Organization of Family and Friends of Women in Prison.

The Santa Cruz Women's Prison Project was a collectively organized, statewide network, for the most part united in our socialist-feminist outlook but with diversity amongst us. The collective process was challenging. Some of us had more experience and knowledge of the institution and a more sustained commitment than others. The prison authorities could not grasp the collective concept and wanted some of us to speak for everyone else. The distance between the three central locations of activity caused some communication delays and difficulties. But we never lost the ideal of working collectively, we routinely engaged in the process of criticism/self-criticism, and there were few actual conflicts over the years. The coordinators from all three locations cooperated with each other's initiatives, and although we didn't always arrive at a consensus concerning program policies and had to make compromises, we avoided most of the problems of centralized power which serve to subvert the principles of collective decision-making. We didn't model ourselves after any existing program, but in form and content we resembled (and sometimes worked in coalition with) the "People's Colleges" and "Universities Without Walls" which operated out of storefronts in the San Francisco Bay Area during the late 1960s and into the 1970s. Apart from very small grants, we all covered expenses out of our own pockets; volunteers who could afford it would sometimes contribute a few hundred dollars to assist with gas expenses, postage, teaching materials, telephone, film rentals and so on. We sought donations for everything we needed: IBM, for example, donated a typewriter to our work.

Few of us who worked with the Santa Cruz Women's Prison Project qualified as "professionals," but those of us who were graduate students expected (accurately) to enter various professions upon completion of our studies. Many of us were working class, and some of us were very poor either temporarily or as class inheritance. A number of us were single parents, and in terms of material and familial circumstances many of us were intimately familiar with the problems of the women in the prison. Most of us brought class consciousness to our work, most of us considered ourselves leftists of one stripe or another, and lesbian feminists did most of the organizational work. As a group we did not adhere to any party line. Those who went to the prison included: Caucasians, African-Americans, Natives, Hispanics and Latinas; heterosexuals, bisexuals, gays and lesbians; people from a wide age range, with most in our twenties or thirties; people inexperienced with the criminal justice system and former prisoners; many renters who lived communally (for both economic reasons and as a political lifestyle choice) but also nuclear family people and people living alone; and so on.

In the first years of the project we were both male and female, but by the end it was almost entirely women who went in. Given that we were a distinctly feminist project at a stage in the Second Wave women's movement when many feminist women were separatists, and given that we were working with women in a segregated institution, the initial decision to include men was made with careful thought, and the men who joined us were very conscious and supportive of feminist issues. As articulated by one of these men, Arnie Fischman, in retrospect:

> . . . being a man in the context of women building a strong feminist consciousness—it may seem strange, but that was always one of the most comfortable parts of the project for me. It really felt good. Most male or mixed groups, including political groups, fall into a tone or style or "feel" of masculine aggressiveness, intellectuality, heaviness and competitiveness, showing off and so on, that has always made me feel awkward, uncomfortable and inadequate, or else I hate myself when I find myself trying to be part of it. In the prison or at our meetings outside there was always a very powerful quality and spirit that I felt so much more at home in, and longed for. Of course there were moments in the prison when I had that disturbing experience of being Other, but there were always so many strange and intense emotional things going on there that that feeling was never sustained or very important to the experience.

Our cultural diversity was our strength. Over the four-year life of the program, several hundred women and a few dozen men volunteered occasional or regular weekends to teach, facilitate workshops or perform in the prison. We became a strong support system for one another in part because of our lack of resources. For example, volunteers from Santa Cruz and the Bay Area got to know one another very well in the ten-hour drives to the prison and through improvised housing over the weekend. Sometimes we would get a couple of motel rooms with bodies in sleeping bags covering every inch of the floor. Sometimes we stayed on the floor of a church basement. On occasion we were allowed to sleep dormitory-style in a closed-off hospital section of a neighbouring men's prison. As a non-funded program we had to be resourceful, and despite significant differences among us we did that in a spirit of mutual support.

At any given time, approximately one hundred women, one-sixth of the prison population, enrolled in academic courses (or "workshops," as they were called generically) for university credit. Some classes had only a few participants, others were packed with up to sixty students. Several hundred more women, that is, the majority of the prison population, participated in informal workshops, attended concerts and other events sponsored by the SCWPP, and in other ways showed their support for the project. Accredited workshop attendance varied according to interest, but whenever attendance at "extra-curricular" events was low we had to consider the reasons: were women being intimidated by staff against association with the Santa Cruz group? were we losing touch with what the women were interested in? We were continually challenged to understand the prison environment in its fluctuating "moods" and to make adjustments and respond accordingly.

Although we were only one of many community organizations which, during the 1970s, brought volunteer projects and sponsorships to the California Institution for Women, we were a regular weekend presence and, for reasons to be discussed later in this chapter, our program stood out from the others. The program was successful from the perspective of most prisoner-students, as evidenced by: their consistent attendance; recruitment of other prisoners to the program; active involvement in guiding the program's direction; enthusiasm expressed directly to outsiders and indirectly through the prison grapevine; prisoners' sustained contact with outsiders following their release from CIW; and, the positive correlation between involvement in the program and chances for a successful parole (of approximately 100 women of one cohort who completed credit courses, within five years only five recidivated, compared to the usual recidivism rate of over 70 percent).

Through the first year of the program, the CIW administrators were publicly appreciative that the University of California was making it possible for women inside to take university-level courses. This was a first in the history of women's prisons, and the CIW administration was glad to take credit for bringing in the program. The California Department of Corrections was similarly supportive, especially because the work was donated entirely through the university, with volunteer labour and barebones expenses covered by individual donations, fund-raising events and small grants from progressive foundations.

Attitudes of the prison guards toward the program were mixed in the beginning. Those few who had themselves gone to college or university, both men and women, were in agreement that education is a sensible use of prison time. Some of those who lacked education themselves were disdainful of the folly of trying to educate "stupid convicts." Other guards were resentful that "the inmates" would be able to get college credits while they did their time, perceived as a reward for committing the crime(s). As working people with families, the staff did not themselves have the luxury of going to school. Complicating this dynamic was the reality that the majority of the volunteers who came to the prison were working-class women for whom education was not a privilege but a hard-earned goal. They were thus less than sympathetic to the disdain of guards who perceived anyone affiliated with a university as "beneath" their own hard-working selves. When this disdain was tinged with perceptible sexism, the sympathy dropped accordingly.

The downhill turn for the project came with some of the male guards' increasing resentment of us as a bunch of "commie-hippie perverts" or "weird, radical kooks." In one of my first meetings with the warden, while engaged with my research, she identified herself as someone who shared the goals of the women's liberation movement; she looked to social causes of crime, rather than individual pathologies. Over time, however, it was clear that many members of her staff, that is, frontline guards, were contemptuous of anyone who did not regard "criminal women" as a breed apart. Although not all the women on the staff were enthusiastic about our presence, and although not all the men on the staff were antagonistic, it was primarily male guards who actively resisted our work. Many of us were (or became) prison abolitionists, and we made that position known inside the prison as well as outside through the media. Much of this story relates to ways by which our work was obstructed by staff who opposed us, but it is perhaps even more significant that so many of the staff did support our work.

Everyone entering the prison from the outside was subject to prior security clearances and routine body searches upon entry and departure, and otherwise reminded of the necessity to obey all prison regulations and to acquiesce without argument to any order by the guards. It was agreed by the prison administrators that the content of the courses would not be censored. This agreement did not, however, extend to the literature we brought to the prison. Books were donated to the project in two ways: publishers sent boxes of texts marked "not-for-resale," and bookstores gave us their paperback throwaway stock with the covers torn off. We observed that the guards didn't examine the content of books without covers; they just "pushed them through." They did, however, react against radical cover titles and graphics and these were the books they confiscated, especially those authored by Karl Marx, George Jackson and other present or former prisoners, or any writer publicly associated with left or Black Power political perspectives. Our solution was to tear off the covers of all paperbacks we brought to the prison. The guards were not interested in the small print. It was the bold titles, evocative images and dangerous names that caught their attention.

The effort to not rock the boat extended to wardrobe, at a time when hippie garb, blue-collar work clothes and African dashikis were in popular-radical fashion both in the prison and in the outside world. This was the normal clothing of many of the volunteers, but they were ridiculed by uniformed prison guards who were generally white working-class conservatives, both male and female. Some of us tried to be more "conventional" in dress and appearance so as to not offend the fashion sensibilities of the guards, but some of us (due to prejudices against skin colour, Jewishness, men with long hair, women with unshaven legs, and so on) were unavoidably "offensive" to certain guards. Most of us, for one reason or another, simply did not fit the majority of the guards' notions of respectable university professor-types. Even those instructors who appeared very proper were tainted by association.

After the first honeymoon year with the prison administration, we experienced increasingly overt expressions of resentment by guards and high-ranked security administrators who wanted us out of there. Our problems were exacerbated by some foolish mistakes by SCWPP volunteers which resulted in periodic, temporary expulsion of the program from the prison. Much of this story, then, is about the constant struggle to keep the program active. On those occasions when the program was in hiatus as a punishment for some breach of prison regulations or protocol (see examples below), the program coordinators and volunteers used their energy to do public education and fund-raising through protest rallies, community meetings and forums, the media and cultural events. We appealed to university officials, public figures and state authorities to examine the extent to which prisons can operate as hidden, autonomous institutions, with the right to deny access to outsiders and to thereby increase the vulnerability of prisoners to human rights violations of the kind described in Chapter Five. The prisoners, meanwhile, were protesting from inside, circulating petitions, holding work strikes, and meeting with the administration to urge that the program continue.

As a collectivist program, the Santa Cruz Women's Prison Project accepted the views of imprisoned women that educational programs and empowering knowledges were the most useful tools that could be offered within the confines of a prison. We also found music and the arts to be the most collectively healing antidotes to (and refuges within) an oppressive environment. The program that I describe could only have occurred within a particular historical and

political context, California in the 1970s, through a specific convergence of
women's liberation and prisoners' rights movements. Unlike the conservatism
of most prison education programs in the 1990s, we began on the premise that
it is not people in prisons who need to change so much as society itself.

Here, then, is the first descriptive account of the first university-level program for women in any prison, conducted at the California Institution for
Women between 1972 and 1976. I go on to describe controversial program
activities and incidents which resulted in conflicts between program participants and the prison staff and administration. Finally, I analyze the means by
which the state resisted encroachment of alternative values and knowledges
within the controlled environment of the prison.

THE "SANTA CRUZ WORKSHOPS"

As discussed in Chapter Three, the establishment of separate institutions for
incarcerated women in England and North America, in the late 19th century,
was one of the first purported reforms in the history of penitentiaries. These
early prisons, to the limited extent that they met their "ideals," focused on
gender-based rehabilitation of "fallen" women, consisting of domestic training
(cleaning, laundry, sewing, food preparation and hygiene), and literacy for the
purpose of moral training through Bible study. In the 1990s, most prison officials, as well as critics, acknowledge the contradictions of attempts to
"rehabilitate" someone within the punitive, custodial environments of prisons,
but in the 1970s, when the Santa Cruz Women's Prison Project was formed,
this goal still dominated "correctional" rhetoric in North America.

The program established by the Santa Cruz Women's Prison Project broke
with all assumptions of traditional penal philosophy. We did not assume that
people in prisons are in any greater need of rehabilitation than any other segment of society. Rather, we analyzed crime as a socially constructed condition,
and criminal justice as a discriminatory system which criminalized people
from the least socially empowered groups. We rejected patriarchal and class-
based presumptions of fixed gender roles, thus we did not accept the common
view that women in conflict with the law *de facto* suffer from non-conformity
to "feminine" standards. We also didn't presume to know better than the
women inside what they needed to make sense of their lives during incarceration or when they were released. We recognized that women in prison are

adults who are no less aware of the world they live in than anyone else, and, despite popular mythology, no less intelligent by any discernible standard. This perception was validated by my review, in 1972, of one hundred randomly selected CIW files which revealed that Stanford-Binet IQ tests, which were administered to all the women, produced an average score of 110. This score, a high average, would probably have been even higher outside the exceptionally stressful conditions of the prison, especially if the scores were adjusted for cross-cultural discrepancies in the test.

It was at the urging of interested prisoners that we arranged to bring accredited university-level courses and cultural events to the prison, and in the collective process of designing the curricula we gave priority to courses which reflected directly on their articulated concerns. In contrast with the existing vocational and school programs in the prison which offered instruction in sewing, hairdressing, office work or Grade 12 equivalency, we introduced the study of critical theory and substantive social issues affecting women's lives. "Women's Lib" had been a hot news item for several years when we began the program in 1972, and women inside wanted to know about it from people directly involved in the movement. We thus developed, in this unlikely circumstance, what became, in effect, one of the nation's earliest women's studies programs. By this time very little contemporary feminist work had been published, but whatever existed was made available to women who took our courses. This included the work of Kate Millett, Shulamith Firestone, Betty Friedan and Germaine Greer, all of whom were critiqued for their limited (white, middle-class) perspectives, and Robin Morgan's edited collection of essays, *Sisterhood is Powerful,* which became the most widely read book at the prison.

A number of us involved in the program had been previously involved in multicultural grassroots community schools, and had studied the work of Paulo Freire, Ivan Illich, Paul Goodman and other liberationist educators. Those of us who at the time were graduate students had also been influenced by the interdisciplinary methods of our History of Consciousness professors, including historian Page Smith, philosopher Norman O. Brown, poet Robert Duncan, and psychologists Bert Kaplan and Ted Sarbin.[4] Most of us adhered to a philosophy of education which was holistic, student-centreed and praxis-oriented, whereby theory was informed by practice with an explicit commitment to social change. To teach was to work together with students to ask critical questions, critique the androcentricity of conventional texts, make political sense of social reality, and effect changes in the construction of knowledge and the analysis of experience. Circle discussions, films and other audiovisual aids, exercises in verbal and written communications, and open critiques of one another's work replaced hierarchical classroom orderings and lecture formats. In these "student-centreed" groups, the prisoners themselves often took initiative for material to be covered or for presentations drawing on their experiences prior to or during incarceration. A minority of the instructors in the program took more didactic or traditional pedagogic approaches in setting up their prison classrooms, with authoritative lectures, formal presentations and conventional methods of examination. In our teaching methods, then, we were relatively autonomous, just as was true on the university campus.

Educational and cultural programs established by the Santa Cruz Women's Prison Project and the University of California were known in the prison, generically, as the "Santa Cruz Workshops." Each credit course consisted of a series of from four to twelve all-day workshops held in the school building on weekends so as to not interfere with the prison work assignments. Special entertainment events, which we called our "celebrations," were held in the recreation room or the prison gymnasium on Saturday and Sunday evenings. Non-credit workshops were generally one-time events which engaged the interest of many women in the prison who were not initially interested in taking courses for credit but who, as a result of contact with the program, gained confidence and enrolled in credit courses in subsequent terms. Prior to each new term, posters were placed throughout the prison "campus," in each of the cell blocks and in all the work and recreation areas, to announce upcoming courses and cultural events. Any woman in the prison was eligible to enrol unless her security level did not permit her to be with the "open" population. The majority of enrollees had not completed high school, as was true of the prison population at large, but many had since completed adult education courses and had otherwise shown interest in advanced education. Attendance varied according to the degree to which a course was a "hot topic"; commonly about a hundred women at any given time would be involved in courses for credit. Every weekend we were at the prison from 8 a.m. to 9:30 p.m. both Saturday and Sunday.

The curriculum offered to women enrolled in the academic component of the Santa Cruz workshops changed from one year to the next (with some courses repeated), depending on availability of instructors and students' stated interests. As an example of the curriculum, following is a brief description of the courses offered during the term October-June, 1973–74:

1. WOMEN AND THE LAW. Organized by Catherine Cusic, with law students Tanya Neiman, Abigail Ginsberg, Judith Kurtz, Ann Grogan, Peggy Baker, Chris Epifania, Ellen Chaitin, Mary Brutocao, Judy Meyer and many others, the course was officially taught by Professor of Law and Assistant Dean at Hastings College of the Law, Wyanne Bunyan. She was assisted in rotation by twelve feminist law students (one of whom, Mary Morgan, was later the first self-identified lesbian to be appointed to a municipal judgeship). A boon to jailhouse lawyers at CIW, this course included units on the following: criminal procedure; sentencing; prisoners' legal rights; post-conviction remedies; legal aspects of health care; women and family law; and, outside legal rights concerned with landlord-tenant relations, discrimination, welfare and consumer risks. In addition to imparting useful legal knowledge, this course was singularly successful in demystifying the reasons so many of the women were in prison.

2. ETHNIC STUDIES. Taught by Bill Moore, a leader in the Bay Area African-American community, with seven assistants, male and female, this course included historical and sociological perspectives on Third World women in the US, including Native women, Chicanas, Asian-Americans and African-Americans. This was an exceptionally popular course, in part due to the high ratio of minority women within the prison, many of whom had direct input into the issues to be studied. (The vast majority of guards and other prison staff were white, at a time when the Black Panthers and other Third World struggle groups were posing a challenge to racist traditions in law enforcement; not surprisingly, then, the guards had strong concerns about our offering this course.) One of the most popular units, among black and white students alike, was the audiovisual history of Black music and its influences on US culture, taught by media and music scholar Bill Barlow.

3. RADICAL PSYCHOLOGY. Taught by a progressive Santa Cruz therapist, Theo Alter, with three assistants, this course critically examined assumptions and practices of then-dominant schools of psychology, psychoanalysis and psychotherapy, including Freud, Jung, Transactional Analysis, Gestalt and Reality Therapy. A fundamental principle of both radical psychology and feminism

in the 1970s was that "the personal is political," thus problems of alienation and power relations were examined in the context of the political economy as it affects society's "mental health." The course was designed to provide a safe and nurturing learning environment whereby women could identify trouble areas in their own emotional lives and gain insights into how best to resolve them with appropriate support.

4. POLITICS: US INSTITUTIONS AND POLITICAL CONSCIOUSNESS. The instructor of this course, Michael Rotkin, had been a political mentor to many of us involved in the SCWPP and to the Santa Cruz community at large. In 1979 he was elected to the City Council and later became the first self-declared socialist-feminist city mayor in the USA. This high-enrolment course, repeated over several terms, was taught by Michael with five male and female guest speakers/assistants (including economist John Isbister and sociologist William Domhoff). They challenged students to formulate analyses of capitalism as the underlying institution of North American political structure, with attention to the evolution of monopoly capitalism and economic stagnation in the 20th century. Critical analysis focused on the role of the state in setting and implementing social policy relative to schools, the family, prisons, welfare, the tax structure and income distribution. This course was particularly satisfying to those few women, generally well-educated, who were serving time for political crimes, and who welcomed the opportunity to engage in dialogue and analysis with other critical thinkers. But the instructor was equally impressed "by women in the prison who had never had a formal education." Continuing in his words,

> They'd read difficult texts that undergraduates on campus wouldn't touch. They thought through the readings on a critical level, and I attribute their ability partly to their being in prison. The level of their work was as high as in any class I've taught at the university. The classes were as intellectually challenging as some graduate seminars. Their ability to deal with abstraction was evident—except when someone was on Thorazine! (M. Rotkin, course evaluation, 1976)

Michael's view was echoed by virtually all the volunteer instructors who taught university-level courses with women in the prison.

5. CREATIVE ARTS. This course was taught and organized by Catherine Cusic and Debra Miller, key coordinators of the SCWPP, who offered a broad

survey of the creative arts in part to introduce the women, many of them artists themselves, to some of the woman-identified art and culture that was proliferating in the "free" world. Units focused on music, dance, drama, art, photography, film, mime and puppetry, with over thirty guest performers and speakers. For their final assignment, students were required to create their own artistic piece—painting, sculpture, ceramics, photography, music or dramatic presentation.

In addition to the workshops for registered students, there were well-attended shows where guest artists performed or displayed their work, to which all the women in the prison were invited. Music performances, the highlights of each weekend the SCWPP was at the prison, introduced the women to a wide range of talent and inspiration, including performers from the just emerging "women's music" network. Over time, our prison concerts were held not only at CIW but also at county jails and federal prisons, under the sponsorship of an outgrowth project, Music Inside/Out, coordinated by Debra Miller, Laraine Goodman and myself. Among the featured musicians were the following: Margie Adam, Rebecca Adams, Gwen Avery, Bonnie Bramlett, Linda Carpenter, David Carradine, Meg Christian, Lacy J. Dalton, Tret Fure, Cathy Gates, Infinite Sound (Roland Young and Glenn Howell), Diane Lindsay, Country Joe McDonald, June Millington, Holly Near, Pauline Oliveros, Vicki Randle, Jackie Robbins, George Stavis, Linda Tillery, Mary Watkins and Cris Williamson. In addition to these concerts, there were special performances by the Miss Alice Stone Ladies Society Orchestra, the Santa Cruz Home-Grown Puppets (with Barbara Franklin, Anthony Eschbach, Barbara Gregory, Scott Soares and Tarey Dunn), filmmakers who presented their works, such as Frances Reid of Iris Films (who also served as one of the SCWPP coordinators), and poets, including Pat Parker and Judy Grahn. We also showed films almost every weekend on a broad range of political and cultural themes, such as: labour struggles; many facets of women's liberation; resistance movements of political minority groups (African-American, Natives, Chicanos and so on); health care in China; the Indochina peace campaign; and welfare rights.

These cultural events were a joyful and uplifting contrast to the numbing lethargy induced by day-to-day prison routine. Often they were an opportunity for women who had learned to love other women to celebrate those feelings. According to the type of performance, some events were high-spirited, with everybody dancing and letting off steam; other events were spiritually calming. Women of varied cultural heritage expanded their appreciation of the arts through this course; they also got in touch with their feelings, renewed their hopes for the future, and found camaraderie and friendship among both insiders and outsiders.

6. ON BEING A WOMAN. Jean Gallick, one of the founders of the SCWPP, was the instructor for this course, working with thirteen female assistants plus members of the Berkeley-Oakland Women's Union. With numerous audiovisual aids, including slides, films, poetry and music, the course presented a potpourri of cultural, economic and political dimensions of being a woman, with specific topics as follows: women and their bodies; Third World women and human rights; depictions of women in literature and the media; class analysis of the women's movement; feminism as political ideology; women, money and power; the state and the family (taught by influential political activist Michael Strange); Sappho and "female homosexuality" in ancient Greece vis-à-vis 20th century lesbians; and, women in South East Asia and the effects of the Vietnam war (with author Arlene Eisen-Bergman as guest speaker). The course presented a powerful array of new ways of thinking about women and their many identities; in effect it constituted an early "Women's Studies 101."

7. DRUG USE IN US CULTURE. Almost half the women in the prison had been convicted of illegal drug offences, so this course was indisputably relevant to their preoccupations. Taught by Josette Mondanaro, M.D., Director of the California Health Department Substance Abuse Programs, the course included the following topics: the process of "getting high"; the politics and economics of drug distribution and use; effects on babies born to mothers addicted to heroin or methadone; the physical effects of "downers," including alcohol, barbiturates, sedatives and tranquilizers; the physical effects of "uppers," including amphetamines and hallucinatory pharmacological drugs; the relationship of drugs to prostitution (with Margot St. James, founder of COYOTE—Call Off Your Old Tired Ethics—as a guest speaker); the effects of race, sex and class on drugs of "choice"; analysis of drug abuse treatment programs; the uses of law and the criminal justice system in responding to drug use; and, confronting addiction. One topic that couldn't be critically addressed, given the context, was the pervasive extent to which women in prison were dependent on prescription drugs distributed (legally) to addicts within the institution.

8. CREATIVE WRITING AND LITERATURE. One of the ways some women in CIW maintained their sense of private space or "sanity" was to keep a prison diary or to write poetry or short stories for the prisoner newsletter, *The Clarion*. This course, which was team-taught on a tutorial basis coordinated by Ellen Rifkin (Fischman), encouraged this writing activity. The first section of the course focused on writing skills in the genres of informational articles, poetry, short stories, plays, essays, and autobiography. Tutors offered critical feedback and the students shared their writings with one another and discussed and evaluated one another's work in a supportive classroom environment. The second section of the course introduced the students to literary analysis and criticism in a variety of workshops, with such foci as the interpretation of modern fiction, which explored writers of different ethnic and cultural backgrounds, and primal myths, a study of pre-literature stories of gods and goddesses with themes such as metamorphosis, matriarchal and patriarchal cycles, initiation, rebirth and death. Because dreams have been a rich source of mythic materials, students in this workshop kept written collections of their dreams and examined their usefulness as signifiers of "essential" experience.

Numerous participants in this course were thought by the instructors to have distinct writing talent. Debra Miller, one of the SCWPP coordinators, later gathered a number of these women for a poetry project, which produced a self-published collection of their work. (After what seemed like endless debates on what to call their book, they settled on *no title at all is better than a title like that!*) Among these prison poets was Norma Stafford, whose work garnered expansive praise from instructors and sister-prisoners alike. With the co-sponsorship of the SCWPP and the San Francisco Unitarian-Universalist church she later self-published a collection titled *Dear Somebody* (1975), from which the following is excerpted:

> *Lying in your captive labour bed*
> *womb straining sweat pouring*
> *you deliver your child*
> *within these concrete walls and steel bars*
> *because your infant is born of you/in here*
> *she is labeled numbered and her mug-shot is taken*
> *before she has breathed before the cord is cut*
> *she has a number and she is called criminal*
> *but you and I know you have delivered to us*

another awesome female warrior.
I hear your deep woman's laughter
ring out through every cell block
and my heart is strengthened
my courage renewed because you are here
just as you are everywhere noble warrior
goddess of Death to the Power
giver of life sweet sweet woman soldier.

• • •

In addition to the courses described above, many other popular courses and workshops were presented through the four years of the project. These courses and instructors included:

ART HISTORY *Rory White, Mary Bargion*
THE ART OF MIDWIFERY *Cheryl Anderson, Kimberly Clouse*
ART THERAPY *Georgia Griffin, Joan Hertzberg, Coeleen Kiebert*
CHICANA CULTURE AND COMMUNITY STUDIES *Katia Panas, Mary Thomas, Maggie Martinez*
COMMUNITY CHILDCARE *Michael Strange, Mary K. Blackmon*
CONTEMPORARY CHINA *Lois Goldfrank*
COUNSELLING TECHNIQUES *Jeannette Danaan*
CREATIVE WRITING *Naomi Clark*
DANCE/THEATRE *Suzanne Hellmuth*
DRAWING AND PAINTING *Rachel Ross, Andra Moore*
DREAM INTERPRETATION *Ken Criqui*
THE EQUAL RIGHTS AMENDMENT *Barbara Whitaker*
FAMILY AND ETHNICITY *Nancy Stoller*
FEMALE SEXUALITY *Karen Rian*
FEMINIST ART AND VIDEO PRODUCTION *Frances Reid*
FOLKTALES *David Burks*
JOURNALISM *Paul Krassner*
LATIN AMERICAN STUDIES *Rafael Guzman, Ruth MacKay*
LITERATURE *Madeleine Burnside, Jim Peabody, Madeline Moore (Hummel), Ellen Rifkin, Alice Harriman*
MEDICINE AND SOCIETY *Nancy Stoller, Laurie Hauer*

Music as Social Expression *George Stavis*
Native Women and Culture *Dana Smith-Hedge, Jim Willis, Corky Willis*
Playwriting *Linda Kline, Amielle Zemach*
Political Theory *Bro Adams, Arnie Fischman, Dan Wagman*
Politics and Minority Groups *Diane Lewis, Leslie Patrick-Stamp*
Politics of Culture *Alice Kaiser*
Reading Skills *Mary Hoover*
Sex Roles *Susan Hubble*
Sexism and Racism *Sally Douglas*
Social Theory *Barry Katz*
Survey of The Blues *Bill Barlow*
Women and Economics *Candace Falk*
Women and Film *Jacqueline Christeve, Lorraine Kahn*
Women in US History *Pamela Allen*
Women's Health Issues *Nancy Smith, Cindy Talbot*

Apart from offering regular courses, the program matched women who wanted to do independent studies or who needed academic assistance with volunteer tutors from the History of Consciousness graduate program and from the community. Barry Katz, Sally Popkey, Anne Plone and Maya Stuart were among the instructors who went to the prison to meet their students and prepare their program of study, but whose teaching was primarily conducted by mail. There was considerable initial enthusiasm for the correspondence tutorials, and dedication from the instructors, but we found over time that some of the women had difficulty keeping up with their work in this mode. They wanted or needed more personal contact and lost their incentive after some months. Some of these women became absorbed into the regular weekend workshops and others dropped out altogether.

Overall, the response of the students to the courses, the "extra-curricular" activities and the contact with the volunteers was consistently positive, as indicated in the following sampling of comments:

You have allowed us to grow and expand through this class and that was a real compliment to us. We don't usually grow in here. We die in here. This has been fantastic.

My plans for parole have changed because of the workshops. When I get out I will be going to college.

I would have attended even if college credit had not been offered, but the credits really meant a lot to me and were quite an incentive and measure of accomplishment. The whole workshop program has put a lot of life into this place.

I was an academic failure in high school but because of the workshops I'm entering college as soon as I get out. I hope my future studies will be with instructors as warm and human as the Santa Cruz group. They give me incentive to study. Thank you for the dictionary and White's Elements of Style. [While on parole this woman earned a graduate degree in engineering. She was one of a number of women in the workshops who later achieved significant academic goals.]

The "Black Studies" workshop introduced me to a man for whom I have the deepest esteem. The films were wonderful. The music gave us a chance to loosen up and the fruit you brought in was the most colourful, natural, lovely sight I've encountered since I've been incarcerated.

This is my first workshop [on illegal drugs] but I will be attending all of them in the future. It has definitely been a rewarding, informative, educational experience. I want to be a drug counselor when I get out, and this is getting me on track.

You all have inspired us to start thinking positively about continuing our education on the outside. With these classes we come alive. I began to realize where I was and what a predicament I had let myself fall into. I began picking up on the real strength of the women I was coming into contact with. Every week day I am so damned impatient waiting for the weekend to come and the workshops. I draw strength and courage from them.

The workshops kept me from flipping out. I seemed to be able to make sense out of things that had never made sense. I was able to get information about racism and to air some feelings and meet with Black sisters on calmer ground.

I want to thank all of you so very much for this past weekend. You gave me and every woman at this institution a beautiful gift, the gift of love and, somehow, the gift of freedom. This [prison] world we live in has a macabre unreality. There is constant ugliness and cruelty in a prison. We build a deeper, darker prison inside our hearts than the one that, in fact, surrounds us. . . . You brought the magic and all the walls came tumbling down. We need you. I need you.

The enthusiasm was reciprocal. Course instructors and their assistants, tutors, workshop facilitators and performers consistently established rapport and trust between themselves and the women, with considerable one-to-one contact. Into the prison we smuggled uncensored knowledge resources, revolutionary ideals, and unqualified support for women trying to define themselves in a confusing, hurtful situation. The instructors appreciated the opportunity to learn firsthand how prisons operate and to discover the fallacies of stereotypes of "criminal" women. They were also energized by the women's enthusiasm for the program, and were glad to accept the women's frequent handmade gifts of appreciation. Karen Rian, for example, was given an elegant small painting on wood, stained in blues, greens and burnt oranges, of naked women dancing as background to a poem etched in black-ink calligraphy:

> *My Body is the*
> *Reality of this*
> *Life . . . Not an Altar*
> *for Love's Sacrifice. . . .*
> *It Houses Me and*
> *Affords*
> *My Spirit*
> *A Voice*
> *To Sing*
> *A Song*
> *of*
> *ALIVE!*
> *ALIVE!*

One series of workshops that had a lasting outcome was conducted by women from the University of California at Los Angeles film school, who taught women how to use video equipment and who facilitated the production of a documentary on life in this women's prison. This video, titled *We're Alive,* became a major fundraising tool for the SCWPP. More importantly, for participants the processes of reflecting on and then documenting their experience of incarceration was personally validating. As individual women were released from prison they would attend public showings of the video and afterward speak to their own experience, and take direct questions from the audience. The dehumanizing effects of prison, with the loss of identity that afflicts so many prisoners, were countered by this opportunity to convey their own images to the thousands of people around the state who viewed their video and were moved by it.

Apart from the stimulation and diversion from the prison routine, the rapport with people from the outside, and the opportunity to commence or make progress toward a degree, the accredited courses were important to some women because, for a short period in the beginning of the program, course completion could positively affect their chances for parole. Whereas some of the guards were skeptical of or disturbed by our course topics, some members of the state governor-appointed parole board, like the prison administration, recognized the value of "relevancy" in education. Indeed, the board's enthusiasm proved to be a problem. It was discovered that some women serving indeterminate sentences were receiving release dates because they had gained academic credit, while others were being denied parole on the grounds that they hadn't yet completed courses in which they were enrolled. This practice stopped when the workshop coordinators effectively protested that the success of the program, as demonstrated by student enthusiasm, was based in part on its administrative independence from the institution and the Department of Corrections, and that our purposes would be defeated if parole was contingent on course completion. Such a contingency would have had negative implications not only for women enrolled in courses but even more for women who were not enrolled. Fortunately, the board chairman listened to our arguments and the problem didn't recur.

One of the most moving experiences for many of the volunteers in the program was the opportunity to bring workshops to women in the Special Security Unit (SSU). This isolated small building, located at the far edge of the prison grounds with its own security force, had served as Death Row until, in 1972, the US Supreme Court temporarily abolished the death penalty (to 1976). The unit was occupied by three young, attractive, intelligent and unexpectedly endearing and vulnerable women who had been convicted in the Charles Manson murders and who, after waiting three years to be executed, were now condemned to life in prison rather than death. The warden was concerned that they should have constructive activities to break the monotony of their interminable solitude, and since they could not be released from their isolation cells to participate in the regular courses, she encouraged me to set up tutorials with them. I had begun this work during my initial months at the prison while doing research. With the development of the Santa Cruz program, Jean Gallick and then numerous others joined in.

Over the years of the program, many of us conducted workshops and special events in the Special Security Unit. At first, instructors were positioned within the narrow corridor separating their barred cells; when it became clear that it was working out, we were allowed to meet together in a little "school room," an empty cell which, as a gift from the father of one of the women, was carpeted, so we could sit comfortably on the floor. We offered tutorials in subject areas that directly or indirectly challenged them to rethink the philosophies with which they had been indoctrinated by Manson (with the aid of heavy, daily doses of LSD), and to turn their minds to critical and transformative endeavours. All these women loved music and several times over the years, in the space of their solitary confinement, they were given private concerts by Cris Williamson, Holly Near and others.

Everyone who engaged in this component of the university project was deeply affected by their contact with these women, who had been brainwashed by this century's most infamous cult leader and who, twenty-five years later, are still doing time. As punishment for their horrific crimes they were condemned to decades of prison confinement and a lifetime of penance, but over the years they cultivated new interests and intellectual and spiritual strengths. The men and women who watched over these few prisoners, as guards in the Special Security Unit, were extremely respectful and supportive of the work of the SCWPP volunteers. They routinely served us cool fruit drinks, treated us as special guests, and went out of their way to make us as comfortable as possible within the humanly intimate but physically cramped and sterile "death row" environment. Some of us came to know the women well as individuals, and friendships developed which have lasted to the present.

INSTITUTIONAL RESISTANCE

It was perhaps inevitable, given mutual antagonisms between some of the more aggressive male guards and SCWPP volunteers who refused to be intimidated by them, that problems would erupt. In a political climate that drew negative attention to the state prison system at large, any outside group seeking

to ameliorate the harshness of the prison environment was perceived as potentially threatening to the routine of the institution and the authority of the
guards. During this period many outside groups, conservative and progressive
alike, had been barred from various prisons for what to outsiders seemed like
trivial reasons. Many participants in our group, in particular, were correctly
identified as radical rabble-rousers, and although some of the staff strongly
defended our presence, others were unrelenting in their intolerance. That we
were affiliated with the university, and had the support of liberal state officials
as well as the prison administration, only served to exacerbate resentments
against the group as a whole. As one of the coordinators I was frequently
alerted by prisoners to ways that the project was kept under surveillance, with
unfriendly guards lying in wait for someone to trip up and discredit the program so as to justify our expulsion from the institution.

During the first year of the program, I was temporarily banned from the
institution, and the program was temporarily suspended, because I had ended
a letter to a prisoner with the Spanish word "Venceremos," a popular collo-
quialism which signified the overcoming of obstacles to freedom. I was at that
time, in my work at the university, helping to coordinate teams of students
who were going to Cuba to assist with the sugar harvest, a program that was
called the "Venceremos Brigade." However, the guard who had read the letter,
as part of the usual censorship procedure on all incoming mail, came to the
false conclusion that I was connected with another group called "Venceremos,"
which had claimed credit for assisting with an escape from a neighbouring
men's institution. The warden telephoned me to tell me what had happened,
and she readily accepted the truth that I had nothing to do with this group.
However, she also warned me that, given the seriousness of the charge, an associate warden in charge of security would not be satisfied until an investigation
was completed, and that meanwhile none of us would be permitted to return
to the institution. (The warden, who had been our strong ally from the beginning, subsequently "resigned" under pressure; the associate wardens in charge
of security, usually men who had worked their way up from line staff, proved
to be the nemesis of the Santa Cruz project.)

While I was barred from the institution over the "Venceremos" fiasco,
women in the prison who had been working with me and Jean Gallick, on
curriculum plans for the university program, organized a strike: they refused
to work, and sat on the ground in front of the warden's office until herded off
to their cells. Only after a thorough investigation of my background, one of

many that were to plague the Santa Cruz project, was the warden able to officially assure the staff that I did not represent a (violent) political threat to their institution, and could be trusted to proceed with the university program.

Following is a representative sampling of incidents involving Santa Cruz program volunteers which presented problems to the prison staff and which resulted in periodic expulsions. In retrospect some of these incidents seem almost comical, more akin to guerrilla theatre (with actors from both sides of the fence) than to a serious academic and cultural program. Some of the issues seem trivial, and to anyone who knows prisons the actions of some of the Santa Cruz project volunteers seem naïve. However, at the time, each of these events was taken very seriously indeed, given the repercussions for the Santa Cruz program and the importance of the program to the women inside.

1. It was the prerogative of the security staff to search not only the bodies, clothing, briefcases, instruments and so on of volunteers when they entered and departed from the institution, but also to thoroughly search our vehicles left in the prison parking lot. On one occasion, while rifling through suitcases in the trunk of a car, they found a small amount of marijuana which had been carefully concealed within a sock. The young woman who owned the suitcase was not a regular participant in the work of the SCWPP but she had been invited to participate as a contributor to one of the workshops. Given her affiliation, the entire project was suspended following a dramatic show of force by the administration, which included the arrival of a state helicopter which circled above the prison grounds, three state police cars which arrived on the scene with their sirens turned up full blast, and the sheriff, who arrested the woman responsible. The volunteers inside, who to that moment had been engrossed in the quietude of the classroom, were routed out, searched, and sent home when nothing more was found on their persons or in their cars. The prisoners, we learned later, were sent to their cells in a state of agitation because they didn't know what was going on. As it turned out, the culpable woman's boyfriend, unbeknownst to the SCWPP coordinators, was the son of the head of the state parole board. When this official heard the story he was as annoyed with the prison administration for their over-reaction as he was with the woman who, potentially, was his future daughter-in-law. After negotiations in the capitol in Sacramento, the program was reinstated.

2. It was the custom of some of the performers who came in with the SCWPP to invite talented women from the prison to join them on stage at the entertainment events that concluded the weekends. One such occasion had

been especially moving. The prison administration had given us permission to arrange an empty recreation room in the mode of a "nightclub," with candlelit tables arranged around the room and rented spotlights lighting the makeshift stage. As was usual for these events, we had brought in a store of much-valued healthy foods to enhance the celebratory atmosphere: a variety of cheese, crackers and wheat breads, fresh fruit and vegetables, juice and nuts, as well as chips and dips and other delectables rarely seen by women inside.

The concert, performed by Cris Williamson, was energizing and spiritually uplifting, and had moved women to tears. As she ended her program, she invited a young African-American woman to join her. This woman was much appreciated for her vocal talents, and on this occasion she chose to sing the classic, haunting spiritual "Sometimes I Feel Like A Motherless Child." Everyone in the room, insiders and outsiders alike, was transported by the beauty and poignancy of her voice, which filled the darkened, candlelit room . . . until, very suddenly, in the middle of her song, the guard who, until then, had stood quietly at the back of the room, abruptly turned on the overhead fluorescent lights and interrupted her song by shouting "That's it, girls. Time's up. Go to your cottages [cell blocks]. You outsiders pack up and get out of here." He utterly shattered the ambience of communion among women that had prevailed in the room to that moment.

If we had all simply obeyed the guard's stern orders that would have been the end of it. But the deep emotions aroused by the music turned to anger, and many of us, prisoners and outsiders alike, shouted back at him to turn off the lights until she was finished. Of course he didn't comply. Fortunately, none of the prisoners was punished; blame was put on the outsiders, and our punishment for "acting out" was, again, expulsion.

Amazingly, the decision to suspend the university program on the basis of this incident was buttressed by claims by the guard that he had discovered window screens on the ground outside our makeshift-nightclub room. He speculated that the outsiders were planning to facilitate an escape. This was strikingly ludicrous both in fact and on the face of the evidence, because the outside door to the room was at no time locked, and the women were free to walk out any time to go to the grounds or to the "cottages." As for escaping from the prison, even had someone exited from the recreation building she would still have had to get through the tightly secured and guarded central control building or climb over the high chain-link fence topped with coiled razor wire. There had been no escape plan, and, as it turned out, the window screens, which had most probably just fallen out of their frames, had been on the ground for months. The window issue was a smokescreen for the furious man whose authority had been momentarily challenged by a roomful of unruly women. In his mind, and with apparent agreement by the security officer, the show of lack of respect was sufficient cause to suspend the university program in another unwilling hiatus. Once again, the coordinators had to appeal to Department of Corrections officials in the state capitol, and wait out another investigation, until it was agreed that there had been no plan for an escape and the program could resume.

3. Most of the SCWPP's episodic expulsions from CIW lasted no more than a few weeks, and were resolved informally. A more serious and telling incident occurred in our second year, in conjunction with an academic exercise which resulted in a several-months-long break in the program and our first major concern as to whether the program could continue at all. In this case, Nancy Stoller, a medical sociologist, and her assistant Laurie Hauer, were teaching a course on women's health issues which included units on nutrition and medication. A questionnaire was distributed to the fifteen students in the course, who were asked to keep a record of food and beverage consumption, cigarette smoking, medication and vitamin intake, exercise, work environment and sleep patterns for a one-week period, as a basis for an overall health analysis.

It was not surprising that the health officers did not want to risk having information about drugging go uncensored into the public world. Even women who had not been addicted to illegal drugs prior to imprisonment became addicted to legal drugs in the prison. Given what we perceived to be over-drugging for the purpose of maintaining a placid population, it made sense that the authorities would censor questions about this aspect of the prison regimen.

However, the administration also made it clear to us that we had overstepped our boundaries by inquiring about the food. As is typical of any group in a total institution, women routinely complained about their overcooked, high-starch, low-protein diet and the lack of fresh fruit and vegetables (despite the institution's location in one of California's garden and orchard paradises). I had myself taken my meals with the women in the "feeding unit" during the initial months of my research at the prison, and when a woman described their usual fare as "white bread, soggy macaroni and greasy slop" I knew she wasn't exaggerating. (Those with sufficient funds, in the form of chits, supplemented

their diet with such edibles as canned sardines, which they could purchase at
the prison commissary.) No one, including the authorities who blamed the
problem on an inadequate budget, defended the prison diet; thus, we were
taken by surprise when this component of the questionnaire was treated as a
major subversive action. In the end, after over two months of negotiation,
during which time the prison administration was undergoing more changes,
the new warden disallowed the continuance of the health course but, with
pressure from university and state correctional authorities, the rest of the program was able to resume its activities.

4. Sex was a matter of high interest at the California Institution for Women,
as in any other prison, as everywhere. As discussed in Chapter Four, most
women in prison form primary relationships with other women, and, given
the almost constant surveillance of prisoners, these are generally platonic
sources of emotional support. At the same time, most women serving lengthy
sentences at CIW had experienced same-sex physical and romantic attractions.
It was not uncommon for two self-identified heterosexual women to fall in
love with one another, despite the disciplinary risks attendant on physical dis-
plays of affection. Women who had "an 'H' on their jacket" (whom the prison
intake staff had identified as "homosexual" as noted in the prison file) were
subject to particularly close scrutiny. Any women caught in "compromising
positions" with one another were sent to solitary confinement and punished
with loss of good time. But despite the risks, intimate friendships were commonplace.

On the outside, during the early to mid-1970s, elder "bar dykes," long-
time closeted lesbians, "baby" lesbians and "recovering heterosexuals" of all
ages were coming out in droves in the United States, in consonance with the
simultaneous rapid growth of the women's liberation movement and catalyzed
in part by the 1969 Stonewall rebellion (the riotous response of gays and lesbians to a police raid on a gay bar in New York City). It was not surprising
that some prisoners and some volunteers would experience mutual attraction.
Prisoners were often openly interested in both male and female instructors and
performers. And some of the young female volunteers, in particular, were
responsive to the charms of women they met in prison. The coordinators
advised all new volunteers against indulging in or cultivating romantic feelings, as illustrated by the following excerpt from a newsletter distributed by
the coordinators to all the volunteers:

In various meetings with administrators at ciw we have been repeatedly admonished against establishing "personal" relationships with the women who come to our workshops. . . . I think we all know that the principal reason for our "successes" at ciw is precisely our refusal (inability) to remain cool, aloof and authoritarian in our relationships with the women who are our "students." . . . An essential ingredient of our work at ciw, then, is that we do engage in a reciprocal process of sharing our selves—who we are, what we feel/think/experience. . . . In some cases, however, [personal relationships] have led to emotional involvements which have been very difficult for the women at ciw to handle. . . . [F]or a woman in prison to have her hopes raised and then crushed can be excruciatingly painful and cruel. Where can she go for relief? . . . We can't make promises we can't deliver. . . . [W]e can't go to ciw as a way to fill voids in our outside lives. (scwpp, 1974: 8)

Eventually, inevitably, one of the guards observed an outsider and a prisoner, who were mutually infatuated, suggestively flirting with each other. In the outside world it would have been harmless, and would perhaps have led to a meaningful relationship. Within the prison environment, however, it became a scandal. To our collective relief, this particular incident did not result in interruption of the university program, only a scolding. It was agreed by all concerned that the "guilty" party wouldn't return. The coordinators were sternly admonished, warned of the consequences if there was any recurrence of such a display, and that was the end of it. Still, it was always lurking—the conundrum of choice and desire made evil by the prison.

5. A non-credit workshop was organized by a professional masseuse for the purpose of teaching interested women the techniques of therapeutic massage. With concern for the excessively routine use of prescribed sedatives and tranquilizers as "treatment" for the profound tensions that pervaded CIW, and given the rising interest in alternative forms of health care in the outside world, this workshop was designed to train women to give one another foot and neck-and-shoulder massages. The only intent was to impart in a straightforward way some simple methods of relaxation.

After a brief demonstrated lecture on the history and therapeutic value of massage techniques to the approximately two dozen women in attendance, the therapist organized the women in pairs to take turns practicing foot-massage. She turned out the harsh fluorescent classroom lighting and lit candles to produce a soothing atmosphere. She lit a stick of incense for its olfactory benefits, and turned on a cassette of gentle, instrumental music. One knew from the moans and sighs of satisfaction that ensued, and the candlelit glow of relaxation on women's faces, that the massages and the overall peaceful ambience were having the intended effects. However, to a passing guard, the scene smacked of a "sex orgy" and he reacted with a show of fury. The instructor of the workshop was innocent in her shock and indignance. It was a clear case of cultural dissonance; the instructor represented the holistic healing methods of the counter-culture, methods which by the 1990s are increasingly integrated with the techniques of modern medicine. But even today, no less than in the 1970s, there is no legitimized place in prison for physical nurturance, and any gentle touching can be equated with sex.

That was the end of the workshop, and SCWPP coordinators were again subjected to what by now, in our third year, had become a routine disciplinary meeting in which we were scolded by irate prison administrators. It was "admirable" for us to bring university courses to the prison, and the concerts and other cultural events were "nice for the girls," but we could "never under any circumstances encourage the women to touch one another." Once again, the program was temporarily exiled from the institution. It had become something of a joke in the Santa Cruz community that whereas most people tried to stay out of prison, we were continually fighting to get back in. Meanwhile, with every expulsion, the women in the prison would organize among themselves to exert pressure on the authorities to let the workshops continue. A woman who had served a long time in prison got a letter out to the project coordinators during one of these breaks, and she wrote:

I witnessed something I would have believed [three years ago] was impossible. We had an [unauthorized] meeting where Black and White were united, under one common cause. There were women there who in the past would never have spoken to each other but here they were standing together, agreeing, touching shoulders. The tone of the meeting was not loud or wild. It was a confident approach to bringing back the workshops. It is something we all want. It was beautiful. We elected a six-woman committee to speak for the group. We are not afraid. Everything is in a suspended state pending the outcome of the [coordinators'] meeting with [the administration]. We're ready to act.

• • •

The above examples are by no means an exhaustive list of all the incidents that provoked conflict between the workshop volunteers and those members of the security staff who objected to our presence in the prison. As just a few more examples:

1. Everything we brought into the prison had to be approved in advance; on one occasion a performer couldn't bring in guitar strings because we didn't have prior approval.

2. Because we brought in fruit (together with other healthy foods) for our weekend celebrations, we were wrongly blamed for a pail of "hooch" (home brew) found in a prison cell, and told we couldn't bring food ever again. (This decision was reversed by the warden before the next weekend.)

When some new volunteers arrived to do workshops, before entering they stopped to take snapshots of each other in front of the prison and a guard came out and blocked them, threatening to cancel their workshops. They pleaded, he relented.

4. Two men arrived at the prison as volunteer workshop instructors, of whom one was brown-skinned. He was scheduled to do a workshop on "Third World" politics and the admitting guard interpreted this to mean that he belonged to some kind of revolutionary organization called "The Third World." The guard thus thought he shouldn't be admitted, not realizing that to be a member of the Third World is, as the man's companion put it, "something one is born into rather than joins."

Due to the constant surveillance and suspicions, some of the volunteers, in their cautions, acquired the "inner cop" that is part of the institutionalization process, so as to not risk making a mistake and putting the project in jeopardy. As one woman put it, in reflecting on the deep rapport between women that was experienced in the workshops and, especially, during the evening cultural celebrations: "What I remember most from those evenings is the very contradiction that I guess made the project important: the incredibly powerful feeling of love and connectedness exploding inside me, and the guard at the door, and the guard who'd been installed within me, trying to kill that power."

Despite the chronic irritations volunteers presented to wary staff, and vice versa, it should be pointed out at this juncture that some disruptive occurrences were occasions for reaffirming that we did have allies among the guards and a strong base of staff support. Indeed, it was a source of particular amazement to me that we maintained the project for so long, given that as a group we were so openly critical of prisons and that our values were correctly perceived by the prison staff as antithetical to those of correctional philosophies. As just two examples of instances where we were defended:

1. When we showed the women a documentary film (called *The Woman's Film*) which depicted newly unionized women fighting for their rights as labourers, they were aroused to loud cheering when the union women got the better of management. The guard who watched over the showing of the film, a married man approaching retirement, was himself persuaded, as he said to me, that "women's liberation is a good thing; it gives you women some self-respect and gets you to stop thinking you have to do everything for the man." A male colleague, upset by the women's noisy reaction, did not share this point of view. The issue got staff talking among themselves and more than a few male guards were speaking up about women's rights, to the undisguised pleasure of their female colleagues.

2. Following from a history class taught by an African-American scholar (who happened to be very tall and handsome, with a commanding presence, and who was highly respected by the women), the staff responsible for searching us before our departures showed particular hostility toward us. He kept delaying our search and then insinuated that this instructor had committed some impropriety and would not be cleared for release from the prison until "the matter," which was never revealed to us, was settled. As the weekend coordinator, I was told I would have to remain with him. With our encouragement, the other volunteers left in the cars for the long drive back home. After some hours in a holding room, with no explanation, we worried that we were going to miss the last return flight to Santa Cruz, where our families and jobs were waiting for us. Finally, we were able to flag down another staff member passing by. This particular man respected our work, and he broke rank to pointedly agree with us that it was a case of racist harassment. He not only defended our right to leave the prison immediately, but also offered us an official state corrections car to get to the nearest airport. Thus we found ourselves in the improbable situation of speeding wildly over the narrow country roads with a screaming siren until we made it to the small airport, deposited the car as per instructions, and were able to dash onto the small plane at the last possible moment. "Free at last," my friend kept repeating like a mantra with intended comical irony, as the plane left the ground, "Free at last."

• • •

There was no single incident that resulted in the final demise of the Santa Cruz program, but rather a combination of political and organizational shifts. Another newly appointed warden (this one a former department store marketing director with no prior experience in corrections) decided that outside volunteers were simply more trouble than they were worth. She was strongly supported in this view by a man who, as the officer in charge of security, had vehemently opposed us from the beginning. The law course was allowed to continue because correctional authorities were then under public and judicial pressure to inform prisoners of their legal rights. Yet even this course was soon phased out.

It is important to emphasize that we were not the only outside group subject to dismissal. Simultaneous with the final expulsion of the SCWPP in 1976, at least a dozen other community volunteer groups were likewise forced to cease their in-prison work at CIW, including conventionally conservative religious and arts and crafts groups. A special committee of the legislature, state senators, a variety of celebrities and many attorneys, professors and other professionals joined their voices to the outcry of prisoners, ex-prisoners and Santa Cruz project volunteers to demand more scrutiny of the administration of prisons. The director of the Department of Corrections and his associates went through the motions of listening to the complaints, but did nothing to implement a practical means of integrating the work of outside groups with the day-to-day life of women in prison.

Even if we had not been officially expelled, those of us coordinating the Santa Cruz Women's Prison Project would have had to reduce our activity. After four years many of us were close to burn-out, and the logistical complications of commuting 500 miles for weekend work was taking its toll on our personal lives and our pocketbooks, given that few of us had full employment and we had to cover most of the project's expenses from our own limited incomes. Prior to the final expulsion from the prison, several of the project coordinators had been meeting with faculty and administrators at community colleges within easy commuting distance from the prison. We wanted to ensure that when it was time for us to leave, the women committed to their studies would not be left without a program. We also helped organize a College Program Advisory Council at the prison, with the support of the authorities, to assist with the coordination of higher education at the institution into the future. Several of these colleges had begun offering one or a few courses at the prison by the time we left for good. They too were suspended temporarily, but were later readmitted. They developed more limited and conventional programs than that offered by the University of California through the Santa Cruz workshops, and far fewer women participated. But, given the demonstrated commitment of a solid block of women to academic work, the viability of higher education in a women's prison was no longer an issue.

POLITICAL EDUCATION IN PRISON

We went to the prison with the idea that anyone, ourselves included, can benefit from becoming critically aware of social reality, and confident enough to act on that awareness. Education is for raising social consciousness as much as for gaining marketable skills. We believed social responsibility to be the purpose and the prerequisite for empowerment and liberation. We saw both universities and prisons as agencies of social control. The curricula (programs), student (prisoner) selection, and reward (punishment) processes are all determined by hierarchies, through which men and women are made to fit their class-divided niches as human commodities. We understood that schools have systematically deprived the majority of education without which political power (self-rule) is impossible. We agreed with Cicero's ancient dictum that "The authority of those who teach is often an obstacle to those who want to learn." Our purpose was to facilitate rather than obstruct the learning process.

No one expects a prison to be an easy-going environment, but volunteers with the Santa Cruz Women's Prison Project who were novices to the prison system were invariably shocked at the level of power held by both male and female guards, and the perceived pettiness of their concerns. Traditionally, teachers have been similarly perceived as holding unilateral power over students, but our experience at the unusually progressive University of California at Santa Cruz had inculcated notions of genuine democracy in education. When subjected to what they interpreted as unreasonable controls over their classes and workshops, instructors and facilitators reacted with visceral if not vocal indignation. When prisoners were treated in humiliating fashion by guards, the outsiders wanted to defend them, to somehow empower them against insults and cruelties. The prisoners, for their part, took a certain pleasure in these outraged reactions by volunteers. For the prisoners, the pettiness and arbitrariness of prison discipline was par for the course and they would shrug it off with the attitude that "It's no big deal; we live with this every minute of every day." A common mantra among the women, in response to shows of force by the guards, was "they can take my body but they can't take my mind."

The intended purpose of the SCWPP was to extend to women in prison the benefits of higher education and the empowerment that accrues from gaining political knowledge, recognizing constructive life choices (despite structural goal limitations) and acquiring skills to act on them. However, the program had at least as much educational value for the volunteers as it did for the prisoners. The volunteers came to understand *who* is in prison, and *why,* beyond the fact of having broken a law. The volunteers also received an education in the power of the state to delimit options for those judged criminal. Most of the volunteers, male and female, had never encountered such utter lack of control over one's own environment as is represented by the structure of prisons, but they also commonly experienced the women themselves as exuding exceptional strengths. It was an education in the politics of punishment. It was also an education in education, as indicated by the following excerpts from instructor evaluations of their experience:

I got far more out of this work than the prisoners. As a person who genuinely likes teaching, it was a dream come true. These students gave back at least as much, really more, than they got. They were creative, thoughtful, analytical and forceful, capable of warmth, cooperation and amazingly enough, ambition. I really felt this to be one of the most powerful experiences of my life.

I had some fears about going to the prison and was surprised to see [the prisoners] looked like an ordinary group of women, sitting in a circle and talking about ordinary things. All the faces were familiar. I had seen them everywhere I had ever been. One middle-aged white woman was dressed like one would expect from a housewife from Orange County. I tried to hide my shock and my embarrassment at my shock when she told me she was in for life for killing her husband.

We learned an enormous amount about how the state operates and the potential strength of women's resistance. The women at ciw made me understand how those women who are the most oppressed by this imperialist society—Blacks, Latinas, Native Americans and poor whites—can be the strongest and clearest force for change.

The women in my classes were my sisters and I loved each one of them. I did not idealize prisoners; many were in there for serious crimes. But their crimes were nothing compared to what I saw done to women, poor people, Black people, Natives, every day.

Reading material gets devoured. I had taken just enough copies of the articles for the workshop participants [about 40], but Saturday night at the dance celebration in the gym dozens of women, who were not in the workshop, asked for copies.

The classes brought a good analysis to the prison. We set a context which helped people move from anger at themselves, individual guards or the prison, or even the "middle class," to an understanding of the system of capitalism, its relations to other institutions and what might have to be done to overcome it. In balance, we probably eased day-to-day tension in the institution by increasing long-range radicalism against the broader system.

I was inspired by how the prisoners organized demonstrations whenever there was a possibility they would not be able to have the Santa Cruz project coming in. . . . Both personally and politically it was incredibly important work. I think I learned more and grew more in my political awareness faster than ever before, being thrust into the kind of intensified experience that is prison work.

Education seems to offer the best hope for individual women to rise above class oppression, defy racial discrimination, or approach some more equal competitive level with men. We tried simultaneously to discourage individualistic tendencies, encourage individual dreams, demystify education, open it up, critique it, and offer it.

We put together a booklet of their letters to and responses from the Vietnam Women's Union ("We Are Sisters"), and it meant a lot to them to have that communication.

It was inspiring to see unity developing across racial lines among the women inside and with the volunteers. The women in the United Indian group, the Chicana group, the Afro-American organization, and the mixed Long-Termers received a lot of support from the project and they invested a lot in it.

The more effective you are politically in a prison, with community back-up, the more likely you are to get kicked out. The women learned to write their own writs and became educated about their own skills. The more you really develop collaborative learning, and people effectively take power over their lives, the less likely they are to go to or stay in prison.

Politically this work is more sensitive, fragile, ugly, awkward, beautiful and compelling than any I have known. I was so relieved to be at the prison with so many rebellious women [in contrast to] the straight world—that part I loved. But then I'd see things that made me feel horrible—my heart would break. Some of the classes were gripping. We would all be totally there, completely involved in each moment, every antenna alert. That kind of concentration is exhilarating and sustaining.

One of the values of the program was that it linked those associated the most elitist social institutions with the most disreputable of social institutions and located common denominators among them. It created a bridge across which people from very different social elements could walk, and meet, and engage in discourse related to social change. This happened for women who were incarcerated together, and for the volunteers among themselves, just as it happened between insiders and outsiders. Some of the volunteers had more in common with prisoners than with other volunteers, but differences among other participants were pronounced and in other contexts could have been the basis for mistrust. Instead, in the prison environment, potential antagonism based on real power differences of culture, class, race, ethnicity, age, gender, sexual orientation and social status were deconstructed through the unifying processes of building the program. The women inside either initiated or were consulted about every decision concerning academic curriculum and cultural workshops; their priorities affected and often dictated the program's direction. It was a collective investment, and whenever the program's continuity was disrupted for another investigation or penalty, everyone's education was at stake. At no time did the volunteers assume that they were giving more to the women inside than they were receiving from them.

Still defending the right of the SCWPP to continue the work at CIW after years of conflict, we pointed to the positive effect the program was having on the women's chances for a successful parole. Given the unorthodox nature of the program we were not always able to persuade authorities of its value as a counter-cultural model. We could, however, boast of success based on low recidivism, the most conventional (if flawed) means of evaluating the success of any prison program. Of approximately 100 women who completed the credit courses and with whom we remained in touch for at least five years following their release on parole, only five were recidivated (that is, were returned to prison for a new crime or a violation of the terms of parole), compared to the normal CIW recidivism rate which exceeded 70 percent. It was partially on these grounds that the coordinators of the project, immediately following our expulsion and for many years thereafter, were invited by state officials to serve as consultants on matters pertaining to women in prison. At the time this struck us as ironic (or, more cynically, as a means of trying to co-opt us before we tried some other "revolutionary" project inside prisons), but in fact it was consistent with the contradictions in the ways that policies and power relations are constructed within the broader correctional enterprise.

It is reasonably argued, given the social obstacles that face anyone with a prison record, that recidivism should not be a measure of whether or not an in-prison program is worthwhile. At the same time, even given the self-selection of these highly motivated students, one cannot discount the value of a program that clearly does cultivate strengths with which to face and overcome those obstacles. In the 1990s the word "empowerment" has become a catch phrase, and those who use this word bring many different meanings to it. The Santa Cruz workshops were symbolically empowering in that they challenged the relationship of criminal justice to social divisions based on class and race. They generated understanding of abuses of power based on institutionalized hierarchies of authority. And simultaneously they opened up empowering understandings of ways that life choices are expanded to the extent that individuals can maximize their abilities within the context of collective and community support systems, even given structural obstacles.

As integral to the work of the SCWPP as the courses and cultural events inside the prison was the public education work of demystifying prisons and serving advocacy for prisoners, and the cultivation of community outgrowths from our work. The network of support groups grew through the four years of the program, and through these contacts women gained assistance in exiting from and staying out of prison, with focus on practical issues such as finding jobs and housing, regaining child custody, and gaining admission to college/university. Women coming out on parole also found emotional support through these contacts, and they entered into the organizational work of the

Santa Cruz project. They did radio talk shows, spoke at community forums and joined in the work of coalitions.

In 1976, following the final expulsion of the SCWPP from the prison, over one thousand women from throughout the state, and their male supporters, marched on the state capitol in Sacramento for a rally to call attention to abuses against incarcerated women, and to address a special legislative committee investigating prison conditions (Faith, 1976). In support of these actions, ten thousand individuals signed petitions demanding greater public access to state institutions. Stimulus for this action came with the refusal of the prison to allow a previously scheduled and highly anticipated CIW concert (to be produced by Marianne Schneller, Davina Colvin and Frances Reid for Women on Wheels, a feminist cultural production company), with performances by Margie Adam, Meg Christian, Holly Near and Cris Williamson. People with limited authority (including young female lawyers who as students had conducted SCWPP legal workshops inside CIW) appealed to people with greater authority, including then-Governor Jerry Brown, to pressure the prison authorities to allow the concert. The rally was also an occasion for publicizing other, more ongoing concerns about abuses at the prison.

The rally was organized by a newly formed statewide Women's Prison Coalition (with leadership by Laurie Hauer, Patti Roberts and Catherine Cusic) with important input from ex-prisoners and the Bay Area Legal Education group of the Santa Cruz Women's Prison Project. Other co-sponsors included the United Prisoners' Union, the Berkeley-Oakland Women's Union and the National Alliance Against Racist and Political Repression (led by Victoria Mercado and Angela Davis). The issues we presented to the legislative committee and the press included: community access to prisons; the unlawful refusal of the CIW administration to allow new mothers to keep their infants with them; obstructions to open visitation by family members; harassment of lesbians; abuses of foster families against children of imprisoned women; the lack of advocacy for women punished for in-prison rule infractions; classification procedures which were used punitively to silence dissident women; arbitrary use of solitary confinement for "troublemakers"; violation of mail rights, including delays of mail deliveries for non-English-speaking prisoners; the inadequacy and inaccessibility of the prison law library; and medical abuses such as indiscriminate hysterectomies, cosmetic surgery and drugging.

In particular, speakers at this rally included ex-prisoners who came to protest the establishment of a new closed-custody behaviour modification unit at CIW. Women identified as "disruptive," because they exercised political leadership within the prison, openly identified themselves as lesbian, or in any way refused to conform passively to the authoritarian prison structure, were being subjected to the latest techniques of psychological control. Women in prison were organizing among themselves against this "Alternative Program Unit" (APU), which was seen as a way to divide the women and silence those who were seen as effective advocates for change within the prison. Media coverage of the rally generated public outrage over the discriminatory criteria by which women were being selected for the behaviour modification unit.

At this late date in the history of the Santa Cruz project, we came to a significant realization that there was a pattern here. Namely, numerous times over the years when the project was expelled from the prison, the authorities were simultaneously developing or reviving plans to establish an experimental behaviour modification unit. The earlier plans for an "Intensive Program Unit," and later a "Management Unit," had not gotten off the ground in part due to internal conflicts within the state correctional enterprise concerning "meddling" with prisoners' brains. The establishment of the APU was a victory for those who had no qualms about using prisoners as subjects in mind control experiments. However, publicized pressure from outside protesters organized by the Women's Prison Coalition, including ex-prisoners, combined with the resistance of women inside and the disapproval of influential state officials, led the prison authorities to close down the unit soon after the rally and hearing, and women who had been confined in this "prison within the prison" were transferred back to the general population. In the wake of significant media attention to the issue, the prison administration relented on the concert, which was allowed to proceed as scheduled. In effect it was the farewell concert for the work of the Santa Cruz Women's Prison Project.

CONCLUDING REFLECTIONS

We should not be surprised that of the 1,250 references cited in the 1992 annotated bibliography on prison education (Duguid, Fowler and Shewfelt, 1992), only 31 are concerned with women. Prison educators have not written about women's institutions because so few significant programs have been developed within them, on the grounds that there are too few women in prison to justify a full range of educational choices (This is not to suggest that the wider range of programs in men's institutions are consciousness-raising or useful for post-prison employment.) Most women who are incarcerated serve very short sentences. It is women serving long sentences (two years to life) who most often articulate a frustration with the limited program opportunities within institutions.

Behind bars, the loneliness and craving for books, serious discussion and cultural stimulation can be as great as the craving for an old drug. To return momentarily to history for a more lyrical analogy, I quote Josephine Butler (see Chapter Two) on the need of some women (I would say most) to feed and exercise their mind. (This is the same 19th century feminist who defended English women against inappropriate police surveillance, based on the suspicion that any woman could be a diseased prostitute.)

> The desire for education . . . is a desire which springs from no conceit of cleverness, from no ambitions of the prizes of intellectual success as it is sometimes falsely imagined, but from the conviction that for many women to get knowledge is the only way to get bread, and still more from the instinctive craving for light which in many is stronger than the craving for bread. (Butler, 1868: 7–8)

With few exceptions, when women in prison want to enrol in college or university courses their only choice is to study through distance education programs. In the 1990s, distance educators are in the vanguard of democratizing education through advanced communications technologies and generally high standards for tutorial guidance and the quality of print materials. Home study has opened the doors of advanced education to women all over the world who are confined in the home or are otherwise unable to attend regular classes. However, I've also been "home study" used as a way to keep inquiring female minds in their place (Faith, 1988). Using domestic confinement as a metaphor for imprisonment (or vice versa), one can understand why women who are literally incarcerated crave the "freedom" of open interaction with other students and/or the instructor, in a classroom. The kind of learning partnership between teacher and student, and students and students, as exemplified by the Santa Cruz workshops, requires a level of direct, personal engagement that can only occur in shared physical space.

By the 1990s, after over two decades since the University of California sponsored the work of the Santa Cruz Women's Prison Project, many feminist-minded women and male allies have joined the staffs of various women's prisons in North America. In Canada, in particular, the status of "correctional officers" has risen in tandem with an increase in employment qualification standards. Although there are still few examples of effective program choices in women's institutions, increasingly it is understood that women, no less than men, must be prepared to support themselves and their families. Women under the punishment of imprisonment who are seeking change in their lives have the need and the right, as do men, to programs which do not conform to the typically low expectations authorities have of people with criminal records. "Vocational training" was instituted in prisons in the 19th century from the tradition of putting slothful "criminal types" to work, in keeping with the Protestant work ethic. People sent to prison are mistakenly stereotyped as having less inherent ability than others. But all women must have access to higher education if they are to have real choices in the real world.

By higher education I refer not only (and not necessarily) to college and/or university study, but to political education and consciousness-raising which expand one's understanding of social choices and lead to skills required to sustain one's equilibrium as well as livelihood. Impetus in the 1970s for improved programs in North American prisons came primarily from prisoners themselves, first men and then women. One of the students in the SCWPP program who worked hard to keep the program going commented that prison had had the effect of "limiting my sense of the possible." How could prison do otherwise? How can anyone leaving a total institution, after years of forced dependency and subservience, be expected to recognize, much less act on, opportunities in the "free" world upon release? Even college graduates who do not have a criminal record find it difficult to position themselves in meaningful vocations within a capitalistic framework. Without significant support, the infantilization of adults who already have extremely limited choices upon entering the prison cannot readily be reversed.

Given that so few women, relative to men, are convicted of serious crimes which endanger others, we have a strong basis with women prisoners for setting up models of decarceration, which could be extended to minimum custody male prisoners. Whatever her (or his) illegal offence, unless a woman (or man) is clearly a danger to society it makes much more sense to provide community services, to address the reasons for the offence than to lock someone away in an institution—which can only exacerbate or postpone addressing the problems that put the person in prison in the first place. In particular, there is a clear need to address economic inequities and gender relations, especially as they affect women.

The women who participated in the Santa Cruz program became conscious of themselves as political subjects in their own educational process. Although they were living in conditions not of their own choosing, they were learning ways by which the choices they did have could work not only to their own advantage but could also bring them closer to community with other women who likewise resisted confinement. Outsiders in the project who lacked prior knowledge of criminal justice were similarly recognizing choices, and ways by which they had themselves been confined by self-serving dichotomies: good people and bad people; the right way to live and the wrong way to live; the right way to think/look/act/be and the wrong way. Such judgements set up walls which are concretized by the very existence of prisons.

State policies, particularly those engendered by criminal justice systems, rarely empower the least privileged populations in any meaningful way. Specifically, there is little cause for hope that state agencies and institutions will themselves ever take the initiative to deconstruct the bureaucracies which sustain penal traditions. It is also dubious whether educators who receive substantial grants for prison education or research programs are likely to promote empowering, grassroots initiatives as enacted by the volunteers of the Santa Cruz Women's Prison Project. The liberal democratic state educates not for independence, freedom and equality, but for the duties of citizenship accorded to one's (usually inherited) social position. The rhetoric of the liberal state is the guarantee of individual rights, but it is the rights of individuals within politically dominant groups that are protected. The state, in its hierarchical modes of social organization, has a vested interest in discouraging dissident political minority populations from demanding the same guarantees for themselves.

The state is not a singular, omniscient entity containing unitary power. It is a network of agencies, dispersed through a body politic, with conflicting priorities and abundant contradictions. Within single institutions these same contradictions are played out. In the university, for example, senior administrators such as Deans, Vice-Presidents, and Presidents, are more accessible to the public and, seemingly, more flexible, than those who hold middle-management positions. Those at the top are concerned with public image and relations, especially as it affects funding, and they must be sensitized to contemporary trends of thought and exercise diplomacy with both liberal and

conservative trend-setters. As decision-makers they must, at least tokenisti-
cally, accommodate trends while at the same time sustaining the existing
power relations upon which their own position is dependent. Middle-management, for its part, must work at maintaining the lower levels of the status
quo, and resists change in order to keep things running with minimal bureaucratic disruption. In prisons, similarly, the people at the top are invariably
more aware of and at least superficially in support of changes which will
appease public opinion. Middle-management officers, conversely, resist wardens who "rock the boat."

Ultimately, within the liberal democratic state, crass abuse of power is manifest most overtly not at the top levels of decision-making but in the lower
ranks of armies of bureaucrats, prison guards and other underlings in the class-
based chains of command. The only real power held by prison guards is a
negative power, which capitalizes on institutionalized orderings of subordination. The frontline guards, who are generally working-class people whose
status in the prison is just a step above the prisoners', are caught between two
antagonistic forces. Certain guards at the California Institution for Women,
generally women with some feminist consciousness, were in all ways supportive of the Santa Cruz workshops. Others, generally men who were on
guard against challenges to the status quo, were resentful of the powerful influence of the program on the life of the institution. It would be generally
unrealistic to expect prison guards to be supportive of programs which are perceived as giving social advantages to prisoners, especially when the substance
of those programs is accurately perceived as subversive of mainstream values.

In the spirit of Paulo Freire (1970), who introduced the idea of "pedagogy
of the oppressed," I witnessed women in dialogue with one another, and with
their teachers, locating and naming themselves within the social context of
their lives, beyond the prison. They refined their understandings (consciousness) of how society is constructed, and gained insights (conscience) into how
they could individually and collectively challenge their exclusions through
political (as opposed to criminal) activism. They demystified a theoretically
complex process. African-American women who studied African-American
history became advocates of Black Power. Women who wore the cloak of lifetime poverty gained class consciousness and an energizing commitment to
social change. Women who had been raped and battered gained feminist consciousness and a basis for unity with other women. Women who were mute
from years of silencing found their voices.

The Santa Cruz workshops came to symbolize resistance, by insiders and outsiders alike, to shame, blame, condemnation, labeling and powerlessness. Cumulatively and collectively, the workshops, through the conduits of knowledge-sharing, culture, artistry and friendship, promoted *analysis* in place of shame, *responsibility* in place of blame, *solidarity* in place of condemnation, *unity* in place of labeling, and the *nurturance* of power-*with* (contra power-*over*) in place of perceived powerlessness. Outsiders who came in with stereotypes of people in prison cast them off. Insiders who held stereotypes of professors, students, socialists, feminists, Jews and so on likewise "turned their heads around." The most reactionary of the guards, in turn, resisted a program that symbolically weakened their own authority, legitimacy and indispensability.

In Chapter Three I referred briefly to the institutional chaos which ensues when prison staffs suffer from low morale due to weakness or discontinuity in administrative leadership. Through the years of the Santa Cruz workshops, the prison lost one warden after another due to the internal politics of the "correctional enterprise"; at one point there were five different wardens in less than two years. Guards become more authoritarian and inflict more arbitrary discipline on prisoners (and outsiders) to the extent that the upper reaches of the hierarchy are in disarray, and the guards' superficial power is reentrenched with each new shift in claims for authority. A prison warden may profess a priority of running a smooth ship and giving staff a voice, or she may hold to a humanitarian philosophy and want to do what's best for the prisoners, but she (or he) will be perceived as useless to either staff's or prisoners' interests unless opportunities for direct consultation and appeal are readily available to them.

One of the paradoxes of the Santa Cruz program was that, in offering university credits and feminist pedagogy to imprisoned women, we were explicitly challenging the class privilege which normally excludes low-income people from educational advancement, but it was working-class guards and security officials, themselves excluded from higher education, who were most directly obstructive to this process. When the Santa Cruz project was just forming, one of the CIW guards had asked if our group would be willing to let staff take the classes, also for credit. We said no, because one of the reasons the women were keen on the program was that it was independent of the custody, security and punitive functions of the institution, and we knew if guards were in the classes the prisoners wouldn't enrol.

In retrospect, I regret that we did not set up a separate program for the staff, or appeal to the women to open up certain classes. Certainly, in the broader picture, the guards were not our enemy, and if they had had a vested interest in the program's continuance, more of them would have supported it. It would have been a process of demystification, on both sides, if the guards and volunteers had gotten to know one another within an egalitarian and collaborative study environment. As it was, numerous male and female guards who were assigned to handle security at non-credit evening cultural celebrations (which were attended not just by the students but by a majority of the prisoners) became among our strongest allies.

For those who participated, the Santa Cruz workshops generated a spirit of community and solidarity and many of us, students and instructors alike, are still in touch with each other and still enrich one another's lives. Most of us, whatever our occupations, are still political activists who have not abandoned our ideals, and who look back on our work together at the prison with satisfaction that on a micro-level it was useful. Many of us have continued to do work with prisoners in various institutions, to sit on committees working to reduce the numbers of people sent to prison or to improve conditions for those who are incarcerated, to do research, teaching and public education on criminal justice, and to otherwise put to use the knowledge we gained from and with women in the California prison. The prisoners, for their part, have similarly continued to show their commitment to the beliefs that were collectively developed through the project, and to use their experience to educate others. Most of them were paroled and have never returned; instead, most went on to live productive lives in a wide range of occupations. Many of them completed college degrees on the outside, but more importantly they gained a sense of community and became important allies in work for social change. Not every story has had a happy ending, but most of our lives, insiders and outsiders alike, were changed for the better.

Education for liberation and empowerment of confined groups, wherever and however rarely it occurs, is an exercise in counter-hegemony which calls for a more equitable and transformative share in social power and decision-making. As Catherine Cusic and Debra Miller summed up our work, we engaged in "education as the practice of freedom, as opposed to education as the practice of domination" (SCWPP, 1975: 10). People sent to prison may have offended society, but by virtue of their incarceration (together with inmates of mental illness institutions) they signify the least socially empowered of all adult human groups. When these people are also women, they are the least visible and the most silenced of all. As women and men who in the early 1970s were finding our voices as feminists and feminist allies, we could do no better for ourselves than to support their reclamation of their lives.

NOTES

1. An earlier version of this essay was prepared for Howard S. Davidson (Ed.), *Schooling in a Total Institution: Critical Perspectives on Prison Education* (Henry Giroux series of Critical Studies in Education and Culture). Westport: Greenwood Publishing Group, forthcoming.

2. In the 1980s, the CIW population was to exceed 2,000, more than triple its capacity. Influenced by the governance of Ronald Reagan, a conservative government in a notoriously carceral state invested heavily in law enforcement and criminal justice industries. Increasing numbers of young women and men were (and still are) serving time for many crimes, such as personal drug possession, or relatively minor theft, which might formerly have resulted in diversion rather than a prison sentence. Women at CIW were sleeping on cots in linen closets, storage rooms, corridors, laundry rooms and in the gymnasium. Every cell was double-bunked. Rather than having the effect of encouraging the courts to be less draconian, the state responded to the overcrowding by building two new "correctional" facilities for women, but as of 1993 the overcrowding at CIW has been scarcely ameliorated.

3. One of the unique features of the Santa Cruz campus of the University of California is a marking system by which students either receive a Pass and credit for their work or, if they fail to complete the work at an acceptable standard, they get no credit and it doesn't go on their record. Although standards for admission are higher than at most other universities, once admitted the students do not have to compete with one another according to arbitrary judgements about what constitutes an A or a B. Instructors write detailed narrative evaluations for each student in each course, giving clear indications of strengths and areas in need of improvement. The benefits of this system are that students strive to achieve their "personal best," students learn the value of cooperative learning, "cheating" is virtually unheard of, students are spared the constant tensions and anxieties of a competitive environment, and the rewards of study are intrinsic rather than measured by an external ranking system. Although traditionalists were initially skeptical as to the viability of this system, it has proven highly successful, not only in the arts but also for students in professional programs such as

pre-med studies. As the Santa Cruz campus goes toward its fourth decade the system remains intact. This Pass/No Record system was particularly useful to women in the prison, where competition for marks would have defeated the purpose of the program.

4. Scholars later associated with the History of Consciousness program included Gregory Bateson, James Clifton, Stephen Heath, Gary Lease, Jerry Neu, Paul Niebanck, Herbert Marcuse, Hayden White, Sheldon Wolin and, finally, notable women. Donna Haraway was the first woman to join the faculty, in 1981, and she has since been joined by Bettina Aptheker, Angela Davis, Teresa de Lauretis and Barbara Epstein.

REFERENCES

Butler, Josephine (1868). *Education and the Employment of Women.* London: Macmillan.

Duguid, Stephen, Terry A. Fowler and John Shewfelt (1992). "An Annotated Bibliography on Prison Education," in *Yearbook of Correctional Education.* Burnaby: Simon Fraser University Institute for the Humanities, 139–420.

Faith, Karlene (Ed.) (1975). *Soledad Prison: University of the Poor.* Palo Alto: Science and Behavior Books.

Faith, Karlene (1976). *Inside/Outside.* Los Angeles: Peace Press.

Faith, Karlene (Ed.) (1988). *Toward New Horizons for Women in Distance Education: International Perspectives.* London: Routledge.

Freire, Paulo (1970). *Pedagogy of the Oppressed.* New York: Seabury Press.

Miller, Debra and Twenty-Two Women in the California Institution for Women (1974). *no title at all is better than a title like that!* Santa Cruz: Women's Prison Project.

Santa Cruz Women's Prison Project (SCWPP) (1974). "An Important Message For All Of Us." *SCWPP Newsletter* (February): 8.

Santa Cruz Women's Prison Project (SCWPP) (1975). "Santa Cruz Workshops: Course Schedule."

Stafford, Norma (1975). *Dear Somebody: The Prison Poetry of Norma Stafford.* San Francisco: Unitarian-Universalist Service Committee.

NAME INDEX

Adam, Margie, 291, 315
Adams, Rebecca, 291
Adler, Freda, 59, 60–68, 85, 86
Allen, Hilary, 234
Alter, Theo, 289
Anderson, Cheryl, 294
Arrington, Marie, 77
Avery, Gwen, 291

Barlow, Bill, 289, 295
Barry, Kathleen, 83
Baunach, Phyllis, 210
Beattie, J. M., 25, 33, 34
Belknap, Joanne, 164
Belleau, Charlene, 188
Belmas, Juliet, 269
Bentham, Jeremy, 146
Bertrand, Marie-Andrée, 60
Blackbridge, Persimmon, 242–43
Blackmon, Mary K., 280, 294
Blais, Jean-Jacques, 140
Blondin-Andrew, Ethel, 201
Bly, Robert, 14

Boguet, Henri, 19
Boudin, Kathy, 159, 216–17
Boudouris, James, 207
Bowker, Lee, 221, 236
Boyd, Neil, 89, 95, 99
Bramlett, Bonnie, 291
Brooks, Virginia, 212
Brown, Governor Jerry, 315
Brown, Norman O., 287
Browne, Angela, 103, 104
Bugliosi, Vincent, 264
Burkhart, Kitsi, 61
Butler, Josephine, 24, 317

Cain, Maureen, 69
Callwood, June, 246
Carlen, Pat, 64–65, 69, 70, 143, 144, 175, 176
Carlson, Norman, 221
Carpenter, Linda, 291
Carradine, David, 291
Carter, Barbara, 218
Cassidy, Mary, 145

325

SUBJECT INDEX

Aboriginal peoples, 186–87, 188, 191, 203; as matrilineal, 199–200; Australian, 128; elders of, 144, 193, 196, 200; in Canada, 184, 187, 189, 201; in prisons, 196; inherent rights of, 187; justice system of, 176; self-determination and, 176, 194, 199, 201; *see also* Alcohol; Assimilation; Native spirituality; Racism

Aboriginal women, 186–203; as prostitutes, 28, 75; discipline of in prisons, 233; history of sexual abuse of, 143; in Australia, 26; in early Canada, 16; in prisons, 165, 184, 193, 204, 277; overrepresentation of in prisons, 90, 136, 138, 184, 185, 189; participation of on 1990 task force, 141; reclaiming their heritage, 202; role in society, 188, 201; suicide of in prison, 139, 236, 245; violent crime by, 99; working together, 91–92 (*see also* Native Sisterhood)

Abuses against incarcerated women, 130, 135, 315; *see also* Medical treatment, compulsory; Normalization, compulsory; Psychiatric care, compulsory; Sexual abuse, in prisons; Youth, compulsory interventions with

Abuses of power, 149, 152, 153, 314, 320

Access of the public to prisons, 285, 315

Administrative custody, 147, 152, 240

Androcentrism, 44, 60, 68, 287

Adultery, 30–32, 50, 97, 100, 265

African heritage, women of, 27, 63, 90, 142, 159, 160, 165, 168, 173, 184, 185, 245, 276, 277, 279, 289, 302

AIDS, 79, 80, 83, 84, 159, 173, 222

Alcohol: abuse among Aboriginals, 21, 197, 198; abuse among incarcerated women, 90, 94, 143, 152, 171; abuse among lesbians, 212; addiction as source of state income, 94; addictiveness of, 90; attempts to criminalize, 89; consumption as a factor in crime, 90, 105, 192; consumption by guards, 161, 162; consumption by pregnant women, 92, 198; dependencies among women, 93

Alternatives to incarceration, 124, 175–76, 207, 279

Grandview School for Girls, 246–48
Guards: attitudes of, toward prisoners, 165, 241; attitudes of, toward SCWPP, 283, 284; function of, 123, 149; power over prisoners, 161, 162, 163; sexual abuse of prisoners by, 248–50; sexual intimacy with prisoners of, 215; training of, 166, 318; women as, 160–66

"H" on one's jacket, 216, 304
Halfway houses, 170–71
Healers, 19, 20, 23
Healing circles, 194, 245
Healing Lodge, 142, 144
Heterosexism of media, 270
Heterosexist models, 219
Heterosexual women, 214–15, 304
Heterosexuality and oppression of women, 77, 98, 136
History of Consciousness graduate program, 275, 279, 287, 295
HIV, 79, 80, 159, 173, 222
Holloway Women's Prison, 162, 175, 230, 236
Holocaust: against women, 22, 260; Hitlerian, 13, 241
Homelessness *see* Vagrancy
Homicide, 32, 76, 95, 96, 102, 104, 106; spousal, 99, 100, 103
Homophobia: 79, 98, 185, 213, 217, 219, 223, 231, 262; discursive models of, 213; in film, 98, 259, 262, 265
Human rights: and social movements, 39; of Aboriginal people in Canada, 191; of criminals, 125, 160; of fetuses, 92; of prisoners, 140, 154, 285; of prostitutes, 78
Hygiene training, in prisons, 127, 130, 286
Hysterectomies, 239, 250, 315

Importation theories, 218, 219
Incorrigibility (status offence), 248
Indeterminate sentencing, 133, 167, 248, 298

Indian Act (1876), 187, 188, 189, 200
Indian Agents, 191
Individual guilt versus social responsibility, 36, 48, 50, 96, 99, 101, 105, 126, 175, 236, 284
Industrial Revolution, 21, 37, 38
Infanticide, 33–35, 43, 50, 97, 100
Infanticide Act (England), 33
Infantilization, 65, 122, 152, 318
Inquisition, 15, 16
Insanity provision, of the Criminal Code, 47
Institutionalization, 64, 75, 151, 159, 169, 197–98, 307; and the inner cop, 307
Institutionalized hierarchies, 164, 166, 314, 320
Institutionalized violence, 223–51
Internal causality, 45, 48, 101
International Committee for Prostitutes' Rights, 82
Internationalization of incarceration, 160

Jailhouse turnouts (JTOs), 219
Jews, 13, 73, 195, 241, 245, 321
Jezebel, 73–74
Joan of Arc, 19, 20

Kinship system: of Aboriginals, 187, 203; among prisoners, 217–18

Law enforcement: against women, 44, 61, 63, 85, 92; against youth, 108; and prostitution, 78, 82; and street women, 76
Law Society of B.C., 175
Legal rights, 42, 78, 185, 309
Legalization: of drugs, 94; of prison sex, 222; of prostitution, 80
Leniency, 234; in prosecuting prostitution-related offences, 28; in prosecution for infanticide, 35; in prosecution of battered women who kill their partners, 33; in prosecution of mothers, 61, 192, 205, 207; in prosecution of parents, 62; in prosecution of women, 39, 40, 61, 234; in prosecution,

Opportunity, differential, criminological
theory of, 67, 69, 87, 88
Order: as a function of prisons, 126, 131; in
prisons, 161, 166, 167, 238, 243

Panopticon design of prisons, 146, 261
Paramilitary character of criminal justice
system, 142, 161
Parole, 167–74; hearings, 167–68
Paternalism: essentialist, 45; judicial, 32, 60;
of law enforcement officials, 61, 89
Patriarchal relations: 43; and violence, 101;
and violence against women and chil-
dren, 200, 237; and women's role, 39,
45, 46, 50; familial, 43, 65, 87, 200; in
Aboriginal cultures, 200; in criminology,
44; in religion, 23; institutional, 104,
106; of functionalism, 74; protection of,
32, 33, 65; state, 65
Peer counselling, 217, 244–45
Peer Support Team, 244–45
Penal philosophies, 122, 148, 175, 238,
286, 319
Penitentiaries: design of, 146; early ideals of,
286; naming of, 121
Penitentiary model, 129, 131
Personal Contact, 216
Petit treason, 32–33, 50
Pharmaceutical drugs: addiction and, 90,
238, 292, 303; containing opium, 89;
use of in prisons, 213, 238
Pillory, 25, 29, 40
Pimps, 24, 25, 72, 74, 80, 81, 82
Pinegrove Correctional Centre, 93
Pink-collar crime, 87
PLAN (Prostitution Laws Are Nonsense), 78
Poaching, 36, 40
Policing practices, 69, 71, 75, 190–91
Political economy, 18, 45, 97, 121, 177, 183
Political education at CIW, 310–23
Political minorities, definition of, 6; 49, 64,
90, 92, 93, 165, 173, 174, 183–85, 189,
319

Political prisoners, 159, 193
Potlatches, 194, 199
Poverty: as a factor in crime, 37, 64, 85, 92–
93; as a factor in criminalization, 65,
92–93, 106–7
POWER (Prostitutes and Other Women for
Equal Rights), 78
Power of the state, 311
Power relations: 22, 29, 32, 45, 48–50, 59,
69, 74, 101, 108, 126, 146, 149, 163,
211, 249; between prisoners and guards,
249, 320; in corrections system, 314;
patriarchal, 237
Powwows, 193, 196, 199
Pregnancy: and drug use, 92, 93; conceal-
ment of, 33–34; of lesbians, 212; of
prisoners, 136, 150, 249
Pre-Menstrual Syndrome, 45–49, 102
Prison abolitionists, 175, 284
Prison for Women (P4W): decentralization
of, 140–45; description of, 138–40
Prison reform, 130, 132, 134, 146, 153,
158, 205, 286
Prisoners' rights, 185, 204–5, 221, 235,
241, 276, 280, 285, 286, 309, 315
Private property, 21, 31, 32, 36, 39, 42
Privatization of prisons, 161
Probation, 46, 102, 123, 192
Programs and services in prisons, 154–60
Property crimes, 35–40, 61, 62, 64, 65, 85–
88, 173
Property rights, 32, 36
PROS (Programme for Reform of the Law on
Street Prostitution), 78
Prostitutes Anonymous, 78
Prostitution, 24–29, 35, 43, 50, 59, 62, 72–
85, 129, 256, 292; stereotypes of, 267,
268
Protective custody, 147, 240
Protestantism, 14, 318
Protests: against market economy, 39; and
food riots in England, 39; at California
Institution for Women, 235, 285, 316;

© JUDY VITEK

ABOUT THE AUTHOR

A human rights activist for five decades, Karlene Faith is one of the leading feminist scholars on prisons. Cofounder of the revolutionary Santa Cruz Women's Prison Project in 1972, she earned her PhD in the History of Consciousness at UC Santa Cruz. Author of numerous books on criminology and women's studies including *13 Women: Parables from Prison* and *The Long Prison Journey of Leslie van Houten*, Faith is currently professor emerita at Simon Fraser University's School of Criminology in British Columbia.

ABOUT SEVEN STORIES PRESS